# BEYOND EDEN

ALSO BY
CATHERINE COULTER

*FALSE PRETENSES*

*IMPULSE*

# CATHERINE COULTER

# BEYOND EDEN

A DUTTON BOOK

*Cou*
*C1*

DUTTON

Published by the Penguin Group
Penguin Books USA Inc., 375 Hudson Street,
New York, New York 10014, U.S.A.
Penguin Books Ltd, 27 Wrights Lane,
London W8 5TZ, England
Penguin Books Australia Ltd, Ringwood,
Victoria, Australia
Penguin Books Canada Ltd, 10 Alcorn Avenue,
Toronto, Ontario, Canada M4V 3B2
Penguin Books (N.Z.) Ltd, 182–190 Wairau Road,
Auckland 10, New Zealand

Penguin Books Ltd, Registered Offices:
Harmondsworth, Middlesex, England

First published by Dutton, an imprint of New American Library, a division of Penguin
Books USA Inc. Distributed in Canada by McClelland & Stewart Inc.

First Printing, January, 1992
1 3 5 7 9 10 8 6 4 2

 REGISTERED TRADEMARK—MARCA REGISTRADA

LIBRARY OF CONGRESS CATALOGING IN PUBLICATION DATA:
Coulter, Catherine.
Beyond Eden/Catherine Coulter.
p. cm.
ISBN 0-525-93397-2
I. Title.
PS3553.0843B48    1992                          91–22643
                                                  CIP

Printed in the United States of America
Set in Palatino

Designed by Steven N. Stathakis

*To Robert Gottlieb*
*my friend and my agent for ten years*

# BEYOND EDEN

# ⮾ PROLOGUE ⮿

*Present*    NEW YORK CITY

The sirens were shrill. They pounded into her head. She hated them. She wanted to get away from them but she couldn't seem to move. Someone was squeezing her hand, she felt his fingers suddenly, warm fingers, blunt. A man was speaking softly and gently to her, but he was insistent, he wouldn't stop. He was like the sirens. She wanted to tell him to be quiet, but she couldn't seem to get the words to form in her mind. She didn't at first understand what he was saying, but she recognized the pattern, the repetition, and despite herself, she began to pay attention to him, looking to his voice to force her outward toward him.

"Do you know who you are?"

She opened her eyes. No, just her left eye. Her right eye wouldn't move. It was strange that it wouldn't, but it was so. He was very close to her. He was young and there was a sparse mustache on his upper lip. His eyes were very blue and his ears were big. She thought he was Irish. She realized then she couldn't breathe.

She gasped for breath and the pain seared through her. There was only pain, no air.

"It's all right. I know you're having trouble. Just take real shallow breaths. No, no, don't panic. Shallow breaths.

1

Yes, that's right. I think you've got a collapsed lung. That's why we've got that oxygen mask over your face. Just breathe, shallow and easy. Good. Now, do you know who you are?"

It was hard to breathe even with the shallow breaths. She focused on the mask that covered her nose and mouth. But it hurt so much. She kept trying, and she got air, but the pain nearly sent her into madness. He asked her again who she was. Stupid question. She was her, and she was here, and she didn't know what was going on, what had happened, except she hurt and could barely breathe.

"Do you know your name? Please, tell me. Who are you? Do you know who you are?"

"Yes," she said, just wanting him to be quiet. "I'm Lindsay." God, it hurt to say those words, hurt so much she wanted to yell with it, but she couldn't. She whimpered, fear sharpening the sound, and the man said quickly, his voice calm and low, "Just take shallow breaths. Don't try to do anything else. Just breathe, that's all you have to do. Do you understand me? That's an oxygen mask over your face to help you. Don't fight it; let it help you. We think you've got a collapsed lung. That's why it hurts so much. But you've got to stay awake and pay attention, all right?"

God, it hurt so much. She tried to hold her breath, to stave off the horrible jabbing pain, but that didn't work either. He was speaking to her again. Why had he repeated the same thing? Did he think she was stupid?

"I know you hurt, but hang in there. We're nearly to the hospital and they're waiting for you. Don't worry. Just keep taking those little breaths. I'm glad to meet you, Lindsay. I'm Gene. Just lie still. We'll be at the hospital very soon now. No, don't try to move."

"What happened?" It hurt so much to speak. And talking through the white plastic mask made her feel like she was speaking from a long way away.

"There was some sort of explosion and you were hit by falling debris."

"Am I going to die . . . collapsed lung?"

"Oh, no, not you. You'll be fine. I promise."

"Taylor. Please call Taylor."

"Yes, I will, I promise. No, don't try to move. I've got an IV in your arm. We don't want you to rip it out. Just keep breathing."

"There were so many screams."

"No one else was hurt, but everyone was scared. You were standing right next to that fake rigging when it blew. Tell me again. Who are you?"

"I was there because I'm Eden."

He frowned, but she didn't see it. It hurt too much and she didn't want him to see her lose control. She turned her head away from him. The pain continued. She'd never imagined before how it would feel not to be able to breathe. For every small intake there was such pain that her whole body shook with it. She closed her eyes and concentrated on holding on.

"How is she, Gene?"

"She's doing fine, at least I hope to God she is. The pain's bad, but she's hanging in there." He turned away from the driver to her. "I'm sorry, Eden, but we can't give you anything for the pain yet. The trauma team has to check you out first. Just hold on, hold on. Squeeze my fingers, think about my fingers and squeeze when you hurt real bad. We're almost there, almost there." Gene wondered if Taylor was her husband. Dear God, the man would be in for a shock when he saw his wife. She was a model. He looked at the right side of her face. It was difficult to tell how bad it was smashed because of all the blood. He held her hand more tightly. Gene O'Mallory wanted her to be all right. He wanted it very much.

She eased away from the man then, pulling back to avoid the pain, pulling back deeper and deeper into her mind. Her mind could breathe for her . . . breathe, slowly and in shallow jerks. No, no, it was from her chest that those paltry breaths came, her heaving chest that felt blistered raw, as if by a great fire, and that strange hissing was from the plastic cup over her nose and mouth, and it hurt so very much. The pain kept tugging at her. She retreated until she felt the blackness come into her, pushing her even farther, sweet blackness that eased the awful pain. And she let the past float into her, all her thinking directed inward, and it was odd, but she saw the face of that reporter— Kettering was her name—and how she'd seen her at the funeral and what she'd said, how sorry she'd been about Grandmother.

She went deeper, pulling her memories with her, pushing, always pushing at the pain. She saw the pathetic girl, so unsure of herself, so very clumsy, tall and skinny, all bony knees and elbows, so ugly, there with them, yet not a part of them, just there, watching, wishing somehow that she could belong, feeling the endless pain of it. But she couldn't belong; and she never had.

# 1

## *July 1981* THE WEDDING

Paula Kettering turned the key in the driver's door of her silver BMW, listened to the satisfying thud as both doors locked automatically, and walked the two blocks along Grant to Old Saint Mary's Cathedral, a seasoned relic that had survived the earthquake of 1906 with only minor damage and had the proud distinction of never having been destroyed in any of the many San Francisco fires. Paula loved the old church, built by the first Archbishop of San Francisco, Alemany, in 1853. She also loved San Francisco, including the July weather, which was typically San Francisco today—low sixties, patchy fog that would or would not burn off—no one ever really knew, even though they always said they did. Although, Paula decided, smiling, if the bride had anything to say about it, the sun would definitely be brilliant overhead by one o'clock. Sydney Foxe had the world by the tail, or whatever the expression was. She got what she wanted, and that was what was important.

This was one of the few society weddings she'd been looking forward to. All summer she'd bitched—mainly to herself. All her Saturdays and Sundays were shot because of society weddings. Ah, but this one was a treat, the social wedding of the year. The brilliant daughter of Judge Royce

5

Foxe and stepdaughter of his rich second wife, Jennifer Haven Foxe, was marrying a wealthy Italian prince, Alessandro di Contini. Paula remembered what Albo Gadsby had written in the *Chronicle*—syrupy crap, all of it—and wished she could have added her own touches to that announcement some six months before. . . . Perfect Sydney Trellison Foxe, graduate of Harvard Law School, Phi Beta Kappa, Mensa, a contract lawyer in the international law firm of Hodges, Krammer, Hughes, and about a dozen other names (No doubt Sydney Foxe would, one day in the not-too-distant future, have her name with all the other partners), was marrying a damned prince from Milan. She would become a princess and a lawyer and so damned rich it made a normal person sick. . . . Yeah, Paula thought, that's what I would have written, all of it true and very sickening.

Paula couldn't wait to see Sydney's wedding gown. It was a Brali original from Rome and reportedly cost Judge Foxe a gratifying twenty-five thousand dollars. Well, the philanderer could easily afford it.

Paula chose the most handsome of the groomsmen, a Frenchman of impeccable manners and ink-black eyes that held more worldly knowledge than they should at his age, to escort her into Saint Mary's and seat her on the bride's side. There weren't too many people on the groom's side, understandable since the groom was a prince from Italy. Only his immediate family was present, a tall slender gentleman in his seventies, the grandfather on the mother's side, as patrician as a nobleman in a Renaissance painting. Beside him was the prince's mother, who was the old man's equal in carriage and what Paula called presentation. They dripped money in the understated way of old and comfortable-with-it wealth. Next to the mother sat a young woman in her mid-twenties, the groom's sister, and she wasn't at all patrician-looking. She looked like a tart restrained by elegant clothes that didn't belong to her, just forced on her for the day. She looked sullen, her dark eyes mean with temper. But what was she so pissed about? There was no shortage of straight men in San Francisco. If she happened to ask, Paula would be glad to give her a few tips.

Paula silently pulled her small gold Alton pen from its sheath in her thin leather notebook and began to make her notes for the column that would appear on Sunday morning. She shivered and looked up, annoyed. Every cathedral she'd ever been in was always damp and chill in the foggy summers, and it bothered her fingers. She had Raynaud's Syndrome, and any change in temperature turned her fingers blue with cold. She wrote for a few minutes, then looked up when the four bridesmaids began their awkward assault on the aisle in their muds—mandatory ugly dresses. Time crawled. Then, suddenly, there was almost an electric charge in the air. Anticipation crackled. The organist broke into "The Wedding March" (so Sydney was a traditionalist), signaling the bride's approach. Everyone rose and turned. Paula got her first clear look at the matriarch of the Foxe family, Gates Glover Foxe, an imperious old lady some seventy-six years old. Paula had been told the matriarch looked only about sixty by those in the know, but since sixty was beyond death to Paula, this tribute to the old lady's lasting beauty was meaningless.

Lady Jennifer, the judge's second wife, Paula quickly wrote, was wearing a creation of pale pink silk. Lady Jennifer looked as if she'd gained weight and the dress was designed to minimize the effect. It didn't, at least not to Paula's experienced eye. Lady Jennifer looked older than her forty-one years, and there were wiry strands of gray in her dark hair. Really quite ugly. Why hadn't she had a rinse? Ah, but the breeding was there in her high cheekbones and that special tilt to her chin, which, despite a weight gain, was still firm.

And there was Jennifer Foxe's daughter, Lindsay, standing in her mother's shadow, a tall rope of a girl, fifteen or sixteen, who'd exploded in growth too fast and was all awkward bones and angles and hollows. Her hair was frizzy and looked to have been sprayed, then smashed flat against her skull by very determined hands. Her complexion was sallow, her mouth too big. She had one redeeming feature that was, unfortunately, overshadowed by the girl's general air of homeliness—quite incredible sloe eyes of a very deep blue. Well, the kid had gotten at least one good thing from dear old dad, his deepset midnight sexy eyes that could seduce the socks off any woman between the ages of sixteen and sixty.

Paula, always methodical, finally turned her full attention now on Sydney, who was walking next to her father, her bright hazel eyes flashing with excitement, her radiance spilling onto everyone in the cathedral. Paula caught her breath, along with everyone else—it was impossible not to. If there was such a thing as a fairy princess of the true sort in San Francisco, Paula knew she was looking at her. As women's bodies went, the prince didn't have a thing to bitch about. Sydney was blessed with full breasts, small waist, and long legs. Unlike most redheads, Sydney had creamy white skin, no freckles, they wouldn't dare invade such perfection. She looked healthy, utterly exquisite, and elegant. She had class. Her long auburn hair was piled like a Gibson Girl's on top of her head, with two long tendrils spilling down each side of her face. Her wedding gown was so simple it nearly defied a decent description—all lace. No frills for Sydney Foxe, no plunging neckline, no ribbing to heave her breasts out further. The gown had fitted sleeves down to her wrists and the longest train Paula had ever seen. It sounded boring, but the gown was anything but boring. It was actually quite perfect. She wasn't wearing a veil. That should have been tacky, but it wasn't.

Paula wrote quickly, just impressions really, for Lady Jennifer's secretary would be handing out full descriptions of the gown to the press. She then turned her attention to the judge. Royce Foxe was a handsome devil, his bearing as patrician as the prince's grandfather, only Royce wasn't seventy-something—he was in his late forties—and it was common-enough knowledge about town that he was as horny now as he had been when he was thirty, and he never hesitated to do exactly what he wanted, wife or no wife. He'd just given up a mistress some two months before, a young fashion photographer no older than Sydney, who had done pictures of Jennifer and Lindsay. Word was he was on the prowl again.

Paula remembered to look toward the prince, her pen poised, to record his expression at the arrival of his bride.

He had no change of expression. He remained calm in look and manner; how odd, she thought, his eyes were dark and had that liquid look some Latin males achieved, but they looked flat to Paula, not a single excited sparkle appeared as he watched Sydney come down Saint Mary's aisle. God, he was handsome, and Paula, who was a fine cockswoman from way back, knew intuitively that he would know how to give a woman pleasure. He would also, she knew, keep his body in shape until the day he died. A beer gut on this man would be a travesty. No, no beer gut for him, not ever. It was odd, she was thinking, her pen still quiet over the paper, that he wasn't slavering over Sydney; nor was he looking the least bit jubilant or triumphant because he was the lucky man who'd gotten her. Sydney Foxe was a prize. Not only was she gorgeous and smart, she also had money, a trust fund—with the expectation of lots and lots more when old lady Foxe finally died. Of course he and his family were very, very rich, probably even richer than the Foxes. Still, why didn't he look the least bit smug, that or sexually excited or something? . . .

Jennifer Haven Foxe watched her stepdaughter turn to Royce and smile up at him as he placed her hand in her groom's. He chastely kissed her cheek, then patted her chin. He was still smiling when he eased into the seat next to Jennifer.

"She's incredible," he said, his eyes still full on his daughter.

"She's you," Jennifer said.

"Yes, she's all me and she's beautiful, brilliant, she's married exactly the type of man I would have chosen for her, and now her life will be perfect, just as I planned."

"How complacent you sound. Would be that life worked out that way. But it never does. I, of all people, know that. You will be around to see all the mistakes, all the pain, all the blunders. I promise you that, Royce."

"You speak like a bitter old woman. Nothing bad will come to Sydney. You're quite wrong. Just look at her. Nothing bad will ever happen to her. Her body, of course, like mine, is also perfect."

9

Jennifer stiffened at the blatant contempt in his voice, but said nothing.

Royce was smiling again. Bishop Claudio Barzini, specially imported for the wedding from Chicago, a longtime friend of Gates Foxe, was speaking now, a radiantly deep voice that reverberated full and rich in the cathedral, bringing gooseflesh to even the most cynical. Royce hadn't objected when the prince had naturally assumed he and Sydney would be married in a Catholic ceremony. Royce decided, looking with complaisance at Sydney, that the pomp, the superb costuming, the elegance of the priest and his minions, were the perfect setting for his gem of a daughter. Much better than a simple Presbyterian ceremony or a Catholic one at the violently modern new Saint Mary's Cathedral on Gough.

Jennifer stared at her stepdaughter, listened to her clear lovely voice saying her vows to the prince. So sure of herself she was, so arrogant and confident. She always had been, even when her new mother, Jennifer, had come into the Foxe mansion when Sydney had been only six years old. She'd looked up at Jennifer and smiled and said so quietly that only Jennifer could hear her, "You won't replace my mother. You won't replace anyone. I'll see to it."

Jennifer smiled now as she watched the prince slide the di Contini family wedding band on her finger. And she thought: At last you will be far away from me now, you damned destructive bitch.

Lindsay Foxe could feel her body growing, particularly her legs. They ached and cramped and pulled and hummed with growth. The unfamiliar panty hose just made it worse, as did the low-heeled pumps that hurt her toes. She squirmed on the hard wooden bench, trying to get comfortable. Her mother gave her a reproving look and she subsided. How tall would she get, anyway? She tried to focus on the wedding, but all her attention was really on the prince.

"Alessandro, do you take this woman, Sydney Trellison Foxe, to be your wedded wife . . . ?"

Lindsay looked at her mother's profile and saw a

pleased smile on her mouth. She wondered what she was thinking. She looked toward the prince again as he repeated his vows. She didn't really want to, but she couldn't help herself. She was sick in love with him, and had been since the first time she'd seen the photograph of him aboard his yacht, the *Bella Contini*, off Corsica, sent by Sydney some eight months ago. He'd been dressed all in white, and his black hair, dark eyes, and swarthy skin made him look like a devil masquerading as an angel. In bed at night she fantasized that he kidnapped her and took her on his yacht and sailed with her far away. He sang to her, told her how much he loved her, and fed her grapes and cantaloupe. When he and Sydney had finally arrived last week, Lindsay saw that he was more beautiful than his photo. She hadn't giggled like her girlfriends, or swooned when she'd seen him and rolled her eyes. No, she'd been struck dumb, and had backed away whenever he'd come near her. Seeing him in person, she simply couldn't imagine him loving her, singing to her ever, or feeding her anything. He was a god, far beyond her reach.

It was odd, though, but he never gave her that indulgent amused look he gave to her girlfriends. No, he would just nod to her, his look grave, his beautiful mouth unsmiling. He was normally quiet around her. Lindsay recognized he was handsome, a true prince fit for a princess, but it wasn't entirely his superb good looks that made her numb and sweaty and tongue-tied. When he did speak to her, he was unfailingly kind, his voice pitched low and soothing, as if what she was and who she was mattered to him, as if he didn't notice that she was a gawky teenage girl who was nearly as tall as he was. He didn't appear to notice her stupid behavior, and most probably he didn't. She wasn't important enough to notice. After all, she was a kid, clumsy and stupid, ugly as sin with her frizzy hair, and he was marrying beautiful Sydney, who didn't have a bumbling bone in her perfect body. Ah, but lately it seemed that Sydney had garnered a lot of mean bones; Lindsay would have wagered that the prince had never seen a single one of them.

The prince was speaking in his firm deep voice, swearing fidelity and his love to Sydney forever. His voice was as beautiful as the bishop's. Why should he care if Lindsay had decided she would willingly give her life for him? He had Sydney; he had the world.

Lindsay looked away from him, swallowing tears. It hurt too much. Her knees creaked and ached and she shifted her legs. At sixteen she had come to the conclusion that life was made up of very few happy bits and big-doses-of-misery bits. She thought about her dreams of the prince. Silly and absurd. They were pathetic.

". . . forsaking all others until death do us part."

The sun was brilliant overhead outside the church. It was just one o'clock in the afternoon. Paula Kettering shook her head at the accomplishment of her own private prediction. A lovely wedding, perfectly planned, perfectly executed. She drove her BMW to the Foxe mansion on the corner of Pacific and Bayberry for what would undoubtedly be the most elegant, the most sumptuous reception of the entire year.

Princess Sydney, as her friends were already calling her, was upstairs in the Foxe mansion in her bedroom, studying her reflection in the mirror.

She was flushed with pleasure, her cheeks a glowing pink. Everything had gone off perfectly. Of course, she never left anything to chance, it wasn't in her nature. She was thorough. That was one reason why she was an excellent attorney, that and the fact that she was so beautiful, the opposing attorneys many times forgot why they were there, they were so intent on staring at her. They lost big, usually. As for the female attorneys who opposed, she usually managed to intimidate the hell out of them, poor homely bitches.

She turned from the mirror after applying another coat of lip gloss to see Lindsay coming awkwardly into the room. She frowned.

"For God's sake, pull your shoulders back! You look like a hunchback. At least you don't have a teenage complexion. That would put the topping on the cake, wouldn't it?"

Lindsay's hand went to her face; then she dropped her too-long arms back to her sides. Her hands felt big and useless, and the knuckles ached. "Yes, it would. You look beautiful, Sydney. The prince asked me to see if you were ready to come down. Mother wants the cake cut now."

"Lady Jennifer can wait until I'm ready. It'll do her good. Besides, she's fat. That wedding cake is the last thing her waistline needs."

Lindsay fidgeted, wishing Sydney would hold her tongue. But she couldn't let it pass, and said, "Mother's not very happy, you know that."

Sydney shrugged and gently eased a flap of lace over her wrist. "If she didn't let herself go, then Father wouldn't be screwing around. He told me that making love to a cow wasn't his idea of a good time."

Lindsay turned quickly. "I'll tell them you'll be down soon."

"Yes, you do that. Oh, yes, one thing, Lindsay. Your puppy infatuation for the prince is amusing, at least I thought it was at first. He told me it was getting embarrassing. Father asked me to speak to you. He says it's pathetic. Try to keep your little-girl sighs to yourself, all right, dear?"

Lindsay fled.

"That's a lie and you know it!"

"Why, if it isn't Lady Jennifer. You've stooped to eavesdropping now?"

"There's no reason to make Lindsay feel rotten," Jennifer said, coming into the room. "She's a good girl, sweet-natured, and yet you persist in putting her down. And you just started doing it. When you saw her father doing it, right? You can't act for yourself, can you, Sydney? You have to do what your damned father does, no matter the consequences, no matter who gets hurt. You always assume he's right. Well, in this case he isn't, he's just being vicious and mean and you're copying him just like a little Xerox machine."

Sydney shrugged. "Actually, I don't give a damn about the kid, not a bit more than Father does. She's pitiful, and Alessandro thinks so too. As Father says, she's a weed in his garden, big, gawky and ugly. It hurts him to have to see her here. He plans to send her away, you know."

Jennifer wanted to slap her. She was lying about Lindsay. Royce wouldn't do that to her, he'd never send her away, never. His mother would stop him. She was trembling, her hands fisted at her sides.

"Come down. Cut the bloody cake and then get the hell out of here. The thought of you living eight thousand miles from me is the only one getting me through the day."

"The thought of coming eight thousand miles to visit me in Milan is the only thought getting Father through the day."

# 2

## *August 1981*   EXILE

"No, this can't be true. Sydney told me you were going to send Lindsay away, but I didn't believe her. I never believed her, not for a minute, that's why I didn't say anything to you, but now . . ." Jennifer Foxe waved a thick envelope in front of her husband. "Tell me it isn't true, Royce. Tell me this is a mistake."

"On the contrary, Jennifer, it's completely true. I'm finally sending your daughter away from here. Are those her registration papers? Finally? Good, I was getting concerned that I would have to call that Mrs. Anglethorpe woman who runs the school to see if they'd somehow lost her."

"*Her* has a name, damn you, Royce! Your daughter's name is Lindsay Gates Foxe. For God's sake, when will you stop comparing her to your precious Sydney? So what if she won't be a lawyer or, heaven forbid, another federal judge like her sweet kind daddy? What if she won't marry an Italian prince? What the fuck does it matter?"

"The gutter language doesn't fit a woman of your years and figure, Jennifer. Though, come to think of it, perhaps it does suit a woman who drinks like the proverbial fish. Incidentally, I think nuclear war is more likely than your daughter becoming anything at all useful. That damned ugly weed will be around my neck until I die. Now, if Sydney told you, why haven't you asked about it before now?"

"Because I assumed she was lying, I told you. She did it just to torment me. Tormenting has always come easy to Sydney, but you've always known that."

Royce Foxe merely shrugged. "She wasn't lying. Sydney never lies. Now, as to where I'm sending her . . ." Royce took the envelope from her hand. Jennifer turned quickly away and walked to the large bow window that looked over San Francisco Bay. It was foggy this morning but it would burn off by noon. That was what usually happened during the summer, she thought vaguely, trying to control her fury. She was shaking. She hated it. She hated the helplessness, the damned vulnerability. He always got the better of her, always. She had to get hold of herself.

She was turning back to face him when she heard her mother-in-law, Gates Foxe, say in her clear imperious voice from the library doorway, "Lindsay will be traveling to Connecticut to a girls' school that I have personally selected, Jennifer. You needn't worry. I told Royce this would be the school for her. It's the Stamford Academy and it's very highly regarded. The *weed* should do well there."

Jennifer stared. Royce actually flushed and tried to salvage things. Good God, he was still afraid of her. It was the money, Jennifer knew, it was the money, nothing else. "Mother, I didn't mean—"

"I know exactly what you meant, Royce. Now, enough, from both of you. You might also consider that the girl has two healthy ears and a fully inquisitive nature. I could hear the two of you myself from the foyer."

Jennifer raised her chin. "Her name is Lindsay."

"Yes, dear, I know that."

Jennifer's chin and voice rose together a bit higher. "Her middle name is Gates. After you, Mother."

"I've always wondered why you named the girl after me," Gates said. "Royce did admit to me that it was your idea. You never particularly liked me, Jennifer, you've hated living in this house, hated having to defer to me, an impossible old artifact. For the life of me I can't figure out

16

why you've put up with it. But I suppose it's the status of this house and all that lovely money, not that you don't have enough of your own for several lifetimes, Jennifer. I do wonder sometimes what Cleveland would have thought about all this—our son still here in this house. He always said that a boy should be out on his own, not living off his parents. Or just his mother, in this instance."

Royce looked suddenly as austere as the federal judge he was. Jennifer had always marveled how quickly he could adapt to any situation. He said now, "I assumed that since you are no longer as spry and young as you once were, Mother, you would want someone here taking care of you, someone who cared what happened to you."

"That would be nice, certainly," Gates Foxe agreed.

Jennifer said abruptly, "All of this is nonsense. I don't want my daughter going back east. She's too young, she'd be miserable, she'd—"

"Actually," Royce said calmly, "she is quite thrilled about it."

Jennifer stopped cold. "I don't believe you. You're lying."

"Why the hell should I lie? For one awful moment there I even thought she was going to throw her skinny arms around my neck."

"No, no. It isn't true. She wouldn't want to leave me. I'm going to find Lindsay. She'll tell me the truth, that she doesn't want to be exiled."

"I wouldn't assume that to be true, dear," Gates said, her voice suddenly gentle. "There's no reason for Royce to lie about that. It's too easily verified, you see. And as for you, Royce, despite what you think, the girl isn't stupid. I wouldn't be at all surprised to learn that she was well aware of your plans for her long before you said anything to her, Royce. She hears things, intuits things. She reads people quite well. What Royce said is true, Jennifer. She really is quite excited about going back east to school. She's said nothing as yet because she's afraid of hurting you, Jennifer. But she does want to leave this house. No, Royce, she isn't stupid. She may be homely and too tall and somewhat clumsy and boorish in her silences, but she isn't stupid. I see a great deal of you in her, Jennifer. Unlike you, Royce, I can also see what she just might become in a few years."

"I'm leaving," Jennifer said.

"Don't forget that the Moffitt Hospital committee is meeting here at four this afternoon, dear. You are expected to attend, since you are the secretary/treasurer. As for you, Royce, you will leave before any of the ladies arrive."

"Yes, Mother."

Gates Foxe waved both of them away. The two of them were exhausting. She walked slowly to her favorite chair that was set with its back to the magnificent windows, facing a wall on which hung an oil painting, a fairly good likeness of her long-dead husband, Cleveland, painted by Malone Gregory in 1954. He'd already gotten old, she thought, looking at the slack jaw, the loose flesh beneath his eyes. Ah, but that look in his eyes was still a flame, even though he was nearing sixty, and she wondered if perhaps when it was painted, he was thinking about that silly girl of twenty he'd been sleeping with until his heart attack. Sydney had the look of him in his younger days, that dashing sparkle that ignited people and made them fall into line trying to please her. Now Sydney was married and an Italian princess. Gates wondered if she would give up her law practice and be a wife in the traditional way. She couldn't quite imagine it, but one never knew.

Gates thought again about the endless discord in her home. She wondered how much Lindsay had heard of her parents' screaming match, not that it mattered. Lindsay wouldn't let on; she'd keep everything behind that sullen homely face and not let out a single peep, even to her grandmother.

Lindsay stood very quietly in the shadows underneath the grand central staircase. She watched her mother and then her father leave the library. She still didn't move. A weed, she thought, a weed in their garden. She touched her fingers to her curly hair. It was a mess as usual, frizzed out and oily because if she washed it too often it just looked like dry straw. She suddenly realized that she very much wanted to leave this mansion, even more than she'd realized before. She wanted to go to Connecticut to school. She wanted to be free. Just two more weeks and she would be free. Stamford, Connecticut. It sounded really distant. She felt a brief pang for her mother, then dismissed it. Her mother would have to learn to take care of herself. Lindsay left her hiding place after another fifteen minutes and escaped the Foxe mansion, walking downhill on Bayberry toward Union Street.

Dinner at the Foxe mansion was formal and elegant and followed an unvarying routine. The night before Lindsay was to leave was no exception. Dorrey, the cook, was huffing as she came into the dining room, for the two silver-covered trays she balanced on her forearms were heavy and she was stouter than she'd been just the year before. She carefully set the trays before the master. At his nod, she lifted the silver covers, watched him give the braised sirloin a gourmet's appraisal then turn to the two small bowls of fresh vegetables, small red potatoes and green beans with French almonds and tiny Japanese pearl onions. At his look of approval, she removed the salad plates and lifted the nearly empty tureen of fresh mushroom soup from the table and took herself back to the kitchen. She'd sliced herself a good half-dozen strips of the sirloin, and her mouth watered thinking about it.

Royce sat at the head of the table and Grandmother Gates at the foot. They took turns directing the conversation. Jennifer sat on her husband's right as she'd done for as long as she'd been in this house. She spoke only after her mother-in-law or her husband had begun a specific topic and invited her opinion. Jennifer looked across the table at her daughter, wondering not for the first time what she was thinking, for her silence was absolute. She even made no noise at all eating. Jennifer wondered if she was wise in allowing Lindsay to come to the dining room with the adults. The girl was terribly thin and at that gawky age. She was just as likely to spill the soup in her lap as to get the spoon in her mouth. She would have to improve in appearance soon; she certainly couldn't go much further the other way.

"I had a letter from Sydney today," Royce said after

he'd carefully chewed a piece of braised sirloin. He decided it was time to offer Dorrey a raise.

"She is well?" Jennifer asked, wishing Sydney would magically disappear from her life. Milan, Italy, wasn't far enough away for the girl who'd made Jennifer's life a misery until she'd left home for Harvard at age seventeen.

"She and her husband will be flying to San Francisco sometime during the fall. We'll have a dinner party for them, don't you think, Mother? Small, perhaps only one hundred guests or so."

"Naturally, that would be appropriate. How is Sydney adapting to Italy and Italians?"

Royce took his time chewing a bite of sirloin. He shrugged then, not looking at his mother directly. "She is happy, of course. She and Alessandro just returned from a month's honeymoon in Turkey and some of the islands in the Aegean. She mentions that the Contini villa is very old and needs modernizing, which she will undertake very soon. She mentions also that her mother-in-law appears to be reasonable and that her sister-in-law is a slut."

Gates made appropriate noises as her son continued his panegyric on Sydney. She heard the word "slut" but wasn't really interested. Gates chanced to look up to see Lindsay staring toward her father. There was hunger in the girl's eyes and a strange sort of sad acceptance. Gates quickly turned away. It wasn't right, but then again, she'd never found life particularly right or fair or just. The girls' school was an excellent idea. Lindsay would make friends there. She'd finally belong. Remaining here would be disastrous for all of them. Sydney had always been the only child he'd loved. Yes, it was better that the girl leave San Francisco, at least until she'd grown enough armor to defend herself against her father—armor that she would need until the day he died.

That evening Jennifer followed Lindsay to her bedroom and looked over the new wardrobe she'd bought her for her school, particularly warm things for the cold Connecticut winters.

"Do you like this, Lindsay?" It was a beautiful cable-knit sweater in pale blue. Lindsay gave her that silent nod that aggravated Jennifer no end.

"If you didn't like it, then why did you let me buy it for you?"

"I do like it, Mother. It's just that it makes me look even taller and even skinnier."

"No it doesn't." She paused, knowing Lindsay wouldn't argue with her. "Are you excited?" she asked finally.

"I think so. I will like the school, I hope."

"Yes, you should. Your grandmother selected the school for you personally. You will be happy there."

Lindsay nodded at the ultimatum. Her mother was trying, Lindsay knew. But she was antsy; she wished her mother would leave her and just go to bed. Lindsay was fiddling with a particularly ugly ring on the third finger of her right hand, the kind of thing one would find in a cereal box. It drew her mother's attention. "Where did you get that thing?"

"A friend gave it to me."

"What friend? A boy?"

"Yes."

"Well, what's his name, this boy?"

"Allen."

"Allen what?"

"Carstairs. His family lives on Filbert. He's in my class at school."

"The ring is cheap and disgusting." Jennifer held out her hand. "Give it to me. I will dispose of it."

For the first time in all her sixteen years, Lindsay said, "No. It's mine. It's a gift and I'm going to keep it." She whipped her hand behind her back.

Jennifer felt like a fool with her hand stuck out, palm up, expecting to be obeyed. She knew Lindsay wouldn't give up the foolish ring. God, she hoped the stupid girl hadn't had sex with this Allen Carstairs. That would be all they'd need, a pregnant Lindsay who couldn't even coordinate herself walking down the stairs.

Irritated, she said, "Very well. Keep the junky thing, but it makes your knuckles look even bigger. Just see that you don't allow this Allen Carstairs to get under your dress, any part of him. Your father wouldn't stand for it if you got pregnant."

Lindsay stared at her mother, who had, strangely to Lindsay, lost at least five pounds since Sydney's wedding. "I wouldn't do that, Mom. You know I wouldn't do that."

"See that you don't." Jennifer realized she was being a bitch and absurd. No boy could possibly be interested in Lindsay for sex. This Allen Carstairs was probably gay and saw Lindsay as a friend, nothing more. She felt guilty. She quickly hugged her daughter. "You'll enjoy the school, Lindsay, I know you will. You're a good girl."

## February 1982

Lindsay loved the nose-biting cold. She loved the snow and the absolute silence and the white-laden branches of the pine-tree forests. She'd become an excellent skier and every weekend she and her friends were at Elk Mountain in Vermont. Strange, but she was no longer as awkward as she had been six months before. She moved smoothly and sleekly, particularly on skis. She felt graceful. She said as much to Gayle Werth, her very best friend, as they rode in the lift to the top of the advanced slope called Moron Mountain by the initiated.

Gayle, a knockout blond, was fiddling with her braces, which had just been tightened and would hurt her for at least another week. "Of course you're not clumsy, Lindsay, not anymore. Your hair still looks a fright, but if you'll just come home with me next weekend, my mom will know what to do with it."

Lindsay was wearing a red ski cap. She pulled it off and turned to face Gayle. "Stiff friz," she said, trying to make light of the bane of her life. "She'll know what to do with this?"

"Yeah, she'll know. Just come, okay?"

"I don't have anything else to do. Why not? I'd like to meet your mom, The Wizard."

"You know, Lind, it isn't all that frizzy anymore. And

22

all those waves are really nice, and so thick . . . you don't know how to tame it down. Mom will fix it."

"Race you down!" Lindsay yelled as they slipped off the lift chair.

It was that downhill run that ended Lindsay's skiing for the 1982 season. She broke her leg halfway down the slope, a clean break that left her white and shaking and nauseated. The guy who had slammed into her was a beginner who'd lost control. He was quite unhurt, which Gayle said was par for the course. It never occurred to Lindsay to call her parents until the doctor, a young woman with bright turquoise contact lenses, mentioned it.

"Why don't I do it for you, Lindsay? You're a bit woozy on the painkiller I gave you, and it might scare them even more. You know how parents are."

"Nothing scares my father," Lindsay said.

"Well, then, your mother."

"Nothing scares my mother either. Don't bother, Doctor, all right? It isn't important, really. I'm here and they're in San Francisco, and I don't want them told."

"Nonsense," Dr. Baines said.

To Lindsay's astonishment, it was her grandmother, seventy-seven years old and vital, stylishly dressed in a Givenchy pink wool suit with matching cloche hat, who came to see her in her dormitory some three days after her accident.

"You didn't come home for Christmas," Gates said as she came to a halt beside Lindsay's bed. Her casted leg was up on a chair and she'd been laughing with three girl-friends. Gates looked around at the wadded-up Fritos bag, two empty tortilla-chip bags, and more empty soda cans than she could count at a glance. The place was a mess, and after Lindsay had quickly introduced Gates to her friends, the girls were out of the room within fifteen seconds. Gayle grabbed the empty bag of Fritos on her way, her contribution, Gates supposed, to lessening the chaos. She tried to remember if she'd ever acted this way. She couldn't imagine it. No, she'd always worn a girdle and a slip and nylons. She'd always worn gloves. She'd rarely cursed, but the good Lord knew she'd swallowed many curses in her lifetime.

"Please sit down, Grandmother."

Gates leaned over and allowed Lindsay to kiss her cheek. As she straightened, she smiled, saying, "I suppose I must have done this once upon a time. My mouth has just started watering. Are there any tortilla chips left in either of those bags?"

"I think so, but they're kind of old now and ground down to crumbs. I don't think you'd like them. Let me call Gayle. She can get some more."

Gates declined the treat, though she gave a little sigh. She consoled herself with the thought that her delicate stomach would probably have heaved and cramped. "I'm here first of all to see that you're all right. You are, that's obvious. I'm also here to tell you that your parents are getting a divorce, Lindsay. Your mother is feeling poorly or she would have come to see you herself. I didn't think something like that should be left to a phone call."

Lindsay's heart pounded slow deep strokes. It wasn't a surprise, not really. She could remember the screaming matches, the hideous things they yelled at each other. She could remember her father saying cutting things about her, always comparing her to Sydney, and Jennifer defending, always defending, but still . . . "A divorce? But why?"

Gates shrugged. "They're fools, what else?"

"But I'm not there anymore!"

Gates wasn't surprised that the girl automatically blamed herself. Children were so vulnerable to adult tantrums. "You aren't the reason they're divorcing." Gates looked briefly away, knowing she was lying in a way, but forging ahead. "You never could be the reason," she said, her voice very firm. "Listen to me. You're seventeen now, Lindsay, and not a child anymore. You know your father isn't a faithful man. He wasn't faithful to his first wife either. It was her convenient death that kept her from being divorced from him." She shrugged, thinking of her dead husband, the philandering sod, and said her thought aloud, surprising herself at her candor. "Some men are like that. Your grandfather was the same way. He kept more mistresses than your father could ever dream of. I was just of another generation. I closed my eyes to it. I ignored it. But things are different now. Wives aren't forced to accept things like that. Your mother just got tired of it, at least that's what she says. Incidentally, she's thin now, too thin. Isn't that strange?"

"She isn't ill, is she?"

"I don't know, child. I'm tired, Lindsay, much too old for all this foolishness, but I felt you deserved to hear this in person and not on a telephone. You've changed somewhat, I think, you seem more mature, and I'm pleased. I've asked your father to leave the mansion. It seems strange to have only him there and not your mother. It's a pity, really, but I always liked your mother. It's just that she had no chance with your father, particularly after . . . But that's something that doesn't concern you. Well, anyway, he's bought an elegant old Victorian up on Broadway, near Steiner, and has imported a gaggle of decorators. Your mother has bought a penthouse condominium on Nob Hill."

"You're all alone, Grandmother?"

"Yes, and it feels wonderful. So don't go thinking I'll die of loneliness. Your parents were really quite exhausting. I'd like to spend my golden years in blissful quiet." Gates fell silent, looking out the dorm window at the snow-blanketed landscape. She'd forgotten about snow and cold and frigid winds. God, who could stand it?

Lindsay said abruptly, not meeting her grandmother's eyes, "Father was here just three weeks ago."

Gates looked clearly startled. "He came to see you?"

"No, he didn't see me at all. I saw him quite by accident. I don't know why he was here, maybe just to check that I wasn't shaming the Foxe family with failing grades or doing drugs or something."

"Or something," Gates said. "He never told me he was coming here, but then again, he's well over twenty-one and can go where he pleases. Of course, he did buy into a partnership with the academy owners, so perhaps he was simply here to check on his investment. Yes, that makes sense. He would want to discuss the business aspects with his new partners. That's another reason I'm here as well."

"I see." Why hadn't he at least come to say hello? If only she'd been Sydney, he would have been here in a flash, ready to take her to the best restaurants, ready to give her an expensive gift, ready to laugh at anything she said, ready to hug her. Why had he bought into the academy? She'd overheard one of the secretaries say something about it, but she'd dismissed it. So it was true after all. Was he afraid that she would flunk out and this was his way of protecting the Foxe name? It was embarrassing; she hoped none of the other girls ever found out. Why hadn't he at least called her? "Mother hasn't called since Christmas."

"No, I imagine not. As I said, she's not well. She will call you soon. Oh, yes, Lindsay, Sydney had a miscarriage. She's all right, but the prince is desolated. His mother and sister are quite concerned about him. Actually, it wasn't really a miscarriage, I guess. Sydney was driving somewhere and there was an accident of some kind that brought on premature labor. It was a male child, but it weighed under two pounds. There was no chance to save it."

"Oh."

"Your father flew over to be with her. He's returning again very soon. He says she's going back to the law firm. You knew she was trying to be a traditional wife, to fit in with all the di Contini social obligations in Milan. Who knows if she was succeeding. After she lost the child, it was over. We'll see what happens. Alessandro isn't happy about her decision, but what can he do? Sydney goes her own way. She's strong, always has been, so you needn't worry about her."

Just to hear his name made Lindsay feel terribly exposed, somehow defenseless, made her ache deep inside. Poor Alessandro. She wondered how fast Sydney had been driving, she wondered if it had really been an accident. Sydney was probably driving very fast and it was all her own fault. The poor prince, wanting to be a father, wanting to have his own son, but Sydney had denied him. Lindsay knew, knew deep in her gut, that Sydney was responsible for the baby's death. And now she would leave him and deny her duty to him as his wife.

Lindsay looked toward her desk. Wrapped carefully

inside a silk-screen envelope were the three postcards the prince had sent her over the past six months, each one from a different place, each one precious to her, the first one from Santorini, where he and Sydney had spent several days on their honeymoon. He'd thought of her even then, even when he'd been with Sydney. Everything he'd written had been warm and interesting and he had signed them with love. Not from her brother-in-law, with best wishes, but from Alessandro. *With love.*

Lindsay swallowed. Sydney hadn't deserved him, and now look what she'd done to him. She'd cheated him out of being a father. She'd killed his baby. Lindsay was suddenly aware that her grandmother was looking at her curiously, so she asked her about the hospital committee, asked her about Dorrey and about Lansford, the Foxe butler for thirty years.

The next morning Gates met with Mrs. Anglethorpe, the school's headmistress, a woman in her early forties, black-haired, with a thick streak of silver running over her left temple, all smoothed into a thick chignon. She was deep-bosomed, long-legged, well-dressed, soft in her speech, and direct in her words and manner. After greeting Gates with great deference, as was her due, Candice Anglethorpe gave her tea and the best scones Gates had ever tasted outside Edinburgh.

She studied Candice Anglethorpe. Yes, she could see it, very clearly. The woman was lovely, bright, graceful, assertive, yet sensitive. She would take very good care of Lindsay. "I wish to know how my granddaughter is doing."

"Ah, well, we were all concerned when she broke her leg skiing. I do understand that the accident would have been difficult to avoid, the other skier a man of uncertain skill, you understand."

"I wasn't speaking of her broken leg. How has she adapted? How are her studies progressing?"

Candice Anglethorpe pretended to count off on her fingers. "She's quiet, but not shy. She's bright, but not brilliant. She has two or three friends but only one close friend, Gayle Werth, whose parents are, incidentally, in politics. Gayle's father is Senator George Werth from Vermont and her mother is a state legislator. As I said, the girl is completely unexceptional.

"Lindsay has no interest in boys yet, but of course all the girls giggle and fantasize and dish up tall tales. As for how Lindsay's fitting in here, let me say, Mrs. Foxe, it is my feeling that this was the best thing for her. She's very happy here. She . . . belongs."

"I knew she would be happy. Her parents are divorcing, as I imagine you already know." Gates paused for just a moment, but Mrs. Anglethorpe remained carefully and studiously silent. Gates's right eyebrow raised just a bit. "No, you didn't know? Well, I just told Lindsay. She seemed not to care overly, but who knows about young girls? She might blame herself, which is absurd, as I told her already. I wanted to tell you just so if there were any odd behavior, you would be on the alert."

"I understand. I was also told that you were here on behalf of your son, who is now one of the new partners of the Stamford Girls' Academy. You have only to ask and I will see that you have whatever records you desire to examine. I will put my secretary at your disposal, Mrs. Foxe."

Gates merely nodded and took another bite of the heavenly scone. The Cornish clotted cream was beyond anything imaginable. "Yes," she said after a moment. "Send me the recipe for the scones and the cream."

Candice Anglethorpe laughed. Inwardly she was so relieved she nearly choked with it. The old lady didn't know anything, and if she did, she was apparently going to mind her own business.

Candice had been at the academy for only four years, and in her opinion, her performance had been grand, bordering on phenomenal. But one never knew, though, particularly when a new partner was a federal judge from three thousand miles away. She would have to find out why he'd bought into the ownership of the academy. To him it really didn't seem at all important; to her, it was critical, and it was baffling, this seemingly indifferent attitude of the very rich. Now she was witnessing it in his mother.

"I will, of course, be speaking to the trustees and the school's accountants while I'm here. That's merely business and has nothing to do with you, Mrs. Anglethorpe. Incidentally, you use the Mrs. for the girls' benefit?"

Candice Anglethorpe felt a jolt but quickly suppressed it. The old lady wanted candor—very well, she'd give her just a taste. If she wanted something more, she would have to ask point-blank, because Candice knew never to volunteer anything. "Yes, Mrs. Foxe, I do. It gives me more credibility, both with the girls and with their parents. I'm also a widow."

"A divorcée would never do. It somehow sounds so very imperfect."

"I agree with you completely."

"I don't blame you. I'd do the same for the same reasons. It's wise of you, though, not to try to hide such things, particularly from a nosy old lady. All my life, I've found things out that I shouldn't have known about. Strange, but there it is."

After Gates Foxe had left, Candice saw to it that her secretary sent the recipe for the scones and the clotted cream to Mrs. Foxe in San Francisco. Then she went upstairs to see Lindsay. She could hear the girls laughing and chattering from outside the door. She smiled as she lightly tapped, knowing they probably wouldn't hear it. They didn't. Candice shoved the door silently inward.

Bitsie Morgan was painting a picture of a naked boy on Lindsay's cast. Gayle Werth was holding her sides with laughter. They were trying to decide what to do with the boy's penis. Should they hide it or flaunt it? They decided to wrap it around Lindsay's leg. Candice studied Lindsay for a moment before the girl was aware of her presence. She was flushed, in no pain, and enjoying herself immensely. Yes, she was happy here. She belonged. She fitted in. No, her parents' divorce didn't seem to be affecting her at all. Lindsay looked at her then, and Candice smiled. Ah, those eyes of hers. Lindsay didn't realize it yet, but someday men would go crazy over those incredibly gorgeous eyes of hers. Yes, they were just like her father's. Whenever Royce was pounding into her, raised on his elbows, grunting with the force of his exertion, Candice would look into his beautiful sexy blue eyes and feel an orgasm hit.

# 3

## *April 1983*   THE BETRAYAL

Finally she was going to see him again. Lindsay hadn't
eaten for a day and a half; she was too excited. She'd felt
nauseous whenever she even got near food, even her
beloved cheeseburgers. She'd changed, she knew she had,
but was it enough? He was used to Sydney and she was
perfect. True, Lindsay was no longer the awkward dumb
twit who'd stared at him, unable to say anything, unable
to do much of anything except gaze upon him with adoring
eyes, but that had been nearly two years ago. She'd been
young then, very young and gauche and silly. She was
grown now; she was mature. She was eighteen and nearly
a woman. Her hands were clammy.

She was also in France, riding in a white limousine,
provided by the prince, on her way to the George V, and
she would see him for the first time since his and Sydney's
wedding. She could still see him clearly in his tuxedo, still
remember how the stark white of his dress shirt was so
elegant and sophisticated against his olive skin. And his
dark, dark eyes, looking at her, so intently, so seriously . . .
She shivered with the pleasure of the thought. Of course
Sydney would be there, but Lindsay didn't care. She just
wanted to see him, look at him, know that he was happy.

She pulled out the wrinkled oft-folded letter from her
purse and read it yet again. The limo driver had raised the
glass shield and she was quite alone. The limo's engine was
powerful, smooth, and quiet. She smoothed out the page
and read:

My dearest Lindsay:
Sydney and I will be in Paris the week of April
11. Enclosed is a ticket. We want you to join us.
Do come. I, especially, want to see you again.

And he'd signed it as he had the other cards he'd sent
during the past two years. *With love*, Alessandro. She'd
turned eighteen the month before. She was grown now.
She had a figure too, not as perfect as Sydney's, but it
wasn't bad. She had breasts and a rear end. She was also
awfully tall, but she remembered him as being taller. He
would see her as grown, he just had to. She stopped her
thinking there, as always. Her half-sister was married to
him. That was that.

There had been no more pregnancies, as far as Lindsay
knew. The poor prince. If he'd been married to her, she
would have done anything for him, had as many kids as
he wanted. He was special, he deserved all the good life
could provide him. He was wonderful.

She fell into daydreaming about him, and it was always
the same, with only minor variations. He was carrying her
in his arms and he was telling her that he loved her more
than life itself, that she was so dear to him, that only she
could make him feel so open, so giving. He was carrying
her aboard his yacht and the crew were smiling and nodding, approving of him and of her, approving of them
together, and it was perfect. Somehow Sydney was gone,
magically, not dead, of course, that would never do. She
was just gone and the prince was free and Lindsay was
with him and would be for the rest of her life. Oh, how
she loved him, and in her daydream he loved her even
more. He was Alessandro to her. He was *her* prince. He
was her god. She sighed at the muted sound of the intrud-

ing Paris traffic. The daydream was bliss itself, and she was always loath to let it go.

She had three different news clippings about him, one with a photograph. She carried the photo with her in her wallet. She pulled it out now and stared. He looked grim in the photo, but his magnetism was clear to her, as were his beauty and the sweet tenderness of him. The article accompanying the photo spoke about recent problems in the family munitions factory near Milan, of terrorist acts on arms shipments bound for Iran, perpetrated by Iraq. Lindsay hadn't paid much attention, searching only for personal remarks about him. One article, at the end, had mentioned that he was married to an American heiress and lawyer, Sydney Foxe di Contini, of the international firm of Hodges, Krammer, Huges, etc., now a partner herself. There were no children. It spoke of his antecedents, but nothing of interest to Lindsay.

Lindsay hadn't seen Sydney since the wedding. She hadn't even seen a photo of her. Whenever the prince and Sydney had visited the United States during the past year and a half, Lindsay had never been invited back to San Francisco at the same time. And they had never stopped off to see her. She was certain this was Sydney's doing. Sydney had ceased to like her, had probably never liked her, and finally had just stopped pretending. Lindsay remembered, even now cringing against the black leather of the limo, how Sydney had laughed at her the day of the wedding, telling her that the prince was amused by her silly teenage infatuation. How he found her pathetic. Just like her father. Lindsay cut it off right there.

Why had Sydney suddenly changed her mind? Why did she want to see Lindsay now? She didn't quite know what to make of it. She believed firmly that the prince had put his foot down. It was his doing that she was now in Paris. Sydney hadn't had a choice but to go along with it. He was the boss and Sydney had bowed to his wishes.

As for Lindsay's father, it was as if she no longer existed to him. She knew he was in Italy a good three months of the year, but she knew nothing more, for her father, when he was compelled to speak to her, only remarked that her half-sister was as beautiful and as accomplished as ever. About the prince, his son-in-law, Royce never said a thing. And Lindsay was too intimidated to ask. She'd asked him once, inadvertently, about her mother, and he'd hung up on her.

The limousine was entering Paris proper now and Lindsay pressed the electric button to lower the passenger window. The air was cool and sweet, the sun bright overhead, and it was, after all, April in Paris, the most romantic city in the world in its most romantic month of the year. Lindsay touched her fingers to her hair. The deep waves were in place, with tendrils wisping around her face. Gayle's mother had done little with the thick overly curly masses of hair, but she'd told Lindsay not to worry. By the time she was twenty, she'd said, the fashion world would be ready for her. Lindsay pulled out her compact and studied her face. Too pale, but she didn't have any blusher. All she wore was lip gloss, and that was a soft pink and nearly gone. She was eating it off.

She was so nervous she felt nausea rising in her throat. She swallowed and breathed in the wonderful Paris air and tried to practice what she would say to him. Her mind was sluggish and she felt like a fool. She felt her spirits plummet and knew she would make an idiot of herself in front of him and in front of Sydney. And Sydney would laugh at her. And then she'd tell their father, and he'd laugh too.

She was to go to the reception at the George V Hotel and ask to be escorted to the suite of Prince Alessandro di Contini. She wondered if the prince would be there to greet her or if just Sydney would be there waiting. It wouldn't matter, she told herself, he would be there soon enough and she could look her fill and, she prayed, she would say something witty, something to charm him, something that would make even Sydney look at her with new respect.

Her luggage was old and battered, and for the first time she was embarrassed. The doorman, however, didn't seem to notice. She was led inside, allowed with gentle condescension to try out her French, and then escorted across the grand lobby to the correct elevator.

The bellhop led her down the wide carpeted corridor

of the twelfth floor. Lindsay slowed; her palms were wet and she felt stickiness in her armpits. She'd shaved her legs the previous night and cut herself badly in three places. At least the bleeding had stopped so she didn't have to wear Band-Aids under her panty hose.

The bellhop knocked lightly on the suite door. There was no sound from within.

Lindsay felt frozen with such excitement she thought she would throw up.

The bellhop knocked again. She heard approaching footsteps. Then, slowly, the door was pulled open. He stood there, dressed in dark slacks, white shirt, open at the neck, and he was smiling at her, and he was so beautiful she couldn't see anyone else. There was a small St. Christopher medal on a gold chain around his neck. He motioned to the bellhop to place the bags just inside the door. He gave him a tip. He closed the door on him. She watched every move he made, listened to his fluent French, saw his charm, extended even to the bellhop, saw the man respond to his natural magnetism.

He turned to Lindsay and his smile widened. "You're here," he said. He held out his arms to her and she was quickly pressed against him, just the way she'd dreamed. She couldn't believe it. He was holding her and he was glad to see her and his body was warm and inviting, molding to hers. He was touching her hair, her back, his breath was sweet and warm on her face.

He set her away from him then and looked her up and down, in silence, for a good two minutes. She stood very still and tall, for her grandmother had sworn that if she ever hunched her shoulders to try to minimize her glorious height, Gates would, quite simply, strangle her. Lindsay stood five-foot-eleven . . . well, five-foot-eleven and two-thirds, truth be told exactly.

"My God," Alessandro said.

She smiled tentatively.

"You've become more than I had believed you would. In another two years you will be a very beautiful woman."

She laughed, and poked his arm, just like a kid would,

she thought, and wanted to curse herself out, but it was funny, this ridiculous sweet flattery of his.

"I was a dog two years ago," she said a shade too loud because she was disconcerted. "I'm just not so gross now."

"Nonsense," he said, and hugged her to him again, kissing her cheek. "A pity that you had to grow up. But here you are, nearly as tall as I am."

She resisted the urge to hunch forward.

"No, no, I'm not criticizing, *cara*. It pleases me. All little girls have to grow up. I like your height. With your sister I have to bend over, and I get a crick in my neck. Yes, a tall girl is very pleasing."

"Where is Sydney?"

The prince looked away. He shrugged. "She isn't here."

Lindsay felt the bottom drop out of her stomach. Now she'd have to leave. It wasn't fair. After all this time . . . it wasn't fair. He wouldn't want her here without Sydney. She wanted to cry. She wanted to kill her selfish sister. Damn her for doing this.

"She left for London this morning," the prince said after a tense moment.

"But why didn't she want to see me? She knew I would be here this afternoon! Why?"

"I'm sorry, Lindsay. She did want to see you. But she also wanted to get away from me more. Don't take it personally. I will be honest with you. Sydney doesn't much like me anymore, and that's what makes her do hurtful things like this. You probably heard from your father that she is now working again. In a career! I am rich; I can take care of her, buy her everything she wants, but she claims she wants to be independent of me. I begged her not to, I pleaded with her to remain at the villa, to be my hostess, to become friendly with all the longtime associates of my family, to become pregnant again, but she refused. Ah, sweet Lindsay, I shouldn't speak of these things. Please forget them. Believe me, I swear Sydney didn't leave here because of you."

He saw the blatant worship in her incredible eyes, the anger all funneled toward her sister, and he smiled wearily.

"You're a good girl, Lindsay. Come, let's put your luggage in your room and then you and I can go exploring. This is Paris and there's so much for me to show you. There's no reason to cut your visit short, is there?"

She looked at him and smiled as she nodded happily.

Lindsay tried not to think about what he'd said. Sydney didn't like him now? Why, for God's sake? Did that mean they were getting a divorce? Her mind boggled at that thought. If so, then he would be free. That brought her up short. Jesus, she was only eighteen years old. The prince was thirty-one or two. He wouldn't marry her. It was stupid. She was a kid to him, nothing more. She was his young sister-in-law, nothing more. She was nothing at all.

But if he and Sydney did divorce, then would she never see him again? The thought brought tears to her eyes.

"What's the matter, *cara*? What is this, tears? You don't like the escargots? Come, tell me what's wrong."

What could she say? Lindsay stared dumbly at him across the small table outside Les Deux Magots. The French were loud, she thought, as others' conversations assaulted her ears. So many people, and they were all out on this beautiful mild April evening. He'd called her darling in Italian.

"Here, have some more wine." She didn't want any more. She'd rarely drunk wine in her life, and it was making her feel dizzy. She was afraid she'd throw up. She handed him her glass that was still half-full. He grinned and filled it to the rim.

"Drink it up, Lindsay."

She did, knowing that it pleased him. She wanted to see him smile, to forget, even for a few moments, about Sydney and the hateful things she'd done to him.

"Tell me about school," he said, sitting back and crossing his arms over his chest and his legs at the ankles. "Do you and the other girls tell each other about your dates? Do you tell each other about how talented the boys are? Do you compare your boyfriends' physical endowments?"

She shook her head.

"Come now, you do have boyfriends?"

"No. Maybe when I go to college. My friend Gayle says that's when you're supposed to . . ."

"Supposed to what? Ah, my dearest little love, you mean that's when you're supposed to lose your virginity?"

She couldn't speak; she nodded. His *love*. It was all the wine. She wasn't hearing him right. "I . . . I've never even met a boy I wanted to even, well, to kiss."

It was as if he sensed her embarrassment and quickly backed off.

It began to rain.

They walked through the rain, uncaring, oblivious, the prince with his arm around her, holding her close to his side, getting her even wetter. They laughed a good deal. She felt such adoration for him, such complete devotion, and she guessed he realized it. She didn't care.

When they reached the suite, he didn't try to hold her in more conversation. He gave her a chaste kiss on her forehead and gently pushed her into her bedroom. She didn't want the evening to end, but she realized she was drunk, not serious drunk, but dizzy, and wiped out with jet lag. She smiled and giggled a bit when she brushed her teeth in the bathroom. She pulled her cotton nightgown over her head and climbed into her bed. The room shimmered around her like a mirage in the desert. She felt soft and warm and the dizziness was part of the sweetness of her mood. What a wonderful evening, better than anything she could have fantasized. The best evening she'd ever have in her whole life. He was perfect and warm and so tender. Yes, perfect, and maybe tomorrow would be the same. . . .

She wondered where he would take her tomorrow. This evening they'd wandered through Montmartre and he'd told her wicked stories of the artists who'd lived there at the end of the last century. La Belle Epoque, it was called, and he told her how one artist had painted himself making love to his model and how his wife had come to his showing, seen it, and set it and him and his model on fire. The painting had sold for a stunning sum just three years before here in Paris. Some Japanese had bought it, he said, laughing.

He was the most romantic man in the world.

Lindsay was on the point of sleep, her thoughts drowsy now and vague. The door opened quietly, and a shaft of light fell across her face from the living room.

She sat up quickly, disoriented. "Is there something wrong, Alessandro?"

The prince stood in the doorway, wearing a dark blue dressing gown, his feet bare. Her eyes adjusted to the light. She saw that he was smiling. Tentatively she smiled back at him.

"I've been thinking, *cara*," he said, and took a step into her room. "I've been thinking about you, ever since the wedding. I've never stopped thinking about you."

She saw then that he didn't have pajama bottoms on. His legs were as bare as his feet. They were hairy. Black hair. His feet were long and narrow. Something stirred in her, something alarming, something utterly · alien, something that made her heart pound in her stomach, something that scared the hell out of her. She pulled the covers to her neck and waited, not understanding, not wanting to understand, really, as his words replayed over and over in her brain.

"I've been thinking that it's absurd for a beautiful innocent girl like you to allow a fumbling boy to take your virginity. You wouldn't enjoy it at all. You'd cry and hate it. No, I've decided I can't allow that to happen."

She knew quite clearly at that instant exactly what he meant. It froze her, mind and body and tongue. Her dream of him died in that moment, became ashes, cold and insubstantial. He was a stranger and she was afraid. She'd been more than a fool, she'd been a blind idiot, a silly little girl. Oh, God, what was she going to do? She was alone here with him. She felt cold and numb and terrified.

"You're very lucky, Lindsay," he continued in his warm soft voice, coming ever closer. She measured with her fear each step he took toward the bed. Her breath hitched in her chest. "Don't look at me like that, *cara*. I'm still Alessandro, the man you've loved for nearly two years now. I haven't changed. And I'm going to teach you how to be a woman and you're going to be grateful to me for it. You're going to thank me. Tell me, *cara*, how much petting . . . ?

That is what you teenagers call it, isn't it? Yes, well, you must tell me how much you've let those bumbling boys do to you."

She tried to find saliva in her mouth. She spoke in a desert-dry whisper. "You're married to my half-sister."

He gave an elegant shrug. "Sydney is a castrating bitch. She's frigid and she's really quite annoying with her bourgeois notions of morality. She's also stupid, contrary to what your besotted ass of a father believes about her. She isn't beautiful, she isn't perfect, she isn't anything. She doesn't matter, just as that stupid baby she was carrying didn't matter. She acted like a fool when she was pregnant, like it was so important to her, to me, to my family. She was enough for me to put up with without having her belly bloated out with a brat. Ah, yes, that was much too much to bear.

"I remember when I first saw you, you were all clumsy angles and bony knees and knobby elbows and you were just to my liking. I knew when I saw you at the wedding that you would become quite lovely in the future, but I knew too you would be older and I hated that. I wanted you then, with all your teenage awkwardness, all your little-girl innocence and guilelessness. God, I wanted you and your virginity. I wanted to cover myself in your sweet innocence. I still want you; I want your virginity even more now. I didn't think I would, since you're eighteen now, but I do. Other men will consider you more beautiful in the years to come, but that's for them, not me.

"No, I can't wait any longer, Lindsay. I've already had to wait too long for you. I sweated and worried, thinking it could already be too late. And your damned father gave you freedom by sending you to that school in Connecticut. I know what girls are like today, fucking when they're young, far too young, letting young boys take them in the back seats of their grubby cars. But you managed to make it to eighteen and you're still a virgin. God knows that by the time you're twenty, you'll have let a good half-dozen boys fuck you. They'd all be Americans and clumsy boors. No, I'll not allow that. I'll teach you to be discriminating. I'll teach you how to fuck a prince."

He was standing by the bed now. He leaned over and switched on the Tiffany lamp. He sat down beside her. He took her cold hand and squeezed her limp fingers.

"Tell me, *cara*, have you let boys stick their tongues in your mouth? Have you let them French-kiss you?"

She nodded, her eyes never leaving his face.

"Did you like it?"

She shook her head. He leaned over and his mouth touched hers.

He immediately straightened. "No, you wouldn't have. They're fools, those boys, not like me, not men. No, they're not anything like me. I don't mind you being afraid, Lindsay, because it really doesn't matter to me. Perhaps it even amuses me. Have any boys played with your breasts? Kissed your nipples?"

She stared at him, unmoving, so afraid she was paralyzed.

"Or your crotch? Have they put their fingers in you? No? Well, I'll make it very nice for you. Girls like to have their lips rubbed and kissed. And there's your little clitoris. Have you masturbated much, Lindsay? Have you given yourself much pleasure? Did all the girls at your school talk about it? How much they wanted to do it?"

He leaned toward her again, his lips parted, his eyes intent on her mouth. "Have you any idea what it will feel like when I have my tongue hot on your clitoris?"

Lindsay cried out, the sound of her own voice shoving her back into reality, back into herself. But this reality was ugly and it was right here beside her. She rolled to the side away from him and onto the floor, coming up to her feet.

He was still smiling. He rose and came around the end of the bed. "Why are you afraid? It's me, Lindsay, and you've loved me since you first saw me. Admit it."

"No, no, stay back. Oh, God, you're not what I thought you were."

He moved quickly then, grabbed her upper arms as she tried to dodge past him, and dragged her back onto the bed. "I don't mind if you fight me," he was saying over and over against her cheek, his breath hot, his voice fast and high. "You won't like it as much, but I will. Jesus, I'll love it." He was still smiling and she could see the gold filling in one of his back teeth.

"No, damn you, no!" She saw that words had no effect on him. He was going to rape her. The instant she thought the word, a string of stark images flashed through her mind, and she went crazy. He was ripping her cotton nightgown open at the throat and she felt cold air on her chest. She kicked her legs up; they were strong because she played soccer, and he grunted with pain. Her knees hit his groin and he grabbed her two wrists and now he pressed himself down on her, pinning her legs. He was breathing hard with exertion, trying to hold both her wrists in one of his hands, but she was too strong. She was a big girl and she was in good shape. "You're acting like a bloody American bitch," he yelled in her face. "Stop it, for God's sake! Hold still for me! Don't be like your fool of a sister!"

This was the real Alessandro, the man Sydney had married in good faith, the man Lindsay had fantasized about and dreamed about . . . and he had set this whole trip up and he fully intended to rape her. . . . God, she couldn't believe . . . She twisted and yanked at his hold, tried to bring her legs up again to give her leverage. She was muscular, and she wasn't going to lie there like a victim. She remembered her self-defense courses. Scream, scream, scream. Had he done this before, to Italian girls? And they'd just lain there whimpering and let him rape them? She yelled right in his face, spittle spraying him, and heaved upward, nearly knocking him to the floor off her.

Suddenly he released her left hand, and immediately she was clawing at his face. He struck his fist into her jaw. She felt pain slam into her face, saw flashes of light, and gasped. He struck her again, hard.

She was on the brink of unconsciousness for a few seconds, enough time for him to rip her nightgown open to the hem. He jerked the cotton edges apart.

He was straddling her now, keeping her legs down by sitting on them, and he was staring down at her. He was smiling; there was triumph in his dark eyes. He forced her hands down on her abdomen, holding them there.

"I hadn't thought your breasts would be so large and

your nipples so big," he said now, dissatisfaction clear in his voice. All the softness, the gentleness, was gone. "Most young girls aren't so filled out as you, but it doesn't really matter. It was my choice to wait, so I have only myself to blame." Because he couldn't hold both her hands down with just one of his, he had to force her hands upward with his so he could touch her breasts.

She screamed at the feel of his fingers against her cold flesh.

He released her hand and hit her again with his fist. He was smiling as he hit her.

It didn't register in her mind; she screamed again, gurgling because she was choking on her own saliva.

He grunted in fury and quickly brought his mouth down over hers. It was brutal and it hurt and she tasted blood. She was biting her own tongue. She wished he'd stick his tongue in her mouth. She'd bite it off, but he didn't.

He struck her again, without warning.

Her head flew back and for a few moments she was unconscious. When she opened her eyes, he was between her legs and he was looking at her, his hands on her, probing, hurting. He was ready, she knew it, and he was simply waiting for her to wake up. He saw her open eyes, saw the awareness in them, and he reared back and slammed into her.

Lindsay rose up off the bed, yelling blindly with the pain. He pounded into her, harder and harder still, and she yelled and cried out, but he didn't slow.

Her tears began to choke her. But still she yelled and cried out.

"Shut up, damn you!"

He slapped her hard, sending her head violently to the side. He was heaving now, hurting her more and more, and she realized vaguely that he was enjoying this. This was what he liked, what he was good at. This was what he'd always wanted from her. She screamed again, blood bright red on her lower lip, the coppery taste of it in her mouth. She managed to free her right hand. She slammed her fist into his mouth. He went at her in a frenzy then, striking her in rhythm with his punishing blows inside her. Then, suddenly, he tensed, his whole body freezing, his back arched. She bucked and yelled and pushed. She felt the semen burst from his penis, deep inside her, and in that moment she wished to die.

"My God! Oh, my God, no!"

Lindsay stared at the unexpected voice and yelled again, disbelieving. It was Sydney and she was watching, mouth agape, frozen just inside the open bedroom doorway.

"Help me, Sydney! Please, help me!"

The prince didn't seem to hear his wife's voice. He was heaving and jerking over Lindsay. And then he was groaning, and she felt his body's contractions with the power of his orgasm.

"Help me, Sydney!"

The prince laughed and struck her again, hard on her jaw. He raised his hand again for another blow, smiling, oh he was smiling grandly, his pleasure full to bursting, but his violence still lacking.

There was a loud popping sound. The prince stiffened suddenly and then he was staring down at Lindsay, and he was frowning in confusion. Slowly he swiveled about, still inside her, to see his wife standing not ten feet away, a .32-caliber pistol held straight out toward him in her right hand.

"Sydney? Is that you? Whatever are you doing here? You should be at home. You should be tending my mother. Why did you shoot me? Why?"

Sydney, pale, still now, screamed, "By God, my own sister!" She aimed the gun and pulled the trigger again.

He shuddered when the bullet went into his flesh, then he fell sideways, sliding out of Lindsay, rocking sideways, slipping silently onto the floor.

Lindsay couldn't grasp it. She saw the gun, saw the blood, all over the bed. She leaned over and looked at him. There was blood all over his chest, and then she saw her own blood between her legs and his sperm leaking slowly out of her. She started shaking.

She was cold, out of control, she realized vaguely, but couldn't do anything about it. She hurt inside and out, and she couldn't seem to think. There was Sydney standing there, dead white, eyes dilated, and holding that damned pistol straight out in front of her, and she said, her voice as dead frightening as hell because it was emotionless and singsong, "Are you all right, Lindsay?"

"N-no."

"Jesus, I wasn't in time. I'm sorry, Lindsay. I wasn't in time. God, I'm so sorry. I came as soon as I found out what he'd planned. The bastard really covered his tracks this time, so it took me longer. When I realized he was still after you, I went crazy. I couldn't believe it at first. It was too insane, too much, even for him. Oh, God, what the hell are we going to do?"

"Is he dead?"

"Dead? He should be, I shot him twice." She looked at the prince's sprawled naked body. "I shot him," she said again. "I shot the bastard twice."

Suddenly Sydney sank to her knees. She rocked back and forth, back and forth, a strange keening noise coming from her throat. The pistol fell from her fingers onto the carpet.

It was the sight of her sister—perfect Sydney, brilliant and beautiful Sydney—looking like a crazed woman that gave Lindsay a focus. It gave her a notion of reality and what it was they now faced.

She scrambled off the bed and onto the floor next to her sister. She didn't look at the prince. He didn't matter right now. She was unaware of her nightgown flapping around her body.

She grabbed her sister's shoulders and shook her. "We've got to do something! Stop it, Sydney, for God's sake, stop it, get hold of yourself!"

"I murdered him. There's nothing to do. I murdered him and everything's over now."

She raised her face from her hands then and stared blindly at Lindsay. "Our daddy's a judge. Isn't that something, Lindsay? He's a fucking judge!"

"No, no, listen to me, you saved me. He was raping me and you saved me! It was self-defense. We'll be all right. I swear it, Sydney."

Sydney merely stared at her, shaking her head slowly back and forth, so pale Lindsay thought she would faint. But she didn't.

Sydney said, even as she shook her head as if in denial, "You stupid little idiot." Her voice was now strong and hard, her eyes dark and wild. "You fool girl, you let him think you wanted this. He's not normal. He took your silly infatuation for sexual overtures. For two years you've let him get you ready for this. What did he do, write you his titillating little postcards? Show you how caring and tender he was? How much he appreciated you, a very young girl? No, don't bother saying anything. It's far too late now. I know, you see, he never changes his routine, there's never been any need to, because I let him have his fun. No choice really, once I figured out what he was all about. Don't you know why he married me, Lindsay? Jesus, of course you don't know. He married me for my future inheritance! The interest from my trust fund doesn't begin to satisfy him. And there you are, gawking at him like he's God. You came running, didn't you? He loves young girls, haven't you figured that out yet? He thinks I'm old. He thought I was too old when we got married. Eighteen is really his limit. He had to wait for you because he couldn't get to you before. I'll just bet he was dying, wondering if he could get to you before an American boy had taken your virginity. Oh, it doesn't matter. I would have killed him anyway, whether or not he was raping you. You stupid little fool, Jesus, stupid, stupid."

Sydney began crying into her hands, harsh ugly cries. Lindsay watched her, unable to move, unable to think, her half-sister's words dinning in her mind. No, no time to think about this, it was time to act.

Lindsay shrugged off her shredded nightgown. She felt the awful stickiness between her legs, felt the vague stinging inside her. Her face throbbed from his blows. She wanted to vomit. She was eighteen years old, too young, too young, and yet there was no one else to help her. She might as well have been alone with a dead man.

What to do?

She managed to rise. She felt herself begin to tremble,

knew she was about to lose control, just as Sydney had. She couldn't allow it. She walked to the ornate telephone and picked it up. She stared at it, wondering how to ask for the police in French. Her hand shook; she stopped it. She drew a deep breath. She got a good grip on herself, and said when the operator came onto the line, *"Les gendarmes, s'il vous plaît. C'est très important."*

Suddenly the prince groaned.

# 4

## THE AFTERMATH

Lindsay was on her knees vomiting into the toilet when the police came running into the suite. She staggered to her feet, clutching a blanket around her. Her mouth tasted bitter and dry. Sydney was standing now, pale and still, the .32-caliber pistol in her hand again, and she was staring down at her husband, who was still lying nude on the bedroom carpet, covered with blood, moaning.

Lindsay was aware of men staring at her, at Sydney, at the prince, taking it in. She pulled the blanket more tightly around her. Her face hurt, her insides burned, and her stomach was roiling. She couldn't speak, just stared back at them. She heard Sydney sobbing, saw two more men carry in a collapsible gurney. They put the prince on it, covered him, and wheeled him out. Lindsay's last view of him was of a man with a gray face, black hair plastered with sweat to his head, and he was moaning. There was a man from the hotel, obviously, because he was very nearly distraught, chattering wildly, wringing his hands.

One of the policemen, a young man with thick black hair and a huge mustache, strode toward Lindsay. She backed away, one hand in front of her to ward him away. It was instinctive. He slowed, spoke to her, his voice low, but she couldn't understand his words. She couldn't understand anything. One of the other men said in English, "You are too ill to walk. He will carry you, *mademoiselle*. He will not pain you. I promise, everything will be okay now."

Okay? That was crazy. Said with a thick French accent it sounded even crazier. She closed her eyes when the man picked her up and carried her to the elevator, through the lavish lobby of the George V, to the police car whose front tires sat on the sidewalk in front of the hotel. She lay against him, aware of the siren, aware of the low talk between him and the two men in the front seat. There were avid faces pressing against the police-car windows and there were loud voices. She turned her face inward. This was reality and she couldn't bear it. She wondered where Sydney was. She felt the pain building inside her, the horror of what had happened to her, of what she had allowed to happen to her. She couldn't seem to stop shivering, but she knew she wasn't cold. The man who was holding her continued to speak quietly. She heard his words, but she saw the prince's ghastly gray face, saw the people's greedy faces as they'd tried to get closer.

The police officer carried her into the emergency room of St. Catherine's Hospital—she saw the huge sign—and then into one of the small curtained cubicles. He laid her onto an examining table. She was shaking, her teeth chattering, clutching the blanket to her like a lifeline, clutching now at him. He spoke more, then pulled her arms away from him. He left. A nurse leaned over her and she understood the word *americaine* but nothing more. Then two men were there, standing over her, both in white coats, and they looked harried and impatient. They were tugging the blanket off her. But she was naked, she knew she was naked, and the prince's sperm was on her thighs, still wet and runny, and there was her blood as well, and it was too much. She fought them, yelling at them to leave her alone, tears streaming down her face.

But it didn't help. One of the men just held her down. The other man jerked off the blanket and tossed it to the floor. Then he was bending her legs and pushing them back toward her chest. They were speaking to her, both of them, but she didn't understand.

Lindsay reared up, sent her fist into the doctor's jaw, and sent him staggering back, flailing his arms to keep his balance, knocking over an instrument tray. She tried to grab the blanket, but it was out of her reach. Suddenly there was another man, and the three of them held her down. Her legs were pushed back again and one of the men was holding them back and apart. The nurse was beside her again, her hand lightly stroking her cheek, trying to quiet her. But Lindsay saw those men, and all three of them were looking at her between the legs and touching her and then one of them suddenly stuck two fingers inside her and she felt raw pain rip through her and she screamed and tried to jerk back on the cold table. Then she felt his fingers curling deep inside her. She screamed and screamed but he didn't stop. He scooped her out and she was watching his face, seeing him nod to the other doctor as he looked down at the fingers that had been in her body.

The nurse looked angry and she said something sharp to the men. One of them said something sharp back to her even as he pushed a long instrument into Lindsay's vagina.

The probing went on and on, an instrument inserted and withdrawn, cold and hard and thick, and the talk between the men with an occasional curt word from the nurse. Lindsay saw their frowns and their nods through a haze of pain and humiliation. She felt it burning deep into her. She felt a needle slide into her hip. It felt cold. One of the men patted her thigh as if she was some sort of pet or child. Then she felt nothing else.

She awoke alone in a private room. She was naked from the waist down, her legs sprawled. She cried out, lurching up, but the men weren't here, only a nurse, who was washing her with warm soapy water.

The woman was young and pretty and she smiled and lightly patted Lindsay's stomach, her fingers damp and warm. She said in very clear, unaccented English, "No, please don't be afraid. Just hold still, yes, that's it. Lie back. They said I could finally clean you up. The doctors got all the evidence they needed and made certain you weren't hurt internally. I'm so sorry, but I'll give you another shot in a minute, after I'm done washing you and you've taken your pills. We don't want you to get pregnant from this. That's right, just hold still. No, no more crying. You're still suffering from shock, which is completely natural. Ah, those damned doctors, they scared you badly, didn't they? Stupid men, and after what had happened to you! Giselle said they didn't go easy with you. They have no understanding of what you've been through and they were so very busy."

Lindsay thought: I'm lying here naked and a stranger is washing me and I've been raped and Sydney shot her husband and he's dead. It was simply too much. She closed her eyes, wishing she could also close out all the vicious and bloody images burned into her memory. The woman continued to speak, telling her about how they'd had to deal with her along with a three-car accident and this handsome young man—an American, just like she was—and his poor broken arm. The doctors really hadn't meant to be so rough, but there had been so little time and others were hurt far worse than she was.

Yes, a crushed body from a car accident was far worse than a simple rape. The nurse gave Lindsay the pills and another shot in her hip. She stayed with her, holding her hand until she slept. She spoke softly, hypnotically, "I'm from Kansas City, you know. My name is Ann O'Conner. I've lived here in Paris for eleven years now. I was glad I could be here when they brought you in. Now you have someone you can communicate with. Even the nurses can be short with foreigners. It's too bad, but it's true. Your face is badly bruised, but no broken bones. The bruises will fade in a couple of days. Go to sleep now. You'll feel much better when you wake up. And I'll be back, I promise you."

And she did as nurse O'Conner said. When Lindsay next awoke, it was light outside, the sun high in the sky. Near noon, she thought vaguely, startled, for it had been in the dark of the night when the prince . . . For several minutes she didn't know where she was. She focused on the sunlight, unconsciously leaning toward it, welcoming it into her. She remembered then, everything, though her mind fought against it. She started crying, like a faucet coming on without her permission, but she simply couldn't stop it. Her throat was clogged and it hurt to swallow, and as much as she gulped and wiped her eyes, she couldn't make the tears stop. She finally decided it didn't matter. She was alone. Thankfully, she was alone. Her face hurt dreadfully, and she felt as though someone had battered her insides.

The door opened quietly. She kept her head turned away. She didn't want to see anyone. Maybe it was one of those horrible doctors who had hurt her so badly, who hadn't cared when they'd shoved things into her, who had shamed her to her soul.

A man's voice said very gently, "*Mademoiselle*? You are awake, are you not?"

His English was accented, unlike nurse O'Conner's, but perfectly understandable. Still, she didn't move, said nothing. Maybe he'd go away. Please let him go away.

"I'm sorry to intrude upon you after what happened, but I must. I am Inspector Galvain with the Paris Sûreté. They sent me because I speak English passably well. I hope you will bear with my efforts. *Mademoiselle*? Please, you must speak to me. I am sorry, but it is so. I have no choice and neither do you."

She turned her head slowly on the pillow. She saw the surprise on his face and the flash of pity before he checked it. She raised her hand and touched her fingers to her bruised cheek and jaw. The prince had struck her many times, hard, with his fist.

"Is he dead?"

The inspector didn't hesitate, and his voice was matter-of-fact. "No, he isn't dead. Your sister's aim wasn't that good. Prince di Contini will live. He won't feel particularly well for a week or two, but he will live. But I do not wish to speak of him at the moment. My concern is with you. Please, you must tell me exactly what happened."

Lindsay shook her head. More tears spilled over and she swallowed. Where were they coming from? Her throat hurt so badly.

"Please, compose yourself. That is better. Take your

time, there is no hurry. All so difficult, I know, *petite*. Just take your time."

"You will get nothing reasonable out of her. I will tell you exactly what happened, Inspector."

It was Royce Foxe and he was standing in the doorway, looking strong and sure and confident. Lindsay couldn't believe her eyes. Her father had come to her the moment he'd found what had happened to her. He'd come to her now because it was urgent that he be here for her. He had realized that and he'd come. Relief and love and forgiveness for his past indifference, his past cruelties, flowed through her. Lindsay tried to sit up but was too weak. It didn't matter because her father was here for her. She smiled at him, raising her hand, and whispered, "Daddy."

Her father looked at her, then quickly away. He continued before the inspector could say anything, waving a hand toward Lindsay, "This stupid girl fell in love with Prince Alessandro di Contini nearly two years ago when she was only sixteen, at the wedding between the prince and her older sister, Sydney. She led him on. She worshiped him and showered him with all these silly feelings. She treated him like he was a god, and what was he to do? He is a man, after all. He invited her here, paid for her to come, and she came willingly, never doubt that, Inspector, never doubt that. When he decided to take what she'd been offering, she changed her mind and fought him. My poor older daughter had to protect her. She was forced to shoot her own husband." He turned to Lindsay then and said in a very soft voice, "You are a pathetic little slut. Just look at you—I can't believe any man would even want to touch you. And now just see what you've brought down upon us."

"*Monsieur! C'est assez!* That is quite enough!"

Royce backed away. He was breathing hard, so angry that he tasted the raw harshness of it. The damned girl had come very close to ruining Sydney's life. Now she was trying to climb out of the bed and she was crying and shaking as she tugged at her ridiculous hospital nightgown that couldn't cover those ridiculously long legs of hers, whispering between gasping breaths, "That isn't true, Daddy, you know it isn't true! Sydney said he liked girls, girls younger than me even, that he didn't like her because she was too old even when they got married. She said he had to wait for me because he couldn't get to me before. She said he was sick, that she came as soon as she discovered what he was planning to do—"

"Shut up, you damned little fool!" Royce turned the full force of his authority on her, and his voice turned low and vicious. "Don't you lie to me, Lindsay. You agreed to have an affair with him. When he got a little crude, slapped you up a little bit, you yelled rape and your sister was forced to help you. God, I never thought the time would come when I'd have to protect Sydney from you! Just look what you've done! You've ruined your sister's life!"

Inspector Galvain stepped between father and daughter. He couldn't believe the unbelievable spite of this man. It had taken him so off-guard that he'd found himself tongue-tied. God in heaven, what had the daughter done to deserve it? He said smoothly, very formally, "You will please leave now, Monsieur Foxe. The doctors have told me your daughter is still suffering from shock. This is quite understandable if you would but pause a moment to think about it. She is also still in pain. The prince struck her very hard, as you can see from the bruises on her face. Also she is hurt internally. I would say that 'crude' is somewhat of an understatement. I would say that you need to reassess what has happened. The prince was brutal; he was an animal. I will attend you later, *monsieur*."

Royce wanted to tell the fool inspector to go fuck himself, but he realized, even in his rage, that it wouldn't be smart. The inspector could cause him trouble. It was his country and Royce had no authority here. He stared at the man who looked so ineffective, so damned unlike an inspector should—short and slight, with a nearly bald head and sad brown eyes. Jesus, this was a policeman? Even his voice lacked authority and command. His attempt at stiff formality was absurd. Royce then thought of his sweet Sydney waiting for him downstairs in the car he'd hired, tired and bereft and silent as a ghost, in far worse shape than this little bitch, lying there, staring at him as if struck dumb by what he'd said. Sydney needed him to tell her what needed to be done, needed him to make things right again. He was her father; he loved her. He would take care of everything for her. He nodded to the inspector.

After all, Royce had said what was true; he'd said what he wanted to say, what had needed to be said. He didn't look again at Lindsay, merely turned on his heel and left the room.

The inspector was silent as he looked down at Lindsay. He felt very sorry for her. He'd wanted to slug Royce Foxe in the face. Instead, he said in his soft voice, resisting the impulse to hold her hand and soothe her, "I have a daughter who is just your age. Just like you, *mademoiselle*. Her name is Felice. Last year she got this crush—that's the American slang, isn't it?—yes, this crush on an older man and she acted so foolish and so silly that we all of us were equally annoyed and despairing. But this man, he was a normal adult, you see, with no sickness in his mind, and thus it was that he understood she was merely a young girl in the agony of infatuation. He was kind to her, but nothing more. He didn't take advantage of her. No normal man would. Do you understand?"

She stared up at him, her eyes dull, not caring about his wretched daughter. "Yes, I understand."

"Good. Now, tell me exactly what happened."

Her voice was as dull as her eyes, and it worried him. "My father told you what happened. It's true what he said, only it isn't, not really. The prince wrote to me that both he and Sydney wanted me to visit them here in Paris. I wanted to see him, it's true. I thought he was the most wonderful man in the world. I worshiped him. I thought my stepsister wasn't right for him, wasn't worthy of him—"

"Ah, and you, *mademoiselle*, were the only one who was right for him?"

"Yes. I believed she mistreated him, that she didn't give him what he needed, what he wanted, what he deserved. Of course he told me of the bad things she'd done to him."

"So you stayed when you saw your sister wasn't there?"

"Yes. It seemed so natural, you see. He told me Sydney

didn't like him and had left. He told me not to blame
myself. I felt so badly for him. I was so angry at my sister
for hurting him. He was wonderful and so nice and he took
me everywhere, showed me all through Montmartre, told
me old stories. It was just like all my daydreams coming
true. And then that night, he came in my bedroom and
started asking me questions about what I let boys do to me
and he told me he wanted to teach me all those things. He
told me how he'd had to wait for me. And then I really
saw him. He wasn't handsome anymore or charming or
kind. I was so afraid of him, and then, finally, I realized
that he wasn't what I'd believed him to be. He hurt me but
I fought him, and I screamed and screamed like they taught
me to do in my self-defense classes, and then he hit me
and hit me and then . . ."

The inspector waited. He saw she couldn't get the
words out and said gently, "Then your sister came and she
shot him. He had already ejaculated in you?"

She looked at him.

Galvain searched his mind for another word, saying
finally, "He came inside you?"

She nodded, a spasm shaking her body.

"Your sister fired the gun again?"

"Yes, she had to. To protect me. He fell off me onto
the floor. We thought he was dead, but then he groaned."

Galvain patted her hand, unable to keep himself from
making this bit of human contact with her. He wasn't particularly surprised when she jerked away. Poor girl, he
thought, poor girl. "You rest now, *mademoiselle*, and you
get yourself strong again. All this will fade, you will see."
He prayed it would be true, but he doubted it. Fade, yes,
but she would never forget, never. He wondered what she
would be like in five years, in ten. He added, "Your father
has hired two guards to keep the paparazzi away from you,
those vultures, and the other media people as well. They
will lose interest soon enough. I will talk to you again. Rest,
*petite*."

Royce Foxe's voice was heavy with fatigue, his eyes rheumy
and burning with grit as he opened the suite door. He

stared at the same inspector who'd been in Lindsay's room at the hospital. "What the hell do you want? Is it the damned prince again? I thought you said he was improving by the hour?" Royce hadn't slept much during the past three days. Even now he knew there was much to do. And now this French police inspector was here again, at Royce's suite, this calm little man Royce was beginning to reassess. Perhaps the little man wasn't quite so insignificant after all. But nonetheless, he didn't stand a chance with him, with Judge Royce Foxe. "I've been assured that my daughter won't be charged with murder. She won't be charged with anything. She acted in defense of her sister. I'm an attorney and an American federal judge, and surely you must know that you can't prey on my ignorance, because I don't have any."

"Yes, I know you are a judge, *monsieur*."

"The bastard will live. So what do you want now?"

"It is a relief," Galvain said, looking around. "No, your daughter won't be charged with murder. That has never been an issue. That is not why I'm here, *monsieur*. I want to know if the young *mademoiselle* Lindsay Foxe will be pressing charges against the man. The hospital told me you'd brought her here yesterday."

"What did you say?"

The inspector remained calm and still and patient, saying, "The Prince di Contini raped her. He brutalized her. Is your daughter here, *monsieur*? I must speak with her."

"No, you won't speak to her, there's no need. Do you think I'm mad? There will be no charges against the prince. Good day, Inspector."

"I must hear this from *mademoiselle*."

Royce didn't know what to do. Damned little man with the power of the police behind him. Royce hadn't, quite simply, thought through the consequences. "I will have my daughter get in touch with you tomorrow, Inspector. I thought you were so concerned about her health. Well, prove it, and go away. She is resting now."

"No, I'm awake." Lindsay came slowly into the living room, wearing a nightgown and bathrobe, her feet in soft flat slippers. Her curly hair was tangled around her face, thick and wavy. She looked sixteen years old, except when one noticed the fading bruises and the weary eyes that held too much knowledge for a young girl of her age.

"Go back to bed, Lindsay," Royce said. "Now. You're not needed here."

Inspector Galvain was pleased when she turned to him, ignoring her father. "Hello, Inspector. Is everything all right? Sydney isn't in trouble, is she?"

"No, there is nothing to worry about with your sister."

"Her concern for her sister comes a little late, I should say."

Galvain watched the girl shrink away at the blast of her father's words. The damned bastard, as cold and brutal as the prince had been. Words or fists, it didn't matter. The soul was still shattered. Inspector Galvain wished he could take her home with him, to his wife, Lisse, who would smother her with love and reassure her that she hadn't been to blame.

He said to her now, formality deepening his voice, "I must ask you a question, *mademoiselle*. I must know if you will press charges against the prince."

Her face went slack.

"I told you, Inspector, she won't!"

"*Mademoiselle?*" Even as he looked at her, his expression as neutral as he could make it, he knew it was impossible for her. But he wanted to try. He wanted to see what the girl was made of. If only he could get her father out of the room, but then, the man would still have a chance at her, to batter her even more than the prince had, only his abuse would be emotional, and the good Lord knew that he'd had years upon years to build weapons for his arsenal.

Lindsay didn't look at her father. Suddenly she looked very old and immeasurably tired. To Galvain's surprise, she said in a very calm voice, "If I press charges, Inspector, what exactly would happen?"

He waved his hand to keep her father silent and said gently, "I am proud that you don't immediately dismiss the idea of bringing this man to justice. You are a smart girl."

"I would like to press charges against him. He hurt me badly. He raped me. He isn't normal. I wish I could be sure that other girls who are fool enough to fall for his charm and good looks won't be hurt. He should be forced, at the very least, to have treatment."

"Excellent, *mademoiselle*. I applaud what you say. It is exactly right."

"It makes no difference," Royce yelled. "She won't press charges, damn you."

Galvain ignored Royce Foxe. "As I said, *mademoiselle*, you are a smart girl. You show courage." He hadn't expected this much from her, he really hadn't. But now he had to put a stop to it. He couldn't let her go through with it. Perhaps, just perhaps, her bastard of a father had learned something about his daughter. But he doubted it. He said to her, his voice very gentle, "You wanted to know exactly what would happen. I will tell you the truth that is unvarnished. A trial would mean an international scandal. Your family is well-known in America and the prince's family is equally well-known in Europe. You would be butchered by the press and in the courtroom. Your family would be harassed and hounded to a most painful extent. Your sister would possibly be charged with attempted murder if the rape charge failed to stand in court. Do you understand me, *mademoiselle*?"

She stared at him. He hated to see the brief flash of spirit disappear from her face. He hated to see the dullness return to her eyes.

"Please don't misunderstand me. It would be right to press charges. I am very pleased that you want to consider it. But I also must be very honest with you. By the end of it, you would be destroyed. Your sister would be destroyed. I am truly sorry, but I cannot lie to you. It is what would happen. There is no mercy for a young girl who is unfortunate enough to find herself raped, particularly by a member of her family. Justice doesn't serve us in these cases, unfortunately. I am very sorry for it."

"I would have told her all that."

Lindsay said nothing for a very long time. She looked at the floor at her feet. Finally, her face and voice expressionless, she said, "Thank you, Inspector. You've been kind to me. You told me the truth. I guess I should also thank you for making me face up to what he did to me even though I know if I hadn't been so silly about him it never would have happened. I had thought only I would be attacked if I pressed charges against him, not my entire family. I had thought about it, before you came, because the prince is a horrible man, but now, now that I understand . . ." She stopped, shaking her head.

She walked slowly from the room, her last words hanging sadly in the air, the belt of her robe dragging on the floor. Galvain stared after her, feeling such pain he doubted he would ever forget.

Royce was pleased. He smiled after his daughter, then turned to smile his triumph at the inspector. "Are you now quite through with us?"

"Oh, yes, quite. But the paparazzi will be very busy. They are like the rutting little pigs, are they not? You have already read the papers and seen the television. I would recommend that you take your daughters and leave Paris as soon as possible. Flee the arena, as it were."

"I would agree. However, the prince's family is here, in seclusion now, of course. They've had the prince moved to a private hospital outside Paris, and the place is guarded like a fort. But I can't be sure they'll keep their mouths closed. His mother has informed me, the patronizing bitch, that she is displeased with Sydney. Imagine, she's blaming Sydney! I must remain and guard my daughter's reputation, her interests, see that they don't try to harm her through the press." Royce raked his fingers through his hair, and for a moment he looked vulnerable and overwhelmed. "Tell me, Inspector, what am I to do about the damned bastard?"

"You ask me, *monsieur*? Well, then, I will tell you. I would secure another gun and shoot his balls off."

Galvain gave Royce a small salute and left the suite.

# 5

## T A Y L O R

Taylor ran into the emergency room, pale and looking more terrified than a man should ever look.

The head emergency room nurse, Ann Hollis, was sixty, tough, and more seasoned than a four-star general. She saw the man coming toward her, saw his fear, and readied herself for the outbreak. Screaming, raw and impotent anger, outward fury, the rage brought on by the helplessness of it all. To her utter surprise, when he spoke, his voice was calm and low.

"I would appreciate your help . . ." He looked at her name tag. "Yes, Ms. Hollis. Lindsay or Eden is her name. I understand there was some sort of accident and she was hurt and now she's here, being treated. I'm her fiancé. Please tell me what's going on. This is very difficult."

And Ann Hollis responded to him with the truth. "I will tell you what I know. First of all, stop worrying. You stay here and I'll go check and find out exactly what's happening. All right?"

Taylor nodded and she left him. He didn't move. He waited, knowing that everything that mattered to him, everything that was deeply inside of him, deeply a part of him, hung in the balance.

Nurse Hollis touched his arm. "Two broken ribs, a collapsed left lung, which they're reinflating."

"How's that done?"

"A small incision between two ribs and a tube is inserted that's in turn connected to a lung machine. It makes breathing easier for her."

"Thank you."

"Contusions and lacerations, but those aren't all that bad." Ann Hollis paused, then drew a deep breath. "Then there's her face." Again she touched her hand to his arm. "It's impossible to say right now because Dr. Perry has just gotten to her. He's got examinations to make. He's got to get CT scans before he can make a determination."

"What exactly happened to her face?"

"It was badly smashed."

He flinched from the baldness of the image that word brought to his mind, but nonetheless he was grateful to her.

"However, Dr. Perry is one of the best reconstructive surgeons in New York City. He probably won't wait to operate. There's the problem of swelling, you know."

Taylor didn't say anything. He was trying not to shake. Nurse Hollis patted his arm again. Touch was very important, she knew that, it comforted, it reassured, it gave human connection and warmth. With a touch, the other person was no longer alone.

"As soon as I can find out any more, I'll call you. Please go sit down. I know it's hard, but you must try to stay calm. She won't die. Her face will heal. As I said, Dr. Perry is one of the best in facial reconstruction."

"Thank you, Ms. Hollis."

She watched him walk slowly away from her. She'd seen the young woman's face. They hadn't cleaned it yet, and there was nothing but dried blood and bits of bone and matted blood-dried hair. Yes, it would be difficult to be beautiful when your face was smashed.

Taylor felt the weight of helplessness. And suddenly he remembered how he'd failed her in Paris, the crying young girl who didn't understand what was happening to her, the young girl who'd been raped so brutally, struck repeatedly, and yet she was at a hospital but the hurt was continuing and she was unable to grasp any of it. And he'd been unable to help her. Just as he'd not helped her this time either.

Her face was smashed. Dear God, what had happened? But all he could think of was the eighteen-year-old Lindsay in Paris, hurt and scared and beaten. And none of it her fault. Just as none of it this time was her fault. And he'd been unable to help her this time, just as he'd been unable then. . . .

# 6



*April 1983*  TAYLOR

He heard her screams and reacted immediately because he was a cop. He tried to get up, tried his damnedest to go to her and help her, but he couldn't. He staggered to his feet, then fell back against the examining table, clutching his broken left arm. He felt nauseous and dizzy from the concussion, and the pain in his arm was becoming more than he could handle.

He was in the emergency-room cubicle next to hers and he'd seen a policeman carry her in a few minutes before, a young girl wrapped in a blanket, her hair disheveled, her face terribly bruised, her eyes wild and vague. She was deep in shock. He recognized it for what it was. She'd been raped, he'd heard them saying.

Okay, so she'd been raped. Why was she screaming now? What were they doing to her? He gleaned quickly enough that she was American and didn't speak French or understand it. Taylor spoke French fluently. He was a Francophile; he had flown to France at least twice a year since he'd turned eighteen. This time he'd spent two weeks riding his motorcycle through the Loire Valley, then back to Paris for three days. And now this. What the hell were they doing to her?

She screamed again and again, deep tearing cries that were liquid with pain and fear and hopelessness, and he could hear the doctors clearly now because they had to talk over her. They were pissed that she couldn't understand them, pissed that she was giving them trouble, pissed that she was fighting them and the girl was so strong to boot and they couldn't hold her down. They were impatient and hassled and they wanted her to shut up so they could get it over with. He should go in there and help her, he thought again, at least translate for her, but he knew that if he moved he would fall on his face. He listened now, for they were speaking even more loudly over her cries.

". . . raped by her brother-in-law, the cop said. Look at her face—the man's an animal."

"Help me get this blanket off her. No, stop fighting. Damnation, she can't understand a word. Hold her, Giselle! Jacques, would you look at the mess here. She was a virgin, just look at all that blood. The guy reamed her good. Dammit, hold her still!"

"Get her legs wider, I've got to get my fingers in there. That's it, press her legs back to her chest. Stop it, no, hold her! Damn, she can't understand me! Ow! Jesus!"

She'd struck the doctor. Hard, from the sound of it. Taylor could hear him lurching around, heard an instrument tray fall to the linoleum floor. He smiled. Good for her. He saw another doctor run into the cubicle. The girl had been raped and they were stripping her and prodding her about like she was a slab of meat. She was quite probably terrified, hysterical, and in pain. There'd been a three-car pileup, he'd heard, which was why he was lying here unattended. At least they were seeing to her.

But couldn't they go a bit easier with her?

He could hear her crying, gasping for breath. He heard the nurse, Giselle, tell the doctors to stop being pigs, she was just a young girl and afraid of them because they were men and she'd just been raped, for God's sake. And one of the doctors said, "Not all that little, Giselle. Hold her down, will you?"

"Yeah," another one of the doctors said, "not little at all, and her body doesn't look all that young either."

The third doctor didn't say anything, he was breathing too hard to catch his breath.

Taylor wished he could hit the bastards. But he just lay there listening to the doctors talk about her, listening to them curse because she wasn't cooperating with them. He listened to the girl's cries, his own pain washing over him. He closed his eyes, but it didn't really help, and he knew he wouldn't forget her screams for a very long time.

". . . Two fingers, dammit, you've got to go deeper and clean her out good. The cops want all the guy's sperm and you need to feel for torn tissue. She's probably torn inside."

She was crying helplessly now. He saw the third man finally emerge from the cubicle, wipe his hands on his pants, and come into Taylor's small enclosure. He nodded to him, then asked him a question in French, speaking very, very slowly. Like Americans did, to make themselves understood to stupid foreigners. Taylor answered him quickly in French, fluently and with no accent, saying without preamble, "The girl who was raped, how is she? Will she be all right?"

The doctor muttered something about Americans minding their own business, to which Taylor looked hard at him and repeated his question. The doctor shrugged as he bent over Taylor's arm. "She's eighteen, an American, and her brother-in-law, a damned Italian prince of all things, split her up really good. He bashed up her face, tore her a bit internally, and she's bleeding like there's no tomorrow. But she'll be all right, at least her body will heal in time. I heard the girl's sister shot him and he's upstairs in surgery. Jesus, what a mess." Then he shrugged, a typical French reaction, as if to say: What do you expect from foreigners except endless stupidities?

Then the doctor was talking about his broken arm, Taylor realized, clucking, turning it and making him grit his teeth, punishment, Taylor assumed, for being pushy. Taylor said in a stony voice that did little to mask his pain, "I'm a cop with the NYPD. How long will it take to heal? I've got to get home and back to work."

The doctor raised his head and smiled, and shot off in his fastest French, "Give it six weeks and stay off your motorcycle. As for your head, you're lucky you were wearing a helmet. Damned machines will kill you."

"Not a scrap of luck to it," Taylor said easily. "I'm not stupid."

The doctor did a sudden about-face. "Say, you're French, aren't you? You just moved to the United States?"

"Nary a bit," Taylor said with a big smile. "Born and bred in Pennsylvania." He paused and added, "I'm just good at languages and, truth be told, French is pretty easy."

He wished he hadn't said anything, because in the next instant he sucked in his breath.

"Sorry. I'm sending you to be X-rayed now. No drugs yet, not with that concussion. Wait here a minute and I'll send someone for you. Oh, yeah, I could tell you weren't really French."

Taylor sighed, closed his eyes, and heard the girl sobbing low now. Her throat must hurt badly, for the cries were hoarse and raw. He waited another five minutes. He was still there when she was wheeled out on a gurney. He saw her briefly again—hair in thick tangles around her face, and God, her face, all bruised, one eye puffed shut, her upper lip swelled and bleeding, a lot worse now than when she'd been brought in. She was unconscious, probably drugged. She looked very young. She looked helpless, utterly vulnerable. At least her sister had shot the bastard.

He didn't understand what would make a man do such a thing, but the good Lord knew he'd seen enough of it his past two years on the force, at his home in the Twelfth Precinct.

A bloody Italian prince. Nothing figured anymore. Taylor sighed again, wishing someone would come and just get all the pain over with.

He was discharged two days later, his arm in a cast. He still suffered nagging headaches. He'd paid out eight hundred dollars in cash for all the hospital services. He had just enough to go home to New York. As for his motorcycle, he'd insured the Harley since he'd rented it here in Paris, so he was only out a hundred bucks for the deductible.

He was tired and felt sorry for himself, even though he knew, objectively, that he was lucky to be alive. The guy had gunned his white Peugeot from a narrow side street and smacked him hard, sending him flying, not onto the pavement, thank God, but into a stand of thick bushes. Those bushes had saved his life. The guy had driven away, leaving him there to curse and hold his arm and wait for the cops to come. And they had. They'd brought him to St. Catherine's Hospital and he'd lain there listening to that poor girl screaming and screaming. He was a cop; he should have just endured it with a shrug. But he couldn't, somehow.

In another day, Taylor was at Charles de Gaulle Airport waiting for his Pan Am flight to be called when he saw one of the Parisian dailies screaming headlines about a Prince Alessandro di Contini having survived the two bullets shot into him by his wife. Taylor's flight was called. He left the small kiosk, aware of the beginnings of yet another headache. He left the newspaper on the counter. He accepted two aspirin from a flight attendant, leaned back, and closed his eyes, saying his usual prayer that the plane would make it into the air.

He thought of Diane, his fiancée of four months, wondering yet again if it was smart for them to get married. They'd lived together in Diane's spacious East Side apartment for the past six months. She was rich and he wasn't. He was a cop and she was trying to talk him off the force, but he was young and arrogant and confident and he didn't buy it. She'd come around. It was her responsibility. They were good in bed together. His trip to France was his bachelor's last fling the way he saw it. Diane thought he was nuts because he wanted to vacation by himself, riding a motorcycle all over a foreign country, but she'd only bitched a little bit, content to warn him a good three times not to catch anything with French girls. Everyone knew how promiscuous they were. Taylor didn't, but he didn't bother to correct her. He'd tried to explain that it was the country itself that drew him, that he really couldn't explain it, but when he'd hitchhiked there when he was eighteen, he knew, simply knew that at one time or another he'd lived here, been part of the land, part of the culture. A previous life? He didn't know, but he did know that he felt wonderful when he was riding a motorcycle beside the Loire River, smelling the ripening grapes in Bordeaux, gazing in awe at the ancient Roman ruins scattered throughout Provence.

He'd be home soon, a couple days early. He wondered when he'd be able to go to France again. There was already the longing for it growing in his gut. He would be twenty-five in two weeks and married in three.

He thought again of the young girl in the emergency room. He knew he wouldn't forget the rape, nor would he forget her battered face and her screams. Nor would he forget her name, the name beneath the prince's in that newspaper at the kiosk at the airport—Lindsay Foxe. Not that it mattered, he thought. Not that it mattered.

## 1987 LINDSAY

It was very hot and it was only the beginning of May. Lindsay sat on a stone bench under an oak tree on the Columbia campus. She was wearing loose-legged khaki walking shorts and a short-sleeved white blouse. Reeboks and thick white socks were on her feet. She wore a tennis bracelet on her right wrist, a gift to herself. She admired Chris Evert enormously. Her legs were already tanned from playing tennis every day for the past two months. She was very good but nowhere near great. Her forehand was a killer, her backhand two-handed but still unpredictable. As for her serve, she got an ace at least one in twenty times. She wasn't playing tennis until tomorrow morning with Gayle Werth, her best friend from the Stamford Girls' Academy, also a senior at Columbia, majoring in physical education. Gayle was her doubles partner and the better player.

Lindsay had one more final exam. She would graduate with a B.A. in psychology in two more weeks. From Columbia, a school with a good reputation.

Then what would she do? There had been company reps on campus a few months before, but nothing they had to offer interested her in the slightest, except for the foreign service, which sounded exciting, at least until she'd met the young man who was their primary representative. He couldn't talk about anyplace but Italy. Lindsay was never going to Italy.

Her stomach growled and she realized she hadn't eaten since the previous night at Marlene's apartment. Salami pizza with extra cheese and a can of light beer. It had made her sick.

The pizza had been god-awful, but it alone hadn't done her in. It was also that guy, Peter Merola, a friend of Marlene's, a classmate. He'd been persistent, and when he'd pretended to accidentally rub his hand against her breast, touching her nipple, she'd bolted to the bathroom and been sick in the toilet. When she'd come out, Peter was coming on to another girl and this one looked interested.

She was safe.

Lindsay rose even as she pulled a sheaf of notes from her large floppy purse. It was fine cordovan leather, soft light brown, and it grew softer by the year, four of them now. She carried everything in it, even her calculator, her books, some tennis balls, a razor, and an extra pair of socks and underwear. She fanned the notes out on her lap. This was her last course and it was taught by Professor Gruska, who was an ardent Freudian. He had intense eyes, looked like a professor, and lived with his father on the West Side at Eighty-fourth Street. He was at least fifty and had never been married. He was strange, but he thought she was stranger. Dr. Gruska had come to the conclusion that Lindsay was screwed up after he'd read a short play she had written, an assignment showing how members of a family related to each other. Lindsay had made up a family, but Dr. Gruska had probed and prodded. He'd gone so far as to read some of her play aloud in class. Then he'd called her to his office after class. He'd asked her questions about her father, wondering aloud if she had a thing for him. He suggested to her that he could help her sort things out. They could begin right now if she liked.

Lindsay had walked out, saying nothing. She was shaking and cursing and afraid within five minutes of leaving his wretched little office. Time had dealt with the worst of it, but not her intense hatred of Gruska, hatred coated with a goodly dose of fear. She would have never gone back, but she needed the class to graduate. She'd forced herself to apologize two weeks later; it was the hardest thing she'd ever had to do. He'd nodded, looking grave. He'd said only that she could call him or come to his office at any time. She could trust him. She realized then that he'd probably looked her up in old newspapers, and now he knew she'd been raped by her brother-in-law. She realized then that she wasn't certain what the papers had reported; she'd refused to read any of them. For all she knew, she'd been the one to seduce Alessandro and to shoot him. She closed off her memories. Now she was taking Gruska's final— essays, he'd told the class, because they were graduating seniors, psych majors, and reportedly somewhat literate. She read her notes as she walked toward the cafeteria, thinking it was a great deal of bullshit. She'd never had a thing for her father; all she'd ever wanted was for him just to recognize that she was there and that she was his daughter. Was that abnormal? Probably no more abnormal than her choosing psychology for a major because she'd hoped, deep down, that she would gain some insights, some self-awareness, to help her stop trembling with terror whenever a man came close to her. Some courses, some professors, had been helpful. Outwardly, no one would ever be able to guess what had happened to her—she'd filled herself with insights from every psychological theory; she'd grown up; she understood that the prince was mentally ill and she had been just a helpless girl drawn in by him; she accepted her fear of men as not being normal, but quite natural, of course, because of what the prince had done to her. She accepted all of it, took it in mental stride, smiled occasionally with cool objectivity at the idea of anyone being actually afraid of the opposite sex, but in the stillness of the night, when she was alone, the pain of those memories could still overwhelm her, the pain and the humiliation, her own stupidity. But she handled it now. At the very least, psychology had taught her how to handle it. Except handling Gruska, the jerk.

She was stuffing papers back into her purse when she saw the letter from her grandmother that had arrived yesterday afternoon. She'd forgotten to read it. She pulled it out and put it to her nose, still smelling the faint odor of musk roses, her grandmother's favorite scent, made especially for her in Grasse, France, by one man named d'Alembert, after the eighteenth-century French philosopher. Gates Foxe was eighty-two and d'Alembert had made her perfume for nearly forty years now. Lindsay had flown to San Francisco at Christmas at her grandmother's request. Lindsay hadn't seen her in several years. She'd slowed down, but her mind was still sharp and she still loved life and still tried to control those around her. Only there wasn't anyone around her anymore. Royce had remarried the year before. His new wife had been there for Christmas and it hadn't been very much fun. The new wife, formerly Holly Jablow, widow of the former Washington state senator, Martin Jablow, was thirty-five. She was vain and greedy and when she wasn't focused on her new husband, she was focused exclusively on herself. She loved mirrors. She quickly saw her husband's dislike for his daughter and adapted in the next moment. She was grating and sweetly patronizing, giving Lindsay advice on her clothes, on her hair, on her fingernails. Lindsay had suffered her in silence. As for Jennifer, Lindsay had seen her mother only once. She was too thin, too nervous, smoked incessantly, and was sleeping with a man who was twenty-six years old. Jennifer had been forced to introduce Lindsay to the man when she'd come to her apartment one afternoon unannounced. She treated her daughter like a rival. Lindsay had left quickly, feeling cold and very sad and very alone. She'd felt all ties to San Francisco falling away from her.

Lindsay pulled the two pages from the envelope, a smile on her face, expecting to hear chatty news about friends and vagaries about the rich and richer in San Francisco. Her grandmother had a light touch with her at least. The letter began as she'd expected.

Just news at first, chatter about Moffitt Hospital and how the board of directors was loath to spend enough money to modernize the new radiology rooms. She raved about Reagan, mourned the horrible proportion of Democrats to Republicans in northern California. Then Lindsay stopped smiling.

"I don't think anyone bothered to tell you because you really don't exist to your father, as you well know—his fault, not yours. Sydney is pregnant. I have no idea if the prince is the father, nor does your father know, by the way. I suppose the family will pass the child off as a di Contini regardless. They really have no choice, since Sydney stayed with Alessandro and played the contrite wife wrapped in a coat of endless remorse. I found I could still be surprised, even after all these years. Sydney is different in some ways, Lindsay, but you would have to see her for yourself to understand how I mean it. She was here by herself a couple of weeks ago. There's a brittle hardness about her, but also an inwardness, an awareness, that makes her not quite like her former self. It's as if she were now responsible for the world. Odd, but true somehow. It's been four years, hasn't it, since you last saw her? Since that awful time in Paris?"

Lindsay went still. Her grandmother knew she hadn't seen Sydney since that horrible time in Paris. Why was her grandmother calling that all up? It didn't matter; an intelligent adult with sharpened insight always dealt with things and smiled and went on with life.

"She told me the prince is as he always was, and I take that to mean that he still likes young girls. Forgive me if this makes you uncomfortable, Lindsay, but it has been four years now and it's time for you to face up to it. I saw at Christmas how guarded you were, how you wouldn't even get near that nice boy, Cal Faraday, who is Clay and Elvira's son and a very smart boy in his first year of medical school. I know what your father says, Lindsay, this damnable litany of his, but he's wrong and you mustn't believe him. The rape wasn't your fault, none of it. Grow up, my dear girl, put this behind you. . . ."

Lindsay raised her head and looked out over the Columbia campus. How very easy it was to analyze and to judge, to proffer well-meant advice to another person. That was something else she'd learned as a psychology major.

She quickly folded the letter and stuffed it back into the depths of her bag. She walked to the psych building, up the indented stairs to the second floor and into room 218, and sat down in her usual chair. No one said much of anything. Every male and female in the room scented the finish line. Everyone just wanted it done and over with. Dr. Gruska and his graduate assistant handed out blue books; then they handed out a single sheet of paper with essay questions on it. She pulled out her ball-point pen and began to write.

She wrote for three hours, filled up two blue books, handed them silently to the graduate assistant, didn't look at Dr. Gruska, and quickly left the building. The day was even warmer now. She had no more classes. She was free. She was through with Columbia. Soon she would have a B.A. degree and no job and no ideas for a job.

She took the ferry across to the Statue of Liberty and sat there in the hot sun watching early tourists wander around and exclaim and gawk, and thinking about precisely nothing.

That evening, to her surprise, Cal Faraday called her and asked her out to dinner and a movie. He'd just finished his first year at Johns Hopkins and was in New York for a few days visiting friends. She said no, her voice very friendly, and went to bed with a mystery.

## *1 9 8 7*  T A Y L O R

Taylor was off-duty. He was wearing his favorite dark brown corduroy pants, a white cotton shirt, and a sleeveless down vest. He was on his way to pick up Dorothy Ryan for dinner at her apartment at Lexington and Sixty-third. He was whistling, feeling better about things and about himself. Dorothy was pretty, funny, and quickly climbing the ladder in advertising. He'd first seen her at a Giants game when Montana of the 49ers had carved up his team like a Christmas goose. She'd been yelling and cursing and soon he found himself watching her instead of the game. He'd bought her a beer and a hot dog and they'd gone to bed that night.

She had fun with sex, teasing him, kissing him all over, making him squirm and moan, and then was letting him bring her to orgasm. She was loving and kind and utterly content with her life the way it was. When she said she wasn't interested in marriage, he believed her. It was a relief. He started whistling louder, his step picking up, when suddenly he heard a loud scream, then another, then a series of gulping cries. It was from a two-flat brownstone just to his left, a building with the smoothness of age and an air of discretion. Suddenly an older woman erupted from the beveled front doors and down the six stone steps, her arms flapping wildly, yelling her head off.

The woman looked like a domestic with bad taste, with her hair tinted a violent red, her fingernails lacquered orange, her dress a South Seas print in bright colors. Odd, but she wore old ladies' shoes on her feet and her nylons were baggy around her knees. She was large, her face heavy, her brows thick across her forehead. She wore too much makeup. She was shrieking now, incoherent. Taylor registered all this in a moment; then he was running to her.

"I'm a police officer. What's wrong?"

She tried to get her breath, eyeing him as if she couldn't believe that a cop was standing right in front of her, then frowning as if she didn't really want him there, as if this was her one chance at drama. He tightened his hold on her upper arms and shook her lightly. Another scream, thankfully, died in her mouth.

"Oh, Jesus, Jesus! My little girl, she's up there bleeding to death!"

"Did you call an ambulance?"

The woman shook her head and her eyes rolled.

"Take me to her now."

He had to shove her to get her moving. Several people hurried by them, heads down, eyes averted. It was, after all, New York. Something like this shouldn't be happening in this neighborhood.

Taylor followed the woman up one flight of stairs, wide stairs in polished oak. Beautifully maintained. No filth, no Flatbush Avenue smells, just a dull rich scent of an expensive room spray. The stairs resounded beneath their steps, deep and full.

"Did your daughter cut herself? What happened? Why is she bleeding?"

The woman shook her head and turned down a wide immaculate corridor and shoved open a thick mahogany door.

"Ellie?" she shrieked. "Where are you, girl?"

Taylor heard a wispy cry. He pushed past the woman and ran through the long spacious living room into a hallway. He turned into the first room, and there she was, lying naked on a single bed, a girl of no more than fifteen. Her face was blotchy and swollen and there was blood smeared all over her legs and onto the white sheets. She was gasping for breath, and when she saw Taylor, she grabbed the sheet to cover herself and jerked back against the headboard. Her eyes were dilated with terror and swollen with pain and tears.

Taylor immediately stopped and smiled. "What happened? I'm Taylor and I'm a police officer and I won't hurt you. Let me help you, okay? Tell me what happened?"

"Bandy poked it into me and he hurt me and now I'm bleeding like I'm going to die."

"What's your name?"

"Ellie."

"Ellie," he repeated, smiling. Rape, he thought. He saw a phone on the table by the bed. He smiled at the girl even as he moved toward the phone. "It'll be all right. I'm going to call an ambulance. All right? No, don't cry out. I'm not going to hurt you."

She was frozen with fear but she didn't make another sound. Her small face, if anything, got even paler. Taylor dialed 911 and ordered an ambulance, turning to see the woman standing in the doorway, wringing her hands, her eyes fastened on the girl. He asked her the address. He had to ask her again. Once done, he replaced the phone in its cradle.

"Now," he said, smiling, "tell me about Bandy." He leaned over her and gently pulled the sheet from her fingers. "No, I'm not going to hurt you, but I've got to see how much blood you're losing. Please trust me, okay, Ellie?"

The girl nodded. "Bandy hurt me bad."

"I know, I know. Now, let me see. Hold still." Even

as he said those words, even as he was pulling the blood-stained white sheet down her body, he was remembering that long-ago night in a Paris hospital emergency room. And he knew why Ellie was bleeding.

"Who's Bandy?" he said again as he eased the sheet to her knees. Poor little tyke. He flinched at the sight of man's sperm mixed violently with so much blood, and the blood was still flowing out of her. "Don't move, Ellie." He turned to the woman. "Bring me four towels, quick!"

He lifted the girl's hips and slid two pillows beneath her. When the woman silently handed him the towels, he pressed one of them against Ellie and covered her lower body with another. He sat down beside her, applying as much pressure as he could.

"Tell me about Bandy."

"No!"

It was the woman, and now her face was flushed and she was shaking. "Bandy didn't do anything, not a thing! This stupid girl, she came onto him and what was he to do?"

Oh, God, Taylor thought, that night in the Paris hospital so clear again in his brain, and then the Paris newspaper of several days later, telling how the girl, Lindsay Foxe, had seduced her brother-in-law . . . and then he hadn't read anymore, but he still remembered what that doctor had told him. He'd boarded his plane and come home. He looked down at Ellie. Hell, this pathetic little scrap hadn't cried out a thing, only her fear and her pain. He looked up at her and said again, "Tell me about Bandy, Ellie." And to the woman when she opened her mouth, "Shut up. Go outside and bring the paramedics up when they get here. Go!"

"She's a liar! Don't believe a thing the ungrateful little slut says!"

Jesus, Taylor thought. He raised his right hand and gently touched his fingertips to the girl's soft cheek. "It's going to be all right now, Ellie."

"Bandy's my uncle, my mama's brother. I've known him forever."

Taylor nodded. He didn't think he could have stood it if she'd said it had been her brother-in-law.

"Is this the first time he stuck himself inside you?"

The girl nodded. "He made me do things to him for a long time now, but he never stuck that fat thing of his in me until today. I didn't want him to, but he made me. He made me bend over and he stuck it in me."

"Where is he?"

"He ran off when Mama came back early. He left me." Tears were seeping out of her eyes, falling into her mouth, choking her.

He felt the wet of her blood on his hand, soaked through the towel. He pulled it away, tossing it to the floor. He saw that the flow was still steady, cursed softly, and pressed another folded towel against her. "Just hold still, sweetheart. You'll be fine in just a little while. I'll get Uncle Bandy for you. I won't let him get away with this."

But Taylor knew in his heart that if she hadn't hemorrhaged her mother would never have panicked and come tearing out of the apartment to find him, and the little girl's rape would have gone unnoticed, unreported, and Uncle Bandy would probably have enjoyed her until she managed to escape from home.

When the paramedics arrived not five minutes later, a man and a woman, Taylor told them what had happened and showed them what he'd done.

"Good job, Lieutenant. Come on, Linda, let's get this poor kid to the hospital. You'll be along later, Lieutenant? The doctors will want to speak to you."

"Yeah, I'll be along. Take good care of her." He smiled at the girl and said quietly, "Don't worry. They're going to treat you like you're the president." And added to the paramedics, "I want to nail the bastard who did this to her. Tell the doctors to be careful about how she's examined. We'll need sperm samples. You know the routine."

He called Dorothy from a public phone and canceled out the evening. He heard her sigh, but she was game, and dutifully asked after the girl.

He took a taxi to Lenox Hill and strode into the emergency room. He could hear Ellie sobbing from the moment he walked into the long narrow room. And the memories flooded him. He unconsciously rubbed his left arm where the break had healed long ago.

He hadn't been able to help Lindsay Foxe. He walked into the small cubicle without hesitation. A woman doctor was working on Ellie and she looked up, frowning.

"I'm Lieutenant Taylor. I found her. I was worried and heard her crying. Can I do anything?"

The doctor nodded. "Okay, Lieutenant. Talk to her. Tell her she'll be fine."

Taylor stroked Ellie's face, pitching his voice low and soft. When she shuddered, he held her, never ceasing his meaningless words.

"I'm done now, Lieutenant. Thank you. Oh, here's the mother. Mrs. Delliah?"

"Yes, I'm her mother. She'll be all right, won't she, Doctor?"

"Yes, but I want to keep her for a couple of days. The bleeding's nearly stopped now. I've got all the samples I need for the police."

"No police," said Mrs. Delliah, crossing her arms over her large breasts. "No police."

"I see," the doctor said in an emotionless voice. "Which family member did this to her? Father? Uncle? Brother?"

Taylor looked up, startled. Then he realized that the good doctor had seen her share of ongoing sexual abuse and rape cases. Probably too many. She looked incredibly weary, the anger dull in her eyes.

"Nobody," said Mrs. Delliah firmly. "The girl was playing with a coat hanger. She did it to herself."

Ellie started crying, deep gulping, very ugly sounds. Taylor wanted to strangle the woman.

"Why would she do that?" Taylor asked, still holding Ellie's hand. "No, no more lies. Why are you protecting your brother, Mrs. Delliah? Look what he did to your child! For God's sake, are you just going to let him get away with this? The man's sick."

He was shouting, trembling from the force of his anger. The doctor laid a hand on his shoulder; Mrs. Delliah had backed up two paces.

Ellie cried and cried.

Taylor returned to his apartment on Fifty-fifth Street at Lexington at midnight. He was exhausted and disgusted. But he was going to get Uncle Bandy. Oh, yeah, he was going to nail the miserable bastard. No one was going to stop him.

# 7

## TAYLOR

He took a taped statement from Ellie the next day. He arrived in her private room at just after seven in the morning, early enough, he hoped, that her mother wouldn't have yet made an appearance. Lord knew what the woman would say today.

Ellie smiled when she saw him and held out her hand to him, shy, as a child would to an adult who had been kind to her. He'd thought about his questions, about how to phrase them, and he spoke slowly and gently. Her pitiful tale nearly broke his heart. She'd been abused by her uncle since she was eleven years old. He'd told her that she was his sweet little girl and she had to keep being sweet or she and her mother wouldn't be able to live in this beautiful apartment and she wouldn't be able to go to her nice private school and play with all her nice friends. At least he'd waited to rape her vaginally until she was nearly fifteen. Taylor didn't know whether or not he'd sodomized her and he couldn't bring himself to ask. Uncle Bandy always gave her nice presents, but he hurt her and she was afraid of him. This time he'd made her bleed real bad.

Taylor got all he needed and was just listening to Ellie tell him about her private school and the friends she had there. He delighted in the normalcy of her talk and wished he could take her home with him.

Mrs. Delliah arrived. She was subdued this morning and her clothing was less garish. She was wearing an expensive camel-hair coat over a plain wool dress of expressionless brown. Her face was scrubbed clean and he realized with something of a surprise she wasn't yet forty. Her red hair, less dubious this morning, was drawn back in a bun. She looked even more like a domestic today, one who wasn't a hooker on the side. To Taylor's relief, she didn't verbally attack her daughter. She was stiff with him, but at least she wasn't cruel to Ellie. She kissed her and petted her and told her she wanted her to come home.

Taylor said, "I would like to speak with you, Mrs. Delliah, after you've assured yourself that Ellie is all right. I'll wait for you in the hall."

Ten minutes later, Mrs. Delliah joined him. She looked wary and defiant. He motioned her to a waiting room. He said without preamble, "Your brother is sick. He needs psychiatric treatment immediately. Hell, he probably needed it twenty years ago. He could have killed your daughter. You've got to stop this and press charges and see that he gets help."

She was wringing her hands, scraping her knuckles on the heavy rings. "I can't."

"If you don't, he will continue to rape Ellie. Surely you know that. Didn't you know that he was abusing her for the past four years? Well, even if you didn't know, this is different, this is the real kicker. She's been completely violated now. She has nothing left and soon she will know it and not be able to deal with it. Is that what you want for your daughter? She'll take the abuse only until she can run away, and then she'll be alone and on the streets and then it's drugs and prostitution and God knows what. Is that what you want for her?"

"I don't have any money."

"There are organizations to help you. You aren't stupid, Mrs. Delliah. You can get a job."

"You don't understand."

"I understand that you are pimping for your brother,

using your own little girl. If you don't press charges, I will report you to the authorities and Ellie will be taken away from you."

She started crying. Taylor wasn't moved. She disgusted him.

"Will you press charges or do I see that Ellie is given to a family who will protect her?"

"He'll kill me," she moaned, hugging herself now, rocking back and forth.

"Don't be crazy. Of course he won't kill you. Tell me his name now, Mrs. Delliah."

"I didn't know he was gonna rape her. I didn't know he was doing things to her, I didn't! I just thought he . . ." No, she wasn't stupid. She was smart enough to stop herself.

He wanted to hit her, but said instead, "Will you press charges?"

In the end, she agreed. He took her to the precinct station and she signed a warrant and her statement. It was late afternoon when Taylor and his partner, Enoch Sackett, went to Uncle Bandy's address.

Taylor supposed he really wasn't surprised, but Enoch, tall and thin as a cane, just stood in front of the magnificent brownstone saying, "Shit, Taylor, this guy torments little girls? And he lives here? It looks like a set for the rich and famous. Why? A guy who has all this? Why?"

"I don't know."

Uncle Bandy was Mr. Brandon Waymer Ashcroft of the brokerage house of Ashcroft, Hume, Drinkwater, and Henderson, Water Street, New York, New York. He answered the door wearing a smoking jacket that shrieked London, with soft striped wool pants and leather slippers on his feet. He had a handsome angular face, was sitting firmly in his forties, slender, with a manner smooth as vintage Bordeaux. He appeared bewildered by their presence, a neat dark eyebrow edging up as he surveyed them on his doorstep, but utterly civilized. After inspecting their I.D.'s he stepped back and waved them in. They followed him over a beautiful old Tabriz into a study that was all smooth mahogany

and built-in bookshelves with uncut heavy books covered
in dark rich colors, and the smell of rich pipe tobacco.

"What can I do for you, gentlemen? Please, be seated.
Something to drink perhaps? A sherry? Forgive me. Beer?"

"Perhaps," Taylor said, "you should put on your shoes
and leave the Savile Row jacket in your closet. A nice conservative sport coat might be just the thing. An American
label. You're under arrest, Mr. Ashcroft, for the rape of
your niece, Miss Eleanor Delliah."

His bewildered look intensified, his brow furrowed. He
appeared to be intellectually insulted. He never lost his
smoothness. He worried with a pipe he never lit, a ruse
Taylor recognized to give him time to think. He was content
to let him think until hell froze over. It wouldn't do him
any good. "I really don't understand, gentlemen," he said
at last, adding quickly, "I should call my lawyer, I believe."
He also thought he should see his sister, poor woman, for
an explanation of this madness.

Taylor agreed.

Enoch winked at Taylor and smoothly cuffed Mr. Brandon Ashcroft, his hands behind his back. There wasn't
really any need, but Taylor wanted this touch of humiliation. The man deserved it. On the way to the station, Mr.
Ashcroft told them freely that his poor sister had gotten
pregnant years before and he had forced the man to marry
her—paid him off, actually. But the man had left her and
Ashcroft had freely and willingly supported her and her
daughter for the past fifteen years. They had seen her apartment. It was very nice. Both mother and daughter were
well provided for. Didn't they agree? There had to be some
confusion here.

Taylor turned in the passenger seat to face Mr. Ashcroft. "I do understand, Mr. Ashcroft. You provide housing
and food in exchange for sexually abusing a little girl."

If his hands hadn't been cuffed, Mr. Ashcroft would
have airily waved them. "That is nonsense, Lieutenant,
utter nonsense. I am a successful man. I am a sensible man.
I am an educated man. Why on earth would I, a man of
high station, do something so despicable, something so

completely incomprehensible, as to sexually abuse a child? It makes no sense, gentlemen."

"Perhaps the shrinks will figure that one out."

Mr. Ashcroft was never incarcerated. His lawyer was there within the hour, a judge duly called, a low bail posted, and he was out and free and on his way back to his lovely brownstone.

Taylor was disgusted, but it wasn't anything new. Money was a man's most powerful legal weapon. But he would nail Ashcroft. He had the mother's testimony and Ellie's. He had the doctor's evaluation as well, Ashcroft's sperm, and everyone involved in the case was mad as hell.

Still, Taylor fretted aloud to his captain, Dennis Bradly, a man of singular patience and goodwill, who watched him silently as he paced the confines of his office.

"The man is used to power. He's used to getting what he wants because he's got money. He's going to intimidate his sister and Ellie. You know it. I know it. The D.A. knows it. The question is, how do we protect them? How do we get this bastard?"

"Look, Taylor . . ." Bradly stopped and ran his fingers through his thinning gray hair. "I know you're up to your neck in this thing, what with you finding the girl and all and probably saving her life. You're too close, it screws up your perspective, makes your thinking muddled. You've got to back off."

"Back off what, Captain?"

"Ashcroft's big-time."

"He's a big shit."

"That too. We'll see. Look, the case is strong, airtight for the moment at least. The D.A. will try to keep it that way, but . . ." He shrugged and reached for his cold coffee in a Styrofoam cup. "Don't lose your head over this thing, Taylor. I know that Kreider case a couple months ago really got to you. You did the best you could, we all know that, but the law says that the accused has a right to face his accuser."

"Yeah, what a pity that the accuser gets iced two days before the trial. A real pro job, and our boy walks away with a big smile on his face, and a twenty-one-year-old woman who never did a bad thing in her life except see Kreider shoot another lowlife gets shot in the head because I talked her into testifying against him."

"It wasn't your fault. Things like that happen. We tried to protect her, you know that. Sometimes it just isn't enough. Hell, Taylor, you've been on the force long enough, what is it, six years now?"

Taylor nodded. "Ashcroft won't get away with this, Captain."

"I hope not," Captain Bradly said, but he didn't sound at all certain.

Taylor met with the assistant D.A., a young man who was bright enough but who didn't have a whole lot of experience, a young man who was still capable of burning with righteous indignation. He was pleased with the preponderance of evidence against Ashcroft. He was certain they would have the man bound over for trial. He told Taylor that Ashcroft's lawyer had already approached the D.A. but his boss wasn't going to bend on this. Taylor felt good. He felt hopeful. At last there would be justice. As for his partner, Enoch just looked at him, shook his head, and told him not to expect too much.

A preliminary hearing was set for the following Tuesday morning. Taylor couldn't wait. Ashcroft, with all his money and his slick lawyer, wouldn't weasel out of this one. No way. He'd be nailed.

He was delighted to hear that Judge Riker would be presiding. He was tough as rawhide and mean as a pit bull. Nobody put a thing over on him. He hated violence and criminals. When it came to rapists, he became nearly rabid with fury. The story was that his niece had been raped some ten years before and the punks responsible had escaped because the cops had seized the evidence improperly.

Judge Riker strode into the small courtroom, his black robes flowing, his thick white hair making him look like Moses, and told the assistant district attorney to get on with it.

The assistant D.A. did get on with it, and it went downhill from there.

The samples of sperm that unequivocally matched Mr.

Brandon Ashcroft's to that found in Ellie's body were missing from the lab. No one could find them.

Mrs. Delliah took the stand and told Judge Riker that her daughter, it turned out, had let one of the boys in her school play with her until he'd hurt her and that was what had caused all the bleeding. Ellie had been frightened and blamed her uncle because he was the only man she knew. It was too bad, Mrs. Delliah said, touching a handkerchief to her eyes, because Ellie's uncle loved her very much. And now he had to go through this.

The defense attorney smiled and said there were no questions. He requested that the judge dismiss the case.

Judge Riker stared hard at the assistant D.A., then said quietly, "Do you want the girl to testify?"

"In chambers, Your Honor, please."

"Very well."

Taylor waited, pacing the corridor outside the courtroom for forty-five minutes. It was over quickly when Judge Riker returned.

"I am dismissing the charges against Mr. Ashcroft. Next case."

It was over. Simple as that. Nothing more. Just over and the man was free. Taylor went to the men's room and vomited up the three cups of coffee he'd drunk. Enoch tried his best to calm him.

"Look, Taylor, it happens this way. You know that, I know that. Hell, what else can you do?"

Taylor looked at him and pulled the small cassette tape from his suit pocket. "Play this for the judge," he said.

Judge Riker sat still as a stone as he listened to the tape of Ellie Delliah telling Taylor about her rape.

When the tape was over, Judge Riker reached out a thick finger and pressed the erase button.

"Sorry, Lieutenant, but the girl swore that what her mother said was right. She did refuse to give us a boy's name, however. I believe you. Of course I believe you. I believe the uncle is guilty as sin and he needs psychiatric help. But there's not a thing I can do about it. Forget it, Lieutenant. I'm as sorry as you are, but the law's the law. Get back to work and just forget it."

Taylor rose, still staring down at the now-erased tape. "That little girl's life will be hell, you know that. You can't believe he'll stop now. He'll think now that he can do anything to her with impunity. He just proved he's above the law."

"No, I think the uncle paid off the mother to change her story. Paid her a ton of money, probably. You can take it to the bank that the mother and daughter will be decamping very soon now and heading for parts unknown. So you see, some good came out of it. The girl will be free from him."

Taylor found little consolation in that, but he nodded, shook Judge Riker's hand, and left the building. He prayed it was true. What with the case being dismissed, the social workers couldn't get involved. There was no way to remove Ellie from her mother's care.

Two weeks later, when Taylor had come off a cocaine bust that had left three teenagers dead and a nineteen-year-old dealer still loose, his captain called him into his office, closed the door, and told him that Ellie Delliah was dead.

"I'm sorry, Taylor," he said quietly. The kid had jumped out of a rest-room window in her private school at Eighty-first and Madison. Three flights up. She'd landed on a concrete sidewalk.

The next day, Taylor resigned from the New York Police Department. Enoch Sackett, longtime partner and equally longtime friend, also resigned.

# *1987* LINDSAY

A passing cab sent black slush up in a wide arc, splashing Lindsay's new light brown suede boots. She stared down at them, cursing under her breath. They were splashed, stained, and now bloody ruined. She cursed a bit more. She'd bought them with her last paycheck from Hoffman and Meyers, a small privately owned publishing house where she'd been a fish out of water in the publicity department for the past five months. Frustrated and angry and feeling so down she wanted to bite something or somebody, she went into a discreet-looking bar at Sixty-fifth and Broadway, just up from Lincoln Center. It was an old-fashioned Irish bar called County Cork, all dark and comforting on the inside, an ancient bar worn and lovingly shined that curved around, and a smell that permeated the place—welcoming and old and mellow.

She slid into a booth that was done in black leather, worn and soft and smelling of beer and whiskey with just a hint of salted peanuts. The large room was dim, nearly empty at this time of day. It was just before four o'clock in the afternoon on a Wednesday. Everyone was still at work. Except her. She'd just quit her job and felt relief and depression in equal amounts.

She looked up at the bartender and called out for a white wine. She looked down at her beautiful new suede boots, the stains now drying and ugly as slash marks on the soft golden brown.

She wanted to gulp down her wine when the bartender brought it, but she sipped it, slow and easy. She brooded, looking at the scarred, beautifully polished wooden table. She thought about her boss, the weak-chinned Nathan, and wished she had punched him out when she'd quit an hour before. But she'd been calm and very adult, she'd handled it well, telling him to find another poor soul with a psych degree to pimp for him. She'd left, only to wonder if he would see she was paid for the two days. Who cared? She was out of there. It had been part of her job to play escort and companion/guide to visiting authors, seeing that all nasty and inconvenient twigs were swept from their paths. She was the smoother-over. The last guy was a golfer who was writing a book about the scandals on the pro golf circuit. She'd removed every proverbial rock from the road, smiled at his stories, kept his spirits buoyed. And then he'd tried to get her up to his hotel suite. When she'd walked and reported what the jerk had wanted, her boss had told her to get back there and keep the man happy. She'd said that being a prostitute wasn't part of her job description.

Well, it was over. During the interview with her boss, the golfer had called in a snit, complaining about her uncooperativeness. She had gotten to laugh then in her erstwhile boss's face. She could smile for real again. She was free for a while until she found another job. She looked around the bar. She nursed her wine, looking up to see a man at the bar, by himself, tossing off a Scotch, if she wasn't mistaken. He was carrying on a desultory conversation with the barkeep, a big-gutted man with an apron wrapped around his middle and up under his armpits, and sporting a big brown mustache. The barkeep wiped beer mugs with a soft white cloth, his movements slow and hypnotic. His dark eyes looked dreamy and old. She wondered if he was really listening to the man or was off into space somewhere.

The man was talking about his BMW and how the sucker hated the snow and slush and how it was rotting underneath from all the salt the city laid down after a snowstorm. The barkeep just nodded and kept wiping those beer mugs. The man drank down the rest of his whiskey and ordered another. He spoke again, but Lindsay couldn't make out his words. He was mid-forties, olive-complexioned, a head thick with black curly hair, slender. He had boyish features and his smile held charm. His clothes were expensive. His voice was as soft and mellow as her white wine. She was distracted, and found herself listening without really intending to. Just to pass the time, she told herself, until her boots dried. No more walking on the sidewalks in this weather. She was going out to dinner with Gayle Werth, to her favorite Mexican restaurant on Seventy-first Street, and she still had a couple of hours to wipe out.

A woman came sweeping into the bar—no other way to describe her entrance. Lindsay could only stare at her. She was swathed in black mink and high-heeled black leather boots. She wore a huge mink hat and carried a Sharif bag, which probably didn't hold more than a lipstick. She was gorgeous and self-assured and obviously on a mission. The man turned when the woman came to him and lightly touched her gloved hand to his shoulder. "Ah, redhead," he said, turning to smile up at her. "I'm glad you're here. You want a drink?"

"Yeah, thanks, Vinnie, a ginger ale. Then I want to talk to you. Glen told me you'd be here."

"Glen's got a big mouth. Dickie, make it a Perrier for

the redhead. No calories. Look at those thighs, Janine. I can see the fat dimples through the coat. No more nothing for you today, sweetie, you got that?"

It was then that Lindsay recognized the woman. She was a model. Lindsay had just seen her on the cover of a woman's magazine at her dentist's office a couple of days before. She wasn't quite so beautiful right now. She was fighting mad at the man. She was speaking angrily at the man, her voice rising with each word.

". . . No more, Vinnie, no more, you hear me? Damn you, it was enough!"

No more what? Lindsay wondered, her hearing tuned to high. Then the man cut her off with a wave of his hand, saying quite clearly to her, "Look, babe, you play by the rules, or you fuck off into obscurity."

The barkeep handed the glass of Perrier to the woman. The man said now, "You're getting lines around your mouth with all your tantrums and whining. Cut it out. No more frowns today, you got that?"

The woman threw the Perrier into the man's face. The twist of lemon fell onto his lap. "Another thing, Demos, I'm marrying Arthur Penderley III and I'll be able to buy and sell you, you no-cock little pansy bastard!" She pulled her gorgeous mink coat around her, tossed her head back in a magnificent gesture, nearly losing her mink hat, and walked from the bar.

"Wow," the barkeep said. "That's some lady. She must be wearing ten thou on her back."

"She's a lot of things," the man Vinnie said as he wiped off his face, "but a lady she ain't. At least this stuff doesn't stain. Ah, hell, Dickie, I'm glad she's getting out of the business. She's tired of it, burned down to her wick, and it's starting to show in her work. I've even gotten a couple complaints about her attitude, you know? When a director or a photographer starts to notice a model's attitude, you know you're in trouble. Usually they're so wrapped up in themselves, they wouldn't even notice God if he arrived on a set. Well, that's that. Give me another towel, will you? Thanks."

He was wiping at his pants when the bartender called out, "Hey, lady, you want another glass of wine?"

Lindsay, fascinated, and not wanting to leave just yet, called back, "Yeah, make it a double."

The man slowly looked up. He paused in his wiping. He looked at her for a very long time, then nodded, raising his whiskey glass in a silent salute.

Lindsay smiled at him. Nothing like a little drama to make one forget one's woes, she thought, delighted at what life unexpectedly dished up on rare occasions, and gave him an unconscious wide smile.

Vincent Rafael Demos couldn't believe his eyes. It was too much whiskey, he thought. That was it. That smile of hers was something else. Electric, yeah, that was it. And that damp mop on her head—unruly as Medusa's hair, but thick and filled with colors from the lightest ash to dark brown, colors that seemed to absorb all light, made more intense with deep natural waves. She had big hair with no styling mousse. As for her eyes, well, he'd soon see. "I'll take her wine to her. Oh, Dickie, put it on my tab."

Lindsay watched the man approach, her wine in his right hand, his whiskey in his left. He was looking at her, no longer smiling, and up came a rush of fear. She quashed it. No more fear. At least no more unreasonable fear. If the man wanted to buy her a glass of wine, who cared? She was the one out of a job. It didn't mean he wanted to attack her. Besides, she was depressed.

"My name's Vincent Demos, or just Vinnie if you heard Janine yelling at me. Or just Demos, which I prefer. Here's your wine. I bought it for you. Can I join you for a few minutes?"

"As long as you don't talk about your BMW, sure."

He grinned and slid into the booth opposite her. He raised his glass and she clicked hers to his.

"You a student?"

"Not anymore. I'm a full-fledged professional, newly-out-of-a-job adult. I just quit my first job this afternoon and a taxi ruined my new suede boots. My name's Lindsay Foxe."

They shook hands. His were dry and narrow, his grip firm.

"Nice to meet you, ma'am."

She nodded.

"You have the most beautiful eyes I've ever seen. Sexy as hell and intelligent, a new combination."

"And that's a new line."

"No line. Fact. They aren't colored contacts, are they? No, I didn't think so. How much do you weigh?"

"My fighting weight or in my Reeboks with thick socks?"

"Fighting weight."

"One hundred and thirty pounds. What kind of prize do I win if I answer all the questions right?"

"You're how tall?"

She cocked her head at him. "Five-foot-eleven. Oh, all right, so I'm nearly six foot."

"I didn't think you looked overweight. You got long legs?"

"To Mars."

"Well, you've also got a smart mouth. I like that. My name's Demos, like I said. I own the Demos Modeling Agency on Madison at Fifty-third. I'm legit, just ask Dickie over there, not some sort of punk who hits on women. I'd like to do some layouts on you. Won't cost you a dime. I'll provide the photographer and the outfits. You interested?"

"You don't look like a punk."

"I'm not, scout's honor. And no, you don't have to strip to your skin for these shots. I don't do calendars or provide fodder for the skin magazines. I do fashion stuff, all legit, as I said. If you're good, you'll make a lot of money and so will I. How old are you?"

"Twenty-two, just graduated last spring from Columbia, degree in psychology. I know, worthless, but it's something at least."

"You ever done any modeling before?"

She shook her head, then said, "That woman who was in here. She's a model. I recognized her. She was in my dentist's office."

"That was the *Cosmo* cover for last month. 'Was' is the

operative word here. Yeah, Janine just retired. I still smell like Perrier and lemon."

"You want a replacement Janine?"

He looked at her closely, silent for too long a time. Finally, "No, I want something entirely new and you just might be it." He sat back, brooding now, and tossed down the rest of his whiskey.

"Actually, you've got ageless bones. That's the key in most cases. Well? Do you want to give it a shot, Lindsay Foxe?"

"When?"

"Tomorrow, say at one o'clock?"

"Why not? As of two hours ago, I'm no longer a publicist."

"Are you tied up with any guy?"

She was instantly still. "No."

"Good. Boyfriends can be a real pain in the ass when it comes to scheduling shoots at weird hours."

"No boyfriends."

"You sound like that's permanent."

"It is, Mr. Demos. It is."

"You're into women?"

"No. I'm not into anything."

"Good. If things turn out, you're going to have to knock off about ten pounds, maybe fifteen. The camera adds it on, you know."

"I've heard. Ten pounds is a lot. Fifteen pounds sounds impossible. I'm not a featherweight. In fact, I'm on the light side right now. I don't know if I could do it or if I'd even want to starve myself like that."

"Well, I'm getting ahead of myself anyway. You might look like a geek on film. Those gorgeous cheekbones of yours just might fade away into the sunset. That jaw of yours might look like a ballbuster's on film. Too, you're a little old to be starting all this. You think about it, Lindsay. Call me in the morning and let me know. Don't let those gorgeous eyes get bloodshot tonight, will you?"

"It's hard to believe all this is for real, that you're for real. It's like a B movie."

"I know," Demos said, and grinned, showing two back

teeth filled with gold. "But then again, I've always thought life was based on a B movie. But the thing is, Lindsay, successful models don't just magically appear in my office. It's the dogs that usually come to an office. I found Janine at a party down in the Village. She had crooked teeth and bleached-out hair, but I saw the possibilities. Two of my very successful models I found just like you—in bars. One of them had to have an ear job. One model I spotted at my aunt's funeral, another one my mom had picked out for a blind date. You never know. If an agency is going to be successful—like mine is—why, then, the eyes are always searching. So, call me, all right?"

As Lindsay said later that evening to Gayle Werth over margaritas, chips, and hot sauce at Los Panchos, "Maybe I'll be on the cover of *Vogue* by next year."

"Sure, sweetie. And maybe you'll get elected to the United Nations."

"They don't do elections, Gayle."

"I'm just saying don't get your hopes up, Lindsay. The man could be a real slime bucket, he could be a pervert, a wanted criminal. You'll check him out before you head over there, won't you?"

"I already did. He's very well-known. He's big-time. He's in the phone book and his address is fancy and quite real. I even called *Cosmo* and asked about him." She sat back in her cane chair and stared at the depleted basket of tortilla chips. "I've got big boobs. Don't all models have to look anorexic and be flat-chested?"

Gayle shrugged. "I'm going with you tomorrow. I'm not taking any chances that you'll be too trusting and sign away the farm."

"Me, trusting?" That was truly a surprise to Lindsay. "You're joking!"

"No. You're naive as hell, Lindsay. Oh, yeah, I forgot to tell you. I saw that psychology creep of yours, Dr. Gruska, this morning when I was on campus checking on gymnastic courses. He nearly ran to catch up with me. Can't you just see him with his tweeds flapping? He wanted to know how you were. He wanted your phone number."

Lindsay choked on a tortilla chip and grabbed for her glass of water. "You didn't—"

"Don't worry. I gave him a number, all right, made it up right then and there. He walked away a happy creep."

"I wonder what he wants?"

"He probably wants what every man wants. He wants inside your jeans."

"I don't think so. His father wouldn't allow it."

Gayle waved a tortilla chip at her. "You're an odd duck, Lindsay. I go along thinking you're so unworldly, but then I see this other side of you. All cynical and funny, at least on the surface. Sometimes I just don't understand you at all."

"Nothing to understand," Lindsay said, and called to Ernesto for two more margaritas, frozen, with salt.

# 8

## 1988   LINDSAY / EDEN

It was a hot day in mid-July, not even noon yet, and already in the low nineties. Lindsay was regretting her long walk to the Demos Agency, but she'd gained two pounds, and walking and sweating was the easiest way to get it off. She came around Fifty-third Street and looked up, half-expecting to see Glen waving from the eleventh floor of the pre-World War II building, a solid brick, dark and dirty, needing a good hosing down, like most of the other buildings on the block. She didn't see Glen. Still, she smiled, knowing that today would be as much fun as she could expect from the modeling grind. She was doing a makeup layout for Lancôme and the ad-agency people in charge of the shoot were funny and bright, and practical jokers. Well, today she'd be the one to get the laugh—she looked like dog meat and when they saw her they were going to scream.

Lindsay bent down to pull up her baggy army socks, a nice touch she'd thought, especially with the puke-green stretched-out cotton pulled over the tops of her ragged jeans. When she straightened, she saw a beautifully dressed woman emerge from a taxi, a vision really, in cool pink silk that should have clashed with her shining auburn tapered bob, but didn't. Lindsay could only stare at her. Inside, she

96

jolted, recognition warring with deep, deep pain. She shook
her head, as if to deny what she saw, then said very quietly,
"Sydney, is that you? Sydney?" Her half-sister turned and
stared at her, taking in the moussed-backed ponytail held
with a rubber band, the shiny face devoid of makeup, and
the loose white shirt.

She said nothing, merely stood there looking beautiful
and slender and perfect, as always, now looking at Lindsay's face, her hair, the dangling Coke-bottle earrings.

"Sydney? It is you, isn't it?"

"Hello, Lindsay. It's been a while, hasn't it?"

Lindsay didn't know what to say. There'd been no
warning of any sort, no one had bothered to tell her Sydney
would be here. Pain and anger and hurt rolled through
her. She just stood there staring at her half-sister. This cool
exquisite creature was very different from the hysterical
woman of five years before in Paris. Then that woman of
five years before had become vicious, siding with her father.

"Yes," Lindsay said, still not moving, "it's been quite
a long time. You look beautiful, Sydney."

"And you, well, you're still Lindsay, aren't you?"

"I suppose one doesn't change all that much." Lindsay
was surprised at another feeling that crept through her at
her half-sister's words. Inferiority, that was it, she felt sudden and utter inferiority. She felt ugly and worthless, no
more than a clumsy lump. She straightened her shoulders,
towering over Sydney, who was only five-foot-seven in her
stylish heels.

"It appears you have changed quite a bit. At least in
those glossy photos you certainly look different. How do
they do it—with smoke and mirrors and doubles?"

"Very nearly." Lindsay laughed. "There's the photographer, who can be a pain in the butt and who can have
an attitude, the person directing the shoot, who's usually
yelling and making threats and throwing fits, the makeup
person, the hair person, the clothes person, all the technicians . . . well, you understand. It sounds manic but it isn't.
Normally it all goes pretty smoothly. It's just that everyone
is always talking and yelling. Sometimes I feel like a block

of wood with all these people working on me and around me."

They were still standing on the sidewalk, people walking around them, the sun beating down overhead.

Neither woman had moved.

Sydney said suddenly, "I came to make peace with you, Lindsay."

Lindsay searched her sister's face but found no clue there, only the endless perfection of her features, the startling beauty of her hazel eyes that only emphasized her cool intelligence. "It's hot out here. I don't have to be upstairs for a while yet. Would you like to go across the street and have something cool to drink?"

Sydney Foxe di Contini, known as La Principessa to all those who weren't intimate with her, still didn't move. Five years was a long time, a very long time, she thought. It had come as quite a shock to her to pick up April's *Elle* and see her half-sister on the cover, so hauntingly beautiful, thin, stylish; she'd realized after close study that it wasn't just a beautiful woman she was looking at, not classic beauty anyway. It was Lindsay's face, filled with that elusive, quite indescribable quality that transcended a woman's looks or lack of them. Sydney could only stare then; she stared now at the ordinary creature in front of her. No, not ordinary, a mess. Those high-top sneakers were god-awful. She wondered if Lindsay found it amusing to present herself like this and then undergo the incredible transformations for the fashion photos.

Sydney thought again of that exotically gorgeous creature on the cover of *Elle* with the thick lustrous hair, the arrogant smile, and those sexy blue eyes. That couldn't be Lindsay. No, Lindsay was the awkward pathetic mess of a girl she'd last seen in Paris after Alessandro had raped her. She'd picked up the phone to call her father. Why hadn't he told her about Lindsay? Then she'd slowly replaced the receiver. Her father never spoke of Lindsay. It would only make him angry, and Sydney didn't like his anger, for it was cold and hard and unrelenting. Then she'd gotten an excellent idea, brilliant, really. She was La Principessa, after all, renowned for her beauty, her charm, her taste. It didn't

take her very long to execute her idea to its fullest. Everything had gone just as she'd envisioned it, but then, she'd
never doubted that it would. Three days ago she'd left
Melissa with her grandmother and great-grandfather and
three di Contini servants, and taken the first plane to New
York.

How odd that no one had told her that Lindsay was a
successful model, she'd thought many times on the flight
over. She hadn't known where Lindsay lived, hadn't ever
cared, and she'd been hesitant to ask Grandmother Foxe for
her address because the old lady might think her unloving,
not even knowing where her half-sister lived. How to
explain to anyone that knowing Lindsay's address brought
that horrible time in Paris back to her, in spades? It forced
her to confront those hours of weakness, the dismal
pathetic hysteria, the woman who hadn't really been her.
She made herself sick whenever she thought about what
she'd been in Paris.

She smiled at the very ordinary-looking woman in front
of her. Seeing Lindsay in the flesh brought back her confidence. Seeing her didn't bring back Paris. Lindsay was just
the same. There was no magic in her look or in any of her
features, no elusive qualities. None. She looked a wreck,
tall and skinny and in those disgusting clothes that made
her look like a reject from the seventies. Slung over her
shoulder was an old bulging bag that could hold a kitchen.
Who had dressed her? It was laughable. There was no guilt
from Paris. Nothing. She was vastly relieved. She was soon
to be on her way, the stars the limit.

"Sydney?"

"Sure, let's go over to that little bar. I'm here for a
couple of days—on business—and I thought you and I
should speak together. Are you in a rush? Do you have a
little time, perhaps, now? A glass of wine would be welcome in this ghastly heat. I'd forgotten how much I detested
New York in the summer. I don't know how you stand it."

"No one does. One just puts up with it."

When they walked into Jay Glick's Saloon, Lindsay
immediately went to the phone and called the agency. She
got Glen at his bitchiest.

"Yes, sweetie, I'm here but you're not. Where the hell are you? I looked down and saw you chatting with this utterly gorgeous woman. Is she a woman, sweetie? Or maybe I lucked out. A queen?"

"No, Glen. She's my half-sister. Please tell Demos I'll be there on time. I've still got close to forty-five minutes before the ad people for the Lancôme shoot arrive." She paused, listening to Glen's outpourings. When he slowed, she said, "No, Glen, my half-sister just showed up. Yeah, right, the famous *principessa*. Okay, later. An hour, no longer. No, tell Demos I'm eating éclairs by the dozen. Sure, Glen, give him a coronary at the very least. Harden some of his arteries. And yes, I've got a real treat for the ad folk. Yes, outrageous, and this time I'll get them. You'll declare me the winner of the practical jokers. See you soon."

Lindsay slid into the booth opposite her sister. A glass of white wine was already there. She raised it, then sighed and put it back down. She called for a Perrier. Sydney said, "You know I have a daughter, don't you?"

"Yes, her name's Melissa. Grandmother sent me a picture of her. She's beautiful. She looks just like you."

"I didn't know you were a model."

Lindsay shrugged, clicking her glass of Perrier to Sydney's wineglass. A pool of pain settled in her stomach. Sydney probably thought she was still a nothing. She'd told her mother and her grandmother about her new career, but evidently neither had seen fit to tell Lindsay's father or Sydney. Or he'd been told and he simply couldn't care less, which was no surprise. But why hadn't Grandmother told Sydney?

"I saw you on the cover of *Elle*."

"That was a lucky hit, so Demos told me. The woman at *Elle* freaked out over the shape of my ears or something silly like that."

"You're with Vincent Rafael Demos."

"You've heard of the loose cannon then. How do you know about him?"

"Most women in the upper strata of society know about Demos and his, ah, models, Lindsay."

"Oh ho! *Upper strata!* No wonder I thought he was a New Jersey loan shark." She laughed, delighted with the snobbery, and to her surprise, Sydney flushed.

"I was joking."

"Sure you were, Sydney." For the first time in her life, Lindsay felt an instant of having the upper hand. It felt quite good, remarkable really. "What is this about him and his, ah, models?"

Sydney shrugged. "It's his reputation. Well deserved, I understand."

"Glen arranges all that for him." It was on the tip of her tongue to tell Sydney that Glen was Demos' lover, but she didn't, saying instead, "Glen's his mother, confessor, secretary, assistant, in short, his right and left hand. He decided some twelve years ago that a dicey reputation would be good for Demos' professional image. Demos rarely sleeps with anything other than his toy poodle, named Yorkshire, and three Siamese cats." *And Glen, of course.* "Now, why are you here in New York? To find out if I'm sleeping with Demos?" She paused only fractionally before adding, "You're here alone?"

Sydney nodded, hearing the crack in her sister's self-confidence. She'd seemed a different person, at first. But it wasn't true. But no, some things never changed. She leaned back in the booth, smiling. "You're thinking of my husband, no doubt. Alessandro is in Rome this week. He is rarely at the villa in Milan now. It's just his grandfather, his mother, Melissa, and me and all the servants. His sullen pig of a sister is married to a Greek shipping magnate and spends more of her time now on Crete. I'm involved in the family business now. A munitions factory, just imagine! Father stays at the villa a good three months of the year. He enjoys Melissa and being with me, naturally. His wife is tolerable, just barely. You've met her, haven't you? Holly's a bitch, but as I said, sufferable if you know how to handle her, which I do very well. Last trip, she stayed at home. She's jealous of me, you know. Father took a mistress after he'd been married to Holly only two months. He won't ever be the faithful type, as your mother soon discovered after her marriage to him. You've changed—a bit."

"I'm an adult now. I handle things. He was probably never faithful to your mother either, Sydney."

"My mother died! You know that. He loved her and only her, and when she died, he changed, gave up."

Lindsay opened her mouth, then closed it. She'd overheard Lansford, the Foxe butler, say to Dorrey, the cook, years before, how after the first Mrs. Foxe had run away from the judge, she moved to New Zealand. It appeared she hadn't died. But surely Sydney knew this. Surely she just liked to pretend it was otherwise. She had the upper hand again. She smiled. "Is there something special you wanted to see me about, Sydney?"

"For God's sake, why do I have to have something special in mind? You're my sister."

"I've been your sister for twenty-three years. Why now? It's been five years."

Sydney said nothing. She sipped her tart chardonnay. She found Lindsay's attempt at sarcasm mildly amusing. Five years should have wrought some improvements, so the attempts at sarcasm were a help. What to tell her? She'd dangle her on the line a bit longer.

"Perhaps I'm really here to find some young virgins for Alessandro. He likes a new crop every year. You could probably throw yourself at his feet now and he wouldn't spare you a second glance. You're just too old, your face and your body. Do you know that Alessandro told me that you would become beautiful? He used to say that and I'd laugh because all I ever saw in you were skinny legs, elbows that stuck out, and a mop of hair that looked like a lawn mower had plowed through it. Of course he preferred you all skinny arms and legs and innocence. Seeing you like this, perhaps he would still want you. Perhaps he would even admit he'd been wrong. I'll ask him."

Lindsay was frozen.

"You still think about that night, do you? Really, Lindsay, what's plain old simple sex compared to shooting your husband two times? I do remember the look on his face. Absolute astonishment, and then he toppled off you." Sydney shrugged. "But it has been five years now, Lindsay. Time for you to forget, certainly. But you know, I've regretted many times that I was such a bad shot."

"I don't think something like that is all that easy to forget. Why didn't you divorce him?"

"Scandal, pure and simple. Same reason you didn't press charges against him. Father was busy working on both of us. And there was so much money at stake. But enough about my husband. How did you get into modeling?"

Lindsay was more than glad to leave it. God, so much and yet not enough. How could one forget? It hurt her throat even to talk about it. She became aware that Sydney was watching her and said quickly, "Demos discovered me last year, in a bar. I'd just quit my job at a small publishing company and a cab had splashed dirty slush on my new suede boots. I was drowning my depression when he saw me and came over. It sounds ludicrously trite, but that's how it happened. He told me it wasn't all that uncommon. I like Demos, regardless. He's smart and he's fun."

"More fun than Alessandro?"

Lindsay snapped the stem of the wineglass that held her Perrier. The glass cut into her finger. She sat there looking at the blood welling up.

"Would you like a Band-Aid?"

"Yes, perhaps that would be a good idea." Sydney wiped the blood off Lindsay's finger with a napkin, then peeled a Band-Aid around it. "There, good as new."

"Why did you say that, Sydney? Why do you want to make me feel horrible all over again?"

"I don't, Lindsay, don't be silly. But you did have fun with Alessandro, admit it. You were completely infatuated with him for over two years, remember? And you made no move to leave when you discovered I wasn't in Paris with him, did you? He made you feel so special, didn't he? Ah, his charm is legendary when he chooses to use it."

"I was a dumb teenager!"

"Very true, Lindsay. Did you know that Alessandro claims to this day you seduced him? He said he didn't want you, but he felt sorry for you because you were so awkward and so embarrassing and so, well, damned pathetic, and that's why he had asked you to Paris, because nobody wanted you and you were so lonely. He had no idea that you were serious about him. He claims you seduced him, that you insisted."

Lindsay looked at her bandaged finger. She felt stripped, naked and cold, to her soul. It would never end, she knew it now. It would always be there, dark and ugly, lurking, just waiting for her to remember, waiting for Sydney to make her remember. Her part in it, what her father and Sydney believed to be true. Even after five years . . . She couldn't let Sydney reduce her to nothing, not now, not like she used to. She was twenty-three years old, an adult.

She looked up at her half-sister. She said very calmly, "What you say certainly makes sense to me. Now that I think about it, poor Alessandro didn't have a chance against all my teenage charms. Why, I remember threatening to break his arm if he refused to slap me up; I told him I'd scream for all the hotel staff if he didn't slam a fist in my jaw, not once but at least three times. Yes, it was wonderful. It was a thrill to be ripped up inside. Nothing like it. Something every teenage girl should experience to teach her how much power she has. Well, it's long over now and if it's okay with you, I'd just as soon talk about blood sports or something equally tantalizing."

"You've grown some armor, haven't you?"

"You're growing tedious, Sydney. Why are you really here? What do you really want? To torment me because you're out of practice?"

"Oh, no, you were never much of a challenge. You were always vulnerable and you knew it. You never knew what to say even at the slightest jab. You knew you were ugly."

"Old refrain. Why are you here? What have I ever done to you?"

Lindsay looked at her half-sister, wishing she could understand, wishing she could see into her mind to know what Sydney wanted. God, but she was beautiful. Lindsay felt like a scrub next to her. Beautiful, perfect Sydney with a perfect child and a husband who liked teenage girls.

"Actually, little sister, I brought up my husband just to

see your reaction. You say you're grown up now. I just wanted to test the waters, to see if it was true. Alessandro, believe it or not, is rather a good father, perhaps even a decent husband, as men go. He's sorry he got rough with you. He wanted me to tell you that. Should I believe him, I wonder?"

"Then why did you say all those things to me in Paris? Why did you follow him? Why did you bring a gun? By God, Sydney, you shot him!"

Sydney just shrugged, a supremely European gesture. "I don't recall what I said to you. I was upset seeing my little sister fucking my husband. If you'd been on top, why then I'd probably have shot you instead." Another shrug. "Alessandro is like most men, my father included—forgive me, *our* father. He occasionally roves. He lost it with you. He got rough. As I said, he very much regrets it now. He would like to see you, to mend fences, so to speak."

"No, I will never see that bastard again willingly in my life. And you're lying, Sydney. Why?"

"Lindsay, I can see nothing's changed. Five years is a very long time. You were young and infatuated and silly. He shouldn't have allowed you to stay at the suite, but he did. It's over. Just forget it."

It wouldn't ever be over, not as long as Sydney waltzed into her life every five years or so and peeled the scab off the wound and poked around. She'd be dead before the memories and pain were finally gone; she knew it, accepted it, and dealt with it.

"I came not only to see you but someone else as well. I didn't tell you, and I haven't told Father yet. He'll scream, I'm sure, but I don't really care. I spoke to Vincent Demos several weeks ago after I'd sent him some quite lovely photos of myself. In short, dear sister, he wants us to do this layout together. He thinks I'm beautiful and stylish and very patrician-looking, the opposite of you, who appear so wholesome and outdoorsy with the proper makeup and clothes. He thinks two sisters, one of them an Italian princess, the other a model who's already somewhat established, is very salable. There's a new Arden perfume that will be coming out, and they're very interested in the sister approach. You know, a perfume that appeals to two very different types of women."

Lindsay couldn't believe this. "He didn't say anything to me."

"I told him not to or the deal was off. I wanted the pleasure of telling you myself. Can't you just see it now? *La Principessa and Eden.* Both of us kissing a bottle of perfume or spraying each other."

"But why would you want to be a model? It's not all that much fun, Sydney. It's hard and sweaty and a grind. You're always on a diet and always in bed by nine o'clock because the shoots are usually scheduled in the morning and you have to be there early for makeup and clothes and hair. It's grueling. Lots of times the director is a jerk, the photographer an ass, and they make your life miserable. For God's sake, you're a lawyer, a princess, you run a business!"

Sydney laughed and sipped at her wine. "Did I tell you I like your modeling name? *Eden.* It has panache, class, mystery. Did Demos select it for you?"

"Both of us did, together."

"I see. How interesting. I suppose, like you, I'll have to cut out the alcohol. It's all sugar, you know. Of course, I've never had a problem with my weight."

Lindsay looked at her half-sister and thought: Why is she really doing this? Not to spite me, no, I'm hardly worth her time or her trouble, not on this scale. Lindsay felt mired in confusion. "Why? Why are you doing this?"

"Why not tell you the truth? It doesn't matter. The money, dear, the money. After I shot Alessandro, he was slow to recover. He's never gotten back his full scope of killer instincts. He's changed—all because of you, naturally—and now he's no longer ruthless and callous. He nearly bankrupted us until I pushed him out. So this modeling will add money to the coffers and give me some fame that I will enjoy. No other reason, Lindsay. Oh, yes, the thrill of seeing you again, the thrill of posing beside you. Just think—the two of us actually working together. I wonder who people will think is the elder?"

"I won't do it."

"Of course you will. Or are you still so jealous of me that you couldn't manage to hide it from a camera?"

"I'm not jealous of you."

"As you say. As you say."

"I don't want to talk about it anymore, Sydney."

"Fine. We meet together with Demos at two o'clock this afternoon. Now, about Father's wife, Holly. She's a bitch, don't you agree?"

"I don't want to talk about her either."

"Did you know that she and Father have moved back into the mansion with Grandmother? Holly's got her eyes on all of Granny's bucks. Grandmother is eighty-three this year. She still gives Father hell. But then again, she shouldn't be hanging around all that much longer. He spoke of putting her in a nursing home."

"No, he wouldn't! She's sharp as a tack and has too many connections for him to pull something like that. As for Holly, whatever she does to him, he probably deserves it."

"I think that's why Daddy isn't too fond of you, Lindsay. You've always criticized him, made him feel less than a man, made your dislike of him very clear. You always sided with your mother, who is now, incidentally, an alcoholic and sleeping with men your age."

Lindsay could only stare at her sister. She sliced and cut like a surgeon. Such a fine touch she had. But still, for the first time since Paris, Lindsay didn't think she'd done too badly. She really needed only the one Band-Aid on her finger.

Sydney rose, straightening her silk skirt. "I think I've given you enough to think about. You were never very fast in your mental workings, were you? I will see you this afternoon in Demos' suite. I trust by then you will have done something with yourself. Oh, do allow me to pay."


## 1988    TAYLOR

Taylor bent over the old man, felt for the pulse in his throat. He was dead, a heart attack it appeared, no overt signs of anything else. But he didn't believe it was a natural death for a second. He rose slowly, looking around. The woman was gone. Naturally.

He called to Enoch, who'd just come around the corner of the alley. "Get an ambulance and keep your eyes peeled for that woman and the cops."

Taylor quickly searched the man's wallet. No I.D., no credit cards, no photos, nothing but a folded piece of paper stuffed down in an inner fold of the wallet. Left by accident? Maybe, but Taylor didn't think so. He unfolded it and read: "If you see Gloria, tell her Demos is trying to hide, but not for long. He'll come through. He always does." It wasn't signed.

Taylor looked up when he heard the wail of a police siren. He quickly folded the paper. He was on the point of putting it back in the man's wallet when he stopped. No reason to.

Who the hell was Demos? He sounded like a New Jersey Mafia runner or some lowlife bookie.

Taylor rose when two officers came into the alley, both holding guns.

"Ah, it's you, Taylor," said the older cop, putting his gun back into its holster. He waved at the dead man. "What's going on? Who's this?"

It was Mahonney from the East Orange police, a paunchy guy, balding, cool-headed, and smart as a whip. The guy with him was a fresh-faced rookie with a bad skin problem.

Taylor wished just then he was back in France and not in a dirty alley in East Orange, New Jersey, standing over a dead body. He'd just come home two weeks before after three weeks covering every rocky inch of Brittany on a Harley.

"I found this in his wallet, nothing else, no I.D., no nothing. Maybe when he was cleaned out this was just missed."

Taylor handed Mahonney the paper and watched him read it, then shrug. "I don't know who this Demos character is. You got any ideas, Taylor?"

"Not a one. I was tailing this guy because his wife paid me and Enoch to get the goods on him."

Mahonney dropped to his knees and looked the dead man over closely. "He looks too old to me to have the energy to go playing around with other women. What would you say, about sixty? Heart attack?"

"Looks like. I don't see any blood or bruises. But I don't think his heart just stopped. No, someone did this to him. And yeah, he is too old and I think Enoch and I were set up. This is the first time I've seen him up close. The wife showed us a photo of a much younger man, and this guy always wore a hat. You want the wife's name?"

"The whole thing doesn't make any sense," Mahonney said, scratching his left ear. "Why hire you and Enoch to follow him? If someone killed him, why would they want you as witnesses?"

Taylor shrugged. He studied the dead man again. "You know," he said slowly, "just maybe this killing with us as witnesses is a message to this guy Demos. You know, having two ex-cops around and they didn't make any difference, the guy's still dead. Or maybe it's a message to someone else, who knows? But to use me and Enoch, it does make sense."

Mahonney nodded. "The arrogance of it smacks of the pros. They've got balls to burn. It makes them look invincible, what with you guys dogging the victim. I'm going to talk to the wife. You and Enoch want to tag along?"

"Sure."

It turned out that the wife who'd hired them wasn't the dead man's wife. She accused Taylor and Enoch of following the wrong guy. This old turnip she'd never seen before. He was ugly as sin. She'd have never married him. She was indignant; she refused to pay them a dime. She said they were losers. The cops were suspicious but there was nothing more to go on. Taylor and Enoch thought and thought of ways to nail her but couldn't come up with anything.

Late the next morning, Enoch walked to their small office on the second floor of the Cox Building on Fifty-fourth and Lexington in Manhattan. The front door was opaque glass with "Taylor and Sackett" printed in bold script. He walked in, picked up the mail from Maude's desk, went into his and Taylor's office, and sat down. "All that's junk mail," Taylor said, waving a finger at the slew of papers in Enoch's hands. "Don't waste your time. Let Maude deal with it."

"Yeah, okay." Enoch tossed the pile over his shoulder onto the floor, then looked back at Taylor and grinned. "Shit, man, so now what?"

Enoch slouched forward in the chair, his long arms dangling between his knees.

"Don't worry," Taylor said. "We're not going to starve and Sheila won't rub your nose in it. I've got a computer job coming up on Monday that I just accepted. It's the Salex Corporation and they've got some real bugs in their new export accounting program. They're paying me big bucks to fix it. We'll survive. You go to work on the Lamarck case, okay?"

"Yeah, okay. It's just a matter of finding out who's selling cosmetic secrets, right? No problem. It's a small industry with just a few players." He sighed. "Sheila's not going to like this at all. She has a fit whenever there's a dead body lying around and I'm anywhere near it. I was lucky. She was out playing bridge last night so I didn't have to face her. Jesus, that's probably why I was a cop, just to bug the old girl. As for the money, well, a thou isn't too much to worry about, you're right."

Enoch had lived with his mother all his forty-two years. They fought like a married couple. He never called her mother. He only called her Sheila, at least to her face. Enoch's father had died when he was eighteen, and his mom, Sheila, had inherited a cool ten million dollars and a dozen shoe stores. She was wealthy and acid-tongued and a kick. She was also a very talented musician. Taylor was very fond of her. She was always after him to get married again. As for Enoch, Sheila never mentioned marriage for him. As for Enoch, he never mentioned marriage either, even though he'd had a dozen relationships with women over the years.

Enoch said, "I wonder who that Demos guy is."

"Mahonney told me if they ever found out it would be by informant," Taylor said. "There are a slew of Demoses in the tri-state area. Good luck. As to that, who wrote the bloody note?"

"I think you're right, and so do the cops. We were not only set up, but our purpose was to send a message to someone, probably this poor slob Demos. To show him he shouldn't fuck around with the big boys. I talked to Boggs, the coroner, just before I left home. He said the guy was stabbed with a thin circular blade right in the heart. The hole was very small and the bleeding nearly nil, which is why you and Mahonney didn't see anything. You think the woman did it, this Gloria? Or was it this Demos? Was the woman we saw with him even Gloria?"

"God knows. Mahonney hasn't even identified the dead man yet. You want a beer?"

"Yeah, it'll drive Sheila bananas. I'll even spill a little bit on my coat. She'll shriek and call me a degenerate." Enoch grinned and rubbed his hands. "Then I'll tell her about the body. Give her lots of details."

"You're evil, Enoch."

"It's part of my charm, Taylor, just part of my charm."

# 9

## LINDSAY

Lindsay stood tall and straight and stiff directly in front of Demos' desk. She said again, more calmly this time, "I won't do it, Vinnie. And you won't talk me out of it, so just forget it."

"Did I tell you that you look a real cutie in that outfit, Lindsay? Like a real bow-wow. Is your underwear just as ratty? Glen told me how you've got this running-joke battle with the Lancôme ad folk. You'll win this one, kiddo, hands down."

"Listen to me, Vinnie. I won't pose with my half-sister. I won't be associated with her in any way. I won't tell anyone she's any relation to me. I'll break my contract first and then you'll have to haul me into court and it'll be a real mess. But I mean it, I simply won't do it."

Vincent Rafael Demos sat back in his chair and steepled his fingers together in front of his face. He frowned. Glen always told him his brain was like a chain saw, always hacking and hacking away until the solution to any problem was there, shining clear amid the wreckage. But this time, nothing came to mind.

"You also know why I won't do it."

Vinnie shrugged. "Your sister told me it was because you're jealous of her, that you grew up that way. She also laughed and said she didn't understand it because, after all, you were already a successful model and she was a nobody. Is that it, kiddo? You're afraid everyone will want her and not you anymore?"

Lindsay smiled for the first time since she'd entered Demos' office, a plush but too-stark room with white leather everywhere—sofa, love seat, chairs, even the photos on the walls were framed with white leather. "You know, Vinnie, I thought that too, but just at first. I thought, here she is again, and lo and behold, I've got something she doesn't have, so her first reaction is to outdo me. But no, I've thought about it and that isn't it. I just gave her the idea, that's all. Look, I'm not a kid anymore. I'm an adult. If it were just a matter of jealousy on my part, I could handle it."

Lindsay drew a deep breath.

"Come on, spit it out."

"I won't pose with her for the same reason you and I came up with the name Eden for me. Just Eden and nothing else."

"Oh."

"I know, you forgot."

"It's been five years since Paris, Lindsay. Who the hell would care now? No one, not even the scandal sheets. Geraldo won't be knocking on your door."

"That isn't true, and now that you remember, you know it isn't. I can see it now: 'La Principessa and Her Little Sister, Lindsay/Eden, Together Again. Sharing Photos, Sharing the Same Man, Again. Will Little Sister Scream Rape This Time? Where's the Prince?' No way, Vinnie. Forget it."

"I hadn't realized, Lindsay, really, I hadn't realized you still felt so strongly about it."

"If you want Sydney for the Arden thing, then she'll do it alone." Lindsay tucked her hands into her jeans pockets. They were shaking. She felt cold but she was also determined.

"All right."

"What's all right?"

"She'll do it alone. The Arden people are really high on her. She's so damned beautiful and sophisticated and smart. All those things, and they show on her face, fortunately. I just wish I could have gotten hold of her years ago. If she decides to model, Lindsay, will you be able to handle it?"

"Just as long as no one knows who I am."

"I can't muzzle her. If she wants to tell who Eden is, why, then, she will."

And she would. Lindsay knew nothing could hold her back if she decided to talk.

When she went to the Lancôme shoot, her clothes set the two ad people to screaming and clutching their hearts when they saw her. But winning the latest practical joke only brought a small smile to her face. She went to her apartment immediately after the shoot, turned the air conditioning on high, and brooded with a Diet Coke. What to do?

She knew Sydney. She would turn it all into a droll joke. That or she'd twist things about in a sweetly solicitous way that would make Lindsay look like a teenage hooker. Lindsay could hear her now, telling about what a pity it all was that her sister, poor Lindsay Eden, had misunderstood, how she herself had misunderstood, how the poor prince had felt so sorry for the ugly duckling . . . And everyone would think: She misunderstood? Sure.

Lindsay couldn't bear it. She had to do something. Sydney was staying at the Plaza. She'd see her again, plead with her to keep quiet, she'd agree to do anything, anything . . . Lindsay remembered so clearly when she'd told Vinnie about what had happened. He'd said nothing much, just nodded now and again. He'd offered no sympathy, not patted her hand once. Better than that, he hadn't doubted her once.

"No problem," he said when she'd finished. "You know what, Lindsay? You don't really look like a Lindsay.

You look like an Eden. How about that for your modeling name? Just plain Eden. It evokes wonderful images and promises mysteries and puzzles of a womanly sort. No one will ever know. How about it?"

But now Sydney was here. Lindsay picked up the phone and called information. Within minutes she heard Sydney's voice.

"Ah, Lindsay, is that you? Whatever do you want now?"

"I want to know if you plan to model."

"Why, yes, I believe I will. The Arden people want me badly and the money they're offering turns even my head. After all, I am a real princess, not just a phony name like Eden, for example. It turns out they would have accepted you because Demos was pushing the sister idea. Yes, I think I will be their spokeswoman for the new perfume. Do you know they're considering calling it *La Principessa*? And then I'll be there on all the propaganda material, on TV, in magazines, everywhere. *People* magazine will probably want to do a story on me."

Lindsay's knuckles showed white, she was clutching the phone so tightly. "Will you say anything about me? Do you plan to tell people I'm your half-sister and it's such a pity and your husband, the prince, and . . ." Lindsay ran out of words. She was breathing fast and her hands were so clammy the phone was slipping from her grasp.

Sydney mused aloud. "Do you think it would even come up, Lindsay? That is your real name, isn't it? How depressing for Father to learn that you're ashamed of your name. Of course, on the other side of the coin, he's relieved that you're not connected with him in any way."

Lindsay knew Sydney would remind everyone the moment the opportunity arose, simply because she would be recognized very soon as the wife who shot her husband in bed with her sister in Paris five years before. She'd never take that. She'd shift things and bring Lindsay into it and Lindsay would end up with the blame all over again. She very gently replaced the phone into its cradle. She drank another Diet Coke and went to bed.

At midnight she was still awake, lying in the dark,

thinking, remembering, her breath hitching even as she thought of the man's name. . . .

His name was Edward Bensonhurst. He was a businessman in automotive parts, with two kids and an ex-wife in New Jersey, and now he lived in Manhattan. Lindsay had met him at a party and liked him. He, however, had wanted to have sex. When she told him no, he'd turned ugly. She told him off and got away from him. Then he'd called her two days later and laughed. He knew who she was. He told her he could play a prince if that's what turned her on. He was the same age as the prince had been in Paris. Hell, maybe he could even get his ex-wife to come over in time and shoot blanks at him. He'd even wear leather if she wanted him to.

She never knew how he'd found out and he hadn't said. She'd hung up on him and kept her answering machine on for the next three weeks. He'd called ten more times, cajoling, making threats, but finally he'd just stopped calling. She prayed he'd finally decided she wasn't worth his effort. God, would it never end?

The phone rang and Lindsay grabbed for it. For an instant she thought it was Edward Bensonhurst again. Foolish, so foolish. She answered it and heard her father's voice.

---

Vincent Rafael Demos sat in his office in the dark and in absolute silence for a long time. The air conditioning cut out all the noise from the street, eleven stories below. It was ten o'clock at night. Even Glen had left an hour earlier, in a huff, refusing to cook him any dinner. "Not even a microwave omelet," Glen had shrieked at him.

Demos was sitting there in a very cold office and he was sweating. He'd memorized the brief newspaper account and it played and replayed endlessly in his head.

". . . Unidentified man, approximate age sixty, found stabbed to death in East Orange, New Jersey. No identification was found on the body, just a note reading . . ."

That damned bloody note! God, and someone hoped a reader would recognize Gloria or a Demos and call the police? That was all he needed, to have the cops coming to call. He knew he had no choice, not anymore. If he didn't respond now, there would be new clues released to the cops, and slowly, surely, the net would tighten around him. Just look how they'd set up this private investigator, this damned ex-cop, so Demos would see just how serious they were. Yeah, the guy, Taylor, was even following the victim and they'd killed him, thumbing their noses at the cops and him and this Taylor. He had to do something because if he didn't there would just be another incident. The cops would come. Someone else would probably die and maybe the someone else would be someone Demos knew.

Finally he picked up his phone and dialed the number. There was an answering machine. When he heard the beep, Vinnie said only, "I'll leave the money tomorrow at the usual place."

He thought of the beautiful Stanislas original oil he would have to sell to get enough money together. He'd bought it in 1968 in the Village when it had been dirt cheap and he had been dirt poor. He'd hocked his hunting knife to buy it. He thought about the dead man, probably Ellery Custer. It sounded like poor Custer, killed to send Demos a message, probably stabbed by that bitch Susan with that sterling-silver ice pick of hers, the one that was a gift from her ex-husband, the note doubtless planted by her on poor old Custer's body, giving that phony name, Gloria, and the real one, Demos. Him.

Well, it was over now. He was safe.

Lindsay took a taxi from San Francisco airport to Presbyterian Hospital on Webster Street. It was midafternoon when she arrived. The first person she saw was her new stepmother, Holly, sitting in the small waiting room reading a magazine. She was swinging her leg, her shoes off. She looked up, saw Lindsay, and smiled.

"The dutiful granddaughter is here. Well, good. The old lady's been asking for you nonstop. I didn't want your father to call you—it's such a horribly long trip for you—but he said his mother told him that if you didn't come, she'd blame him and she'd fix him but good, and that, we all know, means money. You see, she knew you'd come, regardless of what you were doing. She's an old witch, God knows, but tough. I have to admire her for that."

"Yes, I'd come for her."

"You think she'll give you any of her fortune, Lindsay? Is that why you're such a little sweetie?"

"No."

"Good, don't ever kid yourself, because she won't. Everything will go to your father and to me. It's only fair. He's her only son. Too, she knows you're making good money now with your modeling."

"I'm going to see her now. Where is Father?"

"He's in court, naturally. He works, you know. He told me to wait here until you arrived. Now that you have, I'm off. Have fun with the old witch. Oh, incidentally, you're to stay at the mansion, Grandma's orders."

Lindsay didn't want to go anywhere near the mansion, but she didn't say anything. She walked to her grandmother's room and quietly pushed the door open. It was a lovely private room, decorated in soft pastels—peach and pale green. Several French impressionist paintings, excellent copies, were on the walls. There was a small sofa and two chairs near the hospital bed and a large window.

She stood there quietly, looking at her grandmother. She looked small, that was Lindsay's first thought. She was eighty-three years old but she didn't look it. Her skin was smooth and soft-looking, supple, her silver-white hair still thick, her eyebrows well-defined, her cheeks pink. Lindsay had seen very old people before, and invariably they looked like fleshless mummies, all seams and bones, with their pink scalps showing through sparse hair. But Gates Foxe looked like she always had. She was wearing a soft yellow bed jacket with antique Carravannes lace around the collar. Lindsay walked quietly to the bed and stood there.

Gates opened her eyes.

"Hello, Grandmother."

"I'm glad you're here, Lindsay."

Lindsay grinned at her. "Why is it you always look so wonderful and make me feel like a grub?"

"It's my bones. Excellent bones, and you've got them too, my dear. Except for my blasted hip. I fell on the stairs, so clumsy of me really, and it snapped like a wishbone. But I'll be up and about in no time at all. No more bed for me than is absolutely necessary. It reduces one, you know, to have to look up at people."

"I believe you. Do you have much pain?"

"No. See this tube here? Whenever the pain is too bad, I simply press this little button and painkiller is released directly into my bloodstream. No waiting for the nurses to decide enough time has passed. Medical practices are improving. Now, my dear, tell me how long you can stay. Tell me how the modeling is going and when you'll hit the cover of another big magazine."

Lindsay had sent her a half-dozen copies of *Elle.*

"I canceled out three shoots. They weren't all that important. I just have to be back in New York in a week and a half. That's a biggie for *Women's World* I have to be there for. I'll be passing myself off as a professional stock-broker, I think, complete with business suit and briefcase, shot down on Wall Street near Trinity Church. As for another cover, who knows?"

"Sit down, Lindsay. You're looming, and it makes me uncomfortable. That's it, pull that chair over. You're so tall, just like your grandfather, and now that you're a model, you stand much taller. I like that. I always disapproved of you slouching when you were younger. Dear me, to see you all grown-up. It makes me feel positively ancient. Your mother was here this morning. You will see her, of course."

"Yes."

"She's about the same, I guess. She's proud of you, but . . ."

"Yes, but."

"She's so very unhappy. She never learned to focus outward. She wallows in her own misery, and alcohol doesn't help."

"No."

Lindsay watched her grandmother gently press the button that would release some painkiller into her arm. She said nothing, waiting for her grandmother to speak.

"I'm tired, Lindsay. Why don't you go to the mansion and get settled in. Come back and see me this evening."

"I'd rather stay someplace else, Grandmother."

"Nonsense. You're a grown woman now, not eighteen years old. You must learn to deal with your father sooner or later. It's time, Lindsay, past time. Stop being a victim to your memories. You're no longer a little girl for him to hurt and wound at his leisure. Deal with the present as you find it. As for your father, there are many things you don't know about, but they aren't important. Just remember, don't let anyone intimidate you anymore, not even Royce."

Easily said, Lindsay thought.

Lindsay wondered if anyone had ever dared disagree with her grandmother. She said, smiling as she squeezed her grandmother's hand, "If I say no to you, you know very well you'll intimidate me."

"That's different. I'm your grandmother and very old and sick and you must show me due deference. Go along, now. Oh, by the way, Holly's a mess. Don't give her any tit for tat. It wouldn't be fair, even though it would probably make you feel good. She's too vulnerable just now."

Lindsay spoke to the doctor on her way out. His name was Boyd, and he was considered one of the best orthopedic surgeons on the west coast, at least that's what Lindsay's father had told her the night before. He was clearly astounded at Mrs. Foxe's progress. He estimated only another week in the hospital if her recovery continued so rapidly. He smiled at Lindsay then and asked her if she would like to have a cup of coffee in the cafeteria. To discuss her grandmother's case more thoroughly. His smile widened. He was a very confident man.

She said no with a sweet smile and left. It was only a short distance from the hospital to the Foxe mansion. Lindsay paid the taxi driver, set her two suitcases on the sidewalk, and stood there a moment staring at the house and beyond it to the clear blue sky over San Francisco Bay. It was an odd day in July when there was no fog. But it was crystal clear today and the air was so sweet and crisp and fresh it nearly made her eyes water. The Golden Gate Bridge looked stark and bold against that painfully clear sky, the barren Marin headlands, brown and gaunt from lack of rain, the backdrop. Lindsay had always loved the fog to curl around the bridge, softening it, blurring the headlands.

The mansion loomed up huge and neat and overwhelming, its pale brick mellow and soft with age. Odd that it seemed bigger to her now as an adult than it had when she was very young. The grounds were immaculate, the bougainvillea and roses and fuchsias and hydrangeas all in riotous oranges, reds, pinks, and whites. The grass was mowed smoothly, the hedges trimmed perfectly. Still, Lindsay didn't move. She saw the front door open and there was a woman she didn't recognize standing there. She waved to Lindsay.

Mrs. Dreyfus, the new housekeeper, showed Lindsay to her old room down the east corridor on the second floor. Lindsay thanked her and asked what had become of Lansford, Gates Foxe's butler for thirty years. He'd retired, Mrs. Dreyfus told her, but Dorrey, the cook, was still here. There were two maids now, since Judge Foxe and his wife had returned to the mansion.

She finally left Lindsay to herself. Lindsay looked out the bow windows toward Alcatraz, then turned away. She lay on her bed and, to her surprise, fell asleep immediately.

One of the maids woke her at six o'clock.

It was time to see her father. She didn't want to. There was no choice.

She washed her face and pulled her hair back into a soft bun at the back of her neck. Curly tendrils of hair fell at the sides of her face and the gentle deep waves flowed back to the bun. She applied makeup lightly and pulled on a silk wraparound dress of dark blue and white. The blue matched her eyes, the salesperson had assured her. Lindsay didn't know about that, but she liked the dress, felt assured wearing it. She put on white heels, sending her to six feet, two inches, the same height as her father. She smiled at her reflection in the long mirror. She'd be right at his eye level. If she tilted her head back, she'd be taller. She felt confident for the first time in her life going to face her father. She wouldn't let him intimidate her. She wouldn't let herself feel worthless. She was ready for him, her grandmother's advice clear in her mind.

Her confidence plummeted the moment she entered the huge living room. Sydney stood there by the fireplace, a glass of wine in her hand, speaking to their father. She was laughing, her left hand going out to touch his sleeve. He spoke more quickly, and when he finished, Sydney threw back her head and laughed deeply.

"Oh, hello, Lindsay, do come in."

Lindsay nodded toward Holly, in pale cream silk lounging pajamas on the sofa, and came slowly, unwillingly, into the room. The last time both she and Sydney had been here was when Lindsay had been sixteen years old, at Sydney's wedding. It lacked only her mother and five hundred guests. But there was Holly, a fine substitute. She'd gained weight; she was drinking what looked to be a double martini.

"Hello, little sister."

"Sydney. Hello, Father."

Royce looked her up and down and frowned. "You've gotten even taller. You look like a damned Amazon."

"The heels make me your height."

"Take them off. You look ridiculous. Not like a woman, but some sort of female impersonator."

Lindsay took off her heels. Intimidation was a strange thing, or was it simply the long habit of a child obeying a parent? She wondered if she'd ever look him in the eye and tell him to stuff it.

"That's better," Royce said. "Not much, but it is the best you can do."

Lindsay laughed. She couldn't help it, she laughed. She leaned down, picked up her heels, and put them back on. She reached upward and stretched her back. "Ah, that feels better. As I said, Father, I'm now your height. You forget I'm a model. I'm supposed to be an Amazon."

Royce wanted to strike her. For a moment he could think of nothing to say. Never had she gone against him, never. Look at her, the skinny beanpole! Damn, he wanted . . . He drew a deep breath. He would pick another time and then she would obey him without hesitation; he would see to it. He picked a piece of lint off his light gray suit coat. "Holly says she saw you at the hospital this afternoon. How was your grandmother?"

Lindsay realized she'd been holding her breath, waiting to see what he'd do. She'd won. This time she'd won. Her grandmother was right: no more intimidation. Now, if only she could stop hurting deep inside whenever he looked at her with his indifferent dislike. She answered in kind, "In good spirits. Dr. Boyd is very impressed at her recovery."

"She'll outlive us all," Holly said, fingering the four gold chains around her neck. She also wore four rings on her right hand. She wasn't wearing a wedding ring. "Sydney says you don't drink alcohol because you're too heavy. Would you like some soda water?"

"Yes, thank you, Holly. I'm surprised to see you here, Sydney."

"I don't see why. She's my grandmother as well, and I was in New York, not Italy. I was just telling Father I would be modeling for Arden—nothing lowbrow or anything to be ashamed of, even for a powerful federal judge. Just imagine, both of us models."

"You'll be wonderful, Sydney."

"Quite probably. I was just telling Father how your jealousy—so unnecessary now that you're grown—clouded your judgment, how I wanted us to do the commercials together, two sisters, both so different—"

Lindsay interrupted her easily. "It had nothing to do with jealousy." Holly thrust a glass of soda water into her hand. Lindsay took a quick drink. "It had to do with what happened five years ago. I told Demos why I didn't want the whole business dredged up again." Lindsay paused, then said, "I am asking you, Sydney, once you make your debut as a model, not to tell people what my real name is and our relationship."

Sydney regarded her silently for several very long moments. She seemed amused.

"Eden," Royce snorted. "That name of yours, it's absurd. It makes me shudder every time I think of it. I do hope none of the past gets raked up. However, the tabloids are sleazy and always looking out for cheap thrills. I don't think Sydney plans on speaking of the past, Lindsay, because it would hurt her, and she knows I don't want her to be hurt. She's had too much pain to bear already because of what you did." He turned to Sydney. "Are you set on doing this modeling?"

"We need the money," Sydney said matter-of-factly. "And Arden will pay buckets, so Demos tells me. Besides, Italy is boring and too far from home. A real live princess is out of the ordinary, Demos says. And one who doesn't look like a dog without makeup is evidently priceless. Since his percentage depends on how much he can squeeze out of them, he'll do his best."

Royce nodded. "I'm still not sure about this. I hope you're right. I trust you won't claim any relationship to Lindsay. I don't want all that garbage raked up again. I don't want you to suffer anymore."

"My suffering is over, Father, I promise."

Royce still looked uncertain. He looked toward a portrait of Gates, painted in 1955. Stylish, cold, so sure of herself and her dominance over him. "God, that old woman will live forever, Holly's correct about that."

Lindsay drank more of her soda water to keep her mouth shut. Then she heard herself asking, "Will you, Sydney? Tell people who I am?"

Sydney smiled. "Father's right, you know. Eden is such a junky name, so silly really, like a kid playing grown-up. Maybe what you need is to have the air cleared, face up to the past and just laugh. Maybe that would really give your career a needed boost. Perhaps I can help you. Then again, perhaps not."

Judge Royce Foxe laughed and lightly tapped his fingers on Sydney's cheek. "I've always loved your sense of humor, you damned little tease."

"Let's have dinner," Holly said, and jumped to her feet. She really had gained weight, Lindsay noticed. At least fifteen pounds. Just like her mother. She watched Holly stop in front of a mirror just beside the door, a mirror that hadn't been there before.

"I don't know what to do, Grandmother."

It was the next afternoon. Summer fog was thick, blurring the scenery outside the hospital window. It felt cozy and warm in here, protected.

"Well, at last you're ready to tell me what's been making you fidget all over my room for the past hour! What is it?"

"I don't like to burden you, truly—"

"I'm bored, Lindsay, just plain bored. Give me a problem, give me something to think about, something to focus on, so my brain won't rot."

"Sydney is going to be a model. Like me."

"That's absurd!"

"No. She even told Father last night. He was unsure about it, but she talked him around. Did you notice that Holly's gaining weight?"

"She's also drinking more. Yes, I know, just like your mother. But about Sydney. Why is she doing it?"

"She told Father she needs money."

"All right, why do you care?"

Lindsay could feel the cramping in her belly as she forced the words out. "People will figure out who she is really fast and she'll tell them who I am and it will all start over again. That's why I'm Eden. I don't have a last name, I don't have Lindsay Foxe's identity in New York. I've been safe the past year."

Gates Foxe didn't say anything. She stared at her granddaughter.

Lindsay kept talking, unable to keep the words inside. "She'll do it in such a way that everyone will think that I seduced the prince, that it was all my fault, that I was some kind of slut and a pervert."

"No, my dear. Actually, Lindsay, she won't say a word."

"But you didn't hear her last night! I don't know what to do! I've tried to plead with her and—"

"How can you be so stupid? One never pleads with Sydney, it's a waste of time. She despises weakness. I'm surprised you haven't ever realized that before. Of course, to be fair, you haven't been around her all that much. There are nine years between you. But with Sydney, my dear, it's pure and simple reason that works, reason and self-interest, nothing else, and that reason must be bottom-line. Sydney has had to deal with quite a lot on her plate, too much, I'd say, for someone weaker than she. But there it is. She copes and she succeeds at what she does. She sets a course and doesn't go off on a tangent. She also enjoys twitting you. You're a wonderful target for her, just as your mother was before you, because you care about feelings, your own and others'. She doesn't."

"But by speaking of Paris and Alessandro, she would be hurting herself as well, wouldn't she? I don't understand why she would even consider doing it."

"You were correct the first time. You would be the one to come out looking like a Lolita. Sydney is so bright it sometimes frightens me. If she chose to speak of what happened in Paris, why, then, you would look like a conscienceless little slut, and Sydney would come out the brave wife/martyr and everyone would praise her and adore her."

"I've got to stop her. I can't . . . deal with it again."

"So you have dealt with it, then. Is that why you majored in psychology? I thought so. Something so juicy is difficult to keep buried."

"I'll kill her."

"A thought, but impractical, my dear. No, Lindsay, I will deal with Sydney. You don't have the ability to do it. At least not yet. Yes, leave her to me."

The following afternoon Sydney came into Lindsay's bedroom. She looked beautiful, immaculate, chic. She looked angry, but when she spoke, it was with rueful amusement.

"You've won this time."

"What do you mean?"

"You got Grandmother to do your dirty work for you. I won't tell anyone about you, that's the deal. You can continue being wholesome Eden with your sweet smile. Oh, sure, the media will find out who I am almost immediately and I'll be bugged about Alessandro and about Paris and about what really happened. But I won't give you away, little sister. But know this, I will outshine you, Lindsay, don't doubt it. Give me six months and you'll be a has-been."

Lindsay wasn't really listening. She wondered what her grandmother had used as bottom line to ensure Sydney's silence. Self-interest, she thought. That meant money.

# 10

## 1991　LINDSAY

It was late October and the leaves were turning. Central
Park was never more beautiful than in the fall. Lindsay toed
aside yellow leaves from red ones as she walked from the
East Side to the West on her way to meet Gayle Werth at
their Mexican restaurant on Seventy-first Street.

The air was crisp, cool, and she was working up a light
sweat walking.

She heard some children and raised her head. They
were arguing over a toy truck, pulling and tugging at it.
Two mothers stood in close conversation, paying them no
heed. Lindsay smiled and continued, saying nothing. They
were cute kids. And the thought she hated came to her
then, with no warning: I'm twenty-six years old. I'm terrified of men. I'll never marry and have children.

Just stop it, she told herself, kicking a large pile of
brittle leaves out of her way. Just stop it, you stupid fool.
Your life is fine, wonderful, no problems, no hassles. You're
handling things just fine. And indeed, the past two years

had been something of a marvel for both her and her half-sister, when one looked at it from a certain point of view.

Sydney, La Principessa, was seen everywhere, not only in magazines, on television, but also at the biggest society bashes in New York. As for the prince, he was never around. "In Milan, running the family business, the dear," Sydney would say in a wistful sort of way. "I get away to see him and my darling daughter whenever I can. But *everybody* wants me! I do try, of course I do. Next weekend you can be certain I'm *off*." But she never went to Italy, it seemed to Lindsay. Then again, she rarely contacted Lindsay, so it didn't matter.

Lindsay admitted to occasional twinges of pure envy when she would pick up a glossy magazine and see Sydney looking out at her, gleaming perfection, every inch of her. It didn't matter that she was now thirty-five years old. It didn't matter that she hadn't even started modeling until she was past thirty. Nothing seemed to matter when Sydney set her mind to something. But she had, thankfully, been wrong about making Lindsay a has-been, though, which was an immeasurable relief. Lindsay was continuing to do well, not one of the top models like her half-sister, but well ensconced in any case. She was popular, well-liked, most directors and photographers worked well with her, and she could usually achieve almost any effect a client was looking for.

As for Lindsay Foxe, she was still well buried. Not a hint that Eden, the New York model, was Lindsay Foxe, the Lolita of Paris. Sydney had kept her word, thanks to her grandmother's bribe. Lindsay thought about a margarita and tortilla chips and her mouth watered. She'd have to starve for two days, but it was worth it.

# TAYLOR

Vinnie Demos stared at the man and wondered why the hell Glen had asked *him*. He'd recognized him immediately, of course, the second he'd walked through the door. He was the P.I. who'd been following Custer nearly three years ago. He was the ex-cop. Oh, sure, he'd told Glen to find him a bodyguard, someone really *good*, and he'd come up with this guy, this S. C. Taylor. Had Glen done it on purpose, to punish him? Demos didn't doubt it. Glen was sometimes a vile bitch, and he was getting bitchier by the month. Vinnie took several deep breaths and told himself to keep calm. He could handle anything. He'd proved that over the years. This guy didn't know, couldn't possibly have a clue, who Demos was. There'd been nothing on that damned note except the single name, Demos. And who would remember that, after all this time? Still . . . shit. Vinnie was up to his eyeballs again, beyond them this time, as Glen screamed at him, all his own dumb-ass fault, of course, but . . .

"Why do you want a bodyguard, Mr. Demos?"

Vinnie scratched his left earlobe. "It's not exactly for me, Mr. Taylor. It's for the upcoming shoot that'll be done in Central Park this Friday. It's a TV commercial for this fancy shampoo. If it's sunny—and it's supposed to be— then they film the sunlight and have natural breezes fluff through the hair. That sort of thing. Have you heard of Eden?"

Taylor frowned and shook his head. "Who's she?"

"A model. A rather well-known model, actually. She's being threatened, both she and the shoot itself, really."

"What did she do?"

Vinnie fidgeted with the white leather lead-weighted paperweight on his desk. Should he tell this guy something of the truth? No, not yet. Just let him use his brawn. Vinnie didn't want a lecture, nor did he want to take a chance that the guy would bring the cops in on it.

"It's rather complicated and I'm hiring you to protect things, that's all."

Taylor knew this lame explanation was no explanation at all, but his brain wasn't on full power, he recognized that, and decided to play it easy for the moment. He'd protect this Eden and the commercial, then he'd see.

"It's only this one particular shoot that's being threatened?"

"Yes." So far, Vinnie thought, but there'd be more

threats until he came through. And he'd have to come through or there would be violence. But he couldn't come through yet. It was like a damned snowball gathering speed. He wished he hadn't had the burst of ethics and sent Sydney to another agent two years before, but he had, dammit, and now he was paying for it. He should have kept her on, he could have handled it. But it was too late.

"Will you take the job, Mr. Taylor?"

Taylor nodded. He told Demos his price, shook his hand, and left.

"Glen, you damned bitch, get your ass in here!"

Glen appeared in the doorway. He was grinning. "Yeah, boss?"

"Why him?"

"Why who?" Glen said, his voice coy, his subsequent shrug elaborate. "He's supposed to be one of the best, I checked. And did you see that body? All hard and long and lean. And that manly jawline?" Glen licked his lips. "Strong bastard, and sure of himself. Nice smile too. I wanted to ask him if I could feel his stomach muscles, but I didn't think he'd understand."

"Oh, he would have understood, all right. You silly jerk, he's the same P.I. who found Custer, God, what was it—three years ago?"

Glen grew very quiet. He wasn't smiling now. "Yes, I know, Vinnie. He's the ex-cop."

"Why'd you do it?"

Glen turned dead serious, leaning over the desk, his hands flat on its surface, fingers splayed, long slender fingers with short buffed nails. "You've got to face things, Vinnie, you've got to get yourself together. Sell another painting. Don't fuck around with these folk. They do horrible things when you don't keep to your end of the bargain. You want to know why I got him in particular? To pin you, buddy, to make you *do* something. I did it because they just might threaten *me* next time. Get off the dime and pay them off!"

Glen left the room, then turned back, saying, "I can't believe you're taking a chance with Eden."

"They didn't threaten her specifically, they threatened

the shoot and the personnel. So don't accuse me of messing with Eden's life. I'm not taking one damned little chance with her. This bodyguard bit is pure overkill. Hey, you think the damned guy's so great, so sexy, why, he'll take good care of her. Why should you be worried?"

"You're a cold bastard, Vinnie. Cold."

"Yeah? Well, maybe he'll even teach her how to like sex. Lord knows, she needs some."

Taylor took a taxi to Valerie's apartment at Lexington and Fiftieth. They'd been seeing each other regularly since July 4, when Taylor had met her on the beach at Hyannisport. He'd admired her form—a wonderful swimmer—and then he'd found she was funny and sexy and smart. And Lord love it, she was beautiful. Masses of auburn hair and green eyes—moss green, and big and deep—and the whitest skin, all over. No tanning for her. He liked her, he'd discovered, liked talking to her. She was a bit older than he was, but who cared? Just last night, after they'd made love two times in rapid succession, because he'd been tied up with a computer puzzle in Minneapolis with the Claymore Corporation for a very long three days, he'd even told her about Diane, his first wife, and how he'd screwed up his marriage.

"We were both too young," he'd said, propping himself up in Valerie's bed. "Of course that doesn't really excuse anything." She handed him a cup of tea and he sipped it.

"Diane was—is—very rich. I think she wanted a common man under her belt. She got me, as common as they come. She'd decided it was too dangerous for me to be a cop. She wanted her common man safe. She hated it more and more with each passing week. She married me against her family's wishes, naturally, but there again, I really didn't know that either, not until later, not until it was over and she wanted to say hurtful things. It only lasted two years. Looking back, I'm surprised we managed to stay together that long."

"No kids?"

"No. She was only twenty-two when we met, right out of Radcliffe. And I was just twenty-four."

"What did Diane look like?"

Taylor grinned at Valerie. Her hair was tousled and falling in curling tangles over her white shoulders. She was naked, the sheets coming only to her waist. He cupped her left breast, lifting it. "Why would you care?"

Valerie shrugged.

Taylor leaned over and kissed her breast, lightly tugging on her nipple. He heard her intake of breath and lay back on his pillows, grinning impenitently at her. "She was fair, her eyes light blue, her hair black as sin. She was—is—lovely, small and dainty, but what a mouth she's got on her. She can swear like a stevedore. In a fight, I could never outcurse her, never. I was always too surprised when she'd let loose to get my own arguments properly together."

"What finally broke things up?"

"I wouldn't quit the force. I got hit one night, just a flesh wound in the side, nothing serious, but she freaked and wouldn't stop. She wanted me to go into her father's business, which is antiques. I didn't know a Sheraton from a Chippendale and I didn't particularly care." He shrugged, and his eyes, looking beyond her, were in the past. "I didn't understand compromise and neither did she."

"But you did quit the force."

Taylor looked as uncomfortable as he felt. "Yeah, I know. But that was a little bit later, after we'd divorced. There were reasons."

"Why?"

"There were reasons," he said again. He finished the tea and set the saucer down on the bed table. He turned back to her and her left breast. "Beautiful," he said, "just beautiful."

"You're not so bad yourself, Taylor."

"Oh?"

They'd made love again, then finally slept. It was with regret that Taylor had left her the following morning to see this man Vincent Demos.

The taxi let him out in front of her apartment building, a wonderful old 1920's building with huge flats, only two per floor. He nodded to the doorman, the thought striking him that Diane had lived in a flat similar to Valerie's. Was it his fate to be attracted to beautiful rich women? Well, if it was, it really wouldn't matter. He had no intention of marrying again, even if he did, occasionally, feel the urge to be a father. To be like most men his age. A family, children, a dog, the whole bit. He shook his head. Enoch had Sheila, his mother, and he was happy as a clam. He was discreet, had relationships that seemed to keep him perfectly content. But Taylor knew he was different from Enoch. He had just turned thirty-two, still young, but getting up there. He felt itchy. Like now. He forced his mind to Valerie. She was the best thing that had happened to him in quite a while. She loved sex, she was undemanding, and although he knew little about her, he respected her right to privacy. She was bright and her wit sometimes too sharp, but still, she pleased him. He hoped, sometimes ruefully, that he pleased her as well.

Diane had been bright and had loved sex. But still it hadn't been enough. Taylor rarely thought of Diane these days. The last he'd heard she was in Boston, owned her own antique business—actually, inherited it from her father—and was doing quite well. He silently wished her luck and wondered just how rich Valerie Balack really was and he wondered just what she did, if anything.

# EDEN

The morning was bright, the temperature just sixty degrees, only a slight breeze in Central Park. George Hudson was the director of the Jezerell shampoo commercial, a job which he hated. He was in a foul mood. He yelled at the photographer, who ignored him more often than not. He was supposed to be in charge of this shoot, not that jerk-off photographer who didn't know rocks from shit. It wasn't going well but it was easy money, good money, but he wouldn't get any raves about it from people who counted.

George Hudson insisted on good technicians, good makeup people, good cameramen, and he always got them, but he was pissed that he had to waste his time with a ditzy model who was six inches taller than he was and a miserable TV spot that would consume all of forty seconds. Too, the people from the ad agency and Jezerell were always in his face, making suggestions, trying to tell him how to do his job. He looked up to see Eden, tall, lanky, striding toward him, legs as long as a damned man's. At least she had gorgeous hair, all thick and long, deep waves, with a wonderful mix of shades that looked completely natural. He knew they'd done some more shading, to lighten the blond in places, but not much. He looked at her while he talked to his assistant. For the moment, her gorgeous hair was clipped back and flattened down. The hair guy hadn't touched it yet. She was frowning. He wondered who had screwed up what. Her reputation was good, whatever that meant. He'd never worked with her before. He wondered, cynically, if it meant she slept around.

"Yeah?"

"Mr. Hudson? I'm Eden." She stuck out her hand and he took it, shaking it, surprised at her and himself.

"Yeah?" His voice and look were suspicious. "You got a problem? Like everybody else?"

"Nothing really, at least I hope not. It's just that Demos isn't here and there's this man—he's over there. I don't know who he is, do you?"

George glanced over at the man standing casually just beyond the shoot area and cameramen. He was dressed neatly in dark brown corduroy slacks, white shirt, and a pale brown leather jacket. He looked clean-cut, respectable. Which didn't mean shit in New York.

George said to his assistant, a twenty-year-old girl who was overweight and worshiped him, "Gina, go see what that guy wants, then report back to me."

Gina licked her lips, nodded nervously, and took off.

"We'll see. You never saw the guy before?"

Lindsay shook her head. "No. I've just learned to be careful. And no one seems to know who he is."

She watched little Gina trot up to the man, for all the world like a tail-wagging puppy. The man smiled down at her and spoke, his posture reassuring, and he actually patted her arm.

135

Gina came back, relief covering her face.

"He says his name is Taylor and he's here on Mr. Demos' orders."

"Doing what?" Lindsay asked.

"He said that Demos would be here soon and speak to you, Eden."

"I see," Lindsay said, not seeing a thing. "Well, then maybe we can get this show on the road."

"We'll begin in about forty minutes," George said, waving her away. "Have them get your face and hair ready, and get into your clothes."

Lindsay nodded and walked back to where the hairdresser and makeup people were grouped around doughnuts and coffee.

Taylor watched her. So this was Eden, his first exposure to a real-live model. She was very tall, nearly six feet. And thin. This was a shampoo commercial and her hair looked unappealing as sin, all brushed down against her head. He hoped they were going to do something with it and with her. She had to have something going for her other than her height. She was wearing jeans and a baggy T-shirt and high-top running shoes. He watched her go inside a trailer, and the door closed. Odd that she'd been the one to question his presence and not one of the others. Was the lady nervous about something? Had he misjudged Demos? Was this Eden the one on the hook and Demos was protecting her?

He scanned the group, taking note of each man's position and what he appeared to be doing. He had a list of all the men and women who were to be involved in the commercial. What a list. He couldn't begin to estimate the cost of this little outing. He'd checked them all off. No one appeared unaccounted for.

He looked up to see the plump little pigeon, Gina, smiling at him. He winked at her.

He didn't like the fact that they were in Central Park. There were more bushes and trees around than could be counted. There was a continuous stream of people strolling by, trying to be cool and act nonchalant, but still slowing and looking. And there were lowlifes everywhere. He prowled continuously, eyes peeled for anything or anyone suspicious. Nothing so far.

He was used to waiting. He was patient and he knew how to keep perfectly still, if the situation demanded it. He heard a noise and quickly turned. There were two black kids with ghetto-blasters, earplugs in their ears, gyrating down a path. He watched them closely until they passed from sight. He leaned back against an oak tree, feeling the comfort of his 9mm automatic tucked close to his body in his shoulder holster. Thirty minutes later the trailer door opened and three people stepped out. They turned, and one of the men bowed and held out his hand.

An incredible woman took his hand and let him help her to the ground. She was wearing a white flowy dress and her feet and legs were bare. Her hair was something else—all full and deeply waving and multicolored and thick and long. Gorgeous. It was her, the model, Eden. Impossible to believe. He gawked at her, unable to help himself. Of course he hadn't seen her up close.

She looked up then and met his eyes. He felt like a kid with a sudden attack of hormones, and a fool. He nodded to her, then resumed what he was being paid for. He scanned the set and all the people who passed by who even looked like they were considering stopping. He looked at men's hands. At men's faces, at the angles of their heads. He'd always been good at seeing intent. Then his eyes came back to her. Demos had said she might be a target. Demos wanted Taylor to keep close to her. Well, looking at her was no problem.

He watched the director throw his weight around, heard him give orders in a churlish manner, heard him criticize Eden, not once but a good half-dozen times. Her smile was all wrong. She wasn't graceful. She was acting all stiff, like a damned puppet. Taylor would have punched the guy out. Eden simply nodded, shook her head, or asked for clarification. She did what she was told with no show of hesitation or disagreement, moving to a certain position, standing calm and still when ordered to do so. He watched makeup people swarm over her, then a hair person was ducking past a cameraman to straighten hair that didn't need straightening. The photographer and the director kept fighting, and Taylor wondered who was supposed to be the boss here. It was chaos and madness.

The shoot took two and a half hours. During that time Taylor had spotted twenty possible suspects, but all of them had faded away. And always he looked back at her. He watched as one man held a fan two feet away from her and blew her hair away from her face. He watched her arch her back, push her breasts forward, watched her move to sit atop a horse, her long bare legs showing. They'd hired from one of the park drivers a docile old bay mare with a white fetlock, patient and long-suffering.

He wondered at her patience. He wondered how she could keep smiling. He wondered how she could put up with the egotistical director. He waited for her to scream at the jerk, but she didn't, at least this time. When it was over, he breathed a sigh of relief. There'd been nothing more suspicious than a man who'd dropped something and spent too long looking for it, to the point that Taylor started to approach him. But the guy took off. Taylor watched her stretch, speak briefly to the director, shake the photographer's hand, then go back into the trailer.

When she emerged some twenty minutes later, she was back in jeans and T-shirt, her hair clipped back at the base of her head. Strangely, he thought she looked more lovely now than with all the wild and flowy hair.

He pushed off the tree he was standing against and walked over to her.

"Demos didn't show up," he said. He stuck out his hand. "So I'll have to introduce myself. I'm Taylor."

"Taylor what?"

"Taylor's my last name. And that's what I'm called." One of her eyebrows was still up in question. He shrugged. "Okay, my full name is S. C. Taylor, but as I said, Taylor is what I'm called."

Because she saw no alternative, Lindsay took his hand. "I'm Eden. Why are you here?"

"Demos hired me to protect you and the shoot."

Lindsay's mouth fell open and there was no mistaking her surprise. "What?"

"He should have come. He said he would, and tell you who I was and why I was here. He's asked me to stick with you for the next couple of days."

"But that's crazy! Protect *me*? But who would—?"

"Yeah, my thoughts exactly. I think friend Demos owes someone money and the someone isn't happy with him at the moment."

"He loves the horses."

"How long have you been with him?"

"About four years."

"You want to call him and check me out?"

She shook her head on a sigh. "Don't get me wrong. It's not that I trust you so quickly. No, it sounds just like Vinnie. I am surprised that Glen didn't let me know, though."

"Shall we go have some lunch?"

Lindsay didn't know what to say. She'd seen him and distrusted him. He looked too sure of himself, too on top of things. He was good-looking, and that always put her on the alert. He was big, and that made her even more wary. The prince had been smaller-boned, slender, but he'd been strong enough to do just as he pleased with her. This man was six-foot-two, she guessed, the same height as her father. She wished she was wearing heels instead of her sneakers, so she could look him straight in the eye. She supposed that sticking with her meant just that. "It's yogurt for lunch. I pigged out on Mexican food last night and have got to pay the piper now."

"No problem," Taylor said. "You ready?"

She nodded. Suddenly she was aware of the mobs of people all around. "It's not dangerous for us to be walking out in the middle of everything?"

"Don't worry. I'm right with you and I'm armed. I don't want you to end up a prisoner in your apartment, afraid to answer your telephone or your front door. That's no good either. We'll be conservative and smart, that's all. And of course, I'll be dogging your heels."

She nodded. She couldn't wait to get her hands on Demos. Could she truly be in any danger? That bastard.

She wanted to kill him. How dare he put her in this kind of situation? And with this man who was a total stranger?

"Maybe I shouldn't have been honest with you," he said, in step beside her, "or rather, speculated about things, but Demos didn't show up like he said he would. I figured you wouldn't buy anything but the truth."

"You're right about that," Lindsay said, her voice stony, striding so fast he had to double-step to stay even with her. "I'll get him for this, the jerk."

Taylor said mildly, "Perhaps I've got it all wrong. He didn't spell it out like that."

Lindsay looked over at him then, the first time, he realized. What was with her? "Yeah, sure. I'm so valuable he's suddenly decided that I'm in danger of being abducted by a Middle Eastern sheik."

"I'd be tempted."

She withdrew. It was the strangest thing. She was simply no longer there. She didn't speed up her pace, she didn't really do anything different, but she was gone from him, completely. He frowned at her profile and said, "I was out of line. Sorry."

She didn't come back, just nodded, not looking at him, and kept taking those long-legged strides.

"There's a good yogurt shop just over on Sixth and Fifty-seventh. You want to give it a try?"

She nodded. The sidewalks were congested with people, all hurrying, because it was the best offense, the streets congested with cars, taxis primarily, all honking, all zigging and zagging, trying to get the best of each other. She found she was studying faces, assessing them, giving them a significance they'd never had before. Her intent different now, suspicious, afraid. Taylor said quietly beside her, "No, don't do that. Everything will be fine. Trust me. I'm good at my job. If it makes you feel better, I was a cop for a number of years."

"Okay," Lindsay said, and tried to keep her glances at strangers surreptitious.

The yogurt shop was full and they had to wait for ten minutes to get served.

Lindsay ordered nonfat banana-nut yogurt, medium

size, and sat down at a small round white table with ice-
cream-parlor chairs recently vacated. He ordered the same
and joined her.

She ate very slowly, cherishing each bite. He found
himself watching her. "You're always hungry?"

She didn't reply until she'd swallowed slowly, with
obvious relish. "No, not really. It's just that I'm forced to
weigh fifteen pounds less than I should carry. It's the cameras that put the weight on you. Those are the rules," she
added quickly when she saw he would say something. "If
I want to be in this profession, I must abide by them."

"I guess I can understand that. Does your family
preach at you about not eating enough?"

"No, they . . . Where did Demos find you?"

"Actually it was Glen—Flaming Glen with the row of
diamond studs marching up his ear—who called me up and
asked me to come in for a job. Does he always wear black?"

Lindsay smiled. She was relaxing again. He'd backed
off, for which she was immensely grateful. Oddly, she also
trusted him to keep her safe. She'd be rid of him soon
enough, just as soon as she got hold of Demos. "Flaming
Glen is a nut case. If he isn't wearing black, well then, it's
violet. He says it complements his eyes. Be thankful you
got the black dose. He's very angry with Demos about
something right now. How was Glen dressed when you
met him?"

"In tight designer jeans, black, ribbed turtleneck, also
black, a western belt with a huge round silver buckle, and
black Italian loafers."

"He adores that particular outfit. You're observant. You
know, I try to stay away from the office. They try to get
me to take sides."

"Well, I'm a private investigator when I'm not a computer hacker. And that's what Demos is paying me for. I
hope you don't mind me hanging around you for a couple
of days."

"Hanging around exactly how? You mean giving me
advice on what to do and what not to do?"

Taylor shrugged. When Demos had called him at home
the previous night, he'd sounded a bit agitated. It was then

he'd asked Taylor to keep a close watch on Eden, after the shoot. He wasn't going to take any chances, he'd said. Keep a close guard on Eden.

Taylor had jacked up his price, to which Demos had too readily agreed. Taylor wondered if he'd try to stiff him. He'd called Glen and asked for cash up front and Glen had come through.

"Hanging around exactly how?" Lindsay asked again.

He smiled at her and it scared her. She very nearly recoiled. The smile was gone in the next instant and he sat forward in the flimsy chair and said in a very low voice, "I don't know what's with you, lady, but I don't intend to spend my time wondering how you're going to react to me, and worrying about what I say. I've been hired to do a job and you're the job. I'll be your bloody shadow until Demos stops paying the bills. If you don't like that, call him. Now, do you want to call him now or are you ready to go? Incidentally, I've got great taste in clothes, so if you want to go shopping, I'm at your disposal."

Lindsay was silent for several moments. "I'm sorry."

He only nodded.

"New York is sometimes scary."

"That's true."

"I have a karate class in an hour."

"How good are you?"

"Third degree."

"How long you been taking lessons?"

"A year now. I saw a mugging last year and I couldn't stand it." Half-truth, she thought, always half-truths. The problem was that they came so easily, more so by the year.

"You know, what the cops say about defending yourself against a criminal is true. It's usually a mistake."

"So you recommend just lying there and taking it?"

"I recommend using your brain and assessing a situation. Fear is the worst enemy because it makes you act stupid in most cases. Machismo is just as bad."

Lindsay got up. "You were with the NYPD?"

"Yes, I was."

"Why'd you quit?"

He smiled then and opened the yogurt-shop door for her. "Where's your gym?"

"Down on Forty-fourth and Madison. It's okay to go there?"

"Yeah, trust me," Taylor said. "Let's go, then. That's a long walk. I assume you walk a lot to keep your weight down?"

Lindsay nodded.

Taylor watched her work out at Lin Ho's Gym. She wasn't bad. She was rangy, well-coordinated, strong, and she had endurance. The problem was, you could see how she was going to move before she did it. Her intentions were as clear as the deep blue of her eyes. Maybe he could coach her a bit about that. Against a serious perp she'd be mincemeat. He'd have to make sure she understood what the underbelly of New York was really like. He winced as he thought that. He, S. C. Taylor, that outstanding cop who was all for law and order, who'd ardently believed in justice and in the system, had waited exactly two months after Ellie's jump from the second-floor bathroom from her private school. Actually, he'd waited one month, three weeks, and two days after Ellie's funeral. Dear God, that funeral— both the mother and Uncle Bandy had been there, hugging each other, and then the black-souled bastard had actually thrown a red rose on top of the coffin. Taylor had nearly gone after him then. But he'd stopped himself.

But not for long. He'd pulled Uncle Bandy from his rich brownstone and beaten the living shit out of him. Odd, but it hadn't made him feel any better. The man had the nerve to threaten him. The man had the nerve to scream that it was all Taylor's fault. Taylor, enraged, had hit him again. But Ellie was still dead. She was buried at Mountain View. He went there occasionally. He'd never checked to see what had become of her mother. He'd simply never cared. But Uncle Bandy, he'd recovered and Taylor knew he carried on as he always had. Power, money, all the trappings.

He left the gym with Eden, his thoughts still on Ellie. Lindsay wondered what he was thinking. He was clearly distracted. She'd called the office from the dressing room and gotten Glen. "The boss is gone, Eden, away for a long weekend, he told me."

"Why Taylor, Glen? Somebody threaten Demos?"

"Yeah, sweetie. Don't get pissed off at Demos and lose the guy. Let him stay close; he's good at what he does. Isn't he cute? Did you get a look at that chest of his? And that darling little dimple in his chin?"

"Yeah, right, Glen. See you next week."

"Take care, Eden. If you get him in bed, I'll scratch your eyes out."

Lindsay dutifully laughed.

# 11

## TAYLOR / EDEN

Taylor called Valerie from Eden's apartment. He asked her how she was, how her day was, to which he got the same response he always got, namely, that she was fine, had enjoyed herself, had gone shopping and bought this and that, she missed him, and then, what was he doing. All in one breath, little variation, at least on her end of it.

"I can't make it tonight," he said, feeling regret and that regret sounding in his voice. "Yeah, I know you wanted to see that show, but I'm on a job and I'll be tied up at least for the weekend, maybe even through next week. I'm sorry, babe. I'll cash the tickets in and get some more for next weekend, all right? Or would you rather have me send them over and you can use them? Maybe invite someone to go with you?"

"I don't want to go with anyone else! You're with another woman, aren't you?"

"Yes, it's the job I have." He added, frowning into the phone at the suspicion he heard in her voice, "Nothing more than the job, Valerie. I told you this would occasionally happen. What's your problem?"

She burst out suddenly, violently, "You're lying! Damn you, what's her name? You're just like every other fucking man! Tell me her name!"

Taylor stared at the phone, jerked it away from his ear. Valerie was yelling at him, actually shrieking. He couldn't believe it. And she kept it up, this endless supply of venom, yelling now, calling him a liar, accusing him of screwing around, of betraying her with a younger woman, of lying, lying, lying. He remained quiet. What could he say that he hadn't said already? Jesus, you never knew a person. He'd thought he had known her. He thought of her laughter, her beautiful body, her sometimes too-facetious wit, the undeniable intelligence behind that perfect face. But never had he imagined this kind of fury running deep in her. How could she be jealous? Had some guy in the past really screwed her up? It seemed incredible to him for the simple reason she seemed so in control. By God, she was the most beautiful woman he'd ever seen in his life. This was madness.

When she ran down finally, he was angry and impatient, and said, "I'm sorry you don't believe me, Valerie. You're entirely wrong. I'll call you on Monday. I'll expect an apology then."

There was just an instant of hesitation before she started up again. He gently eased the phone back into its cradle, looking down at it in disgust.

He turned to see Eden standing in the open kitchen doorway, just looking at him, her head cocked to one side in silent question. He shook his head, feeling slightly sick. "You never really know a person, do you?"

"No," she said, "I don't think you do. Perhaps it's better not to. Skeletons abound. No, better not to. Would you like a diet soda? A cup of tea?"

A beer would be nicer, but what the hell. "Tea would be fine, thank you."

She disappeared into the kitchen thinking that he was involved, and that was a good thing. She wouldn't have to worry now. She wondered why the woman on the phone could possibly be mad over another female she'd never met. And he'd said, quite calmly, that this was nothing more than a job. Strange.

Taylor sat down on her oversized sofa, covered in a bright South Seas pattern with a good half-dozen throw pillows scattered over its surface. He leaned back, getting comfortable, and took in her surroundings. The living room wasn't large, but it was comfortable, cozy, very cluttered, and surprisingly, for he was a person of strict neatness, he liked it. There was a bamboo coffee table covered with novels in haphazard stacks, another pile of novels on the floor beside the sofa, and two beckoning easy chairs opposite the sofa, a reading lamp between them. He looked at the books, paperbacks mostly. Her taste was eclectic. There were mysteries, spy novels, historical romances, science fiction. He counted just about every Dick Francis novel ever written. And, surprising, there were books on architecture, big sprawling books that you'd normally see carefully arranged to impress on coffee tables. But she had a lot of them and they were as indiscriminately set about as all her other books. Big picture books and biographies, at least a dozen of them about such architects as Barry, Pugin, and Dominico—little-known men, surely—and Telford, the man who had built the first suspension bridge.

No nonfiction, no newspapers, no magazines. Odd about the absence of magazines. She was a model and was probably in many of them. He rose and walked to the fireplace. There were photos on the mantel, several of her with an old lady who looked patrician as hell and stylishly dressed, a single photo of a man who looked to be her father—same eyes exactly—and a lone small photo of a woman who was very thin, looking gaunt, deep worry lines furrowing her brow. Her mother? There was no similarity that Taylor could see. No brothers or sisters?

"Anything in your tea?" She sounded wary, suspicious. He turned slowly, aware that she thought he was spying on her, which, actually, he was, kind of, and said easily, "Thank you. Nothing for me. I like my tea clean. I hope it's not one of those wild sorts of tea, you know, with ground mice toes or herbal orange droppings?"

She laughed, disclaimed, then retreated back to the kitchen. He resumed his perusal. The fireplace was black with use and needed a good cleaning. When she came back carrying a tray, he said, "You need to get yourself on the phone and call a chimney-cleaning place. This is a hazard."

147

Lindsay grinned at him, her apprehension banished with his light touch. It was free, that grin, and somehow he knew that it was special. Special from her, a woman, to him, a man.

"You invited me here," Taylor said after taking a sip of jasmine tea that he hated. "I'm surprised."

Lindsay shrugged. "What else was I supposed to do with you? Leave you in the hall? Insist you remain out on the street corner?"

"We could have gone places. I told you I have great taste. We would have gone to Bloomingdale's."

"I'm tired, to tell the truth. Must you really stay with me like this? All the time? What about tonight?"

"You're stuck with me. Since Demos is paying the bills, do you want to go to the movies? I hear *Black Prince* is excellent, at least it got great reviews." What he didn't tell her was that he already had two tickets. He'd weighed the possible risks in his mind and decided he could sufficiently minimize them. He wasn't stupid and he was experienced. He truly didn't want her to think herself a prisoner.

Her eyes lit up; all of her lit up. It surprised him. She was beautiful; she was successful; she had to have lots of men around, men, of course, of her own choosing. Yet she just looked like she'd been offered an unheard-of treat, something glorious, something completely unexpected.

"We could eat Chinese—no calories, they all fade away after thirty minutes."

Then she looked away from him, saying as she sloshed her tea in its cup, "It's just a job for you, right? Not a date or anything?"

"I wouldn't dream of asking you for a date."

He'd meant it as a joke, but she took him seriously. "All right, then. That would be fun."

"I like your apartment."

She looked at him, uncertain whether he was kidding or not. He saw the exact moment when she decided to take his comment at its face value. He should get her in a poker game. He'd win everything she owned, including her knickers, she was so transparent.

"Thank you," she said finally, looking around proudly.

"It's small, but it's all mine and I've done exactly what I wanted to with it. I even got a good price on it."

"I see you also like architecture."

"Oh, yes, particularly the architects themselves, those of past centuries. Their lives are fascinating, and what they did, goodness, it . . ." She broke off, and he recognized embarrassment. She thought she was chattering and boring him.

"Tell me about Telford," he said easily. "Didn't he once create a design for London Bridge and it got turned down?" When she nodded happily, obviously delighted that he knew something, he was pleased that he'd seen that tidbit when he'd opened the book.

When she accompanied him to his apartment, only eight blocks from hers, so he could change, Lindsay felt strangely happy. She hadn't been out with a man in years, actually walking beside a man, talking to him. Not worrying or inadvertently drawing back. And this wasn't really out, it was a job, his job, but still . . . it was so very different for her. Please, she prayed, let him be kind.

Bottom line, his apartment was much nicer than hers. In an older building, it was larger, with high ceilings and beautiful molding that somehow didn't clash at all with very modern furnishings. A big deep green leather sofa and two leather chairs with footstools, glass-and-wood lamps and tables. Clean, uncluttered, orderly, that was her impression, that and good taste. He obviously liked earth tones—rich creams and tans and pale golds. She felt intimidated. He wasn't poor; not remotely. Why had she expected it? Because he was a bodyguard? She became aware, suddenly, that he was watching her take in his apartment.

"I, uh, like it," she said.

"Thanks. Make yourself comfortable." He waved toward the sofa and left her alone.

He wasn't a fiction freak, she quickly saw, not the way she was. And the neatness, the order of everything, made her want to toss all the magazines and books into the air and let them stay where they landed. It made her itchy, all those tidy stacks. Computer magazines were neatly piled on nearly every surface and on nearly every bookshelf. She picked a very thick *PC Magazine* and flipped through pages scored with indecipherable numbers and words and phrases. There was an article titled *The Dizzo Chip* and she knit her brow over that one. She thumbed through more of the pages, saw pictures of things she didn't recognize. She read several sentences about modems because she knew what they were, but still she didn't understand anything but the prepositions and a noun here and there. She laid the magazine back down, very carefully, into its neat stack of other computer magazines, and looked about some more. She felt a shock when she picked up a magazine with a muscle-bound man on the cover. He looked like Rambo, a huge Uzi or some such thing held close to his chest, his eyes mean and hard and . . . Then she saw the gun magazines, hunting and rifle magazines, sporting magazines, international firearm magazines. She opened one of the foreign gun magazines and read about a Glock 17, an Austrian-made plastic gun. There was a caption beneath the big glossy photo of the gun that read: "For Every Homeowner in the U.S.—Now Available." Jesus, she thought, the thing looked like a toy, most of it transparent and flimsy-looking. But it wasn't a toy. One for every household, wonderful. She turned more pages to see more men holding weapons, on target ranges, out-of-doors in forests, with other men in groups, all of them holding weapons, men and more of them, all armed, ready to kill. And several photos of men with guns standing next to women, or looking down at women, arrogant and dominating, in charge. . . . Did Taylor carry a gun? She shook her head. Of course he must have one. He was a private investigator, he was her bodyguard. Did he wear a gun?

She looked up when she heard the shower turn on, muted from another room, but still clear enough to identify. Another person taking a shower, and only a room or two away. It was a strange feeling. She'd been alone for so very long. She prowled his living room, then went into the kitchen. He was a gadget freak. There were appliances she recognized and some she didn't. She looked at a shiny Belgian waffle maker, sparkling clean, open, and ready to use, and felt her mouth water. There was a can opener that was so fancy it made her feel sorry for the can. She opened his refrigerator to get a diet soda. There were lots of raw vegetables, orange juice, cans of tuna fish, many kinds of dressings, a loaf of wheat bread, no-cholesterol butter, sugarless jams, but no diet soda. She looked longingly at a bottle of Balidonne chardonnay and regretfully closed the refrigerator door.

She wandered back into the living room. The shower cut off, and suddenly, in that instant, she realized that he was naked and what that meant. It wasn't just simply odd to be in the same apartment with a man, it was suddenly overwhelmingly terrifying. She wasn't far from a man who was naked. Only two doors away or maybe just one. She looked down at the coffee table and saw a man with a naked chest, holding a rifle, a woman standing behind him, her look one of awe, of worship, her lips parted slightly, her age no more than twenty-two.

A man could hurt a woman. This man, this Taylor, could hurt her. He was big. Taylor seemed nice, but maybe it was just an act to get her over here. And here she was, having trailed after him without hesitation, happy as a pup, meek as a lamb, blabbing on and on about architects in the seventeenth century. She'd been boring, stupid, and now she was vulnerable.

He was naked. He was in his bathroom now, but what if he came out? Would he have on a dressing gown like the prince had worn, choosing to play the game a little while longer? Would she know he was naked beneath it like she'd known the prince was? No, she was certain Taylor would be naked, no Italian dressing gown for him, no fancy games for him, and all she was wearing was slacks and a simple sweater.

Oh, God. He looked like those men in those gun magazines. The self-defense she knew was laughable against a man like him. She'd heard him at the gym, speaking to Lin Ho, her instructor, heard the two of them discussing strategies when faced with more than one opponent and the opponents were both armed with knives. He'd said nothing to her about knowing martial arts, but he did, he had to. Just the way he'd stood when he was talking to Lin

Ho. It was obvious. He was strong and he could fight. He was a man and he was big and she'd never have a chance against him.

Lindsay grabbed her purse, ran to the front door, wrenched it open, and was out in a second. She heard Taylor calling her name.

She ran down the five flights of stairs, afraid to wait for the elevator. He'd catch her if she waited. If it came, he'd be faster and be waiting for her at the lobby, ready to grab her and shove her back into the elevator and bring her back up here. She was winded, a stitch in her side, when she reached the lobby. She was bent over, clutching her purse to her middle. She ran to the corner and waved wildly for a taxi.

She had to get away.

Taylor heard the front door slam, and without a thought, he raced naked into the living room. She was gone. Jesus, could someone have come in and snatched her? No, not possible. He called after her, but, realizing he didn't have a stitch of clothing on, he knew he couldn't run after her.

Why had she run out?

He stood there dripping water, wondering what the problem was. It was weird. She was weird. He sighed, turned back into his bedroom, and quickly dressed. She was alone, no one to protect her, if the enforcers who hounded Demos wanted to go after her.

Lindsay told the taxi driver to drop her off at Gayle's apartment over on the West Side, just opposite Lincoln Center. Gayle lived in a condo on the thirty-sixth floor. Lindsay dashed through the immense lobby to the bank of six elevators. She punched the buttons and collapsed back against the wall. She was safe. But, as it turned out, Gayle wasn't home.

Lindsay leaned against the corridor wall next to her apartment door, her eyes closed. What to do?

She couldn't very well stand here forever. The security was too good in this building. She'd soon be reported by a neighbor. Slowly, slinging her bag back onto her shoulder, she went back down to the lobby. She'd wait there. If she stayed out in the open, looking harmless, they wouldn't kick her out. If Taylor came looking for her . . . Oh, no, no . . .

She was approached by a security guard two hours later. Their patience had run out.

She left, catching a taxi to return to her apartment. In the back of the taxi she remembered for the first time since her flight from Taylor's apartment that she was under threat. She'd been running around like a fool, unthinking, dangerously unthinking. She realized, laughing a bit hysterically, that she had no place else to go, except maybe to an impersonal hotel. She had no other close friends. Even Demos and Glen she'd kept away from when it came to social get-togethers. She'd kept a whole bunch of folk at bay, all those people who'd tried to be nice to her over the years. They were acquaintances, nothing more, because she'd distrusted them, all of them, women included. All except Gayle because Gayle had known her before Paris.

Head down, she exited her elevator. She felt numb and very, very tired. She very nearly walked squarely into him.

His hands closed around her shoulders and her head jerked up. She nearly screamed but his hand was over her mouth.

"Shut up, damn you!"

She tried to jerk away from him. He was strong, she'd known he would be. He wasn't going to let her go. He would drag her into her apartment and . . .

Taylor saw the terror in her eyes. Not terror of a possible enforcer, he realized with a shock, but terror of him. He said very calmly, "I have to urinate. I've been standing here like a fool for the past two hours waiting for you to bring your butt home. Would you please open the door?"

She stared up at him. He didn't look at all interested in ripping off her clothes. What he looked was vastly annoyed. With her. "You have to urinate?"

"Yes. You're the only game around, Eden. I couldn't very well see myself asking your neighbor to use her bathroom. Open the door."

"Oh." She giggled. Her terror . . . God, she'd been paralyzed with terror and . . . all he wanted was to go to the bathroom.

She opened the door and stood aside, pointing straight

ahead. "Just beyond the bedroom." Taylor gave her another long, very irritated look, then went to her bathroom.

She was standing in the same spot when he came out. He stopped a good three feet away from her. "Talk to me." She stared at him instead.

"I'm also tired of standing. Come along and sit down. Talk to me."

"I'm hungry."

"I won't eat another damned yogurt."

"Chinese?"

"Are you going to duck out on me again?"

"No."

"All right." Taylor sighed. This was weird, the entire situation. "Let's go to Chow Fang's, down in Chinatown."

"I like spicy Chinese."

"It's very spicy."

To Lindsay's surprise and relief, Taylor didn't demand to know why she'd run out on him. She'd fully expected it, an attack, a show of anger, a man's anger, all of it, maybe cold sarcasm like her father's, but he didn't say anything, not even a mention of how she'd endangered herself.

He ushered her into a Szechuan restaurant, old and needing a paint job, with dusty red lanterns hanging from a low ceiling. It was set in the midst of Chinatown and known, Taylor told her, for authentic and tasty dishes.

Lindsay ordered green-onion pancakes with peanut sauce.

"My favorite," Taylor said, and doubled the order.

He spoke to her of the owner of the restaurant, a Mr. Chang, who'd come over in the early 1960's from Taiwan. He spoke of Mr. Chang's family, discussing each of the six children in great detail, until Lindsay finally said, "Stop it! You're making that up!"

"It took you long enough. I was running out of descriptions. Another kid and he would have had to be a juvenile delinquent. Chinese Mafia maybe."

She studied his face. No clues there. Open, kind. But as he'd said earlier, who really knew another person? She picked up a fortune cookie, vastly uncomfortable. She unfurled the narrow strip of paper and read: "You need a new environment. Wallpaper your bedroom."

She laughed and handed it to Taylor. "Keep it," he advised, cracked open his own fortune cookie. There were two slips of paper. The first said: "A woman who seeks to be equal with men lacks ambition."

Taylor grinned and handed it to her. Her eyes lit up and she crowed. "Aha! You see, ancient Chinese wisdom still applies today. I see they believe you need a double dose. What's the other one?"

He opened it and froze. "You have finally met the one love of your life. Tread carefully. You don't want to lose her."

He frowned. What utter nonsense. Bullshit. After the way Valerie had yelled at him, calling him a bastard and a liar? No way. He stilled. Oh, no, not this strange creature sitting opposite him, her eyes on his fortune, waiting for him to hand it to her. Her anticipation was endearing and he shied away from it. This was the woman who'd run out of his apartment with no thought to her own safety. With no reason for flight that he could see. Oh, no, that was crazy. Then he laughed. A damned silly fortune cookie. Produced in a factory in New Jersey by Italians, no doubt.

"What is it? You will take a trip around the world? Confucius says something?"

He merely smiled, shook his head, folded the paper, and stuck it in his wallet.

When they came out onto the street, the night was clear and cool. Chinatown had its own smells and sounds, and tonight, both were pleasant. "I love New York when it's like this," Lindsay said, breathing in deeply. "It feels so good in your lungs."

Taylor was busily looking around. Nothing suspicious. Not a single nose seemingly interested in their business. When he turned back to her, she was still wrapped in the wonders of the night. He smiled at her, then hailed a cab.

"I'm seeing you home. I'll see that you're safe. I'll see that you're well locked in. I'll come by tomorrow whenever you're ready to go out."

"Okay."

"You'll be there? You won't do anything stupid? You won't go out without me?"

"No."

"I admit to relief."

She turned on the seat to face him. "Look, it isn't what you think. You don't understand, really, but . . ."

"Just forget it. I wouldn't care to finish that thought either."

She fell silent.

"You won't open your door to anybody you don't know, all right?"

She nodded, but remained silent. He checked through her apartment. Every bit of comfortable clutter was still in its place. Her bedroom was small and square, but light, with white-painted rattan headboard, dresser, chair, and several white carpets over polished oak parquet floors. He smiled at the panty hose and underwear strewn over a chair. One high-top running shoe was sitting on top of a pale-blue comforter, its mate tipped on its side on the floor beside the bed, a sock half stuck in it still. He remembered the small bathroom well enough. Taylor returned to her, instructing her like a child about her locks, of which she had four and already knew everything.

"Do you have an answering machine? Good. Don't answer the phone, screen the calls first, be sure you know who it is before you pick up and speak yourself."

When he left, finally, giving her one long look that she couldn't decipher, she leaned against the front door and closed her eyes.

What had his second fortune cookie said?

Lindsay wanted to go jogging. It was seven in the morning on a bright sunny Saturday and she was bored and antsy and she'd tried to get Demos twice already but he wasn't there. Neither was Glen, evidently. Cowards, both of them. And Taylor wasn't here, nor had she heard from him.

She wandered through her small apartment, absently drinking tea and chewing on an unbuttered slice of wheat toast.

Why the devil hadn't she thought to get his phone number? Well, he'd forgotten as well. No one had called.

She kept looking toward the front door with all its myriad locks securely in place.

When the doorbell rang at precisely eight o'clock, she

nearly dropped her teacup. She was fiddling with the locks, and when the last chain fell, she jerked open the door.

"I've been up for hours! Where have you been?"

"Good morning to you too. Why the hell didn't you ask who it was? I could have been your friendly neighborhood rapist. I could have been Demos' own personal devil."

He saw she simply hadn't thought about that. She was suddenly trembling, and he saw it, and he was sorry to have reminded her. But, dammit, she shouldn't forget. Her teacup rattled.

"Come on, I didn't mean to scare you, but you've got to be more careful." He started to put out his hands to grasp her shoulders, then didn't. No, she'd likely pull away from him as fast as she could.

"No, I'm not really scared. It's just that I'd forgotten about the other. I've just been waiting and waiting, and your ring just startled me, that's all. I want to go jogging and I didn't know your number and I'd promised you that I wouldn't leave the apartment. Is it safe for us to go jogging?"

He would have preferred not to jog, not out in the open like that, making them easy targets, but he saw the excitement in her eyes, so clear to him, and he grinned down at her from a distance of only two inches. "Safe enough, I think. We'll just take a few extra precautions. And I came prepared." He lifted a black canvas bag. "I've got lots of goodies in here, since I didn't know what you normally do on a Saturday morning." He paused a moment, a black eyebrow raised. "Can I change in your bedroom without you running away?"

"Yes."

"Good. How about a cup of very strong coffee?"

"Bacon? Eggs? Toast?"

He said easily, "No, not if I'm going running with you, but thanks for the gracious offer."

"Go change," she said. "All right, I'm sorry for being rude."

They took a taxi to Central Park South and spent the next hour jogging at an easy pace. He'd found out she always jogged the other end of the park, around the reservoir, and told her that predictability was something to avoid from now on. They'd start from here and stay on the southern end of the park. Taylor's shoulder holster was strapped down tight beneath a loose sweat-top. He wondered if she could see the bulge. He found its weight soothing. He kept to the inside of her, closest to any hidden spots where someone might be lying in wait. He was pleased at her endurance. He didn't have to particularly slow himself down. It wasn't a vigorous workout for him, but on the other hand, it wasn't a piece of cake either. He'd seen no one suspicious lurking around. He recognized several questionable characters from his days as a cop, but didn't worry about them. One of them, an old buzzard with no teeth, even waved at him, grinning widely.

She was wearing iridescent orange shorts, a loose green top, ratty running shoes, and a bright pink headband. She was sweating, her hair matted to her head, all the thick deep waves pulled back in a severe ponytail. Her face was clean of makeup. She was heaving, and there was a long sweat stain from her throat down between her breasts.

And all of a sudden he realized he wanted to kiss her, all over, everywhere, not miss a single patch, which would take a good amount of sweet time because her legs were longer than a man's dreams. He pulled back, tossing her a towel.

She grabbed the towel and wiped her face as she said, "You're barely sweating, you pig."

"I'm a man," he said, and to his astonishment, she stilled, withdrawing as she had the day before. He chose to ignore it, adding easily, "Like I said, I'm a man, not some sort of squirt who can barely do a ten-yard dash. Besides, I thought the myth was that females didn't sweat, they glowed or something like that. I just might have to turn you in."

She came back, softly, slowly, but finally she was there again, the wariness, the stillness, quashed for the moment. But always there, always hovering near. What the hell was wrong with her? Maybe it was this threat business, nothing more. Yeah, maybe that was it. But he didn't think so.

No, it was him as a man that scared her.

# 12

## TAYLOR / EDEN

Lindsay always shopped at the Challed grocery market on the corner. Taylor had her write out a list for him. They'd taken enough risks today.

"It's a habit," he said. "Habits we break, all of them. We either go together, which isn't smart, or I go alone."

She gave him a list and he whistled as he added cookies, wine, beer, chips, and cold cuts to the grocery cart. He felt like hardening a few arteries. Maybe he could even talk her into eating a Frito.

She ate a sandwich with no mayo, no butter, and one slice of nearly fat-free honey ham and a glass of Diet Coke. He felt like a junk-food pig, his plate loaded with chips and two salami-and-ham sandwiches, mustard oozing over the sides, a cold Amstel close to his hand.

"You want to see that movie tonight—*Black Prince*?"

She was delighted and again he marveled at the simple joyousness his suggestion brought her. He wanted to tell her it was just a movie, nothing more, but her obvious pleasure kept him silent.

Having been a cop, Taylor found the movie unbeliev-able, downright silly in places, but nevertheless he enjoyed himself. Eden was finally relaxing with him. They came out, he looking about methodically at the crowd of people press-ing near them, at people's hands mainly, and she talking a blue streak about the male lead and how he couldn't be blamed for believing his brother had betrayed him to the drug lords, how he had really been working undercover for the DEA.

Yeah, right, Taylor thought. He made appropriate noises, keeping her close, keeping her to the inside, his place always slightly ahead of hers. If she was aware of his actions, she gave no sign of it.

It took a while to get a taxi and it made him nervous. It would have been brighter not to have brought her out tonight. But no one followed, he was certain, and he breathed easier. When they got to her apartment, Taylor checked every room thoroughly, gave her his phone num-ber, and said as he was turning to leave, "Thanks for a fun evening, Eden. I enjoyed it, job or not. Remember every-thing I told you."

After he'd gone, after she had herself double-checked all her locks, Lindsay made herself a cup of tea and adjourned to her living room. She nestled in among her cushions on the sofa. She wasn't at all tired. In fact, she felt wired, restless, bedeviled by a fit of nerves, as her grandmother was wont to say. She picked up a historical romance but couldn't get herself settled into the novel. She prowled a bit, frowning at herself. Some ten minutes later, as she was showering for bed, she realized what was wrong. It wasn't the threat; it was Taylor. She could see him so clearly, right now, in her mind, smiling at her. She liked him. She'd been sorry to see him leave tonight. She hadn't wanted him to go. A man, and she actually liked him. More than that, she trusted him. At least she trusted him to keep her safe.

On Sunday night, after a day spent watching profes-sional football games on TV, Taylor left, repeating his same instructions, his same admonitions. Lindsay showered and put on her nightgown, then straightened the devastation in her living room, listening with only half an ear to the ten-o'clock news. She dropped the bowl that had held a gallon of popcorn during the second half of the game between the 49ers and the Giants. She whirled around and stared at the TV. The director of the commercial shot on Friday morning in Central Park, George Hudson, age thirty-six, had been badly beaten and locked in the trunk of his car in a long-term parking lot near the Lincoln Tunnel. He was alive but in guarded condition at St. Vincent's Hospital. He suffered broken ribs, injuries to his spleen and liver. His face had been severely beaten. He had a concussion. Police were, for the moment, calling it a vicious mugging or a gang attack, although they couldn't explain why muggers or a gang would leave over two hundred dollars in Hudson's wallet. Drug dealing was speculated upon. But that sounded far-fetched. There were as yet no clues, no suspects. Hudson had been able to tell police just moments ago that he'd been attacked in the parking lot some three hours earlier by two masked assailants. He knew nothing more. They hadn't said anything, just beaten him senseless.

The moment the newscaster moved on, Lindsay's phone rang. She lurched up to answer it, then remembered. She waited, her hand out, for the answering machine to kick in. It did, and she heard Taylor's voice. She picked up the phone immediately. Before she could say a word, he said very calmly, his voice pitched low, "I know. I just saw it. Stay put. I'll be there in ten minutes. Don't move, Eden."

He arrived in eight minutes. Taylor looked at her white face and very slowly put out his arms. Very slowly he drew her against him. "It's all right. It's all right. You're safe."

The phone rang shrilly.

Taylor motioned her to a chair, noticing for the first time that she was wearing a voluminous white nightgown that covered her from throat to toes, and answered the phone himself. It was Demos and he was terrified and babbling.

"My God! Is that you, Taylor? Did you hear? Oh, my God! You can't say anything, Taylor, you can't. You got that? Keep your mouth shut! Oh, my God."

Taylor let the man's shock and fear run itself out. He

said finally, "I have to talk to the cops, Demos. I have no choice, surely you realize that. I would suggest you pay off these thugs and keep clean after this."

"Yes, yes, I swear I will, but don't tell the cops, you can't!"

Taylor stared at the phone. "Why not?"

"You fool, they'll kill me, that's why not! If you tell the cops, they'll be on my doorstep in no time at all. What the hell would I tell them? Give them names and addresses? Are you out of your fucking skull? God, the moment I spit out one single name, I'm history! I'm dead meat. These guys don't know I hired you, Taylor—and they still don't, because they weren't ever after Eden. They believe it's just me who knows. You can't call the cops!"

Taylor sighed. Demos was right. He didn't want the man killed, no matter how much of an ass he was. "Do you promise me you'll pay them off?"

"Sweet Jesus, yes, yes!"

"Tomorrow?"

"Yes!"

"And you'll break your own neck before you ever get yourself into a mess like this again?"

There was a brief hesitation. "I mean it, Demos. Damn your eyes, I don't want Eden in any more danger. If they threatened you, that would be different, but not Eden, not any more innocent people, you got that?"

"Yeah, I got it. I swear, Taylor, I swear. You can trust me."

Very doubtful, Taylor thought. "Good. Don't forget, Demos, that I know. If ever you screw up again, I'll go to the cops and your hide will be on the line. Another thing, if George Hudson dies, it's a new ball game. No covering up. I have to go to the cops then."

"He won't die. Don't tell the cops. I'll do anything, I swear."

"Yeah, right." Taylor hung up, turned slowly, and said to Lindsay, "It's over. Demos has promised to pay his debt."

"That's good," she said, her voice as blank as a sheet of paper.

"I hope Hudson hangs on."

"I do too. I'll visit him tomorrow. Make sure he'll be okay."

He smiled at her. She was getting her balance back. "Good idea. You know something? I still think you need protection. Anyone who prowls in front of the TV biting her nails over an intercepted pass and howling whenever a penalty is called, definitely needs a guard. What it comes down to is this: I want to see you again. A date this time, not a job. How about it, Eden?"

She'd met him two days before. It seemed much longer. He was smiling but she saw the tension in him. He really wanted to see her again. It surprised her and pleased her and made her only mildly wary.

"Yes," she said, not quite meeting his eyes. "Yes, I'd like that."

The following Tuesday, the temperature plummeted to the mid-twenties. It had rained during the night and stopped early Tuesday morning, leaving frozen streets and sidewalks. Traffic was a god-awful mess, taxi drivers screaming and cursing, tempers short and foul, and pedestrians extra careful when crossing the streets even with the light. Lindsay was bundled up to her eyebrows. She was walking toward the library on the Columbia campus to search out articles for Gayle on the dangers of gymnastics for preadolescent children. "The most recent articles only," Gayle had said. "You're wonderful, Lindsay. I love you and I owe you. Call it my Christmas present. Now you don't have to spend a dime on me."

It was so bloody cold that Lindsay had quickly forgotten how wonderful she was. She looked up, but the library still seemed a goodly distance away. She thought of George Hudson and the horror she'd felt when she'd visited him the day before. His face was a battered mess, his nose broken, stitches on his jaw and over his left eye. The bruises made him look a nightmare. He'd been very surprised to see her, but pleased in his way. He was going to live and he would heal. He just didn't understand why anyone would beat him up. It was a mystery. She felt such guilt she'd left as soon as politely possible. She stopped off and ordered flowers sent to him.

Finally, the Columbia library loomed up, its pale brick facade looking as cold and damp and uninviting as it ever had when she'd been an undergraduate.

She took the deep steps two at a time, stopping when she heard a man's voice. "Lindsay! Lindsay Foxe! Wait a minute. Stop!"

She wasn't about to stop. Once she was inside, she unwrapped the scarf around her neck and lower face, not wanting to turn but knowing he would come after her, knowing as she stood there that she'd have to look at him, face him.

There was Dr. Gruska, breathing heavily, his tweeds covered with a Burberry coat, coming toward her.

She forced herself to remain perfectly still. Students were all around. It was warm. She was safe.

He hadn't changed. Of course it had been only four years, but still, she'd expected him to be sporting more white in his hair, more wrinkles on his neck. He looked just the same, only now he must be in his mid-fifties. Old enough to be her father.

"Lindsay," he said, smiling, stopping in front of her. He held out his hands to her but she didn't move. He dropped them. He rushed into hurried, intense speech. "I have tried to find you but you don't have a listed number. I've tried so hard. I even saw your friend Gayle Werth some time ago and she gave me your phone number, but she got it wrong." *The stupid bitch* hung in the air, unspoken but well understood by Lindsay.

He stood there, now in front of her, looking for the world like a hopeful aging puppy. He pulled the expensive fox fur hat from his head and stripped off his expensive leather gloves.

"How are you, Dr. Gruska?"

"Oh, things go along here, but there are changes, horrible changes. Now that my profession has debunked Freud, philistine unenlightened fools that they are, I find I must accommodate myself to approaches of which I do not approve. Can you imagine—it is expected now that a psychologist deal not with the root causes of an illness but only with the aberrant symptoms! The idiots call it eclectic therapy or survival therapy or reality therapy to make it sound legitimate. It's absurd, and then there's all this drug nonsense to control people but not understand them. I am considering private practice since my colleagues are so shallow, but what I have always preferred is dealing with bright students. They, I have always found, grasp the truth of things, and Freud is unvarnished truth."

*Jerk.*

"How unfortunate for you, Dr. Gruska. I trust your father is well?" Old Dr. Gruska, from what Lindsay had heard about him, was reminiscent of the robber barons of the last century. He was still chairman of the board of the Northwestern New York Bank and ruled all with his iron hand, including his only son, Dr. Gruska the Younger. His "doctor" handle had been conferred in the late seventies by Northwestern University. On that day he had become Dr. Gruska the Elder to all and sundry.

"Oh, yes, my dear father, Dr. Gruska, is in top form. He's nearly eighty, you know, but a man of great stamina and fortitude. I still cherish his guidance. If Dr. Gruska knew you, he would send his love, I know. I've spoken of you so often to him. Please, let me buy you a cup of coffee. It's so cold today and I didn't want to come in, but I'm so glad I did! Come, Lindsay, I want to speak to you, I must speak to you. There is so much for us to discuss, for me to share with you."

She forced herself to look at him with clear unafraid eyes. She remembered her father and her heels. She'd won then. No intimidation. Never again. And she said, smiling slightly, "No, thank you, Dr. Gruska. I'm in a rush right now. It was nice to see you again."

"No! Wait, you must give me your address, your phone number!"

There were at least six Columbia students within three feet of them. Lindsay shook her head. "I don't think so, Dr. Gruska. Why would you want my phone number anyway?" She wished immediately that she hadn't asked, for his show of uncertainty was replaced by a confidence that startled her with its arrogance. "So," he said slowly, stroking his jaw, "you are still afraid of men, I see."

She felt the deep corrosive fear. She held herself steady, still smiling at him. "It's none of your business, Dr. Gruska."

He leaned toward her, touching her arm. "Oh, but it is, Miss Foxe. I see now that you're a model, that you're known only as Eden. My dear father, Dr. Gruska, finds you immensely attractive. As I said, I've told him all about you. I've enjoyed seeing all the photos of you as well, but I know what they hide. They change you and you are willing to be changed, to be concealed, to be viewed as another woman, one who is not real. Even your name, Eden—ah, the beginning, the innocence, the purity—it is not you, but just another device to hide you from the world, from yourself. You must let me . . ." He broke off, as if realizing his words weren't achieving the effect he wished, for her face was pale and set. Oddly, there was rage in her eyes, not fear. He continued, his voice gentle now, "I do not mean to distress you. It has been a very long time since your brother-in-law . . . well, since that traumatic time in Paris. So very long ago. If only you would let me help you. I can, you know, professionally as a doctor, and as a friend, a friend who is also a man who would take care of you, protect you, understand you."

A student bumped against her and absently apologized. Lindsay said, her voice as cold as the air just beyond the library doors, "You're an old man, Dr. Gruska. I don't like you. I didn't like you when I was a senior and forced to take your class. I think Freud is full of shit and I think you're contemptible to remind me of a time that was very painful for me."

He didn't move. He smiled and Lindsay felt sick to her stomach. "I know it is painful, my sweet girl. Sometimes we must suffer pain to be cured of our illnesses. Come with me, Lindsay. Come with me now."

He held out his hand to her. She stared down at his hand, then back to his face.

She wanted to strike him. She wanted to pound him into pulp. He was soft; he was old. She could grind him down easily. She wanted to run. She could taste her fear, raw and nasty in her mouth. She continued to look at him, hoping he couldn't see the fear, hoping he didn't know how scared she was. "Perhaps you can become a behavioral scientist and try to intimidate rats. Good-bye, sir." She was out of the library and skipping quickly down the wide stairs.

He called her name out twice before she was lost in a congested mass of students.

"What's the matter, Eden? Dammit, talk to me."

Taylor took her upper arms in his hands and lightly shook her. "Something happened today. Don't you know I can see every emotion that streaks through you? Talk to me."

He'd caught her so soon after the run-in with Dr. Gruska. Just two hours, and she still felt threatened, wanting to hunker down in the corner of her living room and come to grips with what had happened. Deep inside her, pressing against the fear, was her elation at how she'd responded to Gruska. She'd faced him down. Still, there was all the darkness, the pounding emptiness. She wanted no one to see her like this, but here he was.

"No, don't shake your head at me. It's been four days since I met you but I can tell something is very wrong." He frowned, released her, and said easily, changing his tone, his expression, his approach, "Can I brew you a cup of tea?"

"Yes, I'd like that."

He'd verified a very useful fact, he thought as he put on her red potbellied kettle to boil. She responded to lightness, to matter-of-fact calm. Threats made her draw away even more. A raised voice sent her scurrying away, at least her mind, her attention.

"What kind of tea? Good old Lipton?"

"Yes, fine."

"Lemon? Milk?"

"Just lemon."

Two words at a time, he thought a few minutes later

as he poured the boiling water over the tea bag. Go easy, very easy, and slowly. What the devil had happened?

He carried her tea into the living room, Lindsay trailing behind him. He set it down on the coffee table, scooting aside several of her novels to clear a space. One book fell onto the floor, but she didn't seem to notice.

He sat down in one of the easy chairs opposite her and said nothing.

Lindsay sipped the tea. She looked at him over the rim of her cup. He wasn't pushing now. He wasn't doing anything.

She was immensely reassured, she could handle things now, and said, "I was at Columbia today, at the library, looking up some articles for a friend of mine. I ran into this professor I'd had in my senior year, four years ago. I didn't ever like him, in fact I wanted to drop his course, but I couldn't because I needed it to graduate. My degree is in psychology. Anyway, he wanted to see me, like a date or something. I told him off, that's all, and then I left, well, very quickly."

"Why?"

"What do you mean?"

"Why did you leave very quickly? You'd told him off, what else was there to do? Why did you have to run away?"

"I didn't want him to see that I was afraid of him. No! I didn't mean that exactly . . . He's a jerk and a pompous, arrogant creep. Maybe I should have punched his ticket."

"So why didn't you?"

"I wanted to be reasonable, to stand up to him, to handle him like an adult should."

"Were you alone?"

"Oh, no. It was in the Columbia library. There were tons of students around."

"You weren't alone and you also know karate. I bet you could take him with one arm. You wouldn't even need any help. Why are you afraid of him?"

"It's not that . . . it's his mind, the way he thinks, what he's found out, what he now knows, what he threatens with his words."

That was about as clear as a foggy window, Taylor thought, wishing for words that would be wipers.

Lindsay got hold of herself. She was appalled at what had come out of her mouth, all because of Taylor and the way he was and that he'd showed up here before she could get a good hold on herself again. She smiled now, a social person, all bland and empty. "It's the middle of the day. Why are you here? Don't you have people to guard and computers to fix?"

"Yeah," he said easily, sitting back. "Actually I was on my way downtown to Wall Street to a brokerage house. They've got screws loose in their computer brain and called me to fix it. I thought about you and that's why I came."

Truth be told, he'd gotten this feeling that something was wrong. It wasn't unusual; he wasn't psychic, for God's sake, but sometimes, rarely, he'd just get these feelings, nibbling feelings, that wouldn't go away. When he was much younger, he'd forced himself to ignore them. But not after an old woman had gotten mugged on his very street corner. He listened now, and even if the feeling turned out to be nothing at all, he still listened and still acted. This time his feeling had been right on the button. It was just that Eden wasn't going to say anything more. She didn't trust him. Well, it hadn't been all that long. It would take time. With her, he was fully prepared to be patient. But he could also be cunning as hell.

"Well, I'm fine now, really. Thank you, Taylor. This professor—"

"No problem."

"Thank you for making the tea. It's wonderful."

"I'm glad you like it. I don't like any sugar in mine either. Just real hot and strong. No bark shavings. What's his name?"

"Gruska . . . no, no, that is, no, forget it, all right?"

"Sure, no problem. I've got to go now. Are we still on for tonight?"

She nodded, feeling like a fool, but he seemed not to notice that she'd spit out the name. Still, after Taylor had left, she fastened all the locks on her front door.

\*   \*   \*

Taylor left the Wayfarer Insurance Company on Water Street at four o'clock, the problem diagnosed and fixed. He'd been very lucky because the problem had been one a computer hacker buddy of his had just routed out three days ago and told him about. Taylor had come off as a genius, which was a nice feeling. He was good, but luck was never to be discounted, luck and timing and hacker friends. Over the past four years he'd developed a network of computer friends across the country, and when each discovered something not run across before, the information was duly shared.

Mr. Phiffe, vice-president of operations, at least seventy, white-haired, an aristocrat of insurance, was appalled when Taylor presented his bill.

"Five thousand dollars! But you fixed the problem in ten minutes, Jackson told me so!"

"Yes. I also told Jackson what my fixed charge would be up front, regardless of the time I spent here. The problem in the actuarial data-retrieval system would have continued, you know."

"But he didn't think it would take just ten minutes!"

Taylor smiled. "Mr. Phiffe, you hired me to fix your problem. You said if you lost the actuarial data it would require thousands of man-hours to re-input, not counting the manipulations and the affected output programs. You are back in business, and in record time, I might add."

Phiffe smiled slowly. "You're right, of course. It was just a shock. One gets what one pays for, eh? I pay for expertise and I get it. Time isn't the issue." He buzzed his secretary. Taylor shook hands with him and picked up his check on the way out.

Taylor's next stop was Columbia. Dr. Gruska was a professor of psychology and he was in the Adams Building, second floor, room 223. He asked the woman in administration what Dr. Gruska's psychological roots were, so to speak. "Give him a chandelier and he'd swing by his Oedipus complex," she'd said, and laughed. "The thing is, though, he hasn't got a mother. Just this old curmudgeon father who's run his life. Funny how moms always get blamed, isn't it?"

Taylor agreed that it was.

The day was blistering cold. It was very nearly dark now and getting colder by the minute. He really wasn't expecting Gruska to be in his office and it was with some surprise that his knock was answered with a full-voiced call.

"Come!"

He went in, gently closed the door behind him, and surveyed the man who terrified Eden. Harmless-looking gent, tweedy, smoked a pipe, slender, long narrow face, and had a long nose that was now twitching at the sight of him, a complete stranger, fifties, rather pallid complexion, out-of-shape. Yeah, Eden could have taken him to the floor with only one arm.

"What can I do for you? It's late. I was just getting ready to leave."

"Just a minute of your time, Dr. Gruska." Taylor stuck out his gloved hand. "My name's Oliver Winston, Dr. Winston, psychoanalyst. I've heard a lot about you and wanted to meet you. I'm in town visiting friends and family. A Dr. Graham in my hometown of Columbus said to look you up if I had a chance. He said you were the tops."

Dr. Gruska glowed. Taylor was motioned quickly to a chair facing the good doctor.

"Ah, Dr. Graham. Er, which Dr. Graham?"

"Joseph Graham of Columbus."

"Ah, yes, Joe. Nice, solid fellow. Good background. How is he?"

"He goes swimmingly. As I said, he speaks of you with high praise."

"That is a pleasure to hear. I assume that you are embroiled in our very survival, Dr. Winston?"

Taylor had no idea what he was talking about, but he knew enough from Gruska's body language and voice tone to nod with great sincerity. "Yes, indeed. I don't know what to do about it."

Taylor watched, fascinated, the myriad shifting expressions on Gruska's face. Rage, surprise, pleasure, more rage, more pleasure, conspiracy. He sat forward, his hands clasped in front of him. His pipe sent up lazy smoke into the air, its scent pleasant, like a pine forest.

Gruska's voice was warm, low, intense. "Ah, my dear fellow, then you're suffering as I am suffering, as all of us are suffering. The idea of boiling everything down to chemicals! It's preposterous! Certainly those ridiculous MD's who pretend to understand the human mind can, in a very few cases, administer their drugs and make the patient function."

Taylor made an assenting noise and fanned his hands in despair.

"No doubt your friend sent you to see me because he knew I'd understand and sympathize. I will remain a psychoanalyst despite all the opposition, all the absurdities that abound and proliferate now, for what we have is the truth, and this truth explains what makes all of humanity behave in the ways we behave."

Again Taylor looked struck by Gruska's fluency, his tone and manner. He said slowly, feeling his way, "I have found that women in particular are so well-explained by Freud."

"Oh, my, yes, not to say that any of us worship like disciples at any one man's feet, but Freud pointed out the basic truths for us to build upon, which we have done superbly. And women, they are the most easily understood, the more easily explained, for the way they think leads them to act in the sometimes very bizarre ways they do, and all of it is tied to overpowering and dictated subconscious intuition, and then cognition. Children know and adults suppress, particularly women. It's true, ah yes."

It sounded like hash to Taylor, but he nodded, saying, "I have this one patient, a rather young woman, who's terrified of men. She will not confide in me though I've tried and tried to gain her trust. I have tried to take her back to those formative years, but she resists, she refuses to allow hypnotism, which would unblock her. I ask, Dr. Gruska, what do you think I should do?"

Dr. Gruska paused, pondered, ran his long fingers up and down his pipe stem. He looked uncertain. He looked pleased to be asked.

Taylor quickly rose, fanning his hands in front of him in apology. "Oh, goodness. It's dark outside and I've kept you far too long. Forgive me, Dr. Gruska, but listening to you, hearing the depth of your feelings and knowledge, well—"

"Sit down, Dr. Winston, sit down! You can't go yet."

Taylor sat, relieved.

"This young woman, is she beautiful?"

"Very."

"Does she seem outwardly well-adjusted?"

"Yes, until a man gets close to her."

"Is she one of those bitch professional women or a gentle traditional unencumbered woman?"

"Professional, unmarried, but not a bitch."

"Ah, yes, classic, for the most part, certainly close enough to the paradigm. I would probe gently, Doctor, ask her about her teenage years—not her childhood, avoid that for the time being. Ask her about the sexual urges she suppressed, the guilt she felt when she experienced these urges. Get her to admit to masturbation, have her relive the feelings she experienced when she masturbated. Find out how she masturbated, that's very important—manual stimulation or using devices, such as dildos. It is possible that she seduced a relative—even a father—when she was eighteen or so, and now has closed it away deep in her mind. She has rewritten the event, so to speak, to ease her guilt, to justify what she did then and to justify why she is as she is now."

"My God," Taylor said, and meant it. "Your advice is much more than I had ever expected, Dr. Gruska. Have you had, perhaps, a similar patient?"

"Oh, I've seen many girls like the one you describe. All that suppressed guilt and sexual tension, waiting to be released, demanding to be released, but they can't allow it, because to allow it would mean to admit these feelings. There is one girl in particular who desperately needs this release, who needs my help to gain this release, but there is still the lack of trust, her fear of herself and these feelings, her blindness to her own needs . . . Ah, well, it is late, isn't it? My dear fellow, I am delighted you dropped by. By all means give my regards to Joe." Gruska rose and extended his hand. Taylor obligingly took it and gave it a healthy shake.

He returned to Eden's apartment two hours later.

# ↭ 13 ↫

## TAYLOR / EDEN

Even as he rang Eden's doorbell, Taylor knew he wasn't going to say anything to her about meeting Dr. Gruska at Columbia. Not yet. He was fairly certain that the young woman Dr. Gruska spoke briefly about was Eden. She was terrified of men, that was true, and she sure as hell didn't trust Gruska. As for that sod, the man was certifiable. Taylor didn't think Dr. Gruska could even be taken with a half-grain of salt. How, then, to unmuddy the waters?

Lindsay stared through her peephole, then unlatched, unfastened, and unbolted her front door. "Goodness, Taylor! You're early and I'm a mess."

He hadn't realized he was early until that moment. "I'm sorry, but I was in the neighborhood and—"

"Oh, come in, no problem. I just need to jump into the shower."

Taylor saw that she was wearing an ancient white terry-cloth bathrobe and nothing else. She'd tied her hair up in a rubber band. He smiled. "Again, forgive me. Why don't I grab a beer and watch the news?"

She waved him away and retreated into her bedroom. He shook his head at himself as he moved several novels out of the way on the sofa. He didn't turn on the TV; instead, he thought more about Gruska and what he'd said and what he obviously believed. And he recalled Eden's words, seemingly a jumble: . . . *the way he thinks, what he's found out, what he now knows, what he threatens* . . .

His mind latched on to what had really scared her. What Gruska had found out about her. And that something he needed to discover himself if he was going to be of any help to her. Taylor stopped cold with that thought. He'd just made the quite conscious decision that he wanted Eden in his life, that he wanted her whole and healthy, that he wanted her in bed as well as out of bed, that he wanted, quite simply, all of her.

He felt slightly stunned with the realization. Jesus, he was the bugger who'd sworn off a second marriage. Now he wanted a woman he'd known for only four days, and he wanted her forever. He thought of tall lanky-legged girls in white karate outfits with her gorgeous eyes who would be their offspring. Jesus, he was losing it.

Taylor rose and walked to the telephone. First things first. He dialed Valerie's number. It was Tuesday and he had promised to call her on Monday.

She picked up on the second ring.

"Hello, Valerie, it's Taylor. How are you?"

"I'm fine." She didn't continue with her usual spiel. She paused, then said, "Look, Taylor, I'm sorry about the other night, really. I was just stressed out and flailed at you. Will you forgive me?"

"Sure. No problem."

"Are you busy tonight?"

"Yes, I am."

There was another very long pause. "Are you still working on that same job?"

"No, it's been resolved."

"Successfully, I hope." He heard the strain in her voice, recognized her attempt at civilized behavior, and wondered why it was so difficult for her.

"Yes," he said, "very successfully."

175

He could picture her sitting on the plush silk chair beside the Louis XV table. The phone was pseudo-antique in an old-fashioned cradle. He wondered what she was thinking. He was on the point of softening his answer to her when she said, her voice sharp, "It's another woman, isn't it, Taylor?"

"We aren't married, Valerie," he said mildly.

"But I wanted you to come over tonight!"

"Are you free tomorrow night?"

"No, damn you, I'm not!"

"Well, then, as I said, we're not married. How about Thursday night?"

"You just want to see me so you can screw me!"

"I take it the thought doesn't entice you in the least?"

"Eight o'clock. I'll have Carrousel send over dinner. Don't be late."

She hung up on him. Tit for tat, he thought, slowly settling down the phone, since he'd hung up on her the last time they spoke.

When he saw her on Thursday, he'd break it off. He had to because the only person he could see in his present, in his future, was Eden.

Eden, who was terrified of men. When she came out of the bedroom, freshly scrubbed, dressed in a pale yellow silk dress, her long legs in panty hose and three-inch heels, he laughed.

"You're going to look me straight in the eye now? You're going to put me in my place?"

"Intimidation," she said, smiling at him. "I thought you could use a good dose. I should even be a bit taller than you."

"Have at it, any abuse you like. You look beautiful. I like your hair up in an old-fashioned bun like that."

She merely nodded. She stood next to him then quirked her eyebrow at him. "Maybe not just a little bit," she said.

And he was thinking there was so much of her to learn, to explore, to appreciate, finally, to savor. He thought about buying her some four-inch heels.

"Where are you taking me?"

"It's a surprise."

He took her to meet Enoch and his mother, Sheila, 230 Maple Street, Fort Lee, New Jersey, for dinner that evening.

Sheila was going through her muumuu phase and she even served roasted pig in palm leaves in a grill in the backyard. She appreciated the fifty-degree weather, she said, or she and the pig could have been the same temperature. There were yams and poi, gray and thick and disgusting, and wonderful rolls. She gave Eden long looks, then turned on her charm, which she had in abundance. If she occasionally gushed or overwhelmed, they handled it, at least until dessert of scooped out papaya filled with vanilla ice cream. As for Enoch, he just stared at Eden as if trying to figure something out.

"Enoch's six-foot-four. You'll have to tilt your head just a bit."

Lindsay laughed as she shook her head.

"It's nice not to have to crick my neck," Enoch said.

"What's your last name, dear?" Sheila asked as she expertly sliced up her papaya. "I must have missed it. That damned pig required too much of my attention."

Taylor's spoon paused on its journey to his mouth.

"Oh, I don't have one, Mrs. Sackett. Just Eden."

"You entertainers, so coy and elusive!"

"I'm a model, ma'am, not an entertainer."

"It's close enough, I'm sure," Sheila said to the table at large. "More dessert, dear?"

"No, ma'am. This is wonderful."

Too bad, Taylor thought. He'd already made up his mind he wasn't going to find out Eden's real name, no, she would have to tell him herself, when she was ready. He wasn't going to stoop to going through her mail to discover her real name. He wasn't going to muck about in things she evidently wanted kept hidden.

"Is Eden your real name, then?"

"Sheila," Enoch said, waving his fork at her, "it really isn't any of your business. Leave Eden alone."

Lindsay just smiled, but it was hard. The woman wasn't any nosier than others she'd met, but she was persistent and Lindsay was her prisoner for the evening. She slipped a glance toward Taylor and saw, to her surprise, that he understood, for he nodded. Not five minutes later, he said quite loudly, "Goodness, Sheila, would you look at the time."

"What time? It's not even nine o'clock, Taylor."

Enoch, no slouch, said, "Yeah, Sheila, it is late. I've got a meeting in the morning."

"And Eden and I must leave. She's got to be up by five-thirty. She's got a photo session."

Sheila Sackett regarded the three children with grave displeasure. Her son refused to meet her probing eye. She would deal with Enoch later. As for this Eden girl, she was certainly pretty enough for Taylor, and she seemed reasonably nice, but still . . . "I'd planned to have coffee now. Then I was going to play some jazz for you, Taylor, on my sax."

Taylor looked disappointed, and he was. She was very talented. "Next time, Sheila," he said, rising. He came around the table and kissed her cheek. "Great meal, thanks for inviting us. I love your muumuu and the roasted pig."

"I'll bet you two are going out to do some lovemaking, aren't you?"

"Sheila, please."

Lindsay wondered why he called his mother by her first name.

"That's a wonderful idea," Taylor said as he kissed Sheila's cheek again.

"Oh, boy," Lindsay said on their drive back into the city. "She's a real pusher, isn't she?"

"One of the front-runners. She's been after me for years to remarry. She somehow pictures herself as a grandmother to any kids I'd have."

"Remarry?" Lindsay glanced over at him, her back suddenly straight as a witching stick.

"I was married to a very nice woman when we were both very young. It didn't work out. My fault as well as hers. It's been a long time since the divorce."

He'd been married. He'd been intimate with a woman . . .

"How long were you married?"

"Two years and some."

. . . intimate with one woman, for a long time. Lindsay couldn't imagine such a thing. Sleeping with someone, eating every day with someone, sharing thoughts and troubles with another person—the same person always—being crabby and irritable and letting it show. Arguing about who would clean the bathroom or the freezer. She felt a yearning for that complete intimacy, for that incredible freedom to be as you really were without secrets, without mysteries or guile, without having to watch what you said because it might make the other person leave you in disgust. But still she couldn't imagine it, not for herself, not for Lindsay Foxe.

To Taylor's surprise, she dropped the subject entirely, saying, "Sheila truly plays the saxophone? Jazz?"

"She truly does and she's quite good. Blues is her thing. She loves to go to Atlanta and play in the clubs there. Next time, maybe we can have her play. With her mouth full of reed she won't be able to keep chipping away at you. Also, the thought of her playing a sax in a muumuu boggles the mind. Enoch told me she wears long black gowns when she plays professionally, kind of like Kate Smith."

Lindsay laughed. "She and Enoch look so unlike each other. Sheila's short and plump and he's so tall and skinny. Why isn't she after him to marry or remarry?"

"That's entirely different," Taylor said, turning into the underground parking garage beneath his building. "Enoch's off-limits when it comes to a wife. Sheila doesn't mind him having free-lance associations, as she calls them, but no wife."

"Strange."

"Oh, yeah, very." He paused, then added easily, "Of course a Freudian type would think it's classic Oedipal complex. Have I got that right? You're the psych major."

"Yes, you've got that perfectly correct."

He heard the withdrawal in her voice. "Would you like to come up for a cup of coffee or tea before I walk you home?"

She wanted to, he saw that she did, but she shook her head. She didn't trust him yet. It was that simple. Her fear won out.

He left her at her door, lightly touching his knuckles to her cheek.

He'd wanted to kiss her very much. In fact, it had been difficult not to stare at her mouth. Lindsay stood in the corridor, watching him until he disappeared around the corner. She sighed and went into her apartment, shutting and locking the door behind her, sliding each of the chains, clicking the deadbolt. She heard a noise and whipped around terrified, her stomach heaving up into her throat. There, seated in her living room, a glass of white wine in her left hand, a magazine with a full-length photo of her in the other, was her half-sister.

Lindsay's hand was over her galloping heart. "Oh, my God, you scared me, Sydney. However did you get in here?"

"Oh, hello, sister dear. Your super let me in. I've been here before and the dear man hadn't forgotten me. I've only been waiting fifteen minutes. Your date left quickly enough. I assume it was a date. I could hear you saying good night from in here. I must admit surprise at hearing a man's voice. Who is he? Some guy I should meet? Check out for you?"

Lindsay shook her head, saying nothing.

"Ah, well, maybe it was Demos?"

"No. What do you want, Sydney?"

Sydney Foxe di Contini—La Principessa—rose slowly, smoothing her black leather pants. She wore a hot-pink silk shell over the pants, topped with a black leather vest with gold chains clipping the vest over her breasts. She looked exquisite, slender, elegant, perfect as usual.

"I called but you weren't here, obviously. I wondered, that's all. You never go out with men and I was concerned. You have so few friends and I knew you were out with Gayle just last Monday, so she was a doubtful candidate. I just wanted to tell you I'm flying to Milan this weekend."

"You want me to water your plants?"

Sydney laughed. "Oh, no. I just wanted to be able to tell everyone that I'd seen you and that you were in fine form."

"I'm in fine form."

"Excellent. You haven't put on any weight, have you? No? Well, perhaps you should lose just a bit more, a couple of pounds should do it. Who's the man, Lindsay?"

"No one you know."

"Well, considering your taste, which I imagine has remained frozen in time since you were sixteen—why then, this charmer is probably slender, handsome, and suave as hell."

Lindsay forced a smile. "Yes, all of those things."

"Ah, an aristocratic New Yorker. Is he in the business? Perhaps he's gay and you're just too inexperienced to recognize it. Or perhaps he's gay and you feel safer that way. His voice sounded pretty deep to me."

"No, he's not gay. Look, Sydney, I've got an early shoot tomorrow. I'm bushed."

"All right, I'll go. I've canceled the shoots my agent had scheduled. Nothing all that important, I told him. I also keep telling him it's time to become more hard-assed, more discriminating. After all, it's my face and my body, and my time. Maybe you'd better let me meet this guy. I could make sure he won't try anything with you."

"That's a beautiful photo of you in *Self*. Demos commented on it last week. It's certainly discriminating."

"Yes, it turned out nicely. I'm pleased. Drake Otis did the shoot. Too bad he's gay as a . . . well, no matter. I'll see you when I get back from Italy. Oh, yes, just in case you're interested, Father is doing well. He was embroiled in a very high-profile drug case and the defense attorneys were confident he would throw out the major evidence because supposedly the cops obtained it illegally. Father did throw it out, but he allowed great latitude to the prosecutor, with the result that the three men, Colombians all, got a guilty verdict. Father sentenced them all to twenty years, no chance of parole. He told me he threw out the evidence because if he hadn't, he knew the defense attorneys would appeal and the case would probably be overturned. He's laughing his head off, having the time of his life. You know he hates the liberal judges in California. He pulled the rug out from under the defense lawyers. They're screaming to the media, and of course, since the media are all liberal idiots, they're all over Father's back. He's enjoying it all. As for Holly, the poor thing is now as fat as your mother was just before Father kicked her out. He's got a new mistress, a woman about my age. Her name is Cynthia—Cyn for short. Isn't that precious? As for Grandmother, she's just the same. Father thinks she'll outlive us all."

She blew Lindsay a kiss, turning in the open doorway to say, "I will give the prince your fond regards. It will make him grimace, remembering those bullets, which in turn makes Melissa giggle. You see, some good comes out of everything."

Lindsay wished her half-sister would fly to Italy and stay there the rest of her life. Then, to her own surprise, she laughed. Sydney would never change. But Lindsay was beginning to. It was odd, yet it was true.

Taylor dutifully went to Valerie's apartment on Thursday. When she opened the door, he realized that each time he saw her he'd forgotten how absolutely beautiful she was. She was wearing pale blue-ice silk lounging pajamas tonight and her hair was long and thick to her shoulders, pulled back on one side, held with a gold clip.

She looked as rich as his ex-wife, Diane.

"Hello," he said.

"Hello, Taylor. Goodness, you look good enough to eat. Do come in. Our dinner will arrive in an hour or so. Would you like a drink?"

Taylor followed her, wondering what he was going to say and how she would react. He was relieved that she hadn't immediately started on the attack. It sounded like she wanted his pants off, soon, and that would be even more embarrassing. The thing about it was that there was another woman and he was perfectly capable of feeling like a guilty jerk because she'd been right. But not at first, no, not at first.

Valerie didn't attack, seduce, nothing but sparkling conversation until after they'd eaten their way through the lobster thermidor, tossed earth salad with a light vinaigrette dressing, potatoes sliced thin and broiled, and a chocolate mousse for desert that was to die for. The Château le Duc-

Dupress '79 was exquisite, dry and crisp. It tasted like hemlock to Taylor.

Taylor just wanted to get it over with. He hadn't eaten all that much because he didn't want to be here and he didn't want to feel guilty.

"So," she said, sitting back, a brandy snifter in her hand, "tell me about this job of yours."

"The one I no longer have?"

"Yes."

"I was protecting a woman from a threat made against her employer. It turns out another employee was attacked instead. It's over now."

"I see." She rose slowly, giving him a smile that would have made him hard as a stone just the week before. She untied the silk sash at her waist.

He raised his hand, his eyes on that damned sash. "Wait, Valerie, don't. Please don't."

She paused, her eyebrow going up.

"I want to talk to you."

"We've been talking, Taylor." She looked down at her Cartier watch. "For nearly an hour and a half now we've been talking. So, lover, just relax now and let me . . ." She broke off, smiled at him, and put her fingers on her lips. "No, Taylor, enough. Actually, I'm the one who wants to do the talking. Your turn will come. I wanted to speak to you about this all through dinner, but you were enjoying it so much, I didn't want to ruin it for you. I'm so sorry, baby, I don't want to hurt you, but I've found a man who's divine and he's got everything you don't have and he's aced you right out of the race. I just thought a good-bye fuck would be nice. Assuage my guilt. And you are quite good in bed, nearly as good as he is."

Taylor felt such relief he nearly fell off his chair.

"Come on, pretty boy, one last time and then you're gone. My new man is coming later."

He stared at her. "But why would you want to make love with me when there's someone else you're interested in? That's crazy, Valerie."

She shrugged. "I've always liked comparisons and I do think this one would prove very interesting. Maybe you could go see one of your other girlfriends later and do the same."

"No, Valerie, not this time. I wish you luck. You're beautiful and smart and it's been fun." Jesus, he sounded like a trite recording.

Her face was set into a smile that left her eyes cold as a glacier. He hadn't a clue to what she was thinking. Was she angry because he was refusing to go to bed with her, or was that all a game? Possibly.

"Yes, it has been fun, hasn't it, Taylor? Well, babe, I hope you also have fun with your new little cutie. You know, the one you started out protecting and ended up screwing? And don't lie to me now. Does the bimbo have a brain? Or is she all tits and ass? Why don't you call after you've taken her to bed and let me know who's better."

"I don't think so. Good-bye, Valerie."

She watched him go to the front closet, pull his camel coat off a padded hanger. He shrugged it on, then pulled on his brown leather gloves. She watched him, unmoving, as he walked toward the front door without turning back. She watched every move he made. She watched him stride out the door. He closed it quietly behind him. She felt such fury and pain she thought she'd choke on it. She went to the phone and dialed. A man answered.

"Barry? This is Valerie. Yes, lover. Come on over. Who cares what you tell your wife? Tell her you're constipated and need a constitutional. Yes. Thirty minutes, no longer."

Lindsay discovered on Thanksgiving that both of Taylor's parents were dead. He had one older sister, Elaine, who was married with three children and lived with her accountant husband in Phoenix. It was too far to go, he told Lindsay, then asked her about her plans.

She was predictably vague, which annoyed him, but he let it go. They ended up together again with Sheila and Enoch.

Sheila played the saxophone for two hours, letting it wail and moan until Lindsay had gooseflesh with the power of it. Sheila wore a long black dress. She was incredibly good. There was no prodding, no questions of any kind, on Thanksgiving.

That evening Taylor kissed her for the first time.

They were standing in front of her apartment door, and she didn't want him to go. But she was afraid to let him in.

He simply leaned down, catching her chin in the palm of his hand, and kissed her. Lightly, nothing threatening, nothing to make her withdraw.

"Oh."

He grinned at her, eyes warm, wanting trust from her, wanting warmth from her as well. "Did you like that maybe a little bit?"

"I don't know."

"That's honesty. Always be honest with me, Eden, all right?"

"Sometimes," Lindsay said very slowly, looking down at the buttons on his coat, "sometimes it's just not possible."

"When you come to trust me, you'll find it will be easy as chewing gum, at least I hope so. Good night, sweetheart. Happy Thanksgiving. Sleep well."

"I will, since I'm stuffed with more food than I usually eat in a week. Did you know that fashion photo sessions tend to slow down dramatically during the holiday season? It's because models are people too and the temptations are just too great. I've got until December 1 to get rid of my turkey-and-stuffing lining."

He was pleased that she was lingering to talk, very pleased, probably more pleased than the situation warranted, but what the hell. She paused and he picked it up. "Tomorrow I've got to fly to Chicago. A meat packer, of all things, has brought himself and his company into the twentieth century with a computer that should scare every cow on the hoof in the U.S. Unfortunately, there's a major screwup in the programming and he's so teed off with the company that he called me. I'll phone you from there tomorrow night and give you my number."

Before she could say anything, Taylor leaned down and kissed her again, just as lightly, his gloved fingers caressing her cheek. He loved touching her, even with gloves on. He cupped her chin in his palm. "Miss me, all right?"

"I think I will," Lindsay said, and knew it was true.

Taylor didn't have luck or an attack of genius on the meat packer's job. It took him three long days of pure grunt work to diagnose the problem and figure out how to fix it. The man who'd hired him, Mr. Closse, was looking over his shoulder every minute, wringing his fat hands and cursing technology in general.

Chicago was cold and raining. The wind was loud, even through the double windows in his hotel room. Taylor was tired, impatient, and he missed Eden. Missed her more than he'd thought he would. He looked forward to their long talks each night.

When the job was finally done and the five thousand dollars in his wallet, Taylor flew back to New York.

He was at Eden's apartment by six o'clock that evening.

To his surprise, a young woman he'd never seen before opened the door. She stared at him and he stared back.

"Are you selling something? Why didn't the super ring you up?"

"I'm Taylor and I'm a regular. The super and I drink beer together on Thursday afternoons at Clancy's. Who are you? Where's Eden? Is something wrong?"

"You're a friend of Lin . . . Eden's?"

She sounded shocked and plainly disbelieving. "Yes," he said easily, "I'm a very good friend. I even spent Thanksgiving with her. Who are you?"

"I'm Gayle Werth. Please come in. I'm sorry for grilling you, but it's just that Eden didn't say anything about a man or a friend who was a man . . . Oh, dear, let me take your coat."

"Where's Eden?"

"In the bedroom. She's got a great case of the flu and is at very low ebb right now." Gayle studied him for a minute, still not believing that this hunk, this man who was every inch a man and not a gay, was a friend of Lindsay's, that Lindsay would allow such a man to come within ten miles of her. How much of a friend? "I'll see if she's awake. It's been a very long day for her."

"I'm here now. I'll take care of her."

Again the young woman looked incredulous. At his offer? At his very presence? Taylor had the feeling it was the latter.

"You've known Eden long?"

"We went to boarding school together in Connecticut. The Stamford Girls' Academy. Doesn't that sound great? Anyway, we go all the way back to first ear piercings and exchanging formulas to cover zits. Sit down, Taylor, and I'll see what Eden—"

"No, don't bother." Taylor walked past her, aware that she was on his heels, uncertain what she should do.

He walked quietly into Eden's bedroom and stopped short. She was lying on her back, blankets up to her chin, and her face was white as rice paper. Her hair was in a lank dull braid. She was just opening her eyes. "Oh," she said and moaned. "I had hoped you would call so I could tell you to keep your distance. Don't come any closer, Taylor, I'm sicker than a pig."

"I never get sick," he said, and sat down on the bed beside her. He laid his palm on her forehead. "Fever. How long have you felt this bad? What have you taken and when?"

"Dr. Taylor, I presume?"

"Eden, what do you want me to do?"

"Oh, Gayle . . ."

Taylor turned to the woman who was standing there, nearly *en pointe*, looking worried, amazed, and uncertain. He said easily, as nonthreatening a smile as he could muster on his face, "It's been a pleasure to meet a friend of Eden's. You can leave her with me now, Gayle."

If Lindsay hadn't felt like garbage that had already been completely squashed in a compactor, she would have smiled at the utterly bewildered look on Gayle's face. "He's a friend, Gayle. It's okay. I'll call you tomorrow if I'm still alive. Thanks for letting me boss you around and for being such a wonderful slave."

"You're sure, Eden?"

"Very. Taylor will be leaving soon too."

Taylor didn't say anything. He nodded to Gayle and remained silent until he heard the front door close.

"Now, why the hell didn't you tell me you were sick last night when I called you?"

"I wasn't all that sick. It hit me during the night. I even swore along about two A.M. that I'd become a missionary, but it didn't matter. God must have known I was lying because it just got worse."

The words were no sooner out of her mouth than she stared at him, turning whiter than a moment before, and leapt from the bed. He saw long bare legs from beneath a sleep shirt saying *Don't Hit Psychiatrists or They'll Shrink You* on the back.

He followed her into the bathroom, waited until she was shuddering from dry heaves, then lifted her beneath the arms and helped her back into bed.

"You're sick and it's time to call the doctor."

She fluttered her hand but didn't argue. She felt too awful. Then, when he was reaching for the phone, she said, "I wish you wouldn't. It's just a stomach flu."

"I have a friend who'll tell me what's best. Have you been throwing up all day?"

She nodded.

"You haven't tried to eat?"

"Gayle made some Jell-O but it didn't stay where it was supposed to."

"Okay, just lie there and try to keep still." Taylor called Dr. Metcalf, one of the New York City coroners. He had no intention of telling Eden that all the guy's patients were always dead.

He got hold of Metcalf after a five-minute wait.

"Damn, Taylor, I was in the middle of an autopsy."

Taylor told him the problem and asked his advice. He got it, thanked Metcalf, and hung up the phone.

"Okay, here's what we do. First I trundle down to the market and pharmacy. Don't move."

Thirty minutes later, Lindsay looked at him with some surprise. The saltine cracker appeared to be happy in her belly, the weak tea as well.

"You get a cracker every hour and a bit of tea. Then we'll see."

"Thank you," she said, and closed her eyes. "This is so embarrassing. Please go away. I can take care of myself."

He said something very crude about her self-reliance, and her eyes flew open.

"But you shouldn't have to take care of me, that's crazy. You don't even know me and—"

"Just shut up. I'm staying. I'm sleeping here, next to you, and if you have any problems, then I'll handle them. Now, you're to take two of these pills, then go to sleep. Can I use your toothbrush?"

# 14

## TAYLOR / EDEN

She was asleep when Taylor came back into the bedroom. He quietly undressed, taking off his shirt, shoes, and socks and laying them neatly over the back of one of her rattan chairs, next to a pair of panty hose and a bra. He usually slept nude; but not here, not with Eden. He wasn't about to strip down to his skin and scare the daylights out of her.

He made sure there were crackers within reach, as well as nonaspirin, and Nugarin, a drug to help stop her vomiting.

He eased into bed beside her and pulled another blanket over her. He settled himself with a sheet. The apartment was quiet and warm. Her breathing was even and deep. He gently took her hand in his and lay there on his back, staring up at the ceiling. He could hear the soft ticking of her bedside clock and muted traffic from the window.

He awoke with a start at three o'clock. She wasn't there. He lurched up in bed; then he heard her. She was vomiting in the bathroom.

Jesus, he hadn't heard a thing. He discounted the fact he hadn't slept well in Chicago as he ran into the bathroom. He helped her stand up, gain her balance, then wiped her face with a warm damp cloth. "You want to rinse out your mouth?"

She did but it made her stomach cramp. She dropped to her knees again by the toilet and the cramp stopped suddenly. "Oh, Lord," she said, and let him help her back to bed. She rolled onto her side, her knees drawn up with another cramp.

The cramp eased and she lay panting, looking up at him. Surprisingly, she smiled. Not much of a smile, but a good effort. "This is awful. You shouldn't see anyone like this. It's enough to put you off people forever."

"You'd have to be an ax murderer to put me off. No more cramping?"

"No. Not yet anyway."

He fed her another cracker, took her temperature, and was reassured at the low 101 degrees.

"A sip of tea? No, well, I don't blame you. You want to try to sleep some more?"

"Could we just talk?"

"Sure."

They lay side by side in the dark, holding hands.

"You start," she said, and Taylor obliged, hearing the weakness in her voice.

"Did I ever tell you that I'm a Francophile?"

"A what?"

"I love France, always have. I think I must have lived a past life there, maybe as a worker in a vineyard or something. Anyway, I rent a Harley and cruise around wherever the spirit takes me. I was there for two weeks in September, covering every square foot of Brittany, after most of the tourists had gone home. It was beautiful and warm and . . ."

He realized that something had changed. She was quiet, no problem there, but her hand felt stiff and cold. She'd withdrawn from him.

"Eden? What's wrong? Your stomach cramping again? You need to throw up?"

"No. Oh, God, it's not that."

"Then what is it?"

"I hate France."

"Good Lord, why?"

"I was there once, a long time ago, and it was horrible." It was easier than she thought, to say the words aloud. It was dark, she realized, she was protected in that darkness, she couldn't see his face, couldn't see his reaction to the words that had just spilled out of her mouth.

"What happened?"

Silence. Painful silence. Complete withdrawal.

He said after a while, easily, mildly, "When were you there?"

"In 1983."

"Not really all a coincidence, since I'm there every year. I was there in eighty-three as well. When during the year?"

"In the spring. In April."

"I remember it was beautiful, glorious then. But I mainly remember that trip because I was in Paris at the end of it and got myself banged up in an accident. Didn't do me or my Harley any good. Hospital, broken arm, concussion, the whole bit. Were you in some sort of accident?"

He was aware that this was dangerous territory, even prohibited territory, but he kept on. He'd spoken quietly, soothingly, and now he waited, hoping she would answer him, hoping she'd give him more information, hoping for anything.

"Yes, sort of. I'm tired now. Good night."

"Good night, sweetheart."

Her hand relaxed in his again, her flesh becoming warm and soft. A start was a start even though he had no idea if the start would lead anywhere.

The next morning he awoke before she did. He didn't move, just lay there thinking that she was here beside him, that he still held her hand, that he wanted her here beside him forever. Slowly, very slowly, he turned on his side to face her. Gently he eased his hand beneath her back and turned her to face him. She muttered something but didn't awaken. He pulled her into his arms, then turned again to lie on his back, Eden pressed against his chest.

He smiled. This was more like it. He wished he didn't have any clothes on. He would like to feel her naked against him. Instead, her cheek was against his undershirt.

Another start.

He fell back to sleep.

Lindsay awoke slowly. She didn't move because she

was focused inward, on her body and what its mood was. No cramping, no nausea, no headache. Then she realized she was nearly lying on top of Taylor, her head pressed against his shoulder, one thigh sprawled over his.

His head was turned toward her, his chin resting against her hair. She felt his warm breath. She felt too the warmth of his body. She knew instant and overwhelming terror.

She slid away from him, running clumsily toward the bathroom. Let him think she was sick. Yes, that was it. Let him think she was sick rather than crazy. She shut and locked the bathroom door.

She heard him in her bedroom, stumbling over a chair. He knocked on the door, calling her name. No, not her name, that made-up name that she was beginning to hate because Dr. Gruska had been right. It was a shield, a barrier; it was a lie.

She forced herself to calm. "I'm all right, Taylor. I'm going to take a shower and clean up. I'll be out in ten minutes. Don't worry about me."

He retreated and she breathed a sigh of relief and disappointment. As she showered and washed her hair, she thought of the intimacy again. Looking at them, a stranger would have believed them intimate, would have believed them lovers or even husband and wife. But they weren't any of those things. She was a sham and he was . . .

She felt so weak she could barely stand when she came out of the bathroom wearing her terry-cloth robe. She went to the dresser and pulled out a clean flannel nightgown, one she had bought the previous winter that covered every centimeter of her, and returned to the bathroom. She heard Taylor moving around in the kitchen.

She made her way slowly to the kitchen, her hair thick and wet around her face, her skin white and pasty, and she tried for a smile.

He was completely dressed, thank God. He was whistling and looked right at home.

"Good morning," he said, looking up from the coffeepot. He studied her, then motioned to the chair. "Sit down before you collapse. I don't know if I could pick you up.

I'm pretty weak before I've had my morning injection of caffeine."

She sat down and almost immediately listed to the left.

Taylor said, very slowly, very calmly, "You wore yourself out in the shower. I'm going to help you back to bed, all right?"

"The bed's a mess and—"

"No, I changed the sheets while you were in the bathroom. I hope you don't mind me poking around, but I had to find your linen closet. Everything's pristine again."

She looked up at him, the weakness, the fear, the pain of what she was all on her face. Oh, Jesus, he couldn't bear it. It took everything in him not to pull her into his arms and hold her. But she'd probably freak. Not yet, not yet.

Once in bed, he said, "I don't like you having wet hair. Where's your blow drier?"

She fell deeply asleep with the warmth of the hot air in her ear.

When the phone rang ten minutes later, she didn't stir. Taylor caught it on the second ring.

It was Demos, demanding to know where the hell Eden was and who the hell this was.

"This is Taylor and she's in bed, sick with a stomach flu. Cancel whatever it is she's supposed to do, and call back tomorrow for a progress check."

There was silence. "Taylor? You're really there with her? She let you stay? In her apartment?"

How truthful should he be? Demos evidently knew something. Hell, he had to know what her real name was. Maybe that was all he knew.

"Yeah, I'm really here. I'll be here until she can take care of herself."

"That's a surprise," Demos said, and Taylor could picture the incredulity on the man's face. "It really is. So you and Eden got along, huh? I'll tell Glen, he'll be furious with her. He fancies you himself."

"Give Glen my apologies."

Demos rang off after a few more comments about how light her schedule was, so no problem.

"She told me it was because models were people too

and there was simply too much tempting food around during the holidays."

"True. Well, good luck, Taylor. Ah, listen. You take good care of her, all right? No moves on her, you got that? I'll call tomorrow."

"No moves, Demos."

He looked over at her as he lowered the phone. Who are you? he wondered silently.

On Sunday she still tired easily, but felt pretty much back to normal. He'd spent both Friday and Saturday nights with her. When she awoke Sunday morning lying against him, she didn't leap away. She stayed where she was, warm and content, because she knew he wouldn't hurt her.

They were on the point of going out because the Sunday afternoon was bright and clear and not too cold when the phone rang. Taylor motioned for her to sit down and answered it.

"Who is this?"

"My name is Taylor and I'm a friend of Eden's."

"Er, Eden. Oh, I see. This is her grandmother. May I speak with her?"

He handed over the phone. Eden said nothing of consequence and he knew she didn't because he was there and she didn't want him to know anything about her grandmother. It angered him.

When she hung up, he said, "She sounds very nice."

"She is."

"Where does she live?"

She hesitated; then, "In San Francisco."

"Is she old?"

"Very."

"Let's go Christmas shopping." They went to FAO Schwarz on Fifth Avenue because Eden said she had a niece.

"What's her name?"

"Melissa. She's three. She lives in Italy."

"Your sister or your brother?"

"Half-sister."

He accepted the withdrawal. They remained in the astonishing toy store to purchase presents for his two nephews and niece in Phoenix. When he picked up a kite with a dragon tail, she laughed. "It's wonderful. I had one just like it when I was about six years old."

"Oh," he said. "I thought I'd get it for myself."

She laughed some more and he grinned like a besotted fool. They were examining teddy bears when Taylor said, "Do you want to have children?"

"Oh, yes." Then she jerked back, striking a display. At least twenty teddy bears went flying. FAO Schwarz salespeople were known for being unflappable; this accident was nothing to them. The bears were quickly rearranged. Lindsay felt like an idiot. She saw Taylor looking at her, a clear question in his eyes, and heard herself say, "Children are wonderful, really, but all of us can't, that is, it's impossible, and I almost accept it, but sometimes, just sometimes it makes me sad and . . ."

Taylor said easily, as he carefully checked over a set of outdoor darts, "I want kids too. I didn't realize it until recently. Men must have a biological clock as well as women, because all of a sudden I could see myself washing a station wagon, a flea-bitten dog rushing around shaking off dirty water, and three kids all hollering and climbing over me."

"It sounds nice."

"I guess a wife would have to be lurking about in that picture somewhere."

"Unless you're a biological wonder. Maybe she's the one hosing you down."

He set the dart set back onto the shelf and moved to the toy army tanks. "You're still a young woman, Eden. What are you, twenty-five?"

"Twenty-six." She thought he knew that and frowned at him, wondering what he was thinking about now. He was fast and slippery as a snake, getting things out of her so effortlessly that it was terrifying.

"You've got lots of time. Come to think of it, I'm a young sprout myself, a mere thirty-two. Why don't we both wait two or three more years?"

And she said, staring at the 1885 A. E. Mecklin antique train set just to her right, "All right."

He lightly touched his fingers to her cheek. He leaned over and kissed her lightly, in the middle of FAO Schwarz. "Good," he said.

She was exhausted. He was content. Together they'd spent two hundred dollars on the children's toys, and both were delighted. On their way back to her apartment, Lindsay nearly in a stupor, Taylor, without too much difficulty got her to volunteer that she also had parents who lived in San Francisco. Progress, he thought, pleased, feeling not a bit guilty at taking advantage of her while she was still down.

She fell asleep during the Redskins–San Francisco 49ers game, a cliffhanger for the 49ers, but won in the last ten seconds with a pass from Montana to Rice. She was asleep, cuddled against his chest, his arms around her.

He left that night, not wanting to push her in any way. To his delight, she kissed him at the door. Not a passionate, soul-deep kiss, but a kiss nonetheless. "Thank you," she said. "You're very kind." He walked home whistling. Kindness was just fine for a while.

They became a couple after her bout with stomach flu. It scared Lindsay when she thought about it, but she was so happy she refused to heed any inner warnings that he was still a man and he would want her and he was strong enough to do whatever he wanted to with her. They spent time with Enoch and Sheila. They even spent some evenings out with Demos and Glen and Demos and other women, all gorgeous, all beside him so that his reputation for being a ruthless playboy would be continued. Demos loved the "ruthless" part. A columnist had dubbed him that and he kept the clipping, now yellowing, on his desk, under glass.

Lindsay mailed Melissa's Christmas present on December 4. Not ten minutes after she got back to her apartment, Dr. Gruska called. She had no idea how he had found out her unlisted number. She was sweating and clammy after she'd hung up on him. She called the phone company immediately and secured another unlisted number.

She said nothing to Taylor about the call, but she discovered she was watchful and felt low-grade fear whenever she came out of her apartment building. Evidently Dr. Gruska hadn't discovered her address, thank God. She could handle him if he did come, she was certain she could, but she simply didn't want to. She didn't want to have to run again.

Christmas approached in a snowstorm that turned quickly into a blizzard and grounded Lindsay's plane to San Francisco. She wasn't going anywhere and she was delighted. She called up and gave her apologies. For the first time in her adult life she spent a quiet Christmas with a man. It was incredible, the feelings that poured through her. She gave him the newest small portable phone. It fitted neatly into his shirt pocket. He programmed in her number the first thing. He gave her an Epilady razor, telling her that her razors were now his alone.

When Taylor handed her a box that announced Tiffany's, Lindsay hesitated. Her hands began to tremble.

"Open it."

She did, careful not to shred the paper, so careful, so exacting. So frightened. She slowly pulled back the lid to discover another, smaller box nestled inside. It was a ring box. Inside, settled firmly in lush black velvet, was a marquise diamond ring. She gasped aloud, she couldn't help it. It was the most beautiful ring she'd ever seen in her life. And it was more than a ring. Much more. Oh, God. She looked over at him, frozen, scared, excited.

"Marry me, Eden. Marry me."

She stared at him. She wanted to yell that she wasn't Eden. He'd asked a woman who wasn't real to marry him, a woman who was a lie, a fraud, a sham. She was afraid to touch the ring, afraid of what she'd say, afraid she'd fall apart and weep all over herself, all over him. She drew deep upon herself and said slowly, "I can't marry you, Taylor, because I'm not what you think I am, or who you think I am."

He smiled at that, and said, "It doesn't matter that your name isn't Eden and that it's Lynn. Lynn is a nice name, a solid name, a name with substance. I can tolerate Lynn."

"*What?*"

"When you were sick last month, Gayle slipped and

called you Lynn, then broke it off and switched real fast to
Eden. If you prefer Eden, I don't care. Don't you understand, I don't give a damn."

"I hate Eden. As for Lynn—"

"Well, then . . ."

"It's more, much more, and I don't know how to . . .
You're the one who doesn't understand."

He said nothing, forcing himself to wait, forcing himself to patience, endless patience. She remained silent, staring down at the ring. He rose to stir the burning logs in
the fireplace. The room was warm and smelled of holly and
pine tree and hot chocolate. He looked over at the small
Christmas tree, sparkling with multicolor lights. Together
they'd threaded strings of popcorn and argued how best to
place the bulbs. He insisted that half the decorations be
his—a motley assortment of bulbs his sister had given him
a good ten years before, and ancient tinsel, tangled and
faded, looking as if a cat had mangled it. A Santa Claus
bulb without a beard hung next to a very expensive antique
Victorian Santa. He grinned every time he looked at the
two of them side by side. It was the most beautiful tree
he'd ever seen. He remained silent. The firelight made her
candlelit living room glow and shimmer. He'd never been
more scared in his life. Or more certain. He slipped the
poker back in its rack, pulled the mesh back across the fireplace opening, then returned to join her on the floor. He
sat opposite her, not next to her. He had all evening to get
what he wanted.

"The ring is beautiful, Taylor."

"Yes. I wanted the ring to be beautiful since I want it
on your finger for the rest of our lives."

"I'm very surprised. I wasn't expecting . . ."

"A man to propose to you? A man who hasn't yet even
told you he loves you? You're right. I didn't do it right. I
love you Lynn/Eden. Marry me."

She was silent, not looking at him now.

"I could get on my knees and ask you again, but you're
already sitting on the floor so I don't think it would have
much romantic impact."

"Oh, no, no."

"Also, I didn't have to sell my car to pay for the ring. I do have sufficient funds to keep us both very comfortably. My job is steady and the hours aren't bad, except from time to time, as you already know."

She was still silent, seemingly studying the nap of the carpet.

"If you want to keep modeling, that's fine with me. If you want to sit on your rear end and eat chocolates all day, why, I'll bring you a box of Fanny Farmer pecan turtles every night. If you want to start a family right away, that's also fine. I'm easy, sweetheart. Whatever you want. I just want you to be happy. With me."

His heart pounded. His mouth felt dry as dust. He wondered about the nap on the carpet. It must be fascinating, because now she was running her fingers against the grain. Why didn't she say something, dammit? But she didn't. He forged ahead. "If you want to stay here, I'll move in with you. Or if you prefer my apartment, we can live there. However, I think the two of us together need more room. I think we should find a new apartment. I like the East Side, but the West Side is fine with me. I know a number of great hangouts over there. As I said, I'm easy. Whatever you want."

Still she looked shell-shocked. She looked incapable of speech.

"Do you love me, Eden?"

She looked up at him then, so still she could have been a statue. She drew a deep breath and said, "I don't know about love. I do know, though, that you're miraculous, Taylor."

He blinked at her. "You're always surprising me," he said, and that was true.

"I mean it. I never realized before that a man like you could even exist."

"Why not?"

Too much too fast, he realized, and wanted to kick himself. Too straightforward, punching too quickly.

She merely shrugged. She still held the ring box. She hadn't touched the ring inside.

"I guess you could say I haven't had many good experiences with men."

"They're not me, these other men."

"No," she said. "They're not. They weren't."

"Because I'm miraculous and I don't ever want you to forget it. I also love you."

He saw the fear in her and wished he could have the man or men who'd done this to her. And what had this man or these men done? His hands clenched into fists.

Tears were in her eyes. "I can't. Not yet. I'm sorry, Taylor . . ."

He raised his hand and said easily, "I've got an idea. Tell me true now. Have you enjoyed having me around for the past month and a half?"

"Yes."

"Have I ever frightened you?"

"Yes."

"Let me rephrase that. Do you trust me now more than you did two weeks ago?"

"Yes."

"Do you trust me not to hold you down and rape you?"

Hesitation; then, "Yes."

Okay, he thought, she'd probably been raped. And she'd been in Paris in April 1983. He could check that out— French newspapers, magazines—to see if what had happened to her had happened there. He had a war to win and he couldn't afford to have niggling scruples, not anymore. "Are you remembering how I slept with you for two nights? Are you remembering how you woke up in my arms?"

"Yes."

"I didn't try anything, did I?"

"Maybe you were afraid I'd vomit on you."

He grinned at that. "Could be, but I don't think so. I was hard as a rock all night. I'm talking about my penis, in case you don't know. But, Eden, it didn't matter and it won't matter. I would never do anything to hurt you, and that includes forcing any kind of sex on you that you don't want."

"Stop, Taylor, just stop! It's not that. It's just that I

*201*

can't . . . I know what you . . . that all men want sex and they want it often, but I can't, I just can't . . ."

"Not now," he said easily. "No problem. I'm not blind or stupid, Eden. I have known for a good while that you don't want to have anything to do with me, woman to man. No, don't look so surprised. I won't lie to you. In fact, it would be stupid for me to try to lie to you because when I kiss you, I know you can feel how hard I am, especially when you're wearing your high heels. And we're not just nose to nose. We're everything to everything. It drives me crazy. I want you so bad I hurt with it. But I'm not a raving hormonal teenage boy, nor am I a macho fool. I want you the woman, not just your body. Can you possibly understand that?"

No, he saw, quickly enough, she didn't understand that.

"No matter. We'll work on it."

She made a move to thrust the ring box toward him; then, just as quickly, she drew it back again. He was greatly pleased with the show of indecision.

"The ring is yours, Eden, just as I am also yours. You toss the ring away and I'm tossed away with it. You keep it, you also keep me."

"I don't know . . ."

"Listen to me, I've got an offer." He sat back against the sofa, his arms crossed over his chest. He looked very big, very strong, very much a man, and she found herself, having focused on that, pulling back.

"You can go in the other room if it makes you feel any safer," Taylor said mildly. "Is this position frightening you? No, okay, then. Ah, you're looking surprised again. I know you, at least I'm coming to know you more every day. I have to walk on egg shells around you. Well, it's tough and I'm getting tired of it, so I propose that we come to grips with things."

"What do you mean?"

"You're still here? You've decided to show some courage? You're sure I won't jump on you?"

"Stop it, damn you!" She picked up the box that had

held his portable phone and threw it at him. It hit him square on the chin.

"Good shot. Thank God you didn't break it. Here's my offer: I want to move in with you tomorrow. We'll be roommates, not lovers. We'll be as close as any two people can be without having sex. No sex, Eden, no sex until you're ready. That's a promise."

"Where will you sleep?"

"With you. Just like we did those two nights."

Her brow furrowed and she was chewing on her lower lip. Good, he thought, just maybe I've got her.

"That would mean you'd discover all my bad habits," she said.

"I've got bunches myself. We'd be in this together. Do you floss every morning or every night?"

"Night."

"I'm morning. Do you snore like a pig?"

"I don't know," she said with perfect seriousness. "I've never heard myself. Do you?"

"Only when I'm stressed out or dog-tired. I jog three mornings a week and work out at Mueller's Gym up on Sixty-sixth another two days. I won't get fat on you. I'm also a pretty good cook."

"I won't get fat either," she said.

"Yeah, but is that through personal commitment or because you have to starve yourself to make a living? Will you get fat when you stop modeling?"

"I don't think so. I've never had a problem before."

He smiled at her. "Good. I think we've got all the bases covered."

"I don't cook very well."

"No problem. Since you don't eat, why bother learning? I do great things with lettuce and tofu and pork chops."

"All right."

"Give me the ring." He held out his hand.

She handed him the box.

He pulled the exquisite ring from its bed. "Give me your left hand."

She hesitated, and he just waited, his hand still out, palm up.

She thrust her left hand at him. He held the beautiful ring out, staring down at it as he slid it on her finger. It was a tight fit, a very tight fit, and she had to help him, wincing as she forced it over her knuckle. He'd rather thought a size five would do the trick.

"Good, it'll be a real pain to get the thing off. If you're ever really pissed at me and want to throw it in my face, you'll have trouble doing it immediately, in the heat of passion, so to speak. That, sweetheart, will give you time to cool down and me to talk you out of your snit."

"You're miraculous, Taylor. You're also a devious smart-ass."

"Tell me more. Come here now, I want to hug you."

She came between his legs, stretched out, and leaned back against his chest, and his arms came around her waist. He kissed the top of her head. "You are now my fiancée. It's official. How does that sound?"

"Miraculous."

He laughed, pulled her hair back, and bit her earlobe. "Taylor? Why don't you stay tonight?"

He wondered if she was pressed close to him to feel how hard he was. "All right," he said. "We've got our Christmas stocking for tomorrow morning. It'll be nice not to have to come trudging over here in the cold and snow at seven o'clock in the morning. This way, we can sit in bed, drink cocoa, and attack the stockings whenever we feel like it."

"I can't imagine it," she said, her voice low and just slightly bewildered and disbelieving.

"I can," he said, and kissed her earlobe. "Now I can imagine it very easily."

"The last time I had a Christmas stocking, I was eleven years old."

"Oh, yeah? You want a real sob story? The last time anyone gave me a Christmas stocking, I was in the police academy and it was my instructor. Mean bugger, my instructor. Lots of wrapped goodies—things like hand grenades, tear-gas canisters, a toy gun, bullets, handcuffs, you wouldn't believe those handcuffs, all fur-lined—Lord, she was something else, my instructor, especially with those handcuffs. Her name was Marlene 'Ball Buster' Jakoby and she was—"

Lindsay turned and hit him as hard as she could in the stomach. "Handcuffs!"

"Yes, ma'am, I was a slave for an evening."

"I thought you only did Christmas stockings on Christmas morning."

He looked thoughtful at that. "One adapts. Yes, one indeed adapts."

# ❧ 15 ❧

## TAYLOR / EDEN

They saw in Christmas Day, but only just. At ten minutes after midnight, Taylor looked at her and gave a big yawn. Tomorrow morning, early, was Christmas stockings. They needed their sleep. He held out his hand to her as he rose.

She tentatively placed her hand in his, stood up, pulled down her loose wine-colored sweater, and said, trying to hide her sudden embarrassment, "I'll go first, if that's okay. I'll be about ten minutes."

He nodded, turning to face the fireplace, trying to be as laid-back as his computer friends in California. At that moment she felt a spurt of anger at him, for he'd known intimacy with a woman; he knew how to act, what to say, how to speak. He knew what to *do*. She said from the doorway, "This isn't fair. I feel so strange. I don't know how to act, how to joke around about all this like you do. I feel stupid."

He grinned at her, waving her away as he said, "On the other hand, you're wearing a beautiful ring. You've got me at your feet. What else do you want?"

Again, his light touch. She just shook her head at him. Lindsay called out to him when she was through in the bathroom, and after seeing to the candles, the fire, the front door, Taylor went into the bedroom. Only the lamp atop the bedside table was on. She was lying on the left side, flat on her back, the covers to her chin. She was staring at him.

"Hi," he said easily, but he was thinking that she looked the twentieth-century prototype of a vestal virgin. He unbuttoned his shirt. "You kept to the agreed-upon limit, didn't you, Eden?"

"For what?" She was staring at him. He pulled off his shirt. Then he pulled his T-shirt over his head.

"For the presents in our stockings," he said through the cotton. "Just nonsense presents, limit of fifty dollars. Did you stick to the limit?"

She watched the white T-shirt float to the floor. He began to pull the belt from the loops of his dark gray slacks. Taylor had decided while he'd waited for her that he would wear his T-shirt and shorts to bed tonight, then, after he moved in tomorrow, he'd wear sweats, nothing more. That was what he'd thought at first. Then he thought, why the hell hide his body from her? Why the hell pretend the situation wasn't normal? Why the hell pretend he didn't want her and not let her see that he did? Why the hell not have her get used to him, beginning immediately? It was a risk; it was a god-awful risk, but he accepted it, and prayed. His hand paused a moment; then he knew he had to go ahead with it. She had to get used to him. She had to know that even when he was naked there was simply no chance he would hurt her. She had to trust him.

"Did you?" he asked again, not looking up.

The belt landed on the chair, curling around the T-shirt. He sat down and took off his shoes and socks, then rose again, his fingers on the trouser button.

*"What are you doing?"*

"I'm taking my clothes off. I tend not to sleep in them, you know. It makes them last longer. Save on the laundry and cleaning bills. Now, did you stick to our limit?"

"Taylor!"

She couldn't help watching, she simply couldn't help it. The image of the prince flared bright and stark in her memory, and she saw him naked, saw his sex hard and long, remembered the heat of his breath on her face, the coldness of his hands on her body, and felt the old terror, the humiliation and fear, the helplessness.

"I managed to keep it at just $47.69, to be exact. I got you some neat things. You'll see."

She turned her head away.

She heard him whistling "Silent Night."

But she wasn't eighteen anymore. She wasn't helpless. "Damn you, you promised me, you said that I could trust you, that you wouldn't—"

He didn't intend to pretend for an instant, nor did he hesitate to interrupt her. "I didn't lie, Eden. Turn around and look at me. Get used to me, starting right now. I am incapable of pretending I don't want you, so there's no point in trying to hide it and pretend sex doesn't exist and that I'm some sort of eunuch roommate. Look at me and trust me. I won't ever do anything you don't want." He spoke slowly and easily, so calmly, his own voice nearly putting him to sleep. But not Eden. No, she was too terrified.

She turned her head slowly on the pillow. He was standing in the middle of her bedroom, naked, his arms at his sides, looking at her.

"I'm just a man, Eden."

She stared.

"Do you still think I'm miraculous?"

"Yes," she said finally after staring at him for a full silent three minutes. "I suppose you are."

He grinned at her, feeling a whole truckload of relief. "I like a warped woman. Let's get some sleep."

He walked toward the bed, saw her freeze, but continued on his course. Normalcy was the key. He slipped under the covers. "Turn off the light. You wore me out tonight."

"I didn't. Whatever do you mean?"

"Oh, yes, you did. You didn't squeal with incredible joy when you saw the ring. You didn't leap into my arms and kiss my face off and scream that you couldn't wait to marry me, that you were the happiest woman in New York. Oh, no, lady, you nearly forced me to call out the Marines.

Now I've got to regroup. Off with the light. I've got to think, to plan."

The light clicked off. The bedroom was black as pitch. Lindsay moved around a bit, then became quiet. She said then, "Don't you wear pajamas to bed?"

"No."

"If I bought you some, would you?"

"No."

She sighed.

"Speaking of pajamas, I hate nightgowns. If I burned all of yours, would you sleep nude?"

"No."

"Well, there you are. Good night, sweetheart. It's good to be here, where I belong."

"Good night, Taylor. I'm glad you're here. I think."

"Do I get a good-night kiss?"

Silence.

"All right. A special kiss, an engagement kiss, a Christmas Eve kiss."

She leaned over and kissed him, landing on his chin. He reached out to clasp her shoulders and instead brushed against her breasts. Oh, sweet Jesus, he thought. "No, don't pull back. It's dark in here. Now, let's see if we can't get our mouths together properly."

They did and it was a sweet kiss, one that left him profoundly horny and left Lindsay feeling a small flutter in her belly, a sensation she attributed to residue fear.

When Taylor awoke the following morning at precisely ten minutes past seven, she was lying on her back, a good foot separating them. As he'd done before, he pulled her over and settled her against him. He didn't go back to sleep. He lay there, quite happy and so pleased with himself he wanted to yell with it. She mumbled something and moved, coming closer, her thigh covering his legs quite thoroughly now, her palm over his bare chest, her face tucked into his throat. Her hair was thick and soft and wavy in his face.

He waited to see how she would react when she woke up. Unfortunately, she didn't wake up, and by the time it was eight o'clock, he had to go to the bathroom.

"Well, damn," he said as he eased away from her.

He brought hot chocolate, croissants, butter, and Kramer's strawberry jam in on a tray. "Merry Christmas, Eden. Come on, wake up."

Lindsay couldn't believe it. A man's voice, in her apartment, and she was in bed. It took her less than an instant to come fully awake. She stared at this man in her bedroom. He was wearing her white terry-cloth robe, belted at the waist. He was in her bedroom and he was bringing her food. *He lived here.* She must have lost her mind, she must be crazy. She'd lost it on Christmas Eve. He lived here and she'd agreed to it. Then she happened to look down at the blazing diamond on her left hand. Well, hell.

She scooted up in bed and patted her legs. Well, she didn't have to act like a freaked-out fool. "Set the tray down right here, sailor. I'm starving."

"Don't you ever go to the bathroom?"

She ducked her head down.

"Eden, don't be silly. Even though you're gorgeous, your body's a dream, your mind's flawless in its reasoning, your youth's a fountain from whence flows unquenchable wit—"

"Shut up, you fool!"

"Still, even with all these perfections, you've got to go to the bathroom sometime."

"All right," she said, and went.

When she came back, teeth and hair brushed, the two bulging Christmas stockings were on the bed, along with the breakfast tray.

"This is wonderful," she said, and realized with joy that it really was. It was new and different and she simply couldn't believe it. She relished it. She wanted to hug it to her and never feel fear again. Perhaps Taylor was different . . ."I'm trying to show you that you can't live without me. Food to a skinny woman is always a good start."

She bit into a croissant. "Wonderful. Oh, that's real butter. I'd forgotten I had any."

"Kiss me good morning. It's a tradition in my family that goes all the way back to the Spanish Inquisition. And it will become a tradition in our family as well."

She kissed him, tasting of the delicious strawberry jam

and hot chocolate on his mouth. He deepened the kiss just a bit and let it go at that.

Two weeks ago, Taylor never would have believed he'd be in bed with her on Christmas morning, the recipient of a sweet kiss, but here he was.

As she'd so aptly said, it was indeed miraculous. He wondered, as he picked up his first wrapped stocking present, if she loved him and just didn't know it. He guessed he'd happily settle for "miraculous" for the time being. There was lots to do before he asked her again if she loved him.

Taylor quickly discovered that Eden liked to talk in bed, when it was in the dark of the night, when she couldn't see him or his reaction.

He, in turn, could have any reaction he wanted because she couldn't see him. It suited both their purposes for the time being.

Their most memorable late-night talk had been short and had moved him more than he'd expected. She'd said matter-of-factly, "I've always wanted to belong. To have someone who loved me and cared what happened to me. Someone who never questioned me, who believed me, and accepted me."

Jesus, he thought, and swallowed, then reached out his hand and poked her ribs. "Well, now you do. Don't forget, all that still goes even when we have our first knock-down, drag-out fight."

"It's nice," she said, grabbing his hand. She didn't release it.

That was all, and he knew he'd never forget it as long as he lived. Her hand remained in his all night. It wasn't until the second of January that Lindsay remembered about her mail. Most of it was addressed to Lindsay Foxe. It was possible, of course, that Taylor had already looked at incoming bills and letters, but she didn't think so. When he snooped, she imagined he wouldn't resort to sneaking looks at letters. Still, she either had to tell him who she was or do something about the mail. She felt like a fraud, but she didn't do anything about it.

She shied away from admitting she was Lindsay Foxe. On the other hand, the odds were that he wouldn't ever recognize that name, not in a million years, except that he had been in Paris in April 1983. All he'd had to do was look at a newspaper or scandal sheet. How could he not know? Oh, God, she couldn't bear it. But then again, just maybe he would never find out about her even if the name did sound familiar to him. In terms of his abilities, she had no doubt that if he were curious about her name, he'd know all about her within an hour. She wasn't ready to tell him. Not yet. It surprised her that the wound still festered. For eight years now she'd handled it, down to joining self-awareness groups in college and spouting the party line. Before, she'd really thought herself well-armored, despite Dr. Gruska's two appearances, but Taylor was different in her life. He counted. She didn't want to lose him. She didn't want him to look at her and think she'd been a teenage Lolita. He already knew too much, but this . . . she simply couldn't handle this yet.

She didn't know what to do. What she did do, finally, was get a post-office box. It would be a real pain in the rear but she could see no alternative. Except to tell the truth. No, not yet. If Taylor noticed she didn't get a scrap of mail anymore, he didn't say anything.

He noticed, all right, because he'd been wondering if he should initiate a change of address. He wanted to confront her with it, but he decided to wait.

Damnation. Who was she? Why did it matter about her name? When was she going to trust him?

They both admitted to the other on the eighth of January that the apartment was too small for the two of them.

Lindsay was afraid to speak of it, but Taylor wasn't and he got the ball rolling.

"Let's either move to my place—it is bigger, but probably still not big enough—or let's go looking. What are you doing Saturday?"

It was a commitment that appalled her. It was even more real than the diamond that winked brilliantly up at her. It felt very heavy on her hand. She thought suddenly of the look on Demos' face when he'd seen it. Shock, incre-

dulity, and finally, pleasure. Glen had acted wounded, tossing his head, but he'd given her a big hug. Now Taylor
wanted to move. It wasn't a do-or-die decision, but to her
it was close, very close.

"Well?"

She just looked at him, that look that used to drive him
nuts, it was so wary and uncertain.

"Question, Eden. We've been together for two weeks.
Do you realize that last night while I was taking off my
clothes you were sitting up in bed, your arms around your
knees, and you didn't miss a beat in what you were
saying?"

"I was concentrating on what I was telling you."

"I was hard as a rock and you didn't blink."

"Oh, all right. So I'm getting used to you—to all parts
of you! So what?"

"Two days ago, I woke up early. You were lying all
over me. When you woke up, I pretended to be asleep. You
got up, went to the bathroom, came back, and sprawled all
over me again. What do you think of that?"

"I was too groggy to know what I was doing."

"Right."

"I was cold and you're like a furnace."

"Right. Do you remember only last night, you were
talking to me through the bathroom door? Normal as could
be."

"I was creaming my face! Surely you should be grateful
I spared you that."

"Was that all you were doing?" He flicked his fingertips
over her flushed cheek. "No, please don't resort to violence.
Regardless, it's time to go the next step. Let's look in the
paper and see what's available to rent."

She threw the newspaper at him. "All right, just do it
and shut up!"

"Okay," he said mildly, smoothing it out. "How much
can you afford for your half?"

She laughed, flinging her arms out. "Let's splurge. I
make lots and lots of money. I want one of those big old
apartments with high ceilings and lots of molding and old

marble fireplaces and views that make you cry, but, of course, modern kitchen and bathrooms."

They found just what she wanted on Fifth Avenue between Eightieth and Eighty-first streets in the elegant 1926 Bishop Building. It hadn't been advertised, of course. Taylor and Lindsay both had put the word out and it had been Demos who'd called with the lead. The apartment was one thousand, eight hundred square feet, with lots of shining old wood, both on the walls as wainscoting and on the floors. It cost three arms and a dozen legs, Taylor thought, but what the hell. He turned to see her mesmerized, just standing in the middle of the immense living room, staring out the big bay windows to Central Park and the museum.

"How much do you earn?"

Lindsay knew what the rent was. She also realized he was a man, and men, in general, simply couldn't comprehend a woman earning a whopping lot of money. She said, her chin up, "I can afford more than half, with no strain on my budget, if that's what worries you. I can even afford the security deposit, all by myself. I can even afford the whole thing!"

"Good. Half will be just fine. I don't want to miss my trip to France in the spring or have to eat onion soup at the end of the month. Shall we sign the lease?"

Lindsay found that when she signed her name, her real name, on the line beneath Taylor's, to the one-year lease, she didn't even hesitate. But she did notice his signature. He hadn't crowded her. He hadn't looked down to see what she'd written. He'd even walked away while she was signing the lease. When she folded their copy of the lease and stuffed it into her purse, he still remained quiet. She'd tell him when she was ready. Evidently that wasn't just yet. He was surprised when she said, "You signed S. C. Taylor. What does the S.C. stand for?"

"I'll tell you on our wedding night." Didn't she realize he could play a tit-for-tat game? Evidently not. He saw the shock on her face at his words and tried very much to disregard it.

They moved in on the twentieth of January with only the

requisite number of New York moving screwups. Their belongings together didn't fill up the apartment, but Lindsay was coming to realize that it was more fun this way. Now they'd be able to plan, to argue, to decorate and compromise. It was the compromise part, the sheer fun of discussing everything together, that made her life, all of it, immensely fuller and richer. It made her life more normal because her focus now took into account another person's feelings and moods and opinions. It felt odd. It also felt wonderful.

It was also a commitment the size of which she never considered possible in her life. It was a commitment that shouted for honesty. Soon, she told herself, soon. Taylor was too important to play games with, much too important. Important to her.

On February 2 they'd taken an afternoon to look at Persian rugs for the living room, and had argued and insulted each other's taste, all in all having a fine time. They'd bought a Tabriz, all in soft blues and creams and reds and pale yellows and pinks. It was beautiful in the living room. Taylor claimed credit, as did Lindsay. They fought and yelled at each other. They laughed and drank tea even though Lindsay would have given anything to eat some ice cream. And it was that night, at ten minutes past eight, that the phone rang.

Lindsay answered it, cutting off the middle of a sentence to Taylor. She was still laughing when she said, "Hello!"

There was a brief silence; then, "Lindsay, this is your father."

She clutched the phone in her fist, all laughter gone. "What's wrong?"

"Your grandmother is dead. Your mother is dead as well. Your mother was drunk and driving your grandmother to one of her interminable board meetings. They went flying down Webster Street, out of control, and hit four other cars, all empty, thank God. Your mother . . ."

God, she hated him. She stared at the phone. "When did this happen?"

"Yesterday."

"Why didn't you call me yesterday?"

He was silent and she could almost picture his impatient shrug. "I'm calling you now. The funeral is on Friday. You might want to consider flying out here."

"Yes, I will. Thank you for calling me. It's quite decent of you."

"I don't need your sarcasm, Lindsay. It doesn't become you any more than your absurd height does. I spoke to Sydney yesterday. She'll be flying back from Italy."

Of course he'd called Sydney immediately. But not her, not Lindsay. Her mother was dead. Her grandmother, the timeless old lady, was dead. Gates Foxe, a San Francisco fixture, seemingly immortal, always on the move, always active. And her mother. Drunk? No, she couldn't accept that, she couldn't. She hadn't gone to San Francisco at Christmas. She'd been delighted when Kennedy had closed down with the snowstorm. She'd made no attempt to get another, later flight. She didn't get to see either of them. And now they were dead.

"When you arrive, just take a taxi to the mansion. I suppose you'll have to stay here."

"Yes," she said, and gently hung up the phone.

She raised her eyes. Taylor was looking at her intently. She said, "That was my father. My grandmother and my mother are dead. They were killed in a car accident yesterday. I'd best call the airline now for a reservation out tomorrow morning. The funeral is on Friday."

Taylor watched her dial information and ask for United reservations. She was calm, far too calm. But he waited, listened to her voice as she spoke to the reservations person.

When she hung up, she said, "Oh, dear, I've got to call Demos. I won't be able to make that photo session tomorrow. It's sportswear, in January. Isn't that odd? I don't remember . . . was I doing something on Friday? Taylor, do you know?"

He walked to her and very gently drew her into his arms. She was stiff and withdrawn. He didn't know what to do so he just held her and stroked his hands up and down her back.

"Why don't you go take a nice hot shower. I'll call Demos for you."

"Thank you, Taylor." She pulled away from him and walked out of the huge, half-empty living room, down the long corridor to the master bedroom.

He called Demos.

"You going to San Francisco with her?"

"I don't know. She hasn't asked me to."

"Maybe it's best you don't," Demos said after a goodly silence. "I understand her father is a real jerk, her stepmother is a bigger jerk, and there's her half-sister, Sydney, who's . . . well, that's neither here nor there. Oh, God, it's not fair, is it? Take care of her, Taylor."

"Yes, Demos, I will."

He walked into the bathroom. She was lying in a full tub of hot water, her head back against the rich pale pink marble, her hair wet and thick against her shoulders, covering her breasts.

"You all right, sweetheart?"

She was naked but she didn't care. She opened her eyes and turned her face to look at him. He was sitting on the toilet seat, the look of worry on his face real and honest. It touched her deeply.

"I'm all right. It's such a shock. My mother . . . I haven't really been close to her since I was sixteen and she and my father sent me away to boarding school in Connecticut. My father said she was drunk and responsible for the accident. But my grandmother. It's hard, really hard to believe she's gone. She was always there, always."

Still, there were no tears in her. Only a vague worry.

"Do you want me to come with you?"

She shook her head. "No, no, I don't want you to meet my . . . It doesn't matter. I'll be coming back Friday night. I won't stay there, in the mansion, any longer than I have to. I've always hated it there."

The mansion? There was so much he wanted to know, so very much, and she'd been getting closer to him, closer by the day. They'd had a wonderful argument just the day before, and had ended up in each other's arms, laughing and even kissing a little bit. And now this.

"Call me when you arrive."

"All right."

That night he held her close as he did every night. She was very quiet and his impression was that it wasn't pain holding her silent; it was shock and disbelief, a numbness that invaded the brain so that one could deal with the enormity of the loss. Quite normal, he supposed. Two violent deaths at the same time. He wished she wanted him with her. But he wouldn't push. Not now.

She took a taxi to Kennedy.

At least he knew when she was due back. He'd pick her up when she returned. Maybe by then she'd need him, really need him.

San Francisco was sunny, sixty degrees, paradise on earth. Lindsay breathed in deeply as she walked from the baggage claim outside to where the taxis were lined up.

Thirty minutes later the taxi pulled up in front of the mansion. The man whistled. "Quite some digs. You live here, lady?"

"Oh, no. I'm just an occasional visitor."

"It must be great to be the folk who do live here. Can you imagine all the bucks?"

"No, not really."

She didn't want to press the bell. She didn't want to see Holly, her stepmother, or her father. She still felt nothing save that vague stillness that seemed to be coming from inside her. It was only two o'clock in the afternoon. Odd, back home in New York it would be dark now. What would Taylor be doing? Would he be home?

Home. It sounded wonderful.

She rang the bell.

Holly answered the door. A fat Holly, with a double chin, a pasty complexion, and bloodshot eyes. From crying? Lindsay doubted it. She recognized the signs from her mother. The bloodshot eyes were probably from drinking too much for too long too often.

"Well," said Holly, stepping back. "You're here. Come in, Lindsay."

She was wearing a loose flowing top over very tight

knit pants and sneakers. She looked like a forty-year-old woman trying to look like she was twenty-two and thirty pounds lighter.

"Hello, Holly. I hope you're doing all right."

Holly smiled. "It's your family, not mine. I will miss the old lady, though, odd as that might sound."

"It doesn't sound odd at all."

"You didn't have to live here day in and day out as her daughter-in-law, taking orders, not being able to do what I wanted to do, always having to beg, to plead, to get anything I wanted. Your father was her own personal puppy. God, you're lucky you lived three thousand miles away."

"You don't have to stay, Holly. All this was your decision."

She gave Lindsay a malignant look, then shrugged as she walked into the main drawing room. The heavy brocade drapes were pulled closed. The room was chill and damp.

"Jesus," Holly said, and went on a rampage, jerking open every curtain in the vast room. "That miserable housekeeper, I'm going to fire her ass on Monday. Yes, on Monday I'll be the boss here and anyone who doesn't like it can just get the hell out. And that includes your precious Mrs. Dreyfus. All the old bag can do is snivel and talk about how Mrs. Gates would have done this or that! Jesus!"

Lindsay set her single bag down in the hall, then walked to the vast Carrara marble fireplace. "I'll light a fire, all right?"

"Yeah, sure. It feels like bloodly death in here."

Lindsay's hands jerked.

"I need a drink." Lindsay watched Holly walk to the drink tray and pull the stopper out of a Waterford decanter. It was Glenlivet and Holly poured herself a double shot, neat.

"Drinking more, Holly? Really, dear, you should try to control yourself. People will be coming by to offer their sympathy. The last impression you want to give is that the new lady of the house is a lush."

Sydney was wearing a slender black wool dress with three-inch black heels. Her stockings were black with seams up the backs of her legs. Her hair was pulled back from her face and held with gold combs. Her makeup was restrained, perfect. She looked pale and fragile and utterly beautiful.

Lindsay said from where she remained in front of the fireplace, "Hello, Sydney. When did you get in?"

"Last night. It was a very long flight from Milan. You're looking about the same, Lindsay. How was New York when you left?"

"Cold and sunny."

"And Demos?"

"The same."

"Really, Holly, dear, not another shot? Surely you've had more than enough. You're much more in the open about your drinking than Lindsay's mother ever was. You're also fatter than her mother ever was. And this fixation you seem to have with mirrors— isn't it a bit painful to look at yourself now?"

"Go fuck yourself, Sydney!"

Sydney laughed. "I doubt I'll ever have to resort to that, unlike you. Poor Holly. All that fat you're carrying around turns men off, don't you know that? Particularly my father."

"Just stop it, both of you!"

Sydney and Holly both stared at Lindsay. She was on her feet, pale, furious. She'd had enough. "Listen, no more sniping! Sydney, just keep your nasty comments to yourself. For God's sake, Grandmother and my mother are dead! Just stop it, damn you both!"

"Such passion," Sydney remarked in Holly's general direction. "And here I had thought the prince had sucked all of it out of my little sister."

Lindsay dumped the two fat logs she was holding on the floor. She watched them roll over the beautiful golden oak. One log dented the oak badly when it struck. She said nothing more, merely walked out, shoulders straight, feeling like death herself. Nothing ever changed. Things just seemed to get worse, and now that Grandmother was dead, there was no one to put on the brakes.

She didn't see Mrs. Dreyfus.

She went to her bedroom, locked the door, and

unpacked the few clothes she'd brought, putting them away, paying no heed, really, to what she was doing. Her brain was numb and she was grateful for it.

She wondered what her grandmother had been doing with her mother. There'd really been no love lost between the two women, as far as she knew. But she'd been gone a long time. And sometimes things did change. Just maybe her grandmother preferred the ex-daughter-in-law to the current one. Now Lindsay would never know.

Lindsay closed her eyes. She saw Taylor, laughing, pulling her against him and hugging her tight, nibbling her earlobe, whispering that she had abysmal taste in Persian carpets, that Bokaras were too flimsy and far too red for his taste, which was, of course, superb. Then he went on to her fresh-meadow air freshener. It clogged his sinuses, he said, and got under his fingernails. It smelled like a brothel. It smelled like a cat box in a rich house. God, she missed him, his normalcy, his humor, his balance. She saw Taylor as he'd been last night, worry in his eyes, and helplessness, because he didn't know what to do, what to say to her.

Dear God, he was so dear to her.

At seven o'clock there was a knock on her door. Lindsay was dressed, sitting in front of her window, staring toward Alcatraz Island. Waiting for someone to fetch her. Knowing she'd have to see Sydney and Holly again. And her father.

She followed Mrs. Dreyfus downstairs to the drawing room. The first person she saw was her father, Judge Royce Foxe, standing in a stark black suit with white linen, looking handsome and elegant as always and laughing at something Sydney was saying to him. He looked up at Lindsay, and his laughter died.

# 16

## LINDSAY

"I see you came," Royce Foxe said, nodding slightly toward her in acknowledgment. Whatever Sydney had said to make him laugh was dried up, gone, now that Lindsay had shown up on the scene. There was no welcoming smile for her, but she hadn't expected one. She wondered vaguely when a day would come that it wouldn't hurt her very core, this inevitable and inexplicable dislike he had for her.

"Hello, Father, Sydney," she said, and turned toward Holly. She was holding a glass tightly in her hand, a whiskey glass. "Good evening, Holly."

"You want something to drink?"

"A Perrier would be nice, thank you."

Sydney smiled at her. "Yes, just so, Lindsay. Oh, I forgot to have my secretary send you a thank-you for Melissa's Christmas gift. Melissa is so spoiled she didn't pay that adorable bear much attention, but it was a nice thought on your part. The prince thought so as well. He told me to thank you."

"I'm pleased she liked it for even the brief time she gave it her attention."

Mrs. Dreyfus, red-eyed, head bowed, appeared in the doorway to announce dinner.

Royce thanked her, then turned to Lindsay. "You're so thin I can see your pelvic bones, and you're wearing those ridiculous high heels again. I told you before to take them off but you disobeyed me. You looked absurd then and you do now." But he didn't demand that she take them off this time. She'd won again, this time by omission.

Lindsay smiled. It was odd, but this time, somehow, he didn't seem to touch her so closely. She said simply, "I'm sorry you feel that way, Father."

Royce took Sydney's arm, and Holly and Lindsay followed them into the dining room. He didn't say another word. She felt his anger toward her, but again, it didn't come quite so close as it would have before. Lindsay felt a spurt of unaccustomed power. It felt good.

Holly said when they reached the dining room, "On Monday a decorator is coming, a friend of mine. I'm cleaning out this bloody officious room, every heavy dark corner of it."

"Oh, dear, I do trust you won't go with chintz, Holly," Sydney said, looking back at her stepmother.

Holly looked equal parts angry and hurt. She looked toward her husband for support, but he wasn't looking at her, but at Dorrey, the cook, who was placing a large rack of lamb before him on a huge silver serving tray. He was smiling at Dorrey and thanking her, telling her everything would be all right.

He turned to Sydney. "What is this about chintz?"

"I was just wondering aloud how Holly intended to decorate this room."

"Decorate this room?" Royce repeated slowly. He turned to his wife, an eyebrow rising. "Why, she isn't going to touch a thing. Not without my permission, in any case. Though it is rather dark and heavy in here, don't you think so, Sydney?"

"That's what your wife said."

"Well, doubtless she misunderstands the concepts of shadow and light. No matter."

Holly gasped, but father and daughter ignored her. "Tell me what you think should be done, Sydney," Royce said.

"Well," Sydney began, "I should give the room a lightness and spaciousness that the heavy dark pieces preclude. But there's a consideration of effect, Father, and of period." And she continued with a discussion of fabrics and "looks" and methods of changing lighting and tone and the feel of a room. "It takes time and thought and, of course, good taste. I think you should consider taking it on yourself, Father."

Royce nodded to her as he continued to carve the rack of lamb. "I just might, in time," he said.

"Do pass the vegetables, Holly dear," Sydney said. "That's right, pile up your plate with the green beans, not the potatoes."

"What do you mean, Royce, that you'll do the decorating?"

"Why, there was no ambiguity, was there?" Royce said to his wife.

Lindsay said aloud, "I would like to propose a toast. To Grandmother and to my mother. We will miss them."

Royce smiled at that and raised his wineglass. "How very pious that sounds. But as you wish, Lindsay, not that you ever really knew either of them. Of course, you didn't even bother coming home at Christmas, and your grandmother was very disappointed. She mentioned your absence once or twice, didn't she, Holly? As for your mother, I doubt she noticed your truancy, but one never knows with a drunk, does one?" He then sent a toast toward Holly.

It was as if a curtain had come down in a final call. It was as if the past was behind that curtain and wouldn't come into view again. It wouldn't reach her again. It was gone. Lindsay rose slowly, gently pushing her chair back from the table. She was no longer a child. She was an adult and she could do what she wished to do, and what she wished to do was leave this room with all its pain and ugliness. She said to the table at large, "What time is the funeral tomorrow?"

"At noon. Sit down, Lindsay."

"I think not, Father. At St. Mary's?"

"Yes. Sit down, my girl. You may put on your airs in New York, but I won't put up with your bad manners and

ill breeding here in my home. God, you're so much like
your mother."

"Thank you, Father," Lindsay said. "Good night," she
added to Sydney and Holly. A sedate walk, she said over
and over to herself as she walked from the dining room.
Keep it slow. You're an adult, not a child for him to intimidate or order around. Not anymore. She realized once she'd
reached her room that she was quite hungry. Thank God
for back stairs. She walked down to the kitchen, pausing
as she heard Mrs. Dreyfus saying to Dorrey, "The disre-
spect floors me, Dorrey, absolutely floors me. I won't stay
here now that Mrs. Gates is gone, dear lady. I'm giving the
current Mrs. Foxe my notice after the funeral on Friday."

"She'll not like that," Dorrey said with satisfaction.
"That'll leave the weekend for her to do for herself. No,
she'll not like that at all."

Good, Lindsay thought. She wouldn't be here for Holly
to fire her.

"Our Lindsay is better off in New York, I do know
that," Dorrey continued.

Since when had she become *our* Lindsay? she wondered. Dorrey had never shared home-baked cookies with
her when she was a child, the way they described in novels
or showed in movies. Anytime she'd come to the kitchen
she had promptly been ordered out.

"Probably so. Ah, but it's nice to see Sydney," Mrs.
Dreyfus said. "So beautiful, so perfect, and she's in all the
magazines, so lovely she is."

"So is our Lindsay," Dorrey said.

"Yes, I know, and she's a sweet girl. But Sydney is
different, you know that."

"Sometimes different as in plain old nasty," Dorrey
said.

Lindsay came into the kitchen. It wasn't that she was
necessarily averse to eavesdropping, she was simply afraid
if she continued to listen, she'd hate what she heard.

"Hi," she said, dredging up a smile. "I left the table
because it's a sniper's paradise in there. Is there something
I can eat for supper?"

She became the young lady of the house, deferred to,

seated at the butcher-block table, served, not allowed to do anything except lift her fork. No, she thought as she ate a goodly portion of Waldorf salad, she was no longer *our* Lindsay. She was one of *them*.

"You would like New York, Mrs. Dreyfus," Lindsay said, biting into one of Dorrey's homemade rolls that were better than anything Lindsay had ever had at home.

"Ha! That place of crime and sin! Ha!"

Lindsay grinned. "You can avoid crime if you're careful, and sin is fun."

"Miss Lindsay, don't talk like that. You're not sophisticated like Miss Sydney."

"No, that's true."

Once back in her bedroom, Lindsay called Taylor. He answered on the second ring and she was smiling even before he spoke.

"Is this that wonderful fiancée of mine who'd better be all right?"

"Yes, I'm okay."

Pause. "You hanging in there, sweetheart? Really?"

"Yes. My family . . . they snipe and carp and butcher each other verbally, me included . . . but you know something? It wasn't as important this time as it always has been. I'm coming home tomorrow night."

"The midnight flight?"

"Yes. You don't have to come for me, Taylor," she said, not meaning it and knowing she didn't sound like she meant it.

"Okay, I won't."

She sputtered into the phone. "You bastard!"

He laughed. "Of course I'll be there, grinning like a fool at your gate. Now, tell me what's happening there."

She didn't tell him. She couldn't.

After giving her plenty of empty air and encouraging sounds, Taylor gave up. "I had Chinese this evening with Enoch. He loves the apartment, says it's too high-brow for me, but suits you perfectly. He thought the new Persian rug in the living room showed my good taste. Oh, yeah, I thought my fortune cookie was particularly apt: 'You are an angel. Beware of those who collect feathers.' "

She laughed and he grinned into the phone, loving the sound, hearing the tension in her voice lighten. "Enoch and Sheila send their love."

They spoke of the weather, of things that weren't really important to either of them.

"I have a new case," Taylor said, so frustrated with the conversation or lack thereof that he was willing to try anything.

"What is it? Computer or P.I. stuff?"

"The latter. A man wants me to pin his wife. He's convinced she staged a robbery of their house, lifting everything valuable, including all her jewelry. It's weird, but hey, I thrive on weird. Anyway, I meet the lady tomorrow. I understand she's something of a *femme fatale*. Her husband also said straight out that she's got two lovers, not just the requisite one."

"Don't you become number three. Good luck." There was another long pause; then Lindsay said very quietly, "I really do miss you, Taylor, I really do."

"Same here," he said.

The following morning Lindsay didn't go downstairs until it was time to leave for the church.

She didn't own a black dress and decided in any case that her grandmother would have hated black. Unfortunately, she had no idea what her mother would have preferred. She wore pure white. She wore three-inch heels.

For once Sydney didn't say anything.

The service was elegant, discreet, and St. Mary's was crowded. Lindsay's father did, however, point out the young man who had been her mother's latest lover. "At least he put in an appearance. Shows respect. I trust the little bastard won't try for any of her money."

A society columnist from the *Chronicle*, Paula Kettering, came up to Lindsay after the service.

She said without preamble, "Your grandmother was a wonderful woman, Miss Foxe. I wanted to tell you that. She also believed you had what it took to succeed in anything you chose to do, and you have succeeded. She was very proud of you. And of your half-sister too, of course.

As I recall, she said, 'Sydney, La Principessa, will always land where her mink will soften her fall. Lindsay will abide. She's good at that.' Last year she consented to an interview with me and that's what she said. I wanted to tell you that."

Lindsay was stunned and pleased. Abide. Yes, that's what she seemed to be good at. She suddenly pictured her grandmother, very clearly, saying that. To her chagrin, she began to cry. Paula Kettering patted her shoulder. "I didn't mean to upset you, Miss Foxe, just to tell you . . ."

Lindsay got hold of herself and thanked the woman. Finally, aeons later, the family arrived back at the mansion. The only addition to their party was Mr. Grayson Delmartin, Gates Foxe's lawyer since 1959 when a drunk had run into the beautiful rhododendron bushes in front of the mansion and then sued her. Grayson Delmartin had proved to be a crackerjack, Gates said, forcing the drunk man to pay restitution for the destroyed plants.

Lindsay was on the point of going upstairs to pack her few things when Mr. Delmartin called after her, "Just a moment, Lindsay. I know you wish to be alone, my dear, but there's the reading of the will. All family members are required to be present. Please come into the library."

Who cared? But she went and seated herself behind her father and Holly and Sydney.

There were bequests to Mrs. Dreyfus, to Dorrey, and to Lansford, the retired butler. There were bequests to the organizations Gates Foxe had belonged to and helped run over the years. There were charitable foundations, environmental gifts. When the list had finally ended, Mr. Delmartin raised his thin face and removed his glasses. He looked at each of them in turn. He spoke slowly, as if measuring each word, as he probably was, Lindsay thought. "I don't know if even you, Judge Foxe, know the extent of your mother's holdings. They were, in a word, vast. She has always had the knack of choosing good financial advisers over the years and has prospered, adding to the fortune left her by her late husband."

Royce said in his best unctuous voice, "She was a

bright old woman. She was also renowned for her luck. Get to the point, Grayson."

Mr. Delmartin didn't look at all affronted. He put his glasses back on, picked up the thick sheaf of bound papers, and read:

" 'I leave one million dollars to my son, Royce Chandliss Foxe. I leave one million dollars to my ex-daughter-in-law, Jennifer Foxe. I leave one million dollars to my current daughter-in-law, Holly Foxe. I leave one million dollars to my eldest granddaughter, Sydney Foxe di Contini. I leave five million dollars to my great-granddaughter, Melissa di Contini. Finally, I leave my home, located at 358 Bayberry Street, to my granddaughter, Lindsay Foxe. Also I leave to her, free and clear, the remainder of my holdings, both financial and real, to do with as she pleases. She has kindness, and perhaps in the years to come she will gain wisdom and perspective and understanding of those around her. I hope that her inheritance will aid her in achieving happiness and the security she deserves."

There was utter silence, impenetrable and disbelieving. Incredulous silence, silence that was like the eye of a storm. Dark feelings swirled and the silence was thickening, becoming acid and ugly. Then it seemed that everyone spoke at once.

Holly shot up from her chair, nearly knocking it over, her heavy face mottled with angry color. "But that's absurd! Giving Lindsay this mansion! That's impossible, I want to redecorate it!"

Royce grabbed her arm, pulling her back down. "My wife is perhaps unwise in her choice of words, Delmartin, but nonetheless, what she says is true. Leaving Lindsay anything is absurd. Leaving me, her only son, her heir, a paltry million dollars? Explain, now."

Grayson Delmartin went through his ritual of removing his glasses, giving himself time to think before he spoke. "I was Mrs. Foxe's lawyer, Judge Foxe, not her financial adviser or her family confessor—"

"Bullshit! You advised her all the bloody time! Are you responsible for this travesty?" He stared a moment toward Lindsay. His eyes darkened—her eyes—the blue deep now, turbulent with anger. "What's your problem, Delmartin? Do you have a thing for girls who are over six feet tall and naive and stunted?"

Lindsay rocked back in her chair. She stared at her father, knowing she shouldn't be surprised at anything he said, but this ruthlessness, this cruelty . . .

"Judge Foxe," Grayson Delmartin said, "I beg you moderate your language and your opinions. Miss Lindsay Foxe is your daughter, not some sort of interloper who had no claim on the family. She is also Gates Foxe's granddaughter. She is now very wealthy because she is also the sole inheritor of her mother, Jennifer Foxe. Since she is the sole beneficiary, I will cover it with her in private when we have finished with this."

"Lunacy!" Holly shrieked. "Sheer wickedness! I won't have it! That damned old lady! I'll kill her!"

"We won't ever be finished with this," Royce said. He turned to Sydney. "Well, what do you think? You haven't said a word. One million, Sydney, just one fucking million dollars. Jesus, and five million to your daughter! I'll just bet the old bitch tied up that money so you'll never see a dime of it. Probably Melissa won't either until she's twenty-five. What the hell are you going to do?"

Sydney just smiled gently at her father. She looked like the princess she was—cool, aloof, dignified, well-bred to her Gucci-shod toes. She turned toward her half-sister, her posture, her voice composed, gracious, soft. "Congratulations, Lindsay. It appears that you have quite shown all of us, haven't you? Grandmother used to speak of waters running deep in some people. I never really understood what she meant until now. In any case, I do commend you for your outstanding manipulations and congratulate you."

"I didn't do anything. I have no deep-running waters, that's nonsense and you know it, Sydney. There were no manipulations. My God, this is more a surprise to me than to any of you."                                          .

"Ah, at last some truth out of you, Lindsay," Royce said. "Excellent." He rose with swift grace and strode over to stand over her. "Prove your honesty, your sincerity. Sign over your inheritance to me—to your father—to whom it should have gone in the first place. It isn't right that you take my place in line. You will correct it now."

Grayson Delmartin jumped to his feet. "Now, just a moment, Judge Foxe! I highly disapprove of this. You mustn't try to coerce your daughter, particularly at a time like this. Such intimidation tactics are highly inappropriate and—"

"Stuff a sock in it!" Holly yelled at him. "Just shut up, damn you, you worthless old sod! Is Lindsay paying you a percentage for this? Did you doctor up this supposed will in her favor?"

Mr. Delmartin pursed his mouth closed. He gathered the papers together, taking his time, straightening each sheet perfectly, calming himself. He was trembling, which was strange to him, because he'd been in the eye of family will-reading storms before, some much worse in acrimony than this one. But the Foxes were supposed to be different. Money, he thought, money was the very devil. It blackened and tarnished and corrupted. It inflicted wounds that would never heal. He finished his straightening. He turned to Lindsay Foxe, who was sitting like a statue in a straight-backed chair. "Will you please come with me now, Lindsay?"

"Yes," she said. "I'm coming."

Royce didn't step back. His hands were fisted at his sides. His face was pale, his eyes hard and ugly. "You damned little slut, you no-account little bitch! Little, ha! You just stay where you are! I knew you were a hypocrite, a fraud, nothing more than a mealymouthed little thief. Jesus, I can't believe you'd steal from your own father, steal *my* birthright. More fool I . . ." He slapped his palm against his forehead and delivered his blow, his voice low now: "However, blood will tell, won't it? How could I forget? Didn't you seduce your own sister's husband? Didn't you force her to shoot him because of what you'd done? Didn't you prove exactly what you were when you were eighteen years old? Jesus, you're despicable, Lindsay. I disown you!"

"If you disown her, Judge Foxe, you would no longer be a member of her family and thus she wouldn't have any obligation, either moral or legal, to leave you a bloody nickel in her will. Were she to die and leave you nothing, you would have no legal grounds to contest it. You would, in short, be a laughingstock."

Mr. Delmartin was pleased with his own parting shot. As for Judge Foxe, he looked distinctly displeased with himself and his loss of control. Good, Grayson Delmartin thought as he offered Lindsay his arm. Let the good judge stew on that. Together they left the library. Lindsay was stiff and pale as death, and she stared straight ahead. He led her to the drawing room as a person would another who was blind.

He sat her in a chair and pulled up another opposite her. He took her hands in his as he spoke. Lindsay pulled hers away, unable to bear a touch that brought her here, to the present, to the incredible present that had left everything destroyed, in tatters. But there was no lessening of the shock. Jennifer Foxe had left her daughter an estate nearing five million dollars, after taxes, and a paid-for penthouse condominium on Russian Hill.

Lindsay couldn't take it in. She just sat there, her hands folded in her lap, looking at the painting of her grandfather over the fireplace. Her grandmother had appeared to love this painting. Lindsay could remember her standing here just looking at it, not moving, staring and staring. She'd always wondered what her grandmother was thinking.

"Do you understand?" Delmartin asked, his voice gentle.

"Yes, but it makes no sense." She turned and gave him a grave smile. "It really makes no difference, though, does it? To anything. My father has always disliked me. I just didn't realize how much he hated me, how much contempt he felt for me until today. Even if Grandmother had left me a million dollars like everyone else, even if she had left him the bulk of everything, he still would have yelled and screamed at me and hated me."

"Probably," Grayson said, his voice cool and matter-of-fact. "I have heard from financial rumblings that your father needs a sturdy influx of money. It seems he doesn't have your grandmother's cunning."

"But one million—"

"One million dollars is nothing more than a finger in the dam, so I hear. Now, this notion of giving all your inheritance to him—I advise you strongly against it. As you said, what would it change? You think to buy his love? It wouldn't, you know, and I think you're smart enough to realize that. Nor would it buy his respect. It would buy exactly nothing. I think you should return to New York, Lindsay, and do some thinking. Your Grandmother has laid a heavy burden on your shoulders. Here is my card with my private number at home. I will be here for you, Lindsay.

"I shouldn't say this, but I must. Don't let your father intimidate you. Don't let him make you feel guilty. Don't let him destroy you with that old scandal in Paris. I know it was all twisted from the truth. Your grandmother told me that. Will you promise me?"

She gave him a look of naked pain.

"Promise me," he repeated.

"All right. I promise."

"Good. When are you going back to New York?"

"Now."

"Er, what about the house?"

She stared at him blankly.

"This house, the Foxe mansion. You own it. It's all yours, free and clear. Your father and his wife live here. What do you want to do?"

She waved a vague hand. "I don't know. As you say, they live here. Let them stay. I can't quite imagine going in the library now and informing them to be out by three o'clock."

Grayson Delmartin thought evicting Judge Foxe would provide him the most satisfaction he'd had in a good ten years. "Do you wish me to instruct Mrs. Foxe that no changes are to be made without your express permission in writing?"

She looked up again at her grandfather's painting. Would Holly send it to the trash bin if she had her way? "Whatever you believe appropriate, Mr. Delmartin. No, I don't want any changes, at least not yet. Yes, in writing. That makes it very official."

"Good, good." He rose and offered Lindsay his hand.

"I will wait here until you're packed. Then I will drive you to the airport."

She smiled. "Ah, my protector from the ravening wolves."

"Yes, exactly." Telling Mrs. Foxe she couldn't lay a fat finger on the house would also give him some satisfaction. At least enough for now.

As he drove the very wealthy Miss Foxe to the San Francisco airport, Grayson Delmartin hoped that she had a protector in New York. She needed one, at least until she got herself on an even keel. He'd forgotten the scandal about the prince and his rape of an eighteen-year-old Lindsay. He shook his head. Jesus, a father calling his daughter a slut. It defied any logic he knew of and it defied any understanding Grayson could bring to bear on Judge Royce Foxe's dislike of his younger daughter.

The man, he thought dispassionately, was a shit.

It was on the way to the airport that Lindsay realized exactly what it was her grandmother had done for her: she'd given her power, ultimate power, the only kind of power Gates Foxe had understood, and she'd given it free and clear with no strings. Power. Lindsay smiled. Immense power, but now she had no need of it. She wished she could tell it to her grandmother now, but it was too late. Power wasn't to Lindsay what it was to Gates Foxe. To her it was understanding and acceptance of things she couldn't change. It was overcoming fear, putting the pain of her father's words behind that curtain she'd seen so clearly in the dining room the night before. Power was not letting the past obstruct the future. Power was knowledge of oneself, of what one was, of what one could become. Power was seeing her family as they really were, namely, jerks, and accepting that they'd never change. *And it wasn't her fault.* She didn't have to play their endless destructive games. She was free of them. She drew a deep, clean breath. Delmartin looked sharply at her, but when she just shook her head, he remained quiet.

To her utter surprise, Lindsay slept most of the way back to New York. She didn't dream. She didn't cry anymore. She felt numb, then she slept. The last half-hour of the flight, she was in that vague semiawake state, and all her thoughts were focused on Taylor.

She wanted to see him. She wanted to be close to him. She wanted to touch him, breathe in his scent. She wanted to know that she wasn't alone. Always alone, she thought. God, she wanted Taylor.

It was just after midnight when she came through the gate tunnel. She knew she was hurrying, she couldn't help it. She wanted Taylor, and even a second longer to wait was too long. She nearly tripped once and felt a man's hand grab her arm, to straighten her back up. She smiled her thanks, her eyes darting beyond him, and kept hurrying.

He was there, leaning against one of the concrete posts, his arms crossed, his expression intent.

She paused, looking directly at him. For the first time since she'd met him, she really saw him, saw to the bone and marrow of him, to the toughness and kindness of him, to the essence of him, and she felt something wild and heavy beat steady within her.

She took a step forward, still staring at him, not understanding really, but wanting him more than anything. He'd said nothing, hadn't moved. His head was cocked now to one side as he watched her.

She dropped her bag and simply ran to him. He was a man of quick reaction time and he lifted her up against him, squeezing her so tightly she gasped for breath. When he lowered her, he felt the warmth and softness of her body and he felt something else. He felt urgency in her, and power and a frenzy, a wildness that had brought her to the edge. She didn't lose her hold around his neck. Then she was kissing him all over his face, and he felt the heat of her mouth, the heat of her body.

Sweet Jesus, he thought, his mouth opening to her urging. He allowed himself for the first time since he'd known her to let go, to react as he wanted to, to show her how much he wanted her, to forget control, to forget scaring her. He wanted her with all the pent-up madness in him, and . . .

He moaned in her mouth, his hands now frantic on her back. He became aware of a laugh, and slowly, hating to be parted from her, Taylor raised his head. It took him an instant to focus his mind and his eyes. They were in the middle of Kennedy airport and any minute now he imagined he could very easily pull her pants down, open his, and burst into her.

He drew a deep breath, took her face between his palms and kissed her lightly—her nose, chin, cheeks— smoothed her eyebrows with his thumbs.

"Welcome home, sweetheart. I've missed you."

"Take me home, Taylor, now, please, home." He'd never heard her voice so low, nearly ugly in its hoarseness. He felt himself responding with a recklessness he didn't know was in him. He grabbed her bag in his right hand, her hand in his left, and dragged her toward the exit.

They were nearly running, saying nothing. She focused on the utterly alien feelings shocking through her, but not hesitating, no, she wanted this—whatever it was—and there was no fear, no sense of revulsion. There was only Taylor and he would take care of her and give her what she wanted, what she needed. She was breathing hard, then harder still. His fingers tightened around hers.

She looked at his profile, saw the flush on his cheeks, saw his partially open mouth. Dear God, she wanted to touch him, feel all of him, stroke her fingers down his belly, stroke his penis and make him hard and harder still, and bring him inside her. Yes, yes, oh God, yes . . .

Time suspended itself. Traffic went by the car in a blur of midnight sights and sounds. He was driving too quickly, his hands, both of them, clutching the steering wheel, his knuckles white. There was nothing but her, there was nothing in the world but her.

Lindsay stared straight ahead. She felt the strange rhythms in her body, pounding deep and deeper still, and she didn't question them, rather she breathed fast and harsh, feeling him next to her, smelling the man scent of him, her fingers clenching, wanting to touch him, to feel him touching her.

Suddenly, not more than a block from their apartment, she turned to face him and said only, "Taylor." She swallowed; there was nothing else she could say.

"Yes, Eden. Not long now. Not long."

They were breathless with their dash to the front door of their apartment. It took him too long to get the front door unlocked. He dropped her bag to the hardwood floor, kicked the door shut with his foot and grabbed her. She came fully and completely against him and he realized for the first time that they fitted perfectly together. But the clothes . . . God, the damned clothes. He wanted her naked flesh in his hands, pressed against him. All of her, this instant, heated flesh against him, smooth flesh, her flesh . . .

"Taylor," she said again, and this time she grabbed his hand and together they raced toward the bedroom. She drew him on top of her on the bed and he was heavy and hard against her and Lindsay knew she'd never imagined anything so wonderful as this. He kissed her, not lightly as was his habit, but deep, thrusting his tongue into her mouth, feeling her surprise at the touch of him, knowing that she'd never done this before, never allowed it, but now, with him, she did.

He was trembling with the force of his feelings, the surging lust that was making his heart pound and his loins painful and heavy. His hands were on her breasts now, kneading them, caressing them, tugging gently at her nipples through her clothes. "Too much," he whispered. The clothes were too much. "Yes, oh yes." Lindsay bucked him off her to his side and her fingers were frenzied on the buttons of his shirt, then with a whimper of frustration she began yanking futilely on the zipper of his pants.

All that she was, all that had lain buried so deeply within her, was in the open now, raw and painfully sharp, and she was whimpering with the frantic need that was driving her beyond anything she'd ever known, beyond anything she could have ever believed existed.

Taylor couldn't bear it any longer. He reared back off the bed, thrust his hands beneath her sweater to her slacks, and nearly ripped them open. He jerked them down her legs, bringing her panties with them, and her knee socks. He'd forgotten her boots and cursed, then yanked them off. In an instant she was naked to her waist and she was sitting up, grabbing at his pants and watching him as he jerked off his coat and his sweater.

"Taylor, please."

He couldn't stand it for another moment. He unzipped his pants and freed his sex. She stared at his engorged penis and there was such hunger on her face that he moaned. He came down over her, parting her legs wide.

"Eden, oh sweet Jesus, now." And he parted her with shaking warm fingers and came into her, powerfully, in one long sure thrust.

She yelled, arching off the bed. At the same time her arms were around his back and she was pushing upward, helplessly, not knowing what to do, but allowing the sensations to pour through her, and she felt him so deep inside her. She was pulsing and breathing so hard she thought she would die of it, but all she could think of was the power of him, the heat from him, the depth of his sex, pumping hard inside her, and she moaned and moaned, not ever wanting it to stop, but wanting something, something, that was building and bloating inside her, pushing hard at her, pushing . . .

He was over her, his face flushed with his passion, and then he came down with all his weight now, so very deep inside her, and he began kissing her hard, then shuddering and pulling back, and kissing her with a tenderness that made her arch upward against him, drawing him deeper and deeper. And it was simply too much. "Come now, Eden, come to me." In the next instant, his fingers were between their bodies and he'd found her and she was wet and swelled and he thought he'd die with the wonder of it. He caressed her woman's flesh and she was crying now, her chest heaving, her raw moans filling the silent air, and he said again and again, "Come to me now, sweetheart. Yes, come to me. Give it up. Yes, come, come, come . . . trust me, trust me."

She did with a soul-deep shudder. Her eyes went blank and glazed. "Taylor!" She arched upward, her hips moving wildly against his fingers, drawing him even more deeply into her, and her muscles were contracting and he knew that it was all over for him. When her screams burst over him, he let himself go and heaved and threw back his head, yelling his climax, and he knew even as he exploded inside her that this was her first orgasm and that he had given it to her and that something had happened to bring her to him in this wild frenzy, but he wouldn't think of it now, oh no.

And as he quieted, she said into his mouth, "My name is Lindsay, not Lynn. I hate Eden. Please, my name is Lindsay."

"I love you, Lindsay," he said and in so saying it, he offered her all of him, without reservations and forever.

"And I you," she said, her voice hoarse and raw and dazed, her tongue warm in his mouth, and she was licking his upper lip, his tongue, nipping his chin, and she was tightening beneath him yet again.

"I want to feel all of you," he said, and pulled out of her.

# 17

## TAYLOR / LINDSAY

It was beating wildly inside her again, this need, this urgency, this all-consuming wanting of this man. The orgasm that had hit her hard had dazed her, leaving her shaking and hot and strangely fluid, and she hadn't really understood what had happened but knew that it was going to happen again. This frenzy, it was building fast inside her. She didn't question it, didn't hesitate for an instant. She came up and began ripping off her clothes.

"Yes," she said, all her concentration on getting her bra off, "I want to feel you, Taylor, I want to know everything about you, everything . . . to touch you, your belly is so beautiful and hard and . . ."

He paused an instant, his breath coming fast again and faster still as he listened to her. He didn't question that he wanted her again, as fiercely as he had but minutes before. Blood was pumping through him, and his skin felt itchy and hot. He felt incredibly strong. He watched her tugging clumsily at her bra. He laughed and slapped away her hands. It was a front clasp and he slid it quickly open, and he pushed it back and stared at her breasts, just stared, gulping, his lips moving because he wanted her in his mouth, to suck and caress. His hands cupped them, weighing them, holding them, filling his hands with her, and he groaned.

"Hurry," she gasped. "Oh, hurry, please, Taylor."

And he did. When he came over her, her legs parted for him and he fitted between them and he felt all of her, her breasts against his bare chest, her belly against his, the length of her legs against his, and he closed his eyes at the intensity of the feelings crashing through him.

"Ah, Lindsay, damn, I'd thought to make this time slow and sweet."

"No," she said, pushing at him, trying to touch him with her fingers. He pushed up on his elbows and felt her hands thrust between their bellies and close around him. His eyes closed and he felt himself pushing against her soft hands, his breath heaving, quickening, and he had to jerk away because in another moment or so he would come again. "I can't, dear God, stop it, sweetheart. Come over me, now." He pulled her over on top of him.

He saw she didn't understand. "Come up on your knees and bring me inside you. Then you can move the way you want to."

She glowed at his words, her eyes as deep and hot as her body, and he saw the intense passion in her and it was dazzling. He watched her stare at his penis, then clasp him, and still she stared at him, her look absorbed and intent and eager. He watched her come up on her knees, saw her ease him between her widespread legs. He felt the heat of her as she slid him inside her. He'd known that heat would be there for him, and so it was, incredible and dark and smooth, this welcoming of hers. He felt the wet of his seed, and the wet of her, he supposed, a woman's moistness, and the heat that was pouring onto him, and into him, and it eased his way. He didn't think he could hold on. He grasped her hips suddenly in his hands and in a furious downward motion brought her down hard on him as he jerked up.

She yelled, her back arched. He looked up to see her breasts thrusting out, her head thrown back, her lips parted. She looked pagan with all that thick waving hair like a nimbus around her head. She looked like a woman who had no thought beyond his penis pumping inside her and the pleasure she was drawing from him. He worked her, showing her how to move on him, then paused. He raised his hand. He smiled up at her when, lightly, with a tempter's touch, his fingertips found her clitoris and gently squeezed.

"Taylor!" She yelled and bucked and heaved, and he went over the edge.

She was bouncing on him, her palms flat on his chest, and she was staring at him, seeing him climax, and then Lindsay felt the pressure build higher and higher still until she couldn't contain it anymore. His fingers were fast and hard, then slow and easy on her, and she yelled again and again, rocking against him, madly, senseless with the lust that drove her.

He peaked before she did and lay quietly, watching her as her climax took her, watching her as the deep quivers slowly lessened and her legs relaxed their grip around his hips. She was staring down at her hands, palms flat on his belly. Jesus, he thought, gazing up at her. It was unbelievable, this insane and uncontrolled passion, but he would accept it, willingly, as he accepted her.

He released her hips, saw that there would be bruises on her white flesh, and slid his hands upward to cup her breasts. She quivered again and he smiled.

"You're very responsive," he said in the greatest understatement of his life, and he had to laugh at himself. "You're wonderful, Lindsay."

"Not like you," she said, her mouth dry, her mind sluggish, her body growing more limp with exhaustion by the moment. "Not like you."

"Give me your breasts. That's it, lean down. Good." And he took her nipple in his mouth and she jerked with the shock of it, the newness of it, the utter amazement of it, until she could take no more. Her body had stopped.

She fell atop him, sprawling loosely, covering him, and he touched her hair, stroked his hands down her back, and felt himself still deep inside her.

She'd been so tight that first time. Like a virgin. No,

not a virgin, but like a woman who hadn't had sex in a very, very long time.

She'd had two orgasms. He wanted to dance and shout. He wanted to give her ten more. Tonight. Instead, he eased her onto her back and came out of her. She moaned, throwing her arm over her eyes.

"Don't move," he said.

She could only moan again, drawing her knees up.

When he came back, he gently spread her onto her back again and pressed a warm washcloth against her, wiping away his seed, but not the heat, oh, no, not the heat of her. He pictured making love to her in the summer, when the outward heat would consume them and they would sweat and heave together and meld and become one. He quivered at the thought. He looked down at her sprawled on her back, those long legs of hers, so beautifully formed, slender thighs, and the softness of her, the streaked blond hair that covered her woman's mound. She was too thin, but he didn't care. Even her ribs made him want to come inside her again. And her breasts. Fuller than he expected and round, her nipples a light soft pink. He leaned down and took her nipple in his mouth.

She lurched up, gasping. "Please, Taylor. *Oh, God!*"

The responsiveness of her made him want to shout.

She was tugging at his head, whispering, "Goodness . . . why won't it stop? Why, Taylor? I don't understand, oh, God, it's splendid. Don't let it end."

She was babbling with her discovery of it but he knew she was also exhausted. No wonder. He didn't know what had happened to her in San Francisco. Whatever it was had pushed her to him, completely, openly. "No, love. I'm sorry, forgive me, but you're so beautiful. Not now, not yet." He gently pushed her back down, tossed the washcloth onto the floor, and managed to get both of them under the covers. Within minutes they were asleep, wrapped in each other, close and warm and together.

Taylor fought the urge to come inside her again, but he didn't want to sleep either. He had to think because he had this stark feeling that when she awoke in the morning she wouldn't think, she would simply react and that reaction would be one of cold logic, that or cold fear, fear shaped from the past. He put himself to imagining what she would think tomorrow. After she'd behaved in the dark of the night like the most impassioned of lovers, like a woman to whom sex was the greatest thing in the world, and she'd just discovered it and couldn't, quite simply, get enough of him. He smiled, a sated smile, one tinged with a good deal of satisfaction, but it faded as his worry grew. He had to bind her to him. He had to make her trust him. Hell, at least she'd told him her name. But it wasn't enough. The secrets, the puzzles, had to be solved. He shook his head. His brain felt like mush. She'd behaved completely out of the character she'd created for herself. But created when? Why? Nor did he know what had triggered this change in her. Then, quite suddenly, he didn't care. None of the other mattered, just having her with him, next to him, wrapped around him, here now, and now, now . . .

He felt her breasts against his chest, felt her leg between his. What the hell, he thought, and gave in. Slowly, gently, he came over her, spreading her onto her back, and slipped slowly and deeply inside her. This time he could feel the stretching of her flesh to accommodate him. Sweet Jesus, she was soft, and that incredible heat of hers made him want to pound deep and not stop. He'd been so frantic before, he hadn't really felt the tight flesh that surrounded him, the slickness of her, he'd been aware of an incredible tightness that had driven him insane, but he was now aware of every bit of her. He closed his eyes against the wonder of her.

Then she awoke. He felt her muscles clench spasmodically around him. She didn't, couldn't, have any idea what that did to him. He rode her gently, not so deep this time, but still he felt his body clenching, tightening, felt his heart pound harder and harder, and knew he would leave her if he didn't stop, if he didn't pull out of her now. He quickly eased out of her, came down between her legs to put his mouth on her, knowing she would welcome him. She was sleepy, sated, she wanted him again, and it was dark and hidden, and she was safe with him and she knew it.

She came in soft shudders. Then, to his surprise, as he prepared to ease his rhythm, to bring her down, to soothe her, she came again, her hips lurching upward, reaching a higher level, and he felt the deep flexing of her legs, the tightening of her muscles, the rippling of her flesh. Her hands fisted his hair and he breathed his hot breath against her and she came again. Arching and jerking, she was caught, by him, within herself, and when she quieted this time, he slid into her again, riding her deeply and silently, and spilling himself with gentle shudders deep inside her.

He had no more thoughts. She was against him, part of him, her warm breath against his throat, and when he had climaxed, when his own breathing finally slowed, he smiled down at her, for she was asleep. He joined her and they slept deeply.

Taylor awoke with a start, jerking upright, immediately alert. He whipped about, but he knew he was too late. Eden . . . No, not Eden and not Lynn. She was Lindsay and she wasn't there. He felt her pillow. It was still warm, the indentation of her head still clear. God, he prayed she hadn't run out on him. He cursed himself for not waking when she'd left the bed, for not feeling the emptiness when she'd left him. He prayed he wasn't too late.

He threw back the covers and ran stark naked out of the bedroom. He ran down the long corridor toward the front door, and right into her, nearly knocking her down. She was ready to walk out the door, dressed, in her winter coat and boots and gloves, her huge bag over her shoulder.

He grabbed her arm, twisting her around.

Her face was white. Fear filled her eyes, fear and something else—something wrenching and frightening was there in her eyes. He ignored it.

He grabbed her other arm. "Where the hell do you think you're going?"

She tried to pull away but he didn't ease his grip. "Don't you know about lovers' etiquette? Rule one is you don't run out. You don't pull a disappearing act because you can't face things, can't face what you—yeah you, Lindsay—wanted to do and did with great enthusiasm and energy and passion. No, dammit, hold still. I'm not letting you go anywhere, so don't try. Come with me. I'm naked and it's cold and you belong with me, back in bed. Don't fight me, damn you."

He dragged her back to the bedroom. She dug in her boot heels, but it didn't help. He was strong and mad and determined. She hadn't said a word, hadn't made a single sound. There was just her harsh deep breathing. Once he got her in the bedroom, he slammed the door and locked it. He threw the key under the bed. He pulled her bag off her shoulder, then unleashed the strength he'd always controlled around her. He got her out of her coat and gloves and scarf. She was wearing a bulky wool sweater beneath, and tight blue jeans and boots.

He shoved her down onto the bed. She leapt up, only to have him shove her down again. She kicked out and got his thigh. He winced and cursed, realizing in that moment she knew karate, yet she wasn't out to shred him. No, she battered him with her fists, but even then she was careful. A good sign, he supposed as he grabbed her right leg, held it up by shoving her flat on her back, knocking the breath out of her, and pulling off the boot. He got the other one off the same way. "Now," he said, and grabbed her sweater. "Progress, at last."

She began to fight him in earnest now. Still, she said nothing, struggling and twisting and striking out in an eerie silence that he refused to acknowledge. Her blue jeans were tough because they were so bloody tight, but he got them off her despite her fighting him, peeling them down inside out. He'd carry bruises from this, but what the hell. He saw the bruises he'd made on her hips from the previous night. He wondered if she'd noticed, and remembered her frantic movements, riding him, letting him work her up and down on him, his fingers digging into her flesh, all while she'd shouted and moaned and arched wildly in her passion.

He left her knee socks and her panties on. She hadn't bothered with a bra, just a light wool teddy. He was in no mood for niceties now. He ripped it off.

"Now," he said again, and brought her under the covers with him, holding her, stiff and hard and withdrawn, against him. It made him furious and he bellowed, "Feel me, damn you, Lindsay!" He pressed his hand against her hips, pressing her into his belly, against his hard penis. "I'm yours, dammit, and this body of mine is also yours and I'm not about to let you use me to cure whatever devils were chasing you last night. I'm not about to let you enjoy four damned orgasms that I give to you and then run out on me as if nothing happened. Do you hear me, you damned twit?"

"You're yelling, of course I hear you. You needn't use profanity."

"Good, at least now you're talking. Dammit. No, that isn't profanity, that's just appropriate exclamations. No, dammit, don't struggle because you won't get away from me. I like your belly against me; just get used to it. You've already bruised the hell out of me. You're a dirty fighter, Lindsay, and those long legs of yours reached every part of me. But I've got meaner, nastier experience, so forget trying to get away from me again. Put your head on my shoulder and relax. Do it, damn you! There, that's better."

He could feel her hitching breath, nearly taste the uncertainty, the fear in her. Fear of him? No, more probably it was fear of herself, fear of a past that had colored her every action for years now. Finally her breathing slowed. He kept quiet, content to stroke her until she had eased against him, her muscles loose again.

"Now that you're back where you belong, I've got something to tell you."

He didn't say a word. Finally she said, "What?"

He still held silent.

"What do you have to tell me?"

He kissed the top of her head and squeezed his arms around her back. "You're the best lay I've ever had in my life."

She froze on him, going stiff, and he simply held her. Hell, it was the truth, and some unvarnished truth was good for her. "In addition," he continued after several moments of her rigid silence, "it's a relief that you and I are magic in bed, since we're going to be spending the next fifty years together. Don't you agree?"

"I don't know."

"Sure you do. You enjoyed yourself last night. Good God, woman, you had four orgasms!"

"No, no, please don't say that, Taylor. I don't understand any of it, not me, not why or how. Last night . . . all during the night, I just don't know. It was five."

Good start, he thought, grinning as he kissed her ear and said, "Okay, five orgasms. I would have preferred an even half-dozen. Oh, yeah, I like your real name. When I thought it was Lynn, I was willing to accept it because it was who you were. But I must say that Lindsay suits you much better. Yes, I like you as a Lindsay." When she remained quiet, he continued easily, in a chatty voice, "When you feel like telling me the rest of it, I'm here with ears on alert. I suppose that's why you've kept your mail from coming here. I suppose that's why you signed the apartment lease with one eye on me and your hand curved over your signature. No matter, tell me when you want to. I swear I won't go find out on my own, and you know I could, being an ex-cop and a P.I. and a computer hacker on top of all that. I could find out who you are in about three minutes, probably less. I could have found out two months ago. But I didn't. It's been a real test of my beliefs in the right to privacy not to find out before."

She stirred against him, not trying to pull away, just her body showing her restless thought, her uncertainty, but she said finally, "I meant to tell you my name. It's just that it was never the right time and I was afraid that you'd know the moment you heard it, or you'd find out and hate me and—"

He needed time to sort through what she'd said, but he didn't have it. "I know, I got you in a weak moment." What did she mean that he'd hate her if he found out who she was? The Son of Sam's daughter? Jackie Kennedy Onassis' illegitimate offspring? Taylor hated unsolved mysteries. They begged to be resolved and there was nothing he liked better than figuring them out to the very last loose end, the very last question. He regretted giving her his word. Damnable trust.

"I didn't want you to make love to Eden. She isn't real,

she's nothing really, just a chimera, a fake, and I couldn't stand it."

He hugged her again. "Well, you told me soon enough. I knew it was you, and you are real, Lindsay, very real and all mine." He began stroking his hand up and down her back. "I bruised your hips. You can see clearly the outline of my fingers. Did you notice?"

He felt her nod against his throat.

"I didn't use anything, I'm sorry. Seeing you, knowing you wanted me, the urgency of it all . . . well, I lost it and I didn't use anything. Depending on the time of the month it is for you, I could have gotten you very pregnant last night."

He waited, absorbing her silent shock, and hoping. To his utter delight, she didn't blow a fit, nor did she withdraw from him. She was silent as a stone but he was used to that. He knew she was thinking. And she was. Lindsay was remembering the nurse in the emergency room and the pill she'd been given to prevent pregnancy. To prevent her bearing the prince's child. To prevent her having to have an abortion. She closed her eyes, willing the memory away. And now again, only this time she'd been a willing participant. Taylor's child. Her mind chilled and went blank.

He waited.

"I'm hard again, as I'm sure you can feel. Do you want me to come inside you, in the morning light, so I can see you clearly and watch you climax? And you can see me clearly?"

She trembled at his words and he felt a very clean surge of pure triumph.

He turned and looked at her beloved face. No makeup, and she looked beautiful. Her hair was loose and wild and deeply waving, thick around her face and over her shoulders. Her eyes were a deep blue, glistening with what he hoped was burgeoning desire. He would soon see. He kissed her, feeling her draw back for a moment, then lean into him, her breasts heaving a bit as she did so. He deepened the kiss, touching his tongue to her lower lip, urging her to open her mouth. She did, but only for an instant.

Then, suddenly, she lurched back, rolling off the bed in her haste to get away from him.

She made a grab for the covers but went to the floor without them. He laughed and rolled over, staring down at her. "You don't have to leap away from me. All you have to do is tell me what you didn't like and I'll fix it. I'm good, Lindsay, and I do want to please you."

She was sitting there on the six-by-nine Bokara carpet, in the midst of that deep red, clad only in dark blue knee socks and panties. She was panting and her eyes were dilated. Her hands were fisted on her thighs. And she looked humiliated.

Not that, no, anything but that. He couldn't stand that. "Come here, sweetheart. You don't want sex now? No problem. You did have a good dose last night." He held out his hand to her. She stared at his hand, as if trying to determine what it was. His hand was square, the back sprinkled with black hair, the fingers long, the nails short and buffed. Beautiful hands, a man's hands, and a man could hurt her with those hands, hurt her like the prince had hurt her. She sobbed aloud and crawled away from him, then rose and ran for the bathroom.

"Well, shit," Taylor said.

Since he had a clear view of the bathroom door, he wasn't worried that she could sneak out on him again. Besides, the key to the bedroom door was safely under the bed. He pulled the covers to his chest, fluffed up the pillows behind his head, and lay there watching that damned closed door. He began to speak, of anything that came into his mind. "Lindsay? I guess you can hear me through the door. Did I tell you that my mom was an opera singer? She was really quite good—a soprano, you know. She performed with Beverly Sills, Carlo Panchi, and a bunch of other greats. Her stage name was Isabella Gilliam. Have you ever heard of her? She died in the early eighties, my dad too, in a plane crash in Arizona. Dad was also so proud of her, and you want to know something? He hated opera. But he never let Mom know that. Whenever I remember the two of them now, I wonder if she did know how painful every opera was for him to sit through and I wonder if she

simply pretended not to know so he wouldn't realize that
she knew. You know what I mean? Did you want to tell
me what you think?"

Silence. Then he heard the shower go on.

Well, enough conversation. He'd been weaving a hopeful dream of unreal cloth to ever believe she'd answer him.
He got up and put on a thick terry-cloth bathrobe and went
to the kitchen. He couldn't very well lock her in, so he left
the bedroom door wide open and pocketed the key. He
made coffee and took some croissants from the freezer and
put them in the oven. He whistled, one eye on the door.

When she appeared in the kitchen a half-hour later, he
was sitting at the butcher-block table drinking his third cup
of coffee.

She'd dried her hair and she was fully and completely
and modestly dressed, every inch of her covered from her
chin down. In fact, she was so dressed, she looked bulky.
Her attempt at armor, he assumed.

"Coffee?"

She nodded and slithered into the kitchen and sat
down.

"Croissant with that no-calorie strawberry spread?"

"No, thank you, Taylor."

As he passed by her, he smelled the clean freshness of
her and realized that, unlike her, he smelled of sex. Heady
and musky and thick in the air.

He offered his coffee cup up to toast her, but she
ignored him. She picked at her croissant, her head down.

"Would you tell me something, Lindsay?"

Silence.

"Would you tell me where you intended to go this
morning? You live here, your other apartment is rented out.
Where, Lindsay?"

She looked up then, and he saw immediately that she'd
had no idea at all. All she'd thought was to escape from
him.

It was a shitty realization and he hated it.

"Where, Lindsay?"

"I was going to go to Gayle's apartment."

"No, you weren't, at least not then. You would probably have thought of Gayle soon enough, but not then. Don't lie to me, damn you."

She threw her croissant at him. Since she hadn't buttered it, he was left with only a few flakes on his unshaved chin.

"Better a croissant than a left hook," he said, and wiped his chin.

"I would like to go now, Taylor."

"No. Not until we've straightened some things out between us. It isn't fair to me, Lindsay."

She looked at him then, really looked, saw his rumpled dark hair, the dark stubble on his face, the intensity of his eyes, and something else. She saw concern for her. It was real.

"I suppose you're right."

"Yes."

"I'm a millionaire, Taylor. A multimillionaire."

He cocked his head to the side.

"My grandmother skipped my father and my older half-sister. I got the mansion and the bulk of her estate. I was also my mother's only heir. Actually, my grandmother gave them all a million dollars, but that's considered pig dung and they're all ready to kill me off." She shuddered. "It was awful."

"Come here, Lindsay."

She looked at him, saw him pat his thighs, and he said again, "Come here."

She did. She sat on his thighs and he held her very close. She didn't cry. The tears were too deep, too well buried, even from Taylor.

"Do you want to tell me about it?"

"My father dislikes me. He always has. I've known it for a very long time. When the lawyer read my grandmother's will, and my father realized what she'd done, he turned on me. It was awful. His wife, Holly, was screaming and carrying on and he was as he always is—cold and ruthless and endlessly cruel. Odd, my half-sister didn't join in the fray. And she's very good at it. But she held herself in— why, I don't know. Then the lawyer—his name is Grayson Delmartin—he told me about my mother's will. I have a trust fund that's primarily in stocks that supplements my income, but nothing like this, Taylor, nothing at all like this. I don't know what to do."

"Do you think your father will contest the will?"

"He was so furious, he disowned me. But he won't follow through with it because Mr. Delmartin told him if he did that he would have no moral or legal claim on any of my estate were I to die before he did."

"He sounds charming, Lindsay."

"Why does he hate me so much, Taylor?"

"Perhaps if you told me more I could come up with some kind of an answer."

"He's always given everything to my half-sister, Sydney. She's nine years older than I am and she's always been perfect—beautiful, terrifyingly intelligent, she's got a law degree from Harvard—and she married an Italian prince. Now, of course, she's here and . . ."

Taylor waited. Damnation, she'd been talking, but it was over, she'd pulled back again, and he hated it.

"Why did your grandmother leave you her estate, do you think?"

"I don't know. I know she was immensely proud of Sydney. Perhaps she'd begun to think her son—my father—wasn't what she thought he was, I don't know. My father and his wife, Holly, lived at the mansion with her for the past two or three years." She paused a moment, looking at the fancy coffeemaker that Taylor had brought to the apartment. "I do realize some of it, I think. She wanted to arm me against my father, against Sydney, she wanted me to be powerful, and money was the only way she knew. But, you know, I realized that there was another kind of power that has nothing to do with money."

He held her even more closely, waiting, but she said nothing more. "What is your full name, Lindsay? You're going to marry me. I want to know my future wife's name."

Her mouth opened, the words hovered. Power. Yeah, she had loads of power. But Paris, what the prince had done to her . . . Tears pooled in her eyes and she shook her head against his shoulder. "I can't, Taylor. It's too awful, believe me . . . too awful. Please, just give me more time."

"Are you really very, very rich?"

"Yes, very very."

"What the hell are we going to do about that?"

"I don't know."

"Is that what made you to throw me down and ravish me at the airport?"

Withdrawal, but not completely, no, there was more uncertainty there, and he waited. "What happened, Lindsay? What brought you to me?"

He wondered if she had any idea, and said aloud, "The final show of dislike from your father? The understanding that you didn't want him to dominate you anymore? A sort of liberation?" Jesus, he thought, idiot words out of his mouth. He wasn't a shrink and he shouldn't be playing with the words. But he knew she was the girl Dr. Gruska had spoken about. The whole father thing . . . but seduction? He didn't know, and he was terrified to speculate.

"Perhaps. I thought about you, and only you, focused on you, I guess, because I didn't want all the horrible scenes at the mansion to eat away at me. I wanted you even before I saw you. All I could think about was you. And when I saw you standing there, looking so sane, so reasonable, and warm, and you wanted me and didn't hate me, I guess . . . I don't know."

"Lindsay?"

"Yes?"

"Don't leave me. Don't run away from me again. Whatever disturbs you, whatever frightens you, just don't leave me. Talk to me, or just sit and stare at me. Even turn your back on me. Just don't run. I love you and together we can work it out. Could you try to believe that?"

Silence.

"I'll even let you buy me a hot dog down at the museum to celebrate your new wealth."

She pulled back in the circle of his arm. She looked at him, saying nothing, and then she smiled. "Okay, I won't run out on you. It's time to stop that, isn't it? I'm not a stupid kid anymore, something I've told myself a lot lately.

No, not a kid who can be kicked around and carved to the bone with cruel words. No, I'm an adult now, and adults are supposed to think calmly and to exercise power over themselves."

"Amen," he said, not quite certain what she meant.

But that Saturday afternoon, after they'd come back from jogging in the park, Taylor was to learn that life had a way of always serving up new and varied and perverse dishes on one's plate.

# 18

Taylor was in the shower, having beaten Lindsay in the coin toss over who'd be first. The other bathroom in this magnificent, very old-fashioned apartment held an old claw-foot tub and as yet they hadn't hung a shower curtain around it. Neither of them wanted to sit in his own jogging sweat.

He was happy, and whistling and scrubbing, feeling better than he'd felt in his life. Unfortunately, he had his father's voice, but who cared? He soaped up and grinned, feeling real hope for the first time. Lindsay was engaged to him and she'd opened up and given herself to him. He'd had the greatest sex in his life, and that had been the biggest surprise of all.

In truth, Taylor had doubted his sex life would ever be the same again. He'd pictured, in grimmer moments, a willing but terrified Lindsay in bed, trembling when he touched her, lying stiff and cold, suffering him, enduring. It had chilled his blood. But last night . . .

He came out of their bedroom still whistling, dressed in tight jeans and a dark blue turtleneck sweater. He walked toward the living room because he heard a woman's voice. He thought it was probably Gayle Werth.

He was on the point of coming into the room when he saw, not Gayle, but a stunning woman dressed in black

leather that fitted her perfect body perfectly. She was standing in front of Lindsay, who was seated, looking for the
world like a disobedient schoolchild being berated by the
mistress. He couldn't help himself. He stopped and he
listened.

"... oh, yes, Lindsay," the woman was saying in a
sweet voice that made his blood curdle, "Father still wants
your head. He thought—as he made perfectly clear—that
you were a malicious, evil little slut. But you heard him. He
rather lost it, unfortunately. However, I think he's willing to
reconsider his opinion of you if you do what you should,
if you do what is right, and that is, of course, to reverse
the inheritance. The money should have gone to him and
you know it. He's not sure you'll ever understand, which
is why I'm here speaking for him. I told him you would
come about when you'd had time to think about it. I told
him you were very upset by Grandmother's death, and
your mother's, of course, and it was clouding your judgment. I told him not to underestimate you, Lindsay. You
aren't stupid, I told him. You aren't selfish and greedy. You
would do what is right, what is just."

There was complete silence for several moments. Taylor
knew he should come into the living room, knew he should
end this, but he didn't move, not yet. He heard Lindsay
say, vague puzzlement in her voice, "But you didn't say
much, Sydney, just something about deep waters. And now
you're here as Father's emissary. You're here as his
lawyer."

"Yes, to put it baldly. More than that, I'm here as his
daughter and your sister. I'm here to try to mend fences
and make you see reason. You know how proud Father is.
It's difficult for him to bend, to modify his beliefs." She
paused a moment and laughed. "You should have stayed
just awhile longer. Delmartin phoned after he left you at the
airport and told Holly that she wasn't to touch the house or
else there would be swift legal action. The silly bitch was
howling with rage. It was very diverting. I enjoyed watching her drink herself into a whining stupor. Father is
already talking about sending her on her way. She's a drag
on him now. He can't count on her at social functions

because of her drinking. And all the weight she's gained—she looks like a blimp. No, it won't be long now before Holly is gone. But our father, Lindsay, that's different now. He's what's important. It's his money and he must have it. As I said, he doesn't think you'll be reasonable, but I told him I know you better and you would be. You love him and you won't want to hurt him, not like Grandmother did."

"You want me to sign all my inheritance over to him?"

"Oh, keep some of it, certainly, but the bulk should go to Father. Don't you agree? He was next in line, after all. Moreover, you will still have your mother's money. What is that? About five million or so?"

"Am I to keep a million dollars of Grandmother's money?"

"Why not? It's not really an insult to you, just to Father."

"Won't Father believe I'm a selfish slut if I do?"

"I'll speak to him. I'll make him understand."

"Do you really think I could buy his love by giving him all Grandmother's money?"

"Don't be a fool, Lindsay. He loves you. It's just that he came to despise your mother, and unfortunately, that spilled over onto you. But now, why, yes, I think he would certainly come to look at you differently were you to do what is right now."

"It seems strange to think of him behaving any differently toward me now."

"He would. I promise you that. Will you sign the papers? I brought them with me."

"Shouldn't Grandmother's wishes count in this? Don't you believe she should have the right to do whatever she pleased with her money? It wasn't Father's, it was hers."

"He is—was—her only son. Her money is his, by right, by blood, by what is ethical and just. Now, here are the papers. They're very straightforward. I worked with the lawyer myself so that you could understand them. Will you sign the papers now, Lindsay?"

Taylor wanted to rush in, but again he stopped himself. This was Lindsay's problem, her decision. She sounded perfectly calm, so calm in fact that it worried him a bit. He waited, nearly holding his breath.

And she said then, in that same very calm voice, "I don't think so, Sydney."

"Now, you listen to me, Lindsay, I won't put up with any of your—" But Sydney didn't finish. She'd turned as she spoke, to see a gorgeous man standing in the living-room doorway. A man she'd never seen before. She saw that he was fresh from the shower. He looked tough and lean and hard, just the sort of man she enjoyed. Dark and rugged. She realized with a shock that he lived here, lived with her sister, and it astounded her, made her feel like she was in the wrong apartment. Sydney couldn't accept it. There had to be a mistake, the man had to be the electrician or something. Lindsay wouldn't let a man within six feet of her, particularly not a man like this one. This man was dangerous. He'd take what he wanted. Jesus, this man would make mincemeat out of Lindsay. It was then that Sydney noticed for the first time the brilliant diamond on Lindsay's finger. An engagement ring. An incredibly beautiful engagement ring. She couldn't take it in. There had to be some mistake. There had to be another explanation.

"My God! Who is this, Lindsay?"

Lindsay whipped about to see Taylor, smiling at her, looking questioningly toward Sydney. She tried to smile. She tried to make the muscles move, and they did a bit, making the smile a travesty. She'd wanted to keep Taylor away from Sydney, and when her half-sister had come in, she'd known, deep down, that it wouldn't be possible. Very well, then. She said mildly, "This is my fiancé, S. C. Taylor. Taylor, this is my half-sister, Princess Sydney di Contini."

"Taylor," Sydney repeated, staring at the man. She was shaking her head as she said, "Are you really engaged to Lindsay? No, come on now, it's a joke, right? What are you doing here? Are you here to fix the heating? Are you gay? Is that why Lindsay let you stay here?"

Lindsay heard the absolute incredulity in Sydney's voice. She'd even called Taylor a queer to try to justify his presence to herself. It was too much. What would he do? What would he say? She looked from Taylor to her sister, who was regarding him in helpless wonder, looking so beautiful that no man could resist her. She felt jealousy, ugly and deep, knife through her. Was it really so absurd a notion that a man could be engaged to her? Yes, it was.

Now Sydney was staring at Taylor, her hand held out to him, her body leaning forward, that soft invitation in her expression. Taylor, to Lindsay's relieved astonishment, looked at the vision who was Sydney and merely nodded. "Lindsay's half-sister? A pleasure, ma'am."

"Ma'am? What a horrid thing to call me. Like I'm an old bag or something equally distasteful."

Taylor merely continued his slow perusal, and Sydney, unnerved, looked toward Lindsay, who was looking for the world as if someone had slapped her silly. She looked confused and vague and stupid. "Wherever did you two meet each other? And why didn't you say anything about him, Lindsay? I was with you yesterday, for goodness' sake!"

Taylor said easily, "Why don't you sit down? Since you're her half-sister, I guess it's okay to tell you that I met Lindsay on a job a couple of months ago. I was hired to protect her. Now I protect her for free."

"You're a kind of bodyguard? Well, I should have guessed that. Just look at you, after all. Did you become engaged after you found out she was so very rich, Taylor? This all came about last night?"

"No, Sydney, it didn't just come about."

But Taylor was just smiling, and Sydney knew with sudden insight that she'd made a very big mistake. "I've heard a lot about you, Sydney," he said in that mild voice, as if she wasn't worth yelling at. "I can see that you're excellent at what you are. You man all your gun ports, firing at random. An interesting approach. I wouldn't employ it myself, but perhaps you've found over the years that it tends to work. Those occasional hits must be pretty destructive to the enemy."

"You're being quite silly," Sydney said, but Lindsay saw that she was looking a bit wary now. How could Taylor know about Sydney? She'd never said a word about her. Yet he knew, he recognized what she was.

Sydney continued quickly, "Lindsay wasn't wearing an

engagement ring in San Francisco. If you were indeed already engaged to her, then why wasn't she wearing the ring?"

Lindsay said, "I took it off because I didn't want any questions. We were all there for the funerals, not celebrations and congratulations."

Taylor wished she'd worn the damned ring. She'd been too afraid to own up. She'd been too afraid of the attacks, the questions, the mocking. He wondered how long it would take to change that.

"But there was so much more, wasn't there, Lindsay? Have you told Taylor exactly how wealthy you really are?"

"Look, Sydney, I'm sweaty and tired and I imagine that you have lots to do. When are you going back to Milan? When is Father expecting to hear from you?"

Sydney didn't immediately answer. She was staring at Taylor, frowning. "Did you say you were protecting Lindsay?"

"That's right."

"Are you a private investigator?"

"That's right, among other things."

"My God, you're Valerie's Taylor!"

Taylor felt the big punch right in his gut. He wished this damned woman would just shut her mouth, get up and leave, but he knew it wasn't to be. No, he was about to be pinned.

Again his voice was mild, bland with disinterest. "You know Valerie Balack? I'm not really surprised. The two of you are really quite similar. I dated Valerie for a while there, nothing more, nothing less."

But Sydney was staring at him and he knew at that moment that she and Valerie shared confidences and he'd been one of the confidences. His performance? Both in and out of bed?

Sydney sent a sideways glance at Lindsay, who was standing now to Taylor's left, stiff as a cane. She smiled, a pitying smile that made Taylor want to smack her. "Perhaps I should introduce Lindsay to Valerie. The two of them could compare notes. Women enjoy doing that, you know. Valerie was always impressed with your endurance, that, and your ability to bring . . . Well, never mind that. What do you think, Lindsay?"

Lindsay stepped forward now and Taylor had no idea what would come out of her mouth. She said again, "I'm very tired, Sydney. I would like to take a shower. Are you here simply to make me change my mind? If you wish, you can leave your legal papers here. I will read them and think about it. Could you leave now?"

"You are smelling sweaty, Lindsay, and you do look on edge with your hair plastered against your head. But, my dear sister, your fiancé here and this whole business with Valerie—"

"What Taylor did with whom before we met is his business. It doesn't matter to me. Get on with it, Sydney. Do you have anything else to say? Do you want to leave the papers?"

Sydney looked to Taylor, then shook her head. "No, I won't leave the papers today. I'll call and we'll arrange a meeting between the two of us."

"Fine. Good-bye."

"My, but you seem to have gained a modicum of confidence with your guy sitting here. Actually, you showed some guts in San Francisco. I admit to being surprised. Father was quite hurt. Because of the hulk here? Is that why you're going to marry him, Lindsay? Because he'll protect you when you can't do it yourself?"

Taylor rose quietly. He even smiled toward Sydney. "There you go again, firing at random. No hits for you this time. Perhaps you'll excuse us now, Princess. We're both very tired. I'll see you to the door."

Sydney looked triumphant and Lindsay wished Taylor had stayed seated, his mouth shut, and let her deal with Sydney. She could have dealt with her this time. At least she could have tried. At least Sydney hadn't ground her under this time, despite her salvos, her random hits, as Taylor called them. Lindsay fought the familiar tug of the loser, the way she usually felt around Sydney. When would the feelings go away? When could she face Sydney and simply not care what she said? She watched Taylor escort Sydney out of the living room. She heard her sister's heels click on the marble entrance tiles. She could picture Sydney smiling up at Taylor, giving him a look that would turn most men into slave material. But not Taylor.

She heard Sydney laugh, heard her say, "This is a beautiful place, Taylor. Will you let Lindsay pay for all of it now? And that diamond! Goodness, that must have set you back. Valerie told me, though, now that I think about it, that you weren't poor—not up to our standards, certainly, but not poor by any means. And now you're hooked up with my little half-sister. My very rich little half-sister. Has she let you take her to bed yet?"

Lindsay closed her eyes and waited. She heard Taylor say in his easy way, "Good-bye, Sydney. It was interesting to meet you. Family members can be such a treat. You should be careful, though. That strategy of yours becomes old very quickly."

The front door closed. Sydney was gone.

Lindsay eased down into the chair Taylor had vacated, her hands clasped between her knees, staring down at the exquisite golden oak floor. She saw a dust mote. She frowned at it.

"I find it interesting that your half-sister knows Valerie Balack, but not incredible or overly coincidental. They're remarkably alike, they run in the same social circles, so it makes sense that they'd hook up, both of them beautiful, confident, smart, rich. Both with no mercy, both certain that everything and everyone is here just for their pleasure.

"I hate to say this, Lindsay, but your half-sister isn't going to be my favorite person in the future. Is your father even worse? Now, come here and hold me. Your sister is a harrowing experience. I feel shaky. I need some reassurance. I need to know you're still here for me and that you'll take care of me."

She looked up at him and frowned. "Reassurance," she repeated, then rose and walked into his arms.

"Jesus, sweetheart, I need you."

She accepted him and she accepted his words. "It's all right, Taylor," she said, patting her hands on his upper arms, his shoulders, lightly stroking her fingertips over his cheeks. "It's all right. You did well with her. Much better than I ever have. She always leaves me defensive and feeling stupid."

"I thought you said she was in San Francisco."

"She must have come back to New York right after I did. I imagine she and Father got together and decided she was their best shot to get me to sign the money over to him."

"That seems logical, but not overly bright, given her blatant tactics. I wonder what her cut is from your father if she succeeds. Probably a very hefty amount."

"You don't really think . . . Well, maybe you're right. She'll have to regroup now that you're here. I wonder what her new approach will be. And she'll have one, don't doubt it."

"I can wait to find out—twenty years, at least. Think we can put her off that long?"

"I'll try, but I wouldn't count on it."

"Just remember, Lindsay, it's now two of us. For always."

"I'll remember."

They ate at a small Italian restaurant that evening. Lindsay permitted herself one glass of Chianti, a small bit of Taylor's spaghetti, and a big salad.

"I've got a job on Tuesday. We're talking skin and bones here. It's February and I've got to pretend I'm a snow bunny in tight, immensely tight, ski outfits. The spaghetti is wonderful."

He smiled at her, slowing his eating to match her pace. "Yes, it is. I'm sorry about your grandmother."

"Yes, I'll miss her."

"And your mother."

Lindsay frowned as she chewed on a cucumber. "Poor Mother. She wasn't happy. She was an alcoholic and I can remember back when I was sixteen—before they sent me away to school—that she'd gained weight and her drinking had increased. It was my father's infidelities and her own weakness. He wasn't ever faithful, even at first, I don't guess. I knew it and I was just sixteen."

"Tell me."

"I remember once when Sydney was making fun of my mother, the fat alcoholic. She was also mocking Holly, who's behaving just like my mother did before she finally left my father. Sydney laughed and laughed until I pointed out that Father was more than likely never faithful to her mother either. Why should he be? I thought she was going to hit me. She was red and trembling with rage. She believes her mother was Father's only true love, and after she died, all the mistresses and wives who followed her were vague copies of the real thing. Father was searching, ever searching, you see, to try to replace his first wife. I don't even know what her name is."

Taylor wanted to tell her that sounded just like some of Dr. Gruska's garbage. "What happened to Sydney's mother?"

Lindsay frowned, the tomato on her fork forgotten. "Sydney believes her mother died tragically, but she didn't. I overheard that her mother had remarried and was living in New Zealand or someplace like that. I assume my father had to divorce her in order to marry my mother and then Holly. He's kept up the pretense that her mother died. Perhaps to hold Sydney, I don't know."

Taylor smiled at her. "And you don't have the meanness in you to tell her the truth."

"What good would it do?"

"Oh, it might do something. Next time Sydney drops in on us, let's ask her about her mom. It might just throw her off-stride. It just might do her a world of good to be thrown off-stride. I can't imagine that she often relinquishes control."

"No, that would be cruel."

He raised an eyebrow at her. "You've got to toughen up, Lindsay. Sydney needs to be taken down a couple of pegs, she needs to know that her life can't go along according to her dictates."

"No, it hasn't always. Why, even the prince . . ."

"What about the prince? Her husband, right?"

But Lindsay's head was down. A thick tendril of deeply waving hair fell forward, nearly hitting her salad. Taylor leaned over to tuck the hair behind her ear. She flinched, drawing back.

"No, love, don't do that. Remember, you've got to keep me reassured."

"Did you make love to this Valerie Balack?"

"Yes."

He twirled spaghetti around in his spoon and took a big bite. He waited. Please show me some jealousy, he was thinking. Just a dollop of jealousy. Snipe at me. Be a bitch. Turn red and yell.

Instead her shoulders slumped. Defeat fitted her better. She was far more used to defeat.

He said deliberately and slowly, "However, I've never in my entire adult life made love with a woman who was more passionate, more loving, more giving, than you."

She looked up, paling; then her beautiful dark blue eyes darkened further.

"Will you make love with me when we get home?"

She looked at the lettuce now wilted on her plate. When she spoke, she surprised him. "What if I can't feel anything this time? What if that one time was an aberration, an accident . . . ?"

Taylor leaned forward and took her hands between his. He spoke quietly and firmly as a preacher, his voice and look filled with conviction. "I promise you that's just not true. There's no going back now that you've crossed the line with me. There's no more frightened Lindsay, no more flinching when I touch you. I would never lie to you.

"I swear that when you kiss me—any minute now, in fact—you'll want me just as much as you did last night. Once the dam bursts, so to speak, there's no stopping the flow. You'll have a lifetime of pleasure with me now. It's true. You can trust me. You don't have to worry about it ever again."

"I never thought of it like that."

"You're beautiful and you have some lettuce between your front teeth."

She howled, clapping her hands over her mouth, and he laughed, slapping her hands away, drawing her face toward him, and he met her halfway over the table and kissed her, once, then again and again until she was flushed and laughing herself. He felt happier than he could ever remember.

Unfortunately, that evening there was to be no repetition of the previous night. Nor was there any chance Lindsay was pregnant. Lindsay was embarrassed, but his matter-of-factness cast a whole new light on things. She came out of the bathroom so pale Taylor stopped in his undressing and stared at her. "Let me guess. You've contracted the plague."

"No, it isn't plague. It's worse."

"Let me check your armpits just to make sure."

"No, no, it's just that I can't . . . I wondered why I'd put on two pounds and hadn't eaten anything to deserve it, the water retention, you know, and now . . ."

"Oh," he said. "No, that isn't plague. That's just plain bad luck. That's to bring me down off my high and to punish me for being a sex maniac. And you as well."

"At least it didn't happen last night."

"Thank God," he said fervently, and hugged her. "You hurting?"

"A little bit."

"Get into bed and I'll get you some of those magic pills."

And that was that.

When he held her, finally feeling her body relax as the pills worked, he said, "Don't you forget I love you even though your body is giving me the Bronx cheer."

On Tuesday, Taylor cracked "The Case of the Embezzling Wife." He tended to give his cases names, thinking that when he was eighty and his mind was going on him, maybe he could remember his cases if he identified them well, giving them Perry Mason-type names. He met with the husband at noon to give him the evidence he needed. There was no need to commiserate with the man, he was too furious. He'd already called the cops on his wife and contacted the district attorney.

Taylor was whistling, thinking of the solution to a modem hookup problem one of his west-coast friends had called him about the previous day, while he walked down Fifth Avenue to go home. It was a sunny cold day. Beautiful clear air. A perfect day in New York despite the forty-degree tag on the temperature. He thought of Lindsay and smiled. At breakfast that morning, while he ate a bowl of cereal and she a piece of dry toast, she'd said in the most natural way imaginable, "Let's go out on Thursday night, okay?"

"Thursday night? Something special happening?"

She flushed and he frowned over his spoon of wheat flakes.

"Well, yeah, at least for me."

He took another bite of his cereal. "Okay. Let's call Enoch and Sheila and see if they'd like to do something. Good idea."

"That isn't what I meant, Taylor!"

"Oh?" He stared at her blankly.

She flushed more deeply, then saw the laughter in his eyes, and threw the half piece of toast at him.

"You're awful and ought to be . . . corrugated!"

"No, not corrugated! Anything but that, mistress, even the briar patch!"

She frowned. "No, that's not right."

He was laughing so hard he couldn't help himself. He rose from the table, grabbed her beneath her arms, and hugged her so tight she squeaked.

"Let's stay in Thursday night and celebrate for about twelve hours."

He was smiling like a besotted fool as he wondered how her ski shoot was going. At least it was a gorgeous day and she was wearing ski clothes, so she'd be warm enough. He would have thought the best place to take ski pictures would be at a ski slope. But no, they were at Washington Square.

Actually, the shoot wasn't going well at all. Lindsay looked over at the director and sighed. He had an attitude problem, a common-enough malady, but he was both arrogant and ignorant, which made things nearly impossible because the photographer was good but mush. He had no control over anything. Lindsay was nothing more than a stupid bimbo, the crew a useless group of grunts, the makeup people faggots and hags. He was, in short, the nephew of the ski-clothing-store president. The ad people were biting their nails, trying to keep peace, trying to give the jerk suggestions couched in the most diplomatic phrases, but nothing was working. He was demanding and contradictory and just plain stupid. Demos had left, he was so pissed, just giving her a commiserating nod. She'd mouthed, "Coward," at him and he'd agreed.

Lindsay sighed again, leaning against the set, waiting, waiting, waiting. The male model, Barry, had given the director the finger—when his back was turned—and was sitting over at one of the stone tables playing chess. Washington Square was an odd place. Serious chess players, most of them old as the square itself, played chess next to dope dealers who were even now conducting business as usual. Prostitutes eyed her to see what she had that they didn't. Business appeared to be brisk for both sets of folk. And there was the crew, pissed as hell and bored and grousing. The elaborate set, for which the ski clothing company had shelled out nearly sixty thousand dollars, was sitting there dark and heavy and towering some forty feet in the air, and so far unused. After endless hassles with the city, the ad agency had gotten the necessary permits, but the director hadn't figured out yet how to get Eden and the ski lift together in the same shot. There was even a lift chair, but she hadn't sat in it yet. The gondola swung in the light breeze above her head.

She moved away from the fake ski lift and went over to watch Barry. She played a little chess, but the thought of challenging one of the resident graybeards terrified her. She saw quickly that Barry was getting his ski socks knocked off. She stood quietly, enjoying the game, when one of the set men came and whispered she was to go back and stand against the lift and not move. They had to take some lineup shots. She wondered about Barry, but the man didn't say anything to him. Lindsay walked back to the lift and obligingly leaned against the sturdy wooden beams at its base, wondering what Taylor was doing. She smiled. All she had to do was think of him and she'd smile like a fool.

He filled her and made her happier than she'd ever been in her life. He was her life now.

She began humming, closing out the director's whining orders, staring down at her ski boots as she wiggled her toes. They were tight. She looked up when one of the photographer's assistants shouted at the director. Oh, dear, open warfare. The man told him the light would be gone in thirty minutes and to get his shit together. The waiting was costing a fortune and he was a shmuck.

The director raged on and on. The photographer's assistant, an old-timer of immense experience, just looked sardonic and finally shut his mouth. Lindsay knew what he was thinking: Who the hell cared if this jerk cost his dear uncle three times what he should? Who cared if the photographer, a wimp of the first order, just stood there and bit his fingernails?

Lindsay wondered what had happened to the set man who'd asked her to come back here. No lineup shots? She didn't see any movement. She looked up to see Edie, the makeup woman, striding toward her. Maybe, at last, something was going to happen. She started to call out a greeting, something light and funny because Edie looked like the rest of them felt. Then suddenly Edie dropped her bag and stared upward, a scream coming out of her mouth and another. Then she screamed, "Eden! Jesus, move!"

Lindsay started forward, then heard other screams, and she looked up.

The entire ski-lift structure seemed to lift off its base, then burst into flames like some sort of exploding oil rig, spewing orange fire and black smoke upward. The blast sent a rain of steel flying outward, then down, hard and fast. The noise was deafening. Odd, but the people's screams around her were even louder. But this noise was different. It was stark and close and unreal because it was here, above her and all around her and soon . . .

"No," she whispered, terror freezing her in place for an instant. She lurched away.

She wasn't fast enough. A thick support beam struck her shoulder and bounced off, hitting the concrete beside her. She felt an odd sense of warmth, a blankness that was strange, but there was no pain, only this pressure seeming to come from inside her. It intensified, sending her to her knees. Another piece of debris struck her, full on the side of the face, knocking her sideways, her knees crumbling. Pain, sudden and fierce, made her yell out. Planks of wood crashed down from the ruined ski lift, hitting her, flinging her about. She couldn't do anything about it. Pain was there, full and deep and ugly, holding her. Then there was blackness, blessed blackness that was settling over her, blanketing the pain as one would blanket flames.

Odd about the screams. They went on and on. Had a lot of people been struck? Why wouldn't they stop? The screams were closer to her now, she knew that; they were softer, more vague, and she could almost feel those screams touching her, feel them coming even from her, but somehow she was moving away from them toward that wonderful blackness that blanked out everything and left nothing in its place.

# 19

The sirens were shrill. They pounded into her head. She hated them. She wanted to get away from them but she couldn't seem to move. Someone was squeezing her hand, she felt his fingers suddenly, warm fingers, blunt. A man was speaking softly and gently to her, but he was insistent, he wouldn't stop. He was like the sirens. She wanted to tell him to be quiet, but she couldn't seem to get the words to form in her mind. She didn't at first understand what he was saying, but she recognized the pattern, the repetition, and despite herself, she began to pay attention to him, looking to his voice to force her outward toward him.

"Do you know who you are?"

She opened her eyes. No, just her left eye. Her right eye wouldn't move. It was a young man speaking to her, his face very close to hers. His eyes were very blue and his ears were big. She thought he was Irish. She realized then she couldn't breathe.

She gasped for breath and the pain seared through her. There was only pain, no air.

"It's all right. I know you're having trouble. Just take real shallow breaths. No, no, don't panic. Shallow breaths. Yes, that's right. I think you've got a collapsed lung. That's why we've got that oxygen mask over your face. Just breathe, shallow and easy. Good. Now, do you know who you are?"

272

She focused on the mask that covered her nose and mouth. But it hurt so much. She kept trying, and she got air, but the pain nearly sent her into madness. He asked her again who she was. She was her, and she was here, and she didn't know what was going on, what had happened, except she hurt and could barely breathe.

"Do you know your name? Please, tell me. Who are you? Do you know who you are?"

"Yes, I'm Lindsay." God, it hurt to say those words, hurt so much she wanted to yell with it, but she couldn't. She whimpered, fear sharpening the sound, and the man said quickly, his voice calm and low, "Just take shallow breaths. Don't try to do anything else. Just breathe, that's all you have to do. Do you understand me? That's an oxygen mask over your face to help you. Don't fight it; let it help you. We think you've got a collapsed lung. That's why it hurts so much. But you've got to stay awake and pay attention, all right?"

God, it hurt so much. She tried to hold her breath, to stave off the horrible jabbing pain, but that didn't work either. He was speaking to her again. Why had he repeated the same thing? Did he think she was stupid?

"I know you hurt, but hang in there. We're nearly to the hospital and they're waiting for you. Don't worry. Just keep taking those little breaths. I'm glad to meet you, Lindsay. I'm Gene. Just lie still. We'll be at the hospital very soon now. No, don't try to move."

"What happened?" It hurt so much to speak. And talking through the white plastic mask made her feel like she was speaking from a long way away.

"There was some sort of explosion and you were hit by falling debris."

"Am I going to die . . . collapsed lung?"

"Oh, no, not you. You'll be fine. I promise."

"Taylor. Please call Taylor."

"Yes, I will, I promise. No, don't try to move. I've got an IV in your arm. We don't want you to rip it out. Just keep breathing."

"There were so many screams."

"No one else was hurt, but everyone was scared. You

273

were standing right next to that fake rigging when it blew. Tell me again. Who are you?"

"I was there because I'm Eden."

He frowned, but she didn't see it. It hurt too much and she didn't want him to see her lose control. She turned her head away from him. The pain continued. She'd never imagined before how it would feel not to be able to breathe. For every small intake there was such pain that her whole body shook with it.

"How is she, Gene?"

"She's doing fine, at least I hope to God she is. The pain's bad, but she's hanging in there." He turned away from the driver to her. "I'm sorry, Eden, but we can't give you anything for the pain yet. The trauma team has to check you out first. Just hold on, hold on. Squeeze my fingers, think about my fingers and squeeze when you hurt real bad. We're almost there, almost there." Gene wondered if Taylor was her husband. Dear God, the man would be in for a shock when he saw his wife. She was a model. He looked at the right side of her face. It was difficult to tell how bad it was smashed because of all the blood. He held her hand more tightly. Gene O'Mallory wanted her to be all right. He wanted it very much.

There were six people standing over her, three men and three women. They were cutting off her clothes, speaking to each other, jabbing at her, prodding and poking, but through it all, there was someone's hand on her forearm gently stroking and there was a soft woman's voice with that stroking, saying over and over, "It's going to be all right. You're here with us now and we'll make sure you're okay. Do you understand me, Lindsay? It will be all right."

Someone else said, "She's that fashion model, Eden. First things first, but, Elsie, call Dr. Perry. Tell him to get over here on the double."

Elsie said, "Gene called him from the ambulance. Perry's on his way."

Lindsay felt cold on her skin. She knew somewhere in her mind that she was naked, just as she had been so long ago in Paris. But she felt too much pain to care. Just to take a single breath was beyond anything she could ever have imagined. But the gentle stroking on her forearm continued and she tried to concentrate on it.

A man was very close to her face. He said, "Lindsay? Good, listen to me now. You've got a collapsed lung. What happened is, a broken rib punctured it. So we've got to cut a little incision over here between your ribs—near your side, yes, right here—and stick in a tube. We'll hook it up to a lung machine and it will reinflate your lung. It won't hurt. It'll all be over in just a few minutes and you'll be able to breathe again without the pain. Okay? You understand?"

The fingers paused on her forearm.

"Yes, I understand."

"Okay, let's get it done, guys."

Five minutes later, Lindsay took a breath that didn't feel like she was going to die. She even managed a smile at the man bending over her.

"Better?"

"Yes, much better."

"Now, you've got two broken ribs. We'll leave them alone, but they're going to hurt for a while. We've been giving you morphine through the IV. Do you have any more pain?"

It was odd, but she didn't. "My face?"

"Your face . . . yes, Dr. Perry's here and he's going to take over now "

The gentle fingers on her forearm stopped and Lindsay felt panic. "Where are the fingers?"

Someone said, "What's she talking about?"

"What's going on?"

"Oh, she means Debra. Deb, get back over here!"

The fingers were on her arm again. She closed her eyes. It was all right. The voice came again, soft and warm.

Dr. Perry identified himself. He was a plastic surgeon and he specialized in facial reconstruction, he said. They were going to take her to CT Scan and then they'd see exactly what the problems were. She wasn't to worry. If she felt any pain, she was to sing out.

Lindsay was fully prepared to sing, but the pain she

felt was so slight compared to what she'd already endured, she didn't say anything.

Time passed. Debra didn't leave her. Lindsay said to her. "Taylor. He's my fiancé. Could you call him?"

"After I see you safe into surgery, Lindsay. Then I'll call him, I promise. Give me his number."

Dr. Perry was back and he spoke gently and slowly. "You're lucky, Ms. Foxe. The flesh on your right cheek isn't very damaged, which means little to no scarring. However, the blows you took smashed the bones here and here and here." He lightly pointed to his own face to show her. "We need to go in right now and fix them. You'll be good as new in three weeks."

"Can I see?"

"I don't think you should."

Lindsay thought about that. The right side of her face was numb. She raised her right hand, but Debra grabbed it and forced it back to her side. She leaned close. "No, Lindsay, don't. Just lie still, that's it."

Dr. Perry's voice came again. "I'll need you to sign the surgery consent forms, Ms. Foxe."

She did. Within fifteen minutes she was being wheeled to surgery. She felt no pain. Her head was cloudy. She wasn't scared.

The explosion had happened at twelve-thirty.

She was in surgery by five-thirty.

Demos stood in the hospital corridor, leaning against the wall near the door to what would be her private room, once she came out of surgery, once she came out of recovery.

It would be some time now before she was out of surgery. The surgery was on her face, being performed by a Dr. Perry, one of the top plastic surgeons in the country, the nurse had assured him, not once but four times, one of the very best, and he'd said the bones were situated ideally to be slipped back into their proper place and they weren't to worry, which sounded disgusting to Demos. But why, Demos had wondered, why operate on her face now?

The nurse was patient with him, explaining that if they hadn't done it immediately, there would be swelling that would preclude doing it for a week, at least. Lindsay had agreed, naturally.

"But how could she agree?"

"She was conscious, Mr. Demos. Dr. Perry did an immediate CT scan on her face and her head. You'll have to speak to him, Mr. Demos. But she should be out of surgery around seven o'clock and then it's recovery for about an hour. Why don't you go have dinner?"

Demos and Glen went to the hospital cafeteria and stared at each other over open-faced roast-beef sandwiches.

"I'll never forget that damned phone call as long as I live," Glen said, his hands shaking.

They'd gotten the hysterical call from one of the ad-agency people at precisely ten minutes to one. They'd gotten here as fast as they could, but they hadn't seen Lindsay. It wasn't allowed. Everything was being done for her. Not to worry. Demos had filled out paperwork on her. Then he'd realized he had to call Taylor. Let Taylor deal with her family, with Sydney. He was engaged to her, let him do it. Demos knew Lindsay's number by heart. He'd started to punch out the buttons, then stopped. He looked at those numbers, and they didn't mean anything to him.

"Glen, help."

Glen had shoved him aside and quickly pressed the numbers.

Two rings and then, "Hello, Taylor here."

"Taylor, this is Glen."

"Yeah, Glen. What's up?"

"Oh, God, Taylor, you've got to get here right now!"

"What the hell are you talking about? Where's Demos? What's going on?"

Glen had nearly thrown the phone to Demos. "Taylor, this is Vinnie. There's been an accident and Eden's hurt. Hurry, man, get here now. I don't know anything, just hurry!"

Demos hung up the phone and leaned his cheek against the cold steel. He heard a man say, "Does anyone know a Lindsay or an Eden?"

"I do," Glen said.

"I was with her in the ambulance. She asked me to call

Taylor. I've been asking around, trying to find out his phone number, but nobody knows. Do you know who he is?"

"Yes, we know," Demos said. "I just called him."

"Her face," the young man said. "She's so beautiful. Will she live? Has anyone said? Her collapsed lung?"

"She'll be fine," Demos said, praying like a demon as he said the words.

That had been at two-oh-five.

Twenty minutes later, Taylor was running into the emergency room, pale and looking more terrified than a man should ever look.

"We don't know anything yet," Glen said quickly. "They're fixing a collapsed lung, at least someone told us about that, but then there's her face . . ."

"Her face? What the hell happened to her face?"

"She was smashed."

"Jesus," Taylor said, unable to take it in, just standing there frozen. Then he burst into action. "Where is she? Who can I talk to?" He didn't wait, but walked quickly to the nurses' station.

The head emergency-room nurse, Ann Hollis, was sixty, tough, and more seasoned than a four-star general. She saw the man coming toward her, saw his fear, and readied herself for the outbreak. Screaming, raw, and impotent anger, outward fury, the rage brought on by the helplessness of it all. To her utter surprise, when he spoke, his voice was calm and low.

"I would appreciate your help . . ." He looked at her name tag. "Yes, Ms. Hollis. Lindsay or Eden is her name. I understand there was an accident and she's being treated. I'm her fiancé. Please tell me what's going on. This is very difficult."

And Ann Hollis responded to him with the truth. "I will tell you what I know. First of all, stop worrying. The trauma team is working on her and they're the best. You stay here and I'll go check and find out what's happening. All right?"

Taylor nodded and she left him. He didn't move. Demos and Glen came over. No one said anything.

Nurse Hollis patted Taylor's arm. "Two broken ribs, a collapsed left lung, which they're re-inflating."

"How's that done?"

"A small incision between two ribs and a tube is inserted that's in turn connected to a lung machine. It makes breathing easier for her. Contusions and lacerations, but those aren't all that bad. Then there's her face." Again she touched her hand to his arm. "It's impossible to say right now because Dr. Perry hasn't said anything yet. He's got to get CT scans before he can make a determination. My feeling is that since she's a model, they won't wait to operate. She'll probably have surgery done on her face as quickly as possible. This afternoon."

Taylor didn't say anything. He was trying not to shake. Nurse Hollis patted his arm again.

"As soon as I can find out anymore, I'll call you. Please go sit down. I know it's difficult. But you must try to stay calm. She won't die. Her face will heal. Dr. Perry is one of the best in facial reconstruction in the city. She's Eden the model, isn't she?"

"Yes."

"I've seen her picture many times. She's quite beautiful and she will be again."

"Thank you. She is. She's also a lot more than that . . . she's . . ."

She wanted to take his hand but she didn't. "I understand, Mr. Taylor. I will tell you as soon as I know something more." He nodded and she knew he was fighting for control. She hated to see such pain. She hated to see this hidden, deep pain, this completely controlled pain. Sometimes it was better to shriek and curse all the doctors and nurses and rail against God and fate. But this man would always try to control himself and circumstances around him.

Ann Hollis smiled at him, and now she patted his arm again. The poor young woman was a model . . . not anymore, Ann Hollis thought. Oh, no, not unless she was very lucky, very lucky indeed. She'd seen the young woman's face. They hadn't cleaned it yet, and there was nothing but dried blood and bits of bone and matted blood-dried hair.

279

Yes, it would be difficult to be beautiful when your face was smashed.

She watched the man Taylor turn away and walk back into the waiting lounge with two other men.

Lindsay wished she could throw a rock at the light. It was bright and it hurt her eyes. Why was it on? She hadn't turned it on. Why didn't someone turn it off? She didn't want to open her eyes. She didn't want to see anything; she didn't want to be or do anything. She wanted to stay buried deep and warm within herself, within the warm darkness. It was secure here, except for that damned light. She knew, somehow, that if she opened her eyes she would regret it.

Still, the light was there, brighter now, and there was a voice along with it, a woman's voice, urgent and hoarse-sounding, saying over and over, "Lindsay, Lindsay, wake up now, wake up now. Come on, you can do it. Wake up."

"No," she said, and even that one small word was difficult. Her throat was dry and to the point of pain.

"Here, I'm putting a straw in your mouth. Try to suck some water. You need it."

How did the woman know that? She sucked and felt the water fill her mouth and trickle down her throat. It was wonderful until she swallowed. A shock of pain went through her, squeezing the breath out of her, making her tighten and shrink and shudder with its force.

"Oh, God."

"I know it hurts. I'll give you more painkiller very soon now. You've got to get over the anesthesia first. I need to see how your brain is working." There was a smile in the woman's voice; then she said, "Please open your eyes for me."

"The light. It hurts."

The light disappeared. Lindsay opened her eyes. The room was in shadows. There was a woman in white standing over her. There were other people in the room, she could hear them. She couldn't see them, but she could hear them. Their breathing, a few moans.

"That's good. Now, tell what you see."

"You. I see you and you're wearing white and you're pretty."

"Thank you. Now, don't be frightened. You came out of surgery and you're in the recovery room. You pulled through everything great. Dr. Perry will be in to see you in the morning. He said you'll be gorgeous again. Right now, you look like a Q-Tip—your head is all bandaged up and that's why you can't open your mouth very wide. The bandages are to keep everything immobile. Do you understand? Good. Now, I want you to count some fingers for me. Four? Excellent. And now? Good, Lindsay. Very good."

"My ribs hurt."

"I know. And they'll hurt for quite a good while yet. But the painkiller will help immensely. Dr. Shantel will be here in a moment to talk to you. Just hang in there and then we'll give you some more painkiller very soon."

"Taylor. Where's Taylor?" It was so hard to talk. She felt the swath of bandages for the first time. Her head felt tight. It hurt to try to open her mouth, even a little bit.

"He's here. I tried to keep him out but he threatened to break all my moving parts if I didn't let him in." The nurse leaned closer and whispered, "Besides, he's a real cutie. If he has a brother, I sure would appreciate an introduction."

The nurse moved aside. Lindsay felt him take her hand. Then his fingers were on her bare forearm, light and gentle, Taylor's fingers. Odd that he was doing just what Debra had done. She wondered if they'd told him to touch her, to keep human contact.

His face was right above hers. His look was serious and it frightened her, but his voice was soft and low. "Hello, sweetheart. You're going to be fine. Jesus, don't ever give me a scare like that again. Here's your doctor. I'll be right here. It'll be all right."

Dr. Shantel, a woman who was nearly as tall as Lindsay and tanned from a recent vacation to Maui, said, "Stay, Mr. Taylor. Hold her hand. You're quite a calming influence. And we want her calm as she comes out of the anesthesia." To Lindsay she introduced herself, then said quietly, "You're very lucky. I'll take care of all of you except your

face. That's Dr. Perry's area. Now, your ribs aren't bandaged. They'll mend faster just left alone. We've stitched up
some cuts on your shoulders and chest and neck. Nothing,
really. Practically no scarring. You're just fine now. You'll
be with us for a while. I want you to rest and I want you
to hold your head very still."

Dr. Shantel looked at the bandages wrapped around
the young woman's head and face. "Your face will be all
right. You've come out of the anesthesia well. It's time for
some more painkiller, and then you can have a good night's
sleep."

"Taylor?"

"I'm here, Lindsay. Here's some medication for you.
No, I'm not leaving you."

He watched the nurse inject medicine into the IV in
her left arm. He stroked his fingers over her right forearm,
the way the nurse Debra had told him. He wanted to cry.

The nurse said quietly, "I understand you're her
fiancé?"

"Yes."

"Tell you what. I'll speak to the nursing staff on the
fourth floor. No reason why you can't stay with her if you
want to. We'll have another bed moved in there. Does Miss
Foxe have other family you need to call?"

Taylor just stared at her. *Miss Foxe. Lindsay Foxe.*

He said aloud, "Foxe. Her name's Lindsay Foxe. It's a
nice name."

The nurse looked at him curiously. "You don't have to
worry about any paperwork. Mr. Demos provided all the
insurance information."

It was exactly nine o'clock at night when he remembered. He was alone with her in her private room. There
was the soft hissing sound of the lung machine, nothing
else, save perhaps his own breathing. He remembered.
Sharp memories, utterly clear and brutal. He jerked with
the knowledge.

Lindsay Foxe.

The young girl who'd been in the cubicle in the emergency room next to his at St. Catherine's Hospital in April
1983, the young girl who had been raped by her sister's

husband—a bloody Italian prince—and who had screamed and screamed and fought the men who were also doctors. He remembered hearing how those doctors had spoken about her and to her and what they'd done to her. He shook his head. It was beyond anything. And now that young girl was here and she'd grown up and he loved her and she was going to be his wife.

Lindsay Foxe. Jesus, he couldn't believe it, he couldn't seem to accept it—the chance of it happening; but then there was the gut feeling that it was somehow fate. Taylor shook his head. He was losing it. *Lindsay Foxe.*

No wonder she'd changed her name when she'd become a model. No wonder she hadn't wanted to tell him what her real name was. She'd said something about not wanting him to hate her. She'd only tried to protect herself. From everyone and then from him. When would she have told him? When would she have decided to trust him enough?

Jesus. He thought of Sydney di Contini, La Principessa, Lindsay's half-sister. It had been her husband who had raped Lindsay, and Sydney, that sophisticated bitch he'd met for the first time four days before, had been the one who'd shot him.

Taylor saw she was sleeping. He called Enoch, speaking very softly, and told him what had happened. And then he said, "I need a favor, Enoch."

"You got it, Taylor."

"A serious favor, one that you can't ever talk about, even to Sheila."

"What's going on?"

Taylor told him. "Yeah, that's right. Only French newspapers, no American, they're not necessary." He gave him the exact day. Then he hung up. He looked at Lindsay. Her breathing was shallow, her face was flushed. The lung machine—looking for the world like a blue briefcase—hissed and bubbled. He closed his eyes, listening to the sounds of the machine and picturing again that young girl, wheeled out on a gurney past where he sat waiting for a doctor to see to his arm. So young she'd been, so pathetic, and so completely alone. No one there for her, no one.

And he realized in that instant how much she had to love him. After all that had happened to her, she'd still come to him. She'd trusted him with her body, she'd trusted him not to hurt her. Who cared that she hadn't yet told him her name? It didn't matter. He leaned his forehead on her hand. He prayed silently.

It was nearly midnight when Sydney arrived.

"My God," she said from the doorway.

"Yes," he said, looking at her with new eyes. "Speak quietly. She's sleeping." Sydney nodded and came into the room and slipped out of the full-length Russian sable coat. She was wearing a long black dress beneath, with no sleeves, little front, and no back. She was wearing diamonds—a necklace, earrings, bracelet. Her hair was piled on top of her head and she looked exquisite and expensive. He wished she would fall out of the window.

"What happened?"

"It was at a photo shoot in Washington Square. They'd built a ski lift and it exploded. She was standing right there, evidently. The cops and the fire department are working on it. How did you find out?"

"Well, you didn't call me, that's for sure."

"Keep your voice down. It's possible I didn't call you because I don't know where you live."

"Even if you'd known, you wouldn't have called, would you, Taylor? Oh, just forget it. It was on TV and I happened to see my sister being lifted into an ambulance." She walked to the windows, fidgeting with an emerald ring on her right hand.

Sydney turned to look at him. He was pale but it didn't diminish the fact that he also looked mean and angry and hard as nails, his eyes narrowed on her face. He was holding Lindsay's hand, his strong and hard, hers pale and limp.

"Ah, so she's told you how I'm the wicked half-sister."

"No, she's hardly told me anything at all, as a matter of fact. She hadn't yet told me her last name. The hospital needed it and Demos told them."

Sydney just looked at him. He could practically hear her thinking and sorting through things. Finally, "You remembered the old scandal? Good God, it was years ago. Or did Demos tell you about that too?"

"Actually, Demos didn't have to. I just happened to be in the same emergency room in Paris when Lindsay was brought in. I'd been hit and knocked off my motorcycle, and my arm was broken. I'll never forget it as long as I live, her screams, her fear, her pain, and the fact that she was completely alone. I wanted to kill those bloody doctors who were supposed to be taking care of her. Yeah, I wanted to kill them, and she was helpless because they were holding her down, holding her legs apart and prying into her; it was just another rape, dammit! She didn't speak French and they didn't give a shit because she was a foreigner. I also wanted to kill the bloody bastard who'd raped her. Your precious husband, I believe. "

Sydney felt the shock of surprise, then calmed herself. She remembered Valerie telling her how Taylor loved France, how he was there two or three times a year. How he'd even been in an accident there once . . . years ago, and had broken his arm and been in a hospital . . .

She tried to keep her voice down, keep it smooth and calm, but it was tough. "I wasn't with her in the emergency room. I was a bit over the edge myself at the time. Hysterical, I guess, though I hate to think of that word being applied to me. And the bloody bastard who raped her is doing nicely. He still likes young girls. He's still got enough money to command a steady supply and charming enough so that rape isn't necessary for him. He only seems to have problems when he leaves Italy. And that only once, with my little sister here, in Paris. I don't pay much attention anymore. If it makes you feel any better, Taylor, I shot him. I did save her. A pity, but he pulled through."

It was hard to stay calm, difficult not to throttle her. "If that was supposed to be an apology, it's sadly lacking. Even as an excuse, it sucks. Maybe you can explain why you shot him and then turned around and accused Lindsay of seducing him. For God's sake, didn't you see him raping her?"

Sydney shrugged.

"Why did you turn around and attack her? Why did

you let her father attack her? That's what happened, isn't it?"

"Stop being so melodramatic! For God's sake, things are and were very complicated, particularly at that time." Taylor watched her toss her coat over a hospital chair. She tossed her black purse on top of the coat. She walked back to the window. They were on the eleventh floor. "It's very dark out," she said after a moment. "I hate winter. It was very dark out even at five-thirty. I do hate the blackness."

"Complications come out of lies. The truth is usually very simple."

She turned. "A truism, Taylor? You really don't know anything, you're only guessing."

"What do you want here, Sydney?"

Sydney suddenly smiled. "I called our father and told him Lindsay had been in an accident, evidently a very bad one. Would you like to know what he said? He asked me if Lindsay was going to live. I told him I didn't know, didn't have any details on her condition. He told me to call him immediately when I found out. If she was going to die, why, then, he would inherit all her money, and he needed to get the legalities under way."

He was cold with rage. "And what did you say, Sydney?"

Sydney laughed. "Why, I told him I would call him back, naturally."

"Her plastic surgeon is a Dr. Perry. Her other doctor is named Shantel. You may want to speak directly to Perry and to her. Lindsay will live, Sydney. She's got broken ribs, a collapsed lung, and her face—I understand the bones were crushed but she'll be all right. Be sure to tell her father that, won't you? Tell the bastard for me that he can fuck his legalities. Tell him for me that if he comes near her, I'll flatten him."

"You don't care for me much, do you, Taylor?"

"No."

"You really shouldn't hate her father. You don't know him."

"I don't want to know him. He's a shit."

"You cared for Valerie, didn't you? You were with her for three months?"

He said brutally, "I enjoyed fucking her, but only for a while. She was too possessive, too selfish. She had no control over herself. She was like a spoiled child who wanted everything her own way. I met Lindsay, and Valerie ceased to exist. I told Lindsay you reminded me of Valerie."

Sydney picked up her coat and slipped her arms into it. She strode toward the door, her hand out for the knob, when she turned and said, "What happened to Lindsay's face?"

"A falling beam struck her directly."

She looked at him curiously. "Valerie told me how you enjoyed just looking at her because she was so beautiful. Lindsay isn't in her league. What does she have now to hold you?"

"You seemed to think her money would hold anyone."

"Perhaps, but it didn't work for Valerie."

"No."

"Well, then?"

He went still, deeply and utterly silent.

She smiled. "Ah, perhaps it's pity for the sparrow with the broken wing? Don't you think so, Taylor? That fades, pathetic things always do, and all that's left is the damned sparrow and it still has a broken wing. And your guilt because you aren't interested anymore."

Surprisingly, Taylor smiled back at her, a smile cold and taunting as hers. "I find you amazing, Sydney. I find your father amazing. You know something else? The real pity is that none of us can choose who our relatives are. I'd say that Lindsay got all the black cards in the deck." He turned back to Lindsay then, and didn't move until he heard the door close.

It was ten o'clock the following morning. Lindsay was awake and in pain. Taylor was going crazy watching her trying to control it. Finally the nurse gave her more medication. She fell into a light sleep. The nurse told him it was the facial swelling that was causing most of the pain.

He was on the point of going to their apartment to

shower and change clothes when Sergeant Barry Kinsley of Manhattan South walked into the room.

"Jesus," Taylor said, staring at his old sergeant. "What the blazes are you doing here?"

"Taylor? A shock, my boy, but at my age there shouldn't be any more shocks. Why are you here? You know the lady?"

"She's my fiancée. She's sleeping right now. What are you doing here, Barry?"

"Official, Taylor, very official. Someone tried to knock the lady off. The explosion wasn't an accident, it was a bomb, one of those neat little plastic numbers, and it was detonated from about twenty yards away. She was right there, leaning against that ski lift, when someone detonated the explosive. No one else was anywhere near. A setup, straightforward, no muss, no fuss. Clean, sweet."

Taylor saw red. "Excuse me a minute, Barry." He ran out of the room.

# ∽≋ 20 ≋∾

Demos had left Lindsay's room just two minutes before. Taylor ran down the hospital corridor. He saw Demos standing in front of the elevator banks and yelled, "You goddamned little worm! You filthy little bastard! Don't you move!"

Demos turned, horror turning his skin pasty, as Taylor bore down on him. He didn't hesitate. He poked frantically at the elevator button. Taylor grabbed him by his knotted tie and lifted him off his feet, pinning him against the wall.

"You damned little pervert!" He smashed his head into the wall. "That was no accident, that was a bomb, and it was meant for Lindsay! You didn't even bother to warn me this time. Why not? Jesus, she's lying in there because you're a filthy scum and don't pay your gambling debts!"

Taylor slugged him hard in the stomach and then in the jaw. And still he held him up, cursing him and punctuating his curses by banging him against the wall.

Taylor heard nurses yelling, saw people running toward him, saw some, terrified, running away. A patient came out of his room carrying a bedpan and dropped it. Urine splashed upward onto the linoleum floor. Taylor suddenly felt arms trying to pull him off Demos, but he didn't let go. He wanted to kill the damned bastard.

"Taylor, my boy, stop it!"

Barry Kinsley was built like a bull. He was fifty-five, balding, five-foot-ten, and had a chest the size of a pork barrel. He was still one of the strongest men on the New York police force. He'd been one of Taylor's instructors at the police academy and he'd taken him on the wrestling mat every time they'd gone at it. He'd tried to talk Taylor out of leaving the force. He'd remained a friend, distant, but always there, over the past few years.

He pulled Taylor off Demos, grunting with the effort— Jesus, he thought, he was getting too old for this shit—and Demos slid to the floor. He wasn't unconscious; he looked up at Taylor, whimpered, and drew his legs to his chest in the fetal position.

"I didn't do anything, Taylor, I swear it to you."

"You miserable liar! Barry, let me go, damn you! I'll beat the truth out of this little jerk in no time."

"Nope, Taylor. Now, boy, hold yourself still or I'll have to rearrange that sexy face of yours. The ladies won't like that, boyo. That's right, deep breaths, get control of your- self, and tell Papa Barry what gives here."

Taylor was trying to slow his breathing, trying to get back his control. It was tough. Barry loosened his grip just a bit. Taylor didn't try to escape him.

"Good, now behave, Taylor. I'm going to help this little fellow here get to his feet, and then we're all going back to your fiancée's room. Seems to me that's the safest place for Demos here. You wouldn't want to disturb her now, would you, Taylor?"

"He deserves to have his belly ripped out."

"Possibly," Barry said, eyeing Demos up and down. "Yeah, just possibly. Come along, let's get back to the lady's room." He looked up to see the sea of shocked and scared faces. "Show's over, folks. Go about your business now. Hey, what's that smell?"

Taylor walked on one side of Sergeant Kinsley, Demos, still bent over, on the other side.

"I didn't do anything, Taylor," Demos said, feeling safer with Kinsley between them.

"Just hold your horses, sir," Barry said easily. "Just

wait until we get in the lady's room. Then I know Taylor won't rip your throat out."

"Oh, God," Demos said.

"Now, sir, trust me. I'm an officer of the law."

"Oh, God," Demos said again.

Once in Lindsay's room, Taylor immediately went to her bedside. She was deeply asleep. There was only the hissing sound of the lung machine.

He turned back to Barry. "In early November Demos hired me to keep an eye on her—she's called Eden, and she's a model—because he was into the New Jersey boys for a big amount of bucks. He hadn't paid so they threatened to take out some of his players, not just him, more's the pity. I told him to pay because if anything happened to her he'd be responsible and I'd call the cops. Do you remember that man who was found beaten up in his car trunk near the Lincoln Tunnel? Well, that was the boys' demonstration. It was the director of the commercial shoot Eden was in. The guy recovered, lucky for birdbrain here. Demos then swore to me he'd paid up and he'd never do it again. Now, you little scum, who's coming down on you this time? Who has your balls in a vise now? How much are you in for?"

Demos was finally standing straight. He'd regained some sense of himself. He looked Taylor straight in the eye, Lindsay's hospital bed between them, ignored the sergeant, and said, "I kept my word, Taylor. Do you think I would ever take a chance again on having Eden hurt? My God, she's so—"

"Trusting?"

"Yeah, that and—"

"Gentle? Vulnerable?"

"Maybe, but I'd say she's just plain nice and caring. I love her, man. Oh, not like you do, because she's a woman after all, but I feel spiritual love for her." That sounded like a crock, and Demos quickly retrenched. "What I mean is that I care about her. So does Glen. Look at her! I wouldn't be responsible for that! Never, I swear it!"

He started to cry.

"Jesus," Taylor said. He looked at Barry. He sighed. "He's telling the truth, damn him."

"You should be pleased," Demos said, wiping his eyes and looking embarrassed. "You hurt me, Taylor." He rubbed his head and his stomach.

"Well, I'm not at all pleased," Sergeant Kinsley said. "Don't you two dimwits see what this means? The lady's got an enemy, lads, a real live one, one who had no qualms about using explosives with lots of folk around who could have been hurt. No one was, which means he was being a bit careful. Now, gents, let's talk. I need to know who could possibly have it in for her."

"No one," Demos said positively. "Not even . . . ah, no." He broke off and stared at Taylor.

Taylor was stroking the black stubble on his jaw. He said thoughtfully, "She just inherited a fortune—literally—from her grandmother and her mother. Both were killed in a car accident a week and a half ago. She inherited everything from her mother and most everything from her grandmother. She's very rich. Her half-sister's pissed and so is her father. He thinks he should have all the money."

"You're saying La Principessa could be involved?" Demos asked, appalled. "But I thought . . ." He broke off, wise enough now to keep his mouth shut.

"Who's that?" Barry asked.

Demos said slowly, "That's her half-sister, Princess Sydney di Contini. She's also a model. She, ah, well, she and Lindsay/Eden don't get along. It goes way back . . . way, way back."

"Let's call her Lindsay," Barry said. "Okay, from all her paperwork here, I see her full name is Lindsay Foxe. Where's all this family live, Taylor?"

"In San Francisco. They're evidently old wealth, old power. Lots of both, and all the greedy instincts in the world to go along with it."

"Is her daddy that federal judge, Royce Foxe?"

"I don't know," Taylor said. "Is he, Demos?"

"That's him. Smart bastard, from what Sydney says. Real smart, and that's where she got all her brains. She's a lawyer, you know, Harvard Law School, then she married this Italian prince who raped Lindsay in Paris in 1983."

'Whoa!" Barry stared from one man to the other. "This

is for real? She was raped by her brother-in-law? In 1983? But she was just a kid."

There was a knock on the door, then it was pushed open. Enoch's head came around. "Oh," he said. "Hi, Sarge. What are you doing here? Did Taylor call you for some reason?"

"Well, if it ain't old Enoch Sackett. Still skinny as a post, I see. Doesn't Sheila ever feed you?"

"All the time. It's my metabolism. Hey, Taylor . . ."

Enoch fell silent. He looked toward Lindsay, whose head was swathed in white bandages. He swallowed and looked back toward Taylor.

"She's going to be okay?"

Taylor nodded. He said to Barry, "Let me speak to Enoch for a minute, okay?"

"Why don't we just have Enoch spill what he knows right here, right now?"

"It's not about the case. It's personal. I'm not lying."

Sergeant Kinsley looked unconvinced. He looked toward the sleeping woman, wincing unconsciously. He waved Taylor out of the room.

"I heard about the accident on the radio. Why's Barry Kinsley here?"

"It wasn't an accident. It was plastic explosives and meant only for Lindsay."

"Jesus, man! What are you going to do?"

Taylor looked very tired, as tired as he felt. He needed sleep, a shower, and a good-size meal. His head felt heavy. "I don't know," he said finally. "Thanks for getting this stuff, Enoch."

"I got five different French newspapers and tabloids about the rape. Taylor, she was eighteen years old and she was butchered by the press! Another thing, though: none of them agree. Some come right out and say that she seduced her brother-in-law, others say that her half-sister tried to kill her husband in cold blood and the rape was staged so she could murder him, and one even goes so far as to say that the prince was sleeping with both sisters at the same time and his wife got pissed and shot him. Whatever the explanation, she was an eighteen-year-old Lolita. You go figure."

Taylor couldn't figure anything at the moment.

"Oh, yes, they even have an overheard comment supposedly made by the father. He says the daughter is a slut, basically, and that the person who really suffered in the entire matter was Sydney, the wife. This man sounds like a real winner."

Silence fell between them.

Finally Taylor pulled himself upright. "Everything okay at the office?"

Enoch nodded. "Not to worry."

"I'll call you later, then, Enoch. Thanks for all your help."

When he entered the room, his eyes immediately went to Lindsay. She was still sleeping.

Barry said, his voice pitched deep and soft, "Demos can't come up with any suspects for me, Taylor, other than the family. How about you?"

He looked at the woman he loved, the woman who could be dead, killed by an unknown man or woman. He felt so goddamned helpless. It tasted bitter in his mouth, this helplessness.

"Let me think about it. Lindsay has a good friend—I'll speak to her. Another thing, Barry, what about protection for her here in the hospital?"

"I've got two young guys coming down to keep guard. Both of them on the bitter edge of burnout. But they're good, Taylor, so don't frown at me or give me any of your smart lip. Now, I do need to speak to the lady. I'm going to hunt up her doctor and find out when she'll be with it enough to talk to me. See you later."

Demos said, "The people on the shoot said her face was smashed in."

"She'll be fine," Taylor said.

"Do you think she saw anything?"

"I don't know. You can believe that Barry will speak to each and every one of the folk on the shoot. Pray to God someone remembers something."

*   *   *

Lindsay was awake. Her eyes were still closed. She was holding very still. She could hear the soft hissing of the lung machine on the nightstand beside her. Her ribs hurt, a thudding, prodding sort of pain that was with her every moment, and her face felt like she had two tons of concrete pressing down on it. At least she could breathe; at least she was alive. The other she could bear.

She could control the pain. She could and would because she had to think about what had happened. She'd heard this man, this policeman, speaking to Taylor and Demos. What had happened wasn't an accident.

Someone had tried to kill her.

Control the pain. Yes, she had to control the pain because she had to think. But it made no sense. Who? She had no enemies, as far as she knew. Who? She felt fingers on her bare forearm, lightly stroking, making contact, giving her a connection.

"It's all right, sweetheart."

Taylor's voice—soft and calm. She hadn't realized he was here. He was wiping some Kleenex across her eyes. She hadn't realized she was crying. Then he kissed her, gentle as a soft beam of moonlight.

"It's all right. I'm here. Do you have much pain?"

"I can handle it." It was so hard to speak. It hurt her face dreadfully. "Water."

He slipped the straw into her mouth and she sucked on it, feeling shocks of pain as she did so.

He wiped away the tears on her cheeks.

"If you need some painkiller, just press this button here. It's hooked up to your IV. The nurse did that just a couple of hours ago. She said you could take as much as you needed. That's it. Give yourself a couple of licks. Good. No reason to put up with pain if you don't have to."

Taylor fell silent, waiting for the pain medication to kick in. He continued to stroke her arm, a habit now, probably one he would keep the rest of his life. He finally felt the tension begin to leave her body. Finally. "Now, you just lie here a minute, and I'll fetch your nurse. She wanted to know when you woke up. You've got two doctors, not just one, and both of them want to see you."

She closed her eyes, feeling the pain recede, leaving a strange sort of lethargy and numbness in their wake. She remembered thinking how miraculous it was when her grandmother had showed her how she could get as much painkiller as she wanted by just pressing a button. Now she was in the same position. She could still feel the immense weight, the pounding and heaviness of her face, but the pain was removed. Odd, but it was true.

Dr. Perry arrived first. She remembered him and tried to smile. "You're doing just fine," he said first thing.

"My face feels like it weighs two tons."

"I know. It's the swelling from the blow you took, combined with the swelling from the surgery. You'll need pretty heavy-duty painkillers for another couple of days. Then it will ease and feel more normal by the day. Tomorrow we'll change the bandages. We don't want to take any chances with infection. The stitches come out in about nine days. We'll be able to tell then, pretty much, the results of my handiwork."

It was so difficult to speak. She could barely open her mouth with the bandages heavy around her head and beneath her chin. "Will I look horrible?"

"No. You'll probably look just like you did before. As I said to Mr. Taylor here, you were very lucky. The damage was to the bones, not to your skin, which means little scarring. You were very lucky. You'll be beautiful again. Please don't worry."

"Thank you."

Taylor saw Dr. Perry in the hall. The doctor smiled. "I wasn't lying. She'll be fine. As for her beauty, I know she's a model and her face is her living. I think you should prepare her for a change in careers. It might not be necessary, but I can't be certain. It's nearly impossible to predict the exact result. It just seems wise that you get her thinking along alternative lines. The surgery went very well, I'm not lying to you, but still, one never really knows."

Taylor wanted to tell him that Lindsay wasn't a model because of any great desire to be so. But he didn't. He wanted to get back to her. He thanked the doctor and watched him walk away down the corridor. He said to officer Jay Fogel, who was sitting by Lindsay's door, a *People* magazine on his lap, "See anyone suspicious?"

Fogel shook his head, profoundly regretful. "Not even a pretty nurse." Fogel studied the man for a moment, then added, "Besides, Mr. Taylor, you're here. What maniac in his right mind would try to get to her with you here?"

Taylor just shook his head. Fogel was short, wiry, with a baby face that made all women, regardless of their ages, want to mother him. Fogel, from what Taylor had heard, usually took instant and shameless advantage.

"Just keep alert," Taylor said, and went back inside.

He sat beside Lindsay and immediately covered her forearm with his fingers. He stroked the soft flesh. He felt her ease.

"I know," she said, the words difficult to understand because she couldn't open her mouth very wide.

"You know it wasn't an accident?"

"Yes."

"Any ideas?"

He sounded so matter-of-fact, so completely neutral, that she blinked at him.

He smiled at her, seeing that she'd accepted it, that she'd drawn back from hysteria. She was firmly in control. He admired her greatly in that moment. "I want you to think back to the shoot. Go very slowly. Ah, look whose timing is next to perfection. Lindsay, love, this is Sergeant Barry Kinsley of the NYPD. He and I go back a long way, probably too long a way. He looks like a wrestler and he is, but he does have a brain. He's here to find out who tried to hurt you."

Barry looked into her eyes and knew then why Taylor or any man for that matter could fall like a ton of bricks for the lady. They were deep blue and filled with shadows and mysteries, so deep, he thought, and soft and incredibly sexy. Since she looked like a conehead, all swathed around the head in that white bandage, he hadn't thought much about her looks, even though she was a successful model. Now he wanted to see some professional photos of her.

"Hello, Miss Foxe," he said.

Lindsay nodded, then jerked. *Foxe!* She turned to Taylor, her eyes stricken with the knowledge that he knew and she hadn't been the one to tell him.

Taylor said mildly, forestalling anything she would say, "Lindsay Foxe is a nice name, sweetheart, but I think, personally, that Lindsay Taylor is a much nicer one. What do you say?"

She didn't say anything. She was crying with relief, with shame, with regret. She felt him dab away the tears. What was wrong with her? The crying—she'd never cried so much in her life. There was no control, none at all, and now this.

"Shush, sweetheart. It's all right. We'll talk later about it. It's not important. Please believe me, Lindsay. It's not important. Now, poor Barry here wants to ask you some questions. I want you to go real slow and think about everything. Tell us each and every little detail, no matter how silly, even crazy impressions, don't leave out even the bathroom breaks—tell us everything about yesterday morning."

She did, speaking slowly. She forgot things, then remembered. Taylor asked questions and she remembered more. Barry asked questions with a different slant, and more came back to her. It went slowly. ". . . Then I was standing by that stupid fake ski lift and Edie started screaming. I wasn't fast enough. I looked at her, because I didn't understand, then I looked up, following her eyes, and then things started raining down on me."

Barry said slowly, "Then you didn't see anyone who shouldn't have been there? You didn't have any questions about anyone at all?"

"No."

Barry said, "One thing bothers me, Miss Foxe. You were the only one standing against the ski lift when it exploded. No one else was close. Why were you there at just that moment and all alone?"

She closed her eyes. Why? "Oh, no," she said. "Oh, no."

"Tell us," Taylor said. "What do you see? What do you remember?" She heard the urgency in his voice, but his fingers on her forearm remained in their gentle slow rhythm.

"One of the set men came over to me. I was watching a chess game. He said they wanted to do some lineup shots and would I please go stand against the ski lift."

"Ah," Barry said. "Think now, Miss Foxe. Was the man one of the crew? Did you recognize him?"

"No."

"Okay, it's probably our guy. Picture him in your mind. Describe him as completely as you can."

Lindsay placed him in her mind, saw him as clearly as she did Sergeant Kinsley, and said, "He was five-foot-nine or ten. Not more. He was medium-complexioned, light brown eyes, light brown hair and eyebrows, thick eyebrows, and straight. His hair was on the long side, and oily. I know the color because he wore it long and it showed longer than the red wool cap he was wearing." She continued, covering each inch of the man.

Barry was amazed.

Taylor couldn't believe it. He didn't know what he expected, but not this nearly photographic recreation.

"I'm going to get a police artist over here, Miss Foxe. Would you work with him?"

"Yes."

"And mug books, but we'll do that later." Barry said to Taylor, "It sounds to me like this guy was hired to do the job. The explosives weren't professional, but neither were they amateur. He knew what he was doing but he isn't the kind to have this crazy kind of pride in his work. He knew how to keep himself from buying anything traceable. Yeah, chances are he was hired. Miss Foxe, I don't want to frighten you, but this is important. Who can you think of who would want you out of the way?"

"You mean dead," Lindsay said, no emotion in her voice, and was pleased.

"That's right," Barry said. It was that same matter-of-fact voice Taylor had used. It was calming. She almost smiled at both of their tactics, but the pain had been inching back into her consciousness and she just couldn't.

"No one," she said.

Taylor watched her press the button for more painkiller. He didn't say anything. He drew away Barry's attention from her until she could regain her control. He knew it was important to her. It would have been just as important to him.

"Sydney di Contini, Lindsay's half-sister, is supposed to come visiting in a little while. You want to stay around and meet the lady?"

"Who wouldn't want to meet a real-live princess?"

Sydney wasn't alone. Judge Royce Foxe and his wife, Holly Foxe, were with her. Taylor stood when she entered. His eyes went to the patrician older man who stood just behind her. My God, he thought, staring. Lindsay had his eyes. Just his eyes, nothing more. Well, perhaps his height as well. But the eyes, it was like looking into her eyes, until Foxe said, "What is going on here?"

Cold and flat and hard, Taylor thought. No, his eyes weren't anything like his daughter's. There was no warmth, just ice, hot and hard.

Barry introduced himself, then turned to Taylor. "And this, of course, is your daughter's fiancé, S. C. Taylor."

Royce Foxe stared at the man who, Sydney had assured him over and over, was engaged to Lindsay. He didn't know what he'd expected, but it wasn't this sort of man. This man was tough. He'd been around. He'd seen things a lot of men never saw. He was good-looking, Royce supposed, but he looked dangerous, possibly cruel. Certainly ruthless. This man was engaged to Lindsay? He shook his head. It made no sense. He was inclined to think it was all a lie.

He nodded toward Taylor. Holly was introduced. Taylor wanted to beat the living hell out of Royce Foxe, but he knew it wouldn't be smart. Not here, not now. He said easily, "It's rather crowded in here. Lindsay's sleeping right now and I don't want her awakened. Why don't we all go to the waiting room?"

Royce glanced over at his daughter. She looked pathetic, absurd really, with her head wrapped up like an imaginary invalid in a bad comedy. He grimaced, then turned on his heel. Barry looked over at Taylor, saw that he was white-faced with rage.

He winked at Taylor. It made Taylor shake his head. He opened his mouth, then closed it.

Barry wasted no time. When they were in the small private waiting room at the end of the corridor, he said to Judge Foxe, "I understand you're furious because your mother left all her money to Lindsay."

"Not bad, Sergeant," Royce Foxe said. "Not wonderful either, but you might improve with practice."

Taylor winked at Barry. The man was something else.

"Well, weren't you pissed about it? Didn't you try to get Lindsay to sign over her inheritance to you?"

"Certainly. It's only right. I am the only heir, the real heir, not her. My mother was old, she was losing it, quite badly really. I'm not yet certain how Lindsay got to her, but I will find out. Then she will lose all of the money. However, I wouldn't murder my own daughter."

He laughed, a soft, mellow sound. "I've seen a lot of very strange fathers during my years on the bench, Sergeant, but as a federal judge, it simply wouldn't do for me to kill my daughter. For any reason."

Holly said, pointing a beringed finger toward Taylor, "It's absurd! All of it! I'll just bet Lindsay got herself mixed up with *him* and now she doesn't want him anymore because she has money and he hasn't and he tried to kill her!"

"Her mind isn't polished," Royce remarked to Barry, "but she does have rather pointed notions, does she not?"

Sydney said, "This is absurd, Sergeant. None of us would harm Lindsay. Don't you have any real leads? Perhaps it really was an accident after all."

"No, it wasn't an accident," Taylor said. "Incidentally, the police will be getting financial statements on all of you. You talk a good game, Mr. Foxe—"

"Judge Foxe."

"We'll have to see, won't we? I was a cop, and like you, I've seen a lot of strange fathers. I consider you one of the most remarkable and uncommon of any I've ever run into."

"Just what the hell is that supposed to mean?"

"I was referring to Lindsay's rape in 1983 by her brother-in-law, and how you turned on her, how you dished your own daughter up to the press."

Royce Foxe turned pale with anger. "So that's what she told you, is it! That damned little ingrate, that stupid slut, why I'll . . ." He broke off, as if realizing what he was doing, and in front of a cop.

Royce waved a negligent hand, back in control again. "My wife and I are staying at the Plaza. If you wish to speak further with us, Sergeant, we will, of course, oblige. We will remain in New York for only two days. No reason to stay longer if Lindsay is going to live."

"Yeah, you can count out any funeral plans, Judge," Taylor said. He watched, without moving, until Foxe was out of sight. "I would fancy doing something very painful to him," he said to Enoch.

"Me too, boyo."

Later that afternoon when Lindsay awoke, Taylor said to her, "I've made a decision, Lindsay."

He saw fear instantly leap into her eyes and wanted to kick himself.

"Just stop it, do you hear me? I don't give a rat's ass that you didn't tell me who you were. I even understand why you didn't. I know now, and I'd like to punch your father's lights out. He's a shit. You're not. I love you and I'll always love you. If it's okay with you, here's what I want to do—"

"No, stop," she said. Lindsay closed her eyes, feeling the pain swamp her, trying to control it. She did, finally. "I believe you love me, Taylor. I think it's miraculous, but I believe that you'll always love me. You've never lied to me and you never would. You're just not made that way. You say who I am doesn't matter to you. I believe you. I'm very grateful to you for that.

"Now, I honestly can't think of anyone who would want to hurt me, except my family." She paused, looking over his left shoulder. Then her eyes met his and she said very quietly, "If it is my family, then there's a solution. Will you marry me now? As soon as possible? Then if my family is behind it for the money, they wouldn't have a motive anymore because you'd be my beneficiary."

Taylor smiled. He had been on the point of asking her to marry him for the same reason. "You're pretty smart, you know that? How about tomorrow afternoon? You're a Protestant. I know a Presbyterian minister. Is that okay?"

She nodded, relief and happiness overcoming the pain.

Taylor tried to choose his words carefully, but he didn't entirely succeed. "Your father's behavior appears irrational to me. So is your half-sister's. As for your stepmother, she's practically off the deep end. If one of them—or both or all three—were behind the attempt on your life, then once we're married, I really do think you're right. They'll not forgive, but they will forget."

"What about the prince?"

"Sergeant Kinsley has checked. Sure enough, the prince is here in New York. He cleared customs on Sunday. He's staying with his wife. If the motive is money, the police will discover it soon enough." He felt her become rigid, felt the awful fear come into her, saw it in her eyes.

"I'm afraid."

"I am too, but let me tell you something, Lindsay. If that man tries to come near you, I'll hurt him. Please believe me, because I'm telling you the truth."

"Like you hurt Demos?"

"Lots worse."

"I'll look real silly in a wedding veil right now."

"Once you're unwrapped and rid of your cocoon and feeling back to normal, we'll do it again. I love you. Will you marry me tomorrow?"

"Yes." Lindsay closed her eyes. Married to Taylor. She saw her father's face. Saw his rage, for he would be enraged because he'd see himself unable to coerce her once Taylor was her husband. Had he tried to have her killed? She saw Holly and knew she was as furious as her husband. Both of them hated her, blamed her for somehow making her grandmother leave her everything. Lindsay still wondered, she still couldn't figure our why her grandmother had left her the money. She was very tired. Her face throbbed and pressed heavily down. Her ribs rubbed and gnawed. She hated the sound of the soft hissing. The doctor had said perhaps tomorrow she would be unhooked from the lung machine. But Taylor had agreed to marry her. Everything would be all right.

Taylor kissed her and left, telling her he'd be back in a couple of hours.

He'd hired a private nurse, Missy Dubinsky. She entered the moment he left, big breasts bouncing, full hips straining at the white pants, smarmy big smile. Lindsay knew it was wise that she never be alone, but the woman was simply too cheerful and so thrilled to be taking care of a beautiful model. She oozed goodwill. Lindsay ground her teeth and kept silent.

Jesus, she thought. Beautiful . . . she touched her fingertips to the thick bandages that covered her head and the right side of her face.

Yeah, some beauty she was now. She hadn't believed Dr. Perry. She wasn't stupid. Taylor had spoken easily about her career, questioning her about the future and what she wanted. No, she wasn't stupid. He was preparing her. She just prayed she wouldn't look like a freak, with one eye lower than the other. She just prayed Taylor wouldn't feel revulsion once the bandages were off and the stitches taken out. She prayed Taylor really loved her.

At least she was alive.

Who had tried to kill her?

# 21

It was a lovely wedding. Never mind that the bride was propped up in bed wearing a hospital nightgown beneath a satin bed robe—white, of course—holding a bouquet of roses in her right hand and her head wrapped in white bandages.

Still, Gayle Werth and Sheila Sackett had gotten together and in the space of twenty-four hours, along with the help of the nurses and orderlies and doctors, had turned the room into a flower garden of red roses and white carnations. They'd even draped the bed and windows with pink and white crepe paper. The one Monet print on the wall opposite the bed had a big white bow on it.

The staff had done even more. The nurses had given Lindsay a huge box of condoms and wrapped her lung machine with a huge red bow. The card on the condoms read: "Soon to be replaced." The card on the lung machine read: "Soon to be gone."

Dr. Perry had given her an antique mirror-and-brush set, telling her as she opened it that she was going to be beautiful very soon again and he wanted her to have a mirror close at hand to admire herself and to admire him. Demos and Glen weren't to be outdone. They'd provided for home delivery of two dozen gourmet meals from La Viande. Demos said, "Well, I know for a fact that all Lindsay can manage is a salami sandwich. She said you were the cook, Taylor, but I didn't believe her." He turned to Lindsay and took her hand. "I want my models to suffer to stay thin. Did I say that all the meals were seven courses?"

As for Taylor, he laughed at the condoms and was grateful for the meals, since he could count his own ribs now. As for Lindsay, she was a stick. He prayed that Dr. Perry would have a fine life for his kindness.

It was Enoch who remembered one dark wool suit. He had it cleaned along with a white dress shirt, and brought it to the apartment an hour before the wedding at the hospital.

"Cufflinks," Taylor said, scrambling through the dresser drawers.

"Here," Enoch said, and handed him a gold pair in the shape of unicorns. "I thought you'd be too nervous to think about anything on your own. These were my dad's. Sheila always said he was into fantasy. Then she always smiles. It's tough thinking about your parents making out, you know?"

"Thanks." Taylor turned to give his friend a distracted smile. "Thanks too for the piano lessons from you and your mom. How did you know that I wanted to learn and Lindsay already played?"

Enoch tapped the side of his head. "Mom says our brains go back to before the *Mayflower*."

"Yeah, right. Hey, Enoch, do you see any pigs taking off outside?"

In the taxi Enoch said, "Look, Taylor, try out a smile on me. You're getting married, not going to a funeral."

Taylor said very quietly, "I'm scared shitless."

Enoch patted his hand and nodded wisely. "Look, I know you never wanted to get married again, not after Diane, and here Lindsay is probably richer than Diane was, but—"

"I'm scared shitless about the maniac out there trying to kill her."

"Oh. Sorry."

"It's all right." Taylor sighed. "Funny thing is, I probably should be scared about remarrying, but I'm not. I love her and can see both of us together until my brain gives out into mist and my body folds up into bones. It's strange, but there just aren't any doubts. As for her money, we'll deal with it."

"Do you think you'll keep on with the business?"

Taylor turned to look fully at the man who'd been his friend for six years. "Why do you ask?"

Enoch looked embarrassed. He shrugged. "You're rich. You don't have to be a working stiff anymore."

"No, Lindsay is rich. I'm still just me. Now, don't get me wrong. I think a man who scoffs at his wife's money and insists she's to live on his salary alone is an ass."

"That was your attitude with Diane and her money."

"Yeah, I know. I'm trying to be mature about this, Enoch. Lindsay can do whatever she wants with the money. If she wants to make it part of the common pot, so be it. Hey, we might decide to invest in pork bellies or pinto beans. Or we'll buy Kauai. How about a helicopter business? You got any suggestions?"

Enoch laughed. "She's a great woman, Taylor. She's changed a lot since back in November. Come to think of it, you have too."

Taylor remembered the night she'd come back from San Francisco. He could still taste her mouth, feel her surprise when he kissed her and touched her, her passion, her urgency. He could remember the softness of her flesh, the tightness of her when he'd entered her. "Yes, she has," he said. And he remembered just as clearly his feelings when she'd come to him. "I as well."

"Has Barry discovered anything at all yet?"

"You remember the description she gave of the supposed set man?"

"Yeah, I still can't believe it. I've never known a witness that good. If he'd had a mole on his butt, she probably would have intuited it from his accent."

"She'd never thought it was important enough to mention to me before. She does have a photographic memory for faces. I told her we were going to bring her on in the business. Anyway, one of the old guys in homicide saw the sketch and recognized the bastard right off. His name's Bert

Oswald, a little killer for hire, been in and out of prison all his life, a loser most the time, but occasionally he gets a job done and it usually ends up getting him back into the slammer again. He comes cheap and he's not, as I said, very reliable."

"Thank God he wasn't this time."

The taxi pulled up at the hospital.

Taylor said, a touch of anxiety in his voice that Enoch didn't miss, "I look okay?"

"You missed a spot shaving, your eyes are a bit bloodshot, you look skinny, but hey—yeah, just fine. A regular Romeo."

The driver turned around and gave them both a huge grin. "Hey, which one of you cuties is expecting?"

He was still laughing when he pulled away.

"Now, that's better," Enoch said, observing the wide grin on Taylor's face.

Gayle and Sheila were there fussing over Lindsay. She was now wearing a bit of powder and some lipstick. It looked faintly ridiculous in her current condition, but Taylor just leaned down and kissed most of it off. The minister, Reverend Battista, had known Taylor's mom and dad and sister. He was charming, warm, and had no problem with marrying the couple in a hospital. He lived every single day deep in his faith and didn't question life's occasional strange byways too often. He'd discovered long before that it led to absurdities that couldn't be explained. So he smiled and greeted Taylor and told him he was glad to see him after three years.

They were in love, Reverend Battista saw, and he was pleased. He appreciated weddings, particularly when the bride wasn't obviously pregnant. Those he always doubted would last the first round. But these two . . . they'd last. He watched Taylor slide the wedding band on Lindsay's finger. They were . . . attached, somehow attuned to each other.

When Reverend Battista pronounced them well and finally married, Taylor's eyes shone. His severe look melted away. He kissed his bride. There was applause from the nurses and doctors standing in the doorway.

"For someone five days out of surgery, you're a charming bride," Taylor said next to her bandaged ear. "You feel up to a drop of champagne?"

"Oh, yes. It's my wedding day. Dr. Shantel said half a flute."

His eyes darkened. And she knew he was thinking about the one night they'd had together. It seemed aeons ago now. Almost as if it had never existed. But it had, and she could still remember the faint echoes of pleasure, a pleasure so intense it was frightening, and he'd promised her that it would always be like that between them. She believed him.

There were six bottles of Mumms champagne, enough for all the staff who were in and out of the room, Officer Fogel, and Missy Dubinsky. Barry Kinsley came round to congratulate them and tell Taylor that the little shit Oswald was still on the loose but they'd get him soon.

Taylor looked over at this wife, who was speaking to Glen. "I'm not certain it's safe for her to leave the hospital. Her lung machine was unhooked this morning. Dr. Perry says if she has proper rest, she can recuperate at home as well as here. But at home, I don't know how well I can protect her."

"Let's keep her here, Taylor. Easier to keep her safe."

"Yeah."

"One little glass but no more," Dr. Shantel said, smiling down at Lindsay when Enoch tried to give her another half-glass. "Your medication is still a bit on the heavy side for too much alcohol. Congratulations, Mrs. Taylor."

Lindsay fell asleep just after finishing her first half-glass of champagne. Dr. Shantel smiled and shushed everyone. "Our patient's so happy she has to sleep it off."

"Well," Barry said, gazing down at the new Mrs. Taylor. "Nothing like having your bride conk out on you before your wedding night."

"I figure we can make up for it in the next fifty years."

"Good man."

Sheila laughed and gave a very interested look. "Do you like jazz, Sergeant?"

"Well, ma'am," Barry said, turning admiring eyes

toward Sheila, who was wearing a long emerald silk dress, "I like to think I play a mean trumpet. Yeah, jazz is something else. Right now I'm listening every night to Harry Dellios. He's out of—"

"Atlanta! My, my, isn't that a wonderful coincidence, Enoch?"

Enoch groaned. "That's my cousin, Sergeant. But beware, if you spend a lot of time with my mom here, you'll get as skinny as I am."

"Might not be a bad idea," Barry said, looking down at his belly. He turned to Taylor, who was leaning over his wife, just looking at her. "I need to speak to you some more when all the fun's over."

It was over in fifteen minutes. Barry Kinsley asked Gayle Werth to accompany him and Taylor to the waiting room.

He said without preamble, "Taylor told me about this guy Dr. Gruska, a professor who kept trying to track Lindsay down."

"Gayle, do you think he could be crazy enough to turn on Lindsay?" Taylor asked.

Gayle took a turn about the small waiting room, thinking hard. When she turned, she nodded. "Yes. He's a nut case. According to Lindsay, he's deep into repressed childhood sexuality, you know, all that Freud stuff."

"I agree," Taylor said. "At least it's worth a shot. I've tried to track him down. He'll be on campus tomorrow, I was told. I'll talk to him."

"I'd like to come along," Barry said. "No, don't look at me like I'm spoiling your fun, boyo. I just don't want you to rumple his tie if he starts foaming at the mouth and admitting everything."

"You can't think of anyone else, Miss Werth?"

"No. Lindsay's always kept to herself, particularly after 1983, Taylor. You know, after Paris."

"No men?" Barry asked. "None before Taylor?"

"Oh, no. She wouldn't let a guy within ten feet of her. Taylor's the first man she even smiled at. I still can't believe this." She stopped, then reached out her hand and shook

Taylor's. "Thank you. Lindsay's great. I've always been so worried for her."

"The boy will keep her happy, Miss Werth," Enoch said.

"Yes, I think the boy will. He has heart."

After Gayle had left, Barry said, "We finished the check on all the family. No big surprises. Just as we thought. The father is in financial trouble—he's a pistol as a judge but as a businessman he's dog piss. His wife married him for his money and she's not a happy lady now that her stepdaughter got the dough. Word is she's also an alcoholic. The older daughter, Sydney, makes a bundle as a model, but she spends more, and not on her own amusements, in all fairness to her. As for her husband, the prince, the jerk's well on his way to going through the family fortune. Big trouble there. Sydney is sending a good deal of her earnings back to Italy to keep things afloat. Whatever her faults, she hasn't deserted the family."

"She does have a daughter there."

"Yeah, well, the daughter's quite the little princess. Spoiled rotten, from what the police lieutenant in Milan told me. Throws tantrums in public. So, Taylor, it's possible that one of the family or more than one of them would want her out of the way. Jesus, how many times does it all come down to money? Too often, my friend, far too often. But to kill her? I just don't know."

"Well, since we're married now, it's academic. If any of them were behind the first attempt, there shouldn't be another. They won't get a dime if she dies now."

"Who's going to tell them that their fat pigeon has flown to another coop?"

It happened so quickly Lindsay had no time to react. She was groggy from sleep, her mind lulled and calm. She didn't hurt, which was a blessing, but her throat was dry. Six days now since the surgery. She wished she could carve a slash on her bedpost for every day that went by.

And now she was married.

She smiled.

And then the voice came, so warm and so familiar that

she thought she must be making it up in her mind, dredging up a nightmare because she had nothing else to do. But it wasn't a nightmare.

"Little Lindsay. Poor Lindsay. I don't know if you're so beautiful now. You're certainly old, ah, but your poor face. All smashed in, Sydney told me. All blood and smashed bone. But it isn't all that important now, is it?"

Where the hell was Missy? Why the hell had the young police officer outside her door let him in?

Then she saw that Missy was standing in the open doorway, beaming at the prince's back. She saw that Officer Fogel was standing behind Missy, not looking at the prince, but at Missy's rear end.

"Your brother-in-law just wanted to see you for a moment," Missy said, smiling with lots of white teeth, all goodwill. She turned her high-wattage smile up higher when the prince turned at the sound of her voice.

He looked the same, Lindsay thought. No, no, he looked more handsome. He was at least forty now, and he looked like a fairy-tale prince, tall and slender and elegant, his hands long and narrow. He looked like the perfect man.

He liked teenage girls. He had raped her. What would Missy say if Lindsay told her that. Missy would probably beam her big smile, poke out her big bosom, and tell her that the poor man just needed a real woman to show him the proper way.

"Won't you say hello to me, Lindsay?" the prince said, turning back to her. "I came a long way to see you."

In that moment, something odd happened. The old paralyzing fear left her. Something inside her changed as she turned her head on the pillow to look more fully at him. Something grew inside her, something strong and whole. Something powerful. Something mean.

She felt suddenly wonderful. "Hello, Prince. What a long time it's been. Whatever are you doing here? I'm a bit surprised they'd let you into the country. Oh, but they don't know about you here, do they?"

He looked briefly taken aback. He frowned. "Your voice is different. Oh, I see. It's difficult for you to talk because of that bandage under your chin."

"No, not really," she said. "The bandage isn't that tight now. It's something else. What are you doing here? Fresh hunting grounds in New York?"

He said easily, calmly, as if to a cantankerous child, "I'm here to see you. That's all. And to ask you to reconsider your engagement to that proletariat imbecile. Sydney told me about him, Lindsay, and I have to agree with her. It's obvious what he's about. He's marrying you for your money. Everyone can see it's true. He's a ruffian and probably dishonest. He was a cop, wasn't he? He would hurt you. He's used to violence. Don't marry him. Think about it. Give yourself time."

She wanted to laugh. She felt the meanness grow, and the hardness seemed to fill her. She felt strong and stronger still; she felt good. When he reached out his hand to touch her, she didn't flinch, just looked him straight in the eye. "Don't, Prince." She'd spoken calmly, slowly. She smiled up at him. "If you get one inch closer, I'll make you very sorry. I'm not a teenager now for you to intimidate."

He drew back his hand. His eyes changed. They were no longer warm and caressing. His mouth thinned. Odd, but it made him look only the more handsome, added somehow to his charisma, because it made him look faintly dangerous. Lindsay looked beyond him toward Missy and Officer Fogel. They'd retreated a couple of steps but the door was still open. Taylor's order, probably.

The prince bent down just a bit and said softly, his eyes glittering as he looked at her mouth, "Do you like to fuck your peasant, Lindsay? Is he rough with you? Do you suck him off? You like that, don't you? Is that it?"

Lindsay looked up at him. Over the past years when she'd tried to think objectively about him, she'd tried to figure out how his mind worked. She'd wondered why he had become twisted. Had it started when he was a child himself? When he became a man? Who had been responsible? His father? Mother? Genes? Now she simply didn't care. Now all she wanted was to have him gone. Ah, but she felt powerful now, and free, even though she was trapped in a hospital bed.

She whispered, her own eyes glittering up at him, "Oh,

yes, Alessandro, the peasant rapes me nearly every night, holds me down or fastens my wrists to the bedposts with his neckties, don't you know, and he slaps me and makes me bleed sometimes because he's so rough. I love it. You taught me all about that, didn't you? All that neat slapping and pain? By all that's right, I owe you so much, Prince, so very much."

He straightened. "I thought as much. You've changed, Lindsay, and I don't like it. No one likes your attitude now. And you're lying to me about this man. But he'll change on you the minute he's got you married to him. You have money; he doesn't have anything. Don't marry him. I'm here to ask you to come home with me, to Milan. I'll take care of you. You'll be part of my family. You're Melissa's dear aunt. Come to Italy with me, Lindsay."

"Aren't I a bit old for you now, Prince?"

"You're my dear sister," he said. "Nothing more."

"How fickle you are. I fear you're a day late, Prince."

"What do you mean? I don't understand you."

A deep voice came from the doorway. "She means to say that you're the only one going back to Italy. Now, Prince, it's up to you how you return home. You can go flat on your back in a nicely lined casket or you can be a charming little princeling sitting in first class."

The prince turned slowly. Lindsay watched with great interest and a smile. For a moment she felt regret that Taylor had come. She'd wanted to tell the prince that she was free of him, that she was free of the past he'd forced upon her. She'd wanted him to examine her freedom, to recognize it, to react to it.

"Hello, Taylor," she said in great good humor. "This is my brother-in-law, the Prince di Contini. Isn't he absolutely something? For the first time since I met him I realize how truly remarkable he is. He has unplumbed depths. What do you think? He wants to take care of me because I'm his dear sister. Nothing else. I'm very old now, you know. Beyond eighteen is ancient to him. After he raped me, it seems he lost his respect for me. I think now he's willing to swallow my old age because of my new wealth. Do you think he wants me to go back with him so I can buy his little girls for him?"

Taylor looked the prince up and down, from his finely made Italian wool suit to his Gucci loafers, then said easily, "I think you're right, sweetheart. He certainly is something. 'Remarkable' doesn't begin to cover him, though."

"How about 'pervert' then?" Lindsay asked, loud enough for Missy and Officer Fogel to hear.

Missy gasped.

Officer Fogel giggled.

Taylor turned and waved them away from the door, saying, "Show's over." He closed it softly. He turned back and said, "So, Prince, you've been speaking to my wife?"

"Yes, I want her to tell you to go to hell, I don't want you to hurt her, and you will because you're uneducated and a ruffian and I want her to come back with me . . . *What did you say?*"

"My wife. She is my wife. Her name is now Lindsay Foxe Taylor. It has a ring to it, don't you think?" Taylor walked past the prince to stand beside Lindsay. He lifted her hand. Her engagement ring shone brilliantly, highlighting the wedding band.

"No, you can't have married him, you can't have. Oh, Jesus, this can't be . . ."

The prince fell silent, stunned, disbelieving. Lindsay wasn't certain what he was thinking now. Was it about all the money he'd never get out of her now? Had he been the one to want her dead?

It needed but Sydney to complete the drama, and she arrived two minutes later to a thick pool of silence. She looked at her husband and said with disgust and no preamble, "I thought you'd come here, you bloodless fool. I've looked and looked for you. You just couldn't keep your distance, could you?"

The prince looked up at his wife. He showed no interest. A faint line of displeasure marred his brow.

"I told you to leave her alone, damn you! Why can't you ever listen? Jesus, why did you come to New York anyway? I didn't want you to get near her! There's nothing you could say to her that she'd believe!"

"I'm glad he came, Sydney," Lindsay said quietly. "I really am. I see things so clearly now."

Sydney looked at her half-sister and smiled slightly. "Did your pulse flutter anew when he walked in? Isn't he handsome? And his body is as fine as any model's."

"Oh, no, no flutterings. He just wants me to come home with him. He'll take care of me. I tend to believe him, since I'm twenty-six and very old. That was how old you were when you married him, so you should know. I guess he also wants access to my money."

The prince said very quietly, "It doesn't matter now, Sydney."

"What doesn't?"

For an instant Taylor found himself feeling some sympathy for the man at his wife's deadly sarcasm. But only for an instant.

"She's already married to him. Can you believe that? She's already married to him."

Taylor said to a slack-mouthed Sydney, who was shaking her head back and forth, "It's true. We didn't invite you because the screaming and yelling and cursing would have disturbed the other patients, not to mention the minister."

"She's married to him," the prince repeated.

"So," Taylor said, "here's the bottom line. If any or all of you tried to kill her for her money, you can forget it. She dies and I get it all. You don't get a penny. Not even half a lira. Nothing. Do you understand me, both of you?"

"She married him and he'll hurt her. Just look at him, tough as a peasant. How could you marry someone like him, Lindsay?"

"You're fucking disgusting!" Sydney said. She grabbed his arm and tugged him toward the door. "Just shut up. I can't believe this!" At the doorway Sydney turned. "Oh, yeah, little sister, all my best wishes. I'll ask Valerie to call you with some advice. I hope you know what you're doing."

"I think I do, Sydney. I asked him to give himself to me and he said yes."

"I'll just bet he couldn't say yes fast enough."

"That's right," Taylor said. "I was so fast I nearly knocked her bandages off."

"She married him," the prince said, shaking his head. *"Him!"*

"Oh, shut up!" Sydney yelled at him. Then they were gone, the prince still mumbling, but quiescent, Sydney silent and pale, her hand firmly on his arm.

Taylor said nothing for many moments. He was studying Lindsay. Finally, "I'm sorry I ruined your show. I didn't realize then that you had everything under control. He didn't hurt you this time, did he? You saw him clearly, didn't you?"

She raised wondering eyes to his face. "How can you understand things so readily? You're right. He didn't even scare me a little bit. I was kind of sorry when you arrived, but no matter. He's pathetic, isn't he, Taylor?"

"Yes, very pathetic."

He kissed her fingers, her mouth, her nose.

"I like the sound of that, Taylor. Control. Yep, I had control. You know something else? I was a sarcastic bitch. I felt mean and hard. It was wonderful."

He continued kissing her; then, "How's the pain?"

"I feel like brain-dead but I hurt hardly at all."

"Is Missy driving you nuts?"

"No, but she's driving Officer Fogel crazy."

"He deserves it, the horny sod."

They spoke quietly for a while longer, then Taylor looked down at his watch and said, "I'm off now to see Dr. Gruska. Barry's coming with me. Fogel and Missy will be here. I'm going to pin their ears back for letting the idiot prince in. You rest now, okay, sweetheart?"

"Be careful, Taylor."

It was cold in the psychology building. Heat sputtered and hissed from the old radiators along the walls of the long corridor and the linoleum cracked beneath their feet. "This is his office," Taylor said. The door to room 223 was closed but there was a light inside. They paused, hearing voices.

"He's got a student in there," Barry said, raising his hand to knock.

Taylor pressed his hand down. "Just a moment," he said. They stood very still, listening to a girl's intense voice. She couldn't be more than twenty years old, if that. She was speaking softly, leaning forward—they could see her outline through the opaque glass. "I do trust you. Do you truly think you can help me, Dr. Gruska?"

"Ah, Bettina, I know I can. You're young and beautiful and smart. You've repressed so many feelings, my dear, and your father hasn't helped you by ignoring you and pretending not to notice that you're nearly a woman now. But I can free you by releasing those feelings. I'll cleanse you. We'll free them together and I'll show you what it can be like to express yourself, all of yourself, to give all of yourself and not hold anything back."

"I don't believe this," Barry said under his breath. "Is this guy serious?"

"Dead serious, more's the pity. Sounds like he's got another live one."

"Shall we rescue the kid?"

"Yeah, let's."

Dr. Gruska didn't at first recognize the hard-faced man who strode into his office. A harder-faced older man came in behind him. He felt a spurt of alarm. Then he recognized the first man.

"You visited me a while ago. You're a doctor from Omaha, right? Dr. Winston."

"That's right. But I'm really not. I lied to you. My name is Taylor, and this is Sergeant Barry Kinsley with the NYPD."

If Gruska chose to think him a cop, just as well. Taylor paused and looked at the girl, who'd stood and was now staring in sheer fright at both of them. She was small, slender, with long blond hair straight down her back. She wasn't especially pretty but she was as innocent and guileless as a pup. Taylor wondered what Lindsay had looked like at her age. Taylor nodded coldly to her, then said to Gruska, "We'd like to speak to you, Dr. Gruska, about Lindsay Foxe."

Gruska jumped up from his chair and several blue books went flying off the desk. The girl was evidently forgotten. "Oh, God! Is she all right? I saw it on TV but I didn't know which hospital they'd taken her to and I called and called but no one would tell me anything. I thought she was at St. Vincent's but they kept giving me the runaround. Then the news said it wasn't an accident. Is she all right?"

Barry and Taylor looked at each other.

The girl said, curiosity overcoming her fear, "Are you here about the model, Eden?"

"That's right," Barry said. "Dr. Gruska here evidently wanted to help her too. He thought she was too repressed, just like you. He wanted to be the one to, er, free her up, just like you. He's just full of helpfulness. Why don't you leave, miss, and think about him. He really isn't what you think he is."

The girl looked toward Dr. Gruska, her eyes large with fright and doubt, but he wasn't paying any more attention to her. She fled without another word.

Maybe they'd saved one, Taylor thought.

Taylor said, "Lindsay is going to be all right. Someone tried to murder her, that's true. We'd like to ask where you were at the time of the explosion, on Monday, at noon."

"*Me?*" Gruska simply stared at them, shaking his head back and forth. "You think I could have been involved? I wouldn't hurt Lindsay. I love her, I've loved her for years. My father loves her too. I want to take care of her. She needs me, you know, needs me very much. Only I can help her, but she won't let me. Please, take me to her."

"Not much furniture in his living room," Barry said under his breath.

"Perhaps you can tell us where you were, Dr. Gruska?" Taylor asked again. "Monday, at noon."

Gruska waved his hand around. "I was here all day, I was here with these bloody idiot students. You saw one of them—idiots, all! Take me to her now."

"Can you think of anyone who would want to hurt her?" Barry asked, patient as a bishop.

"No one. She's shy, always has been because she was so very hurt by her brother-in-law. When I found out what had happened to her—she was a student in my senior

319

seminar—I tried to help her but she was too afraid. She wouldn't let me. No one could want to hurt her, no one except maybe a man who tried to have sex with her and she turned him down. Revenge maybe, by some man she wouldn't sleep with."

"Do you know of any such man, Dr. Gruska?"

"No, no. So shy . . . she was always so shy, so withdrawn, always trying to protect herself."

Barry said, "Do you know a man named Oswald? Bert Oswald?"

Dr. Gruska looked at him blankly. "You mean like the guy who shot Kennedy?"

"Same last name, sure enough." Enoch sighed and turned to Taylor, who said, "Thank you, Dr. Gruska, for your time. As to where Lindsay is, we aren't allowed to disclose that information, not until we apprehend the person responsible. However, it's best you forget her now because she's found someone to help her. She's married and she's very happy. No more problems, I promise you."

"Married? Oh, no, that's impossible." The man looked panicked, his hands shaking. "No, no, you've got to be wrong. I know her. She wouldn't let a man get near her, no way."

Taylor said very calmly, "She's married to me, Dr. Gruska, and I assure you that she has changed quite remarkably. She loves me and she trusts me. She is no longer the Lindsay Foxe you knew. Now I suggest you forget her."

They left Dr. Gruska standing by his desk, staring at nothing in particular. He looked like a man who had lost his bearings.

"I've met lots of nuts," Barry said. "He's right up there with the best of them. Ain't it comforting to know he's passing on his store of knowledge to the younger generation?"

"Yeah, comforting. And we're not a bit closer to finding out who's behind this. Not old Gruska, that's for sure. And you know something, Barry, deep down, I just can't buy it that one of the family or all of them are responsible. They're pretty disgusting, but not murderers. At least, I don't think they could have come up with the idea to murder her so quickly after the will had been read. It took thought and planning. It took knowing someone to hire to do the job."

"Judge Foxe is bound to know all sorts of talented scum, Taylor. West coast and east coast."

"Yeah, I agree, but the time frame is just too short for them to act so quickly. You see, someone would have had to say it aloud. 'Let's kill Lindsay. Then we'll have her money and we'll be all right.' Then all of them would have had to agree. Then the judge would have to get hold of someone to do it. Not enough time to get it done."

Barry sighed. "Unfortunately, I think you're right. Who, then, Taylor, who?"

"Bloody hell, I don't know."

"Where are you off to?"

Taylor smiled then. "To see my bride."

# 22

"Hold very still, Mrs. Taylor. That's it, just a few more snips."

*Mrs. Taylor.* How odd it sounded. Lindsay tried to focus on her husband, on herself as a wife, but she couldn't. She was tense as a stick. She was afraid. She knew Taylor knew it too because he was holding her hand, squeezing her fingers.

"It's going to be fine," he said, watching Dr. Perry slowly remove the bandages.

He'd asked him earlier in the hallway, "Will you know when you take off the bandages this time what the result will be?"

"Close enough. There will still be swelling and bruising, and that will look strange, but that's temporary. Yes, we'll know this time. *I'll* know this time. Don't worry, Mr. Taylor. I'm really very good."

Her hair was matted down to her head. She'd lost ten pounds and it showed on her face. Her flesh was pale where there was no bruising. She looked like she'd been very ill, which she had. The stitches looked obscene, black thread woven in and out of her flesh. The hair over her right ear had been shaved off and it showed. A small bald spot that made her look so vulnerable he wanted to cry. He looked more closely, along with a silent Dr. Perry. Her eyes were closed and Taylor knew she wouldn't open them until she had to.

There was still the swelling Dr. Perry had spoken about, only it wasn't symmetrical, rather it was lumpy, and the bruising gave her the look of the Italian flag. She looked pretty bad, truth be told, at least to a layman. It was impossible for Taylor to tell how it would turn out. He said now, without hesitation, "You're gorgeous."

"He's right," Dr. Perry said matter-of-factly. "I'm just about the greatest. I hope you've got good insurance because I cost a bundle."

"Really?" Lindsay opened her eyes and looked straight at Taylor. She searched his face. She saw no distaste there, no revulsion. She heard no lie in his voice. She gave him a tentative smile. "Can I have the mirror Dr. Perry gave me?"

"Not yet," Dr. Perry said. "First I want the stitches out, then a bit of alcohol to get rid of all the dried blood. Now, hold very still. This will sting just a little bit."

"Sting" wasn't the right word for it, Lindsay thought, but she kept herself as still as a stone. She closed her eyes again when he was dabbing alcohol against each of the three suture lines on her face. "There won't be any scarring," Dr. Perry said. "Not that I expected any, of course. Good thing you don't smoke, because if you did, that would be out. Also, no vitamin C for three months. That can make scarring. I'll give you a list of all foods to avoid as well. Otherwise, you just need to rest and lie around for the next two weeks. No strenuous activity, no jogging, nothing but having your husband wait on you. Gain back some weight. Now, Dr. Shantel tells me that your ribs are coming alone fine, but all my orders apply to your ribs too. At least two more weeks, okay, Lindsay?"

She touched her fingertips to her face. She felt the cool flesh, strange to her touch, and jerked her fingers back.

"Now, before you look in the mirror, understand that you've still got swelling here and there and the bruising has faded quite a bit, but it looks pretty god-awful. However, your husband has pronounced you gorgeous and you will be in about another week or so. Here, take a look."

She wasn't so sure she wanted to look, given all his disclaimers. She held the antique mirror up and forced herself to look into the glass. She swallowed, forcing herself to focus only on her face. She studied the three suture lines, the curious swelling that made her look like a lumpy frog, particularly around her right eye. It was the strange pale green and sunflower-yellow bruises that finally made her smile. She looked ridiculous. She looked like a prisoner of war. How could Taylor not look at her and fall on the floor with laughter? She was silent for the longest time, merely looking at herself.

Taylor became restive.

Dr. Perry looked ready to gnaw his fingernails.

Lindsay said finally, a small laugh in her voice, "I'm so beautiful I think I'll call Demos to set up a photo session for this afternoon."

"Wash your hair first," Taylor said, leaned down, and kissed her. "Here I was halfway hoping for a little Igor to help me with all my storm and electrical experiments, and you have to go and disappoint me."

Dr. Perry, grinning, said, "I've already spoken to your private nurse on how to get you cleaned up. She knows what to do. Tonight you and Taylor need to have your first regular meal. Demos is having it delivered here from La Viande." He shook Lindsay's hand. "I just thought I should warn you."

"Can I go home tomorrow?"

Taylor said quickly, "Yes. Missy is coming along. We'll put her in the third bedroom. I don't want you alone, sweetheart, not yet. Also Barry is sending Officer Fogel. He'll probably give all his attention to Missy, but there's at least safety in numbers. I don't ever want you alone, not until we find out who's behind all this."

"It isn't Dr. Gruska."

"No."

"It isn't my family either."

"Probably not. Not enough time for the planning of it."

Lindsay sighed. Who, then? She turned and gave her hand to Dr. Perry. "Thank you. When will I see you again?"

They set up an appointment for the following Monday.

Taylor would bring her to his office on Fifth Avenue at Fifty-first Street. "Third floor, suite 306."

When they were alone, Lindsay said, "Please, Taylor, you don't have to pretend that I look great."

"Okay," he said, and grinned at her. "But you know, I really enjoy the Mutant Ninja Turtles on TV. I can now relate."

"You're thin."

"So are you."

"If I wear a bag over my head, will you sleep with me when we get home?"

He wondered if she meant sleep, pure and simple sleep, or sex, not so pure, nor so simple, but loads more fun. "Maybe I'll wear the bag," he said. "You know, Lindsay, we need to get a start on that huge box of supergigantic condoms the nurses gave you."

She hadn't meant sex; he saw that quickly enough. But she was thinking about it now and he looked at her closely, studying the myriad expressions that came across her face. "Okay," she said, and then yawned.

"I just hope they'll be big enough," she added after he'd turned, closing her eyes.

He started, jerking around and looking down at her. He saw a tiny smile quiver on her lips. He saw himself slipping a condom over his penis, saw her smiling at him as he did it, her legs spread for him, and he nearly came right there.

"I've got to go get a drink of water," he said.

Taylor took her home the following morning. She wore sunglasses, at her fervent request, but her hair was soft and shining, so filled with deep waves he wanted to bury his hands and his face in the thick masses.

Fogel brought Missy to the apartment in a patrol car, which, he'd confided to Taylor, tended to make women horny.

To Lindsay's astonishment and chagrin, by the time she was standing in her own bedroom, she was exhausted.

"No complaints about bed, huh?"

She shook her head. "This is stupid."

"No, this is recuperation, babe."

"But what about our wedding night?"

"Our what? Oh, that. I'd forgotten all about it."

She smacked her fist in his belly.

She slept away the morning and into the afternoon. When she woke, Missy brought her lunch. Taylor wasn't there, Missy told her, but Fogel was sitting in the living room. He was probably contemplating seduction strategies for Missy.

At two o'clock the phone rang. Missy answered, then called out to Fogel.

Lindsay heard his voice from the living room, but not the words. He came into the bedroom a moment later, grinning, relief flooding his boyish features. "That was Captain Brooks. He says they caught that Oswald creep and I should come on back in now."

As if this were the first time he realized the meaning of the words, Fogel suddenly sounded very depressed. He looked at Missy and said "Shit" under his breath. "They need me," he added. He shuffled a moment, then said to Missy, "You want to walk me to the patrol car?"

"Just a moment," Lindsay said. "Didn't this Captain Brooks tell you anything else? Who hired Oswald?"

"He didn't say, Mrs. Taylor. Would you like me to call him back?"

Lindsay saw that Missy was fully prepared to give Officer Fogel quite a treat. She smiled and shook her head. "No, give me the number and I'll call him. Thank you for your help, and good luck."

He gave Lindsay the number, then he and Missy wrapped up in coats and left the apartment, arms entwined.

Lindsay dialed. The phone rang once, twice. It was picked up on the third ring, and a man said, "Twelfth Precinct, Johnson here."

"May I please speak to Captain Brooks?"

"Just a moment."

She waited. Her breathing quickened. They'd caught him! They'd caught Oswald. Thank God. Now, who had hired him? Soon it would be over, soon Oswald would tell them. Her palms felt wet and cold. Soon, very soon now, she'd know who wanted her dead. Soon now.

Another man came onto the line.

"Hello? I hear you want Captain Brooks."

"Yes, please."

"He's been on vacation for the past four days, ma'am. He won't be back until Monday week. You a friend of his?"

Oh, God, a lie, a diversion to get Officer Fogel out of the apartment. "I'm Lindsay Foxe Taylor. Captain Brooks just called here to say that Oswald had been caught. He asked Fogel to come back to the station."

Silence.

Then a sudden explosion of recognition. "Oh, damn! Listen, Mrs. Taylor, you make sure your door's locked and bolted. I'll have some men over there in . . . !"

"What? You mean that . . . ? What's going on?"

The phone was dead. Completely and suddenly very dead. No dial tone, just silence, pure and deep silence.

Lindsay eased it away from her ear, held it out in front of her, and just stared at it. Then she knew the man hadn't hung up on her. He hadn't dropped the phone. Someone had cut the wire. She swallowed and stared toward the doorway. She had to lock the front door. She knew that Missy would have left it unlocked when she'd left with Fogel. Had she even left it open? Was she even now kissing Fogel in his squad car?

Oh, Jesus.

She got up, felt her ribs protest with a vicious prod, but ignored it. Fear made adrenaline flood through her. She ran from the bedroom, her long flannel nightgown nearly making her trip, ran as fast as she could toward the front door.

It opened.

She skidded to a stop, her eyes glued to the now-opening door. She couldn't move. She could only stare and pray and stare some more.

She wasn't surprised when the man slipped inside. She wasn't really surprised that he was holding a gun and aiming it at her. It was the same man from the commercial shoot. He smiled when he saw her standing there, her face bruised, wearing a granny gown, looking white and ill and terrified.

"Hi," he said. "You're still around, sweetie, more's the pity. Lucky little bitch, aren't you?" He locked the door behind him. "Oh, don't worry about the girl with the huge tits. She ain't coming back for a while yet. She's too busy fucking that cop down in the patrol car. The little gentleman pulled it in an alley so they wouldn't be disturbed. Who says cops ain't got no sensitivity? It's just you and me now. Lord, do you ever look like an ugly duck now. Wouldn't you rather have died than look like you do now?"

Lindsay felt her insides twisting, heard her heart pounding. Why couldn't he hear it? Did he hear it, did he smell her fear? It was heavy, metallic. She wanted to gag with the smell of her own fear. Did he enjoy it? Seeing her terror? She heard a voice that was deep and small and it asked, "But why? Why do you want to kill me? What did I ever do to you?"

Bert Oswald just shrugged. "It's too bad you look like a freak, or you and me could have a little fun before I have to ice you down but good this time. Hey, I'm sorry, lady, but I kinda have to hurry, you know? From the way that cop was moving out of here with that gal, I'd say he'll probably get his rocks off pretty quick now. Of course, I could have some fun with her when she got back here."

Lindsay turned and ran. She heard a hard pinging sound. Wood splintered into the wall not six inches from her head. She heard him running after her now, heard another sharp pinging sound—oh, God, it was a bullet— and this one struck her in the arm. She felt a searing streak of iciness, then nothing, blank numbness. She made it to the bedroom, slammed the door, and turned the lock. Because she'd watched lots of television and violent movies, she quickly moved away from the door. It was lucky she did. A bullet struck the door and came flying through, spewing out splinters in all directions.

She plastered herself against the wall, wheezing with fear. She knew she had to think, to act, but dear God, she couldn't even bring herself to move. How long before he shot the lock off the door? How long before he came in and shot her?

How long did she have?

She opened her eyes and stared sightlessly around the bedroom. Something inside her recognized there was nothing in here to help her. Without hesitation, she ran to the bathroom. Another lock, more protection. But once he got in here, she was trapped and it would be over.

She slammed the bathroom door and turned the lock. It was thicker than the bedroom door, not hollow. She cursed then, wishing she'd moved some furniture in front of the bedroom door to buy her some more time. Too late . . . too late. She switched on the bathroom light. She saw herself in the mirror and didn't recognize the wild-eyed woman who looked as if she'd stared Satan right in the eye.

A weapon. She needed a weapon. When he came through the bathroom door she wasn't going to just stand here and let him kill her. What? She pulled open the medicine cabinet. She flung bottles off the shelves. The racket dinned around her as bottles hit the tile floor, breaking, shattering, rolling. She heard the bedroom door crash against the wall. He was in the bedroom now. He was looking around. In another second he'd know she'd come in here. Thank God the bathroom was old-fashioned, high ceiling, large. She had some room. There was nothing to help her in the medicine cabinet.

She fell to her knees and pulled open the cabinet beneath the sink. Cleaning supplies. A toilet brush, sponges, one green and one yellow, both shrunk from a lot of use, a can of Ajax, a roll of toilet paper, several toiletries bags for traveling, and a bottle of Pine Sol—oh, yes—but it was nearly empty. She flung it onto the floor. Oh, God, there, in the very back, was a can of Lysol bathroom spray. Basin, tile, and tub cleaner . . . it was foamy, and it came out in wild, thick spurts. She picked up the can and started shaking it. It was nearly full. She pressed down her finger and out poured the foam. Stop, stop, she had to have enough for him.

She heard his voice not three feet away from her; he was pressing his face close to the door.

"Little sweetie? I'm right here and I don't have a lot more time to spend on you. You know? I cut the phone wires, and no telling how long it will be before someone from the phone company shows up. And I'd hate to have to hurt your little nurse with the big tits. Now, you gonna open that door for me? If you do, I'll make it real quick, you won't feel a thing. Otherwise . . ." He let his voice trail off, hoping to terrify her, but she was smiling now, terror at bay.

She was holding the bottle of Lysol. What to do? How to get to him?

Slowly Lindsay rose, smiling a ghastly smile, and walked to the door, careful not to stand directly in front of it in case he fired through it.

"Come on, now," Oswald said again. He sounded cajoling, wheedling. Good Lord, she thought, was he so stupid as to think she'd let him in?

A sharp retort, and a bullet slammed through the wood and came into the bathroom, hitting the tile over the bathtub. Shards of tile splintered and flew outward. She felt some strike her, sharp little bites, but didn't really notice.

It was time. She knew it was time.

She inched over to the door. She stretched out her right hand toward the latch. She saw the blood soaking through the flannel of her gown, lots of blood, but it didn't concern her at the moment. It just looked odd, so ugly and wet and red against the soft white material of her gown. There was no pain. Just when he fired again, through the doorknob, Lindsay clicked the lock open. Another one . . . yes, just one more.

He fired again, cursing loudly now, furious now, and she grasped the doorknob and jerked open the door, flinging it back.

He held the gun limply in his hand. The door struck him and he went careening back. But he still had the gun and he wasn't slow, but he was surprised, and that gave her a second.

He grunted, trying to react, but Lindsay was faster. She brought up the can of Lysol, shoved it into his face, and pressed down. Thick white foam went directly into his eyes, his nose, his mouth. Thicker and thicker.

He screamed and the foam filled his mouth, overflowing now. He dropped the gun, falling back, his hands on his face, his fingers digging out the foam in his mouth, out of his eyes. Lindsay dropped the can. She leaned forward and hit him as hard as she could with her fist in his belly. Then she stepped back, raised her leg, and kicked him in the balls. He yowled and fell to his knees. She raised her right leg and kicked him in the neck.

He was screaming now, lying on the floor on his side, holding his belly. He looked rabid with all the foam coming out of his mouth. She was panting now, and he was looking up at her and there was such pain and fury in his eyes that she felt the paralyzing fear come over her again. She backed up. There was that smell again, that fear smell, and it wasn't coming from her any longer. It was coming from him.

"I'm gonna hurt you bad," Oswald gasped. "God, are you gonna hurt." He was on his knees, trying to stand. He saw his gun on the floor and went flying forward to get it.

Lindsay raised her leg and brought her foot down on his kidneys. He fell flat on his face, screaming.

Taylor came through the front door, two policemen behind him, and all of them froze for a millisecond at the horrible screams they heard.

Taylor crashed against the bullet-ridden bedroom door and flung himself into the bedroom. He stopped. He stared. He watched Lindsay kick the man in the kidneys, and now he fell backward onto the floor, curling up immediately into the fetal position, yelling, bawling. She raised her foot again and he shouted, "Enough! Lindsay, that's enough."

The power surged through her, pulsed through her, making her invincible, making her strong. It was monstrous and it was splendid and she wanted to kill this little worm. She would kill him, now.

"I'm going to kill him!"

She raised her foot to hit him in the head, but Taylor caught her leg, jerking her toward him. He caught her in his arms and pulled her against him. He felt the fierce pounding of her heart, felt the rippling and tensing of her muscles and understood what was happening to her.

"You got him," he said over and over. "You got him and he's very sorry now. You hurt him bad, Lindsay. It's over now, sweetheart. Over."

She was so stiff, so far away from him, from herself. It took several more minutes before the tension eased out of her.

Lindsay looked up at him. "Lysol cleaner," she said. "Foam. I surprised him and got him with the Lysol not an inch from his face. He looks like a rabid dog with all that foam in his mouth." She laughed, a creaky, ugly sound. "Or like a meringue pie. He kept trying to dig it out with his fingers. I don't know if it burned his eyes, though." Then, just as suddenly, she squeaked, "My arm."

Then she stared at the blood-soaked flannel, saw drops fall to the floor. She was very silent, trying to take it in, trying to understand. She blanched, stared vaguely up at her husband, and fainted for the first time in her life.

"Oh, God! Don't do it, you asshole!"

Taylor whipped around. Oswald had grabbed for his gun. One of the officers already had his in his hand. He yelled for Oswald to stop, not to be a fool. "Drop the gun, damn you!"

Oswald, dumb with pain, focused his fury on the source and raised the gun toward Lindsay.

The officer fired.

Oswald made a small mewling sound. He turned his head in the direction of the officer, tried to say something, then fell onto his side.

"I think," Taylor said, "we need two ambulances." He was profoundly grateful that Lindsay hadn't seen this part of it.

He picked her up and laid her on the bed, ripping her flannel sleeve as he said, "Is Oswald dead?"

"No, but he's hurt bad. Dave got him in the head, but not a death wound, at least I hope to God not."

"Good. We've got to keep him alive long enough to find out who hired him."

"How's Mrs. Taylor?"

Taylor bared her upper arm. "The bullet went through the fleshy part, thank God. She's bleeding like stink, but she'll be all right." He looked down at her messed-up face. He smiled. "She saved herself. She probably would have killed Oswald if we hadn't come in time to save his filthy hide. Just keep him alive, guys."

The officer was wrapping a towel around his head.

Taylor leaned down. "I love you," he said, and kissed her mouth.

He heard one of the officers say, "I hope she doesn't ever get mad at me. Just look what she did to this guy."

"It's a media circus," Demos said, panting as he came into the hospital room. "They nearly got me, but Glen pulled me into the service elevator just in time."

"Yeah, a feeding frenzy," Taylor said. And all of it would come out now, he thought, looking down at Lindsay, who was awake but so doped up that she was nearly insensible.

"Taylor, I hate to tell you this, but . . ."

"What is it, Demos?"

"It's her father, the judge. He's down there and it looks like he's going to be a pain in the ass again."

Taylor just stared at Demos. "No, oh, no. What is he saying?"

"Glen is down there listening to him, waiting for us. I just heard him mumbling something about how she always liked publicity even when she was only eighteen and in Paris after she'd seduced her brother-in-law. She loves to show herself off—she's a model, isn't she—always taking off her clothes for everyone to see her. And bad things happen when she's around. Jesus, you'd think she shot herself! I don't know if he's talking now to the reporters. He probably is by now."

Taylor very slowly rose from his chair beside her bed. He smiled at Demos. "That settles it. It's really enough. Father or no father, I'm going to bash his head in."

Demos didn't try to stop him. He wanted to assist him if Taylor would only let him.

Another police officer stood outside the door. "Don't

move a muscle, Dempsey. And don't you even consider letting God or any of his angels in, you got that?"

"Yes, sir." Dempsey had heard about what Fogel had done. Jesus, a fly wouldn't get close to the lady as long as he was here.

Taylor felt calm. He would do what he had to. This hatred of the father for the daughter. He simply couldn't comprehend it. Now he didn't care. He would stop the man once and for all. When he reached the lobby, it was pandemonium. Reporters were yelling questions, cameras were everywhere. And there, in the middle of all the chaos, stood Judge Royce Foxe, dapper and handsome, looking every inch the stalwart judge, which he was, but now he wasn't saying a thing. Sydney stood next to him, her chin high, looking gorgeous and determined. She was pulling him through the throng now, just smiling, her jaw set, looking straight ahead. She saw Taylor and nodded. She said something sharp to her father.

Without a word, Taylor followed her, weaving in and out of the pushing and shoving reporters, just keeping her in sight. It took only a few seconds for a reporter to recognize him, then the pack was on his back. He said nothing, merely kept shoving them from his path. If he'd been a woman, he wouldn't have had a chance. They were merciless. Sydney was headed to the administration section of the hospital. He slipped inside the CEO's office after her and Royce Foxe, Demos behind him. Some bright assistant slammed and locked the door in the reporters' faces.

"Thank you," Sydney said to the three hospital administrators. "Please leave me now with my father. He hasn't been well and I must speak to him."

The men didn't look happy. Taylor said, "Yes, you're needed out there before the media tear up the hospital, and don't think they won't."

That hadn't occurred as a possibility, and the three men were quickly gone. This time Demos locked the door after them.

Sydney said, looking up at her brother-in-law, "It's all right, Taylor. Nothing he said hit the reporters' ears. Just Demos and Glen heard him, and a couple of hospital employees. I stopped him in time. It's all right. Now, I need to get him to the airport and back to California. Demos, you want to help me?"

As Sydney left, Taylor said, "Why did you stop him? Why, Sydney?"

"Because he's mad with hate and . . ."

Taylor stared at her. "And?"

She just shook her head.

"Oh, yeah, Sydney, if he'd opened his trap to the media, he would have ruined all chances of getting any of Lindsay's money, right? That's why you stopped him."

"No!"

"So you were afraid for yourself, afraid that the scandal would hurt you this time, not Lindsay. God, lady, you are a piece of work."

She slapped him hard.

His hands fisted but he didn't move. He just smiled down at her. "Take him out of here before I beat him into ground meat."

"God, I hope she kicks you out!"

Taylor just smiled, shaking his head.

Lindsay sat up in bed, staring toward the darkened windows, thinking about how lucky she was. Her face, after additional CT scans ordered by Dr. Perry, who had been scared into the hiccups, had turned out all right. There were three strips of tape over the suture lines, pulling the skin tight, after her violent exertion. Her ribs hadn't made out quite so well, but they would mend. The bullet wound wasn't bad but she'd lost a goodly amount of blood. It turned out that Taylor had the same type and had donated.

She wasn't in shock, which surprised everyone. She'd come around, stared down at the stitched-up hole in her arm, and simply said to Taylor, "Oh, dear, will I have a scar?"

And he'd laughed. He still was laughing when the nurse had bandaged the wound. She was in a private room. Not the same one as before, but it could have been, except this one faced the river. This one had a Degas print on the wall opposite the bed.

"Let's keep her here overnight." That was Dr. Shantel speaking to Taylor near the door. Why not to her? Lindsay wondered. She wasn't a Victorian maiden to swoon. She ground her teeth. She had swooned. It was rather a shock to know that her body could simply give out on her like that.

"It's been a series of traumas," she heard Dr. Shantel tell Taylor in a much-lowered voice. "Perhaps I can recommend a good psychiatrist, you know, the type of doctor who can help her get over this."

"I don't need a shrink," Lindsay said in a loud voice. "What I need is to know who hired Oswald. If we don't find that out soon, then I will go into shock and I'll go directly to Bellevue."

"She's right," Taylor said. "Look, Dr. Shantel, I'll keep a close eye on her. She's got grit and she can be as mean as Satan, and she's not stupid. She'll tell me if things get shaky. Don't worry. Even if she doesn't, I'm not stupid. Okay?"

When they were finally alone, for the first time since the attack in their apartment, Taylor said, "I just spoke to Barry. Oswald's in surgery. His chances are fifty-fifty. No, it wasn't any of your blows, it was the bullet in the head fired by the officer. Now, wife, how are you doing?"

"Can I get combat pay?"

He was immensely pleased. He wondered how much of her bravado was show, but realized it didn't matter. She was holding up and showing him clearly that she was holding up. That meant a great deal to both of them. He lay down on the bed beside her, turning on his side to face her. "Your face isn't going to fall off. Dr. Perry is relieved. He says the swelling will hang around awhile longer and to keep these three little strips of tape over the suture lines. You got it?"

She nodded. "It's a relief to me too. Do I look really gruesome?"

"Yes, but I'm somewhat nearsighted so it doesn't bother me all that much."

"Do you know something, Taylor?"

He was nuzzling her neck. "What?"

"I haven't been bored since I met you. On the other hand, I don't know if my body can keep mending itself in time for you to come up with new diversions."

He suddenly became very quiet in mid-kiss.

"Taylor?"

He raised himself on his elbow and looked down at her. He said very slowly, "I think, sweetheart, that you've just hit on something."

She just looked up at him, saying nothing. Her arm burned, but it wasn't important. She scarcely even noticed it.

"I can't believe I didn't think of this before. Maybe we've been looking at this from the wrong end. You just said I'm the one coming up with new diversions. What if these attacks on you aren't directed at you but at me?"

She stared at him. "Is that possible?"

"I've made enemies. I was a cop for a good number of years. Yeah, maybe we've been staring in the wrong end of the kaleidoscope. Let me get Barry over here fast."

Barry would be over after he'd finished his dinner. Didn't the two of them ever think about food?

"Now," Taylor said, easing down on the bed beside her again, "I want to ask you a question."

"Shoot."

"Not that, Lindsay. Tell me why your father hates you."

She gave him a clear, honest look. "I don't know, I truly don't. I've wondered and wondered and tried to figure it out over the years. I asked my mother, my grandmother, but they always told me it was my imagination or that my father was just under a great deal of stress. Finally my grandmother did admit that he loved Sydney more than he loved anyone else in the world. He was, she said, a man who couldn't seem to love more than one person. It's like he's almost obsessed with her."

"Did he always treat you badly?"

She shook her head. "No, it started sometime before Sydney's wedding, before I was sixteen, I think. He simply drew back from me. Everything went to Sydney and she wasn't even there most of the time. Now that I think about it, that's when the troubles started between him and my mom too. She gained lots of weight and started drinking too much, just like Holly is now."

"Sydney is nine years older than you."

"Yes. So she would have been in law school when it began. Not even in San Francisco all that much. She was at Harvard."

"You can't remember anything that could have precipitated this behavior of his? This viciousness?"

"No. What are you thinking, Taylor?"

He kissed her. "I'm thinking that we're going to have some answers, finally. Another thing, sweetheart, old Oswald is going to sing like a yellow canary once he's out of surgery. Not to worry."

"Why worry?" she said, and smiled up at him. "I've got another good arm to donate."

# 23

Barry Kinsley stood beside Taylor, hands shoved into his pants pockets. Both of them were staring at the swinging doors, waiting for the surgeon to come through.

"I found a gray hair this morning," Taylor said, never taking his eyes off those doors.

"Yeah, well, I got a good dose of indigestion from all these shenanigans you and your wife have put me through. My wife said if I didn't get the guy responsible today, she wouldn't sleep with me for five months."

"Why five months?"

"That's when our kid goes off to college and she figures she'll be so horny by then she won't care what I've done."

"I didn't know you had a kid. More than one?"

"Four. This is the last one off to college—a real pistol."

The swinging doors were pushed open.

Two nurses came through, talking. No surgeon.

Three more minutes passed. They paced, silent now.

The surgeon came out then, an older man with tired pale eyes. He was still wearing his greens, only they were stained with blood now. He pulled the cap off his head even as he said, "He didn't make it. I'm sorry. It was problematic when I went in. The bullet did a lot more damage than I'd first thought. If he had lived, he would have been a vegetable in any case. I am sorry."

"Well, heigh ho," Barry said, and sighed. "Thanks, Doc."

Taylor headed back toward the elevators, feeling lower than a slug.

He pounded the elevator button with frustration. "Doesn't the guy have any relatives? Maybe someone we can contact who would know who hired him?"

Barry shook his head and stabbed at the elevator button, outdoing Taylor. "Not a single merry soul, more's the pity. I checked on that right away. Jesus, Taylor, back to square one."

"I'm getting slow in my retirement. What are we going to do now, Barry?"

"Well, there's nothing we can do about him croaking, not a bloody thing. Now, you said you had some other ideas. Let's get back to Lindsay."

When they reached Lindsay's hospital-room door, there was Sydney, arguing with Officer Dempsey. He was refusing to let her in. Taylor could tell by the set of her shoulders that she was about ready to take his head off. He could tell by the set of Officer Dempsey's shoulders that he wanted to let her do whatever she pleased, but he was holding firm.

"No, ma'am," Dempsey repeated, looking more miserable by the word. "I'm sorry, but no one gets in here. Not God, not any of his angels. Sorry, ma'am, really I am, but those are my orders. Taylor would have my guts if I let anyone in."

Barry raised an eyebrow at that.

Before Sydney could blast him, Barry called out, "We'll keep an eye on her, lad." He smiled at Sydney and pushed open the door. "Good lad," he added to the officer as he passed him. Taylor said nothing until they were inside.

Lindsay was asleep, the bruised, swelled side of her face up. She looked like she'd been in a war, which she had been.

He immediately lowered his voice to a whisper, asking Sydney, "The judge is gone?"

"Yes, I waited until I actually saw him onto the plane. I even waited until the plane took off." Sydney looked toward her half-sister. "God, she looks like bloody hell. She'll be all right this time?"

"Yes. She tells me she wants combat pay."

"I'm here to cut a deal." She looked toward Sergeant Kinsley. "I don't want him around. This is just between us, Taylor. Once you hear what I've got to say, I don't think you'll want Lindsay involved."

"Okay, I'll bite. What kind of deal?" Before she answered, she looked pointedly at Barry. Taylor said, "Can you wait outside for a bit, Barry? This really shouldn't take long."

"No, it shouldn't," Sydney said.

She said nothing more until the door closed.

She moved away from him, a good twelve feet away, he saw. "Well?"

"It's about my father. I imagine you've been wondering why he hates her so much. Well, I'm here to tell you why."

Taylor made certain Lindsay was asleep, then said, "All right, but keep your voice down."

"Mind you, I didn't know any of this until after Grandmother's death, after the reading of the will, after Lindsay had already left to come back to New York.

"Grayson Delmartin, Grandmother's lawyer, came back to the mansion after he'd dropped Lindsay off at the airport. My father started in on him immediately, telling him he was going to sue, yelling that Lindsay would never get away with it, and he'd tell every newspaper in the state, he didn't care, and the world be damned. The Foxe name would go down the tubes, no doubt about that. He was going to tell, he was going to make a press announcement the following morning, and he was going to get all the money.

"I didn't know what he was talking about. Neither did Holly."

"Dammit, Sydney, get to the point."

"He said that Lindsay wasn't his daughter. He said that he'd found out the truth some ten years ago and told his mother. She already knew, he said. She knew, and she wasn't displeased. She told him to keep his mouth shut, that she wouldn't tolerate him telling anyone about it. He agreed, oh yes, he said he'd keep quiet, but only if she promised to leave him all the Foxe money."

"The judge isn't her father . . ." Taylor shook his head. "That's crazy. I've seen both of them. She's got his eyes—they're identical—that dark blue, mysterious, so deep it's scary. And the shape, completely the same. Identical. Is the man blind? Or are we talking about a long-lost twin brother?"

"He screamed at Delmartin that his first cousin, Robert, was Lindsay's father and he could prove it."

"Cousin?" Taylor said blankly. "Lindsay never said anything about a cousin who looks like her, she's never said a word about other relatives."

"She never met him, never even knew he existed, as far as I know. Why should she? Her mother, the poor bitch, wouldn't tell her, you can bank on that. This cousin was evidently there only a short time and then he was gone, and he never came back. He's dead. He died in the late seventies, in a skiing accident in the Alps. Mind you, this all came from my father while he was screaming at Delmartin."

"Weren't there any photos of this Robert character? Didn't your grandmother ever say a word?"

"Not a photo, not a clue."

"What the hell kind of family is this? Oh, I forgot, you're a big part of it. Go on, Sydney, finish this. I've already got an inkling about your punch line."

"My price goes up every time you're a shit, Taylor. This Robert was the son of my grandmother's younger brother, and evidently the spitting image of him. The eyes, I found out, are hereditary. Of course, I never went sorting through any of my grandmother's things either before or after she died. I remember wondering why Father couldn't stand Lindsay. Of course, I never paid her any attention at all, although I remember thinking that something had changed, but I can't be sure of the time because I was always in and out, usually out of the state. He started cutting her down whenever she came anywhere near him. Of course, he's always adored me—a large part of that was because of my mother. I look like her, he says. He loved my mother more than anything in this world. So, through her, he gave me all his love, all his attention."

"And you followed in his footsteps and became a real bitch to your half-sister."

Sydney shrugged. "She was a pain, always in the way, and besides, she's barely related to me."

"All right, Sydney. I'll bite. You've dropped one shoe. Where's the other? How are you planning on keeping your father from screaming the truth to the media?"

Sydney smiled then. "I phoned Mr. Delmartin before coming back here to the hospital and told him what father had said and threatened. He laughed, said that Grandmother had foreseen his threats and had taken steps to see that he'd be disappointed—her word."

"What are the steps?"

"I don't know."

Taylor said, "Probably some kind of legal adoption, I'd imagine, done between Lindsay's mother and grandmother."

"That sounds like the old lady," Sydney said. "The miserable old biddy and—"

"Get on with it, Sydney."

"All right. For five million dollars I'll keep quiet about this; Lindsay will never find out the truth." He raised his eyebrow and she said, "All right, let me spell it out, lover boy, for five million she won't find out that her dear mother was a slut and she's a bastard."

Taylor laughed. "What makes you think her ex-father won't be here yelling the truth at her just for revenge?"

"He can and will bargain with you himself, don't doubt it. Once he calms down and realizes the potential of what he now knows, he'll be right back here, ready to cut a deal."

Taylor didn't say anything for a very long time. Sydney, an excellent lawyer, knew not to move, not to fidget.

"All right," he said.

"Just like that? You'll come through with the five million just like that?"

"Oh, no, not a bloody dime."

"Don't you realize what this would do to your precious wife? Your precious very, very rich wife?"

"She'll never know, at least from you. As to her father, he's something of a wild card. I'll just have to deal with him when and if he shows up."

"You'll deal with me!"

"No."

"All right, let's just wake up Lindsay and tell her!"

Taylor grabbed her arm as she tried to push by him. "Keep your voice down, Sydney. You won't wake her up. You'll listen to what I have to say to you. You see, I want to cut a deal with you."

"You don't have anything," she said, but she was wary now, he saw it in her eyes.

"Your wonderful mother," he said very quietly. "The woman your father adored, the woman who died, and all the women who came after her were just dull copies of this perfect woman. You're just like her and that's why your father treats you so well, why he worships you."

"What about my mother?"

He heard the fear in her voice, low, masked, but still there. She was good, she really was.

"Would you like to have her address, Sydney?"

She reeled away from him as if he'd struck her.

"You're lying!"

"Keep your voice down or I'll drag you into the corridor."

He didn't have to drag her anywhere. She raced past him and was out of the room in an instant. Taylor followed. He wasn't smiling, but it had to be done and he would be the one to do it. He would be the one to end it.

She was standing outside the room, leaning against the wall, her head back, her eyes closed. She didn't open them, just said very quietly, "You're lying, aren't you?"

"Ask your precious father."

"She's dead. She died when I was six years old. He came and got me at school and told me she was in heaven. He cried and held me. She's dead. I hated Jennifer when he brought her home. She proved what she was, didn't she? A slut, and she had Lindsay, a bastard. She wasn't married to my father for a year before she was screwing around on him! Damn you, my mother's dead!"

"No she isn't." He wanted to tell her that most likely her mother had walked out on him for his infidelity, that she'd also walked out on her daughter, but he simply couldn't bring himself to say the words.

Then, in the space of an instant, her eyes grew as cold as her voice. "So, what deal, Taylor? What you're saying could be true, but who cares? There's no real value to it, none."

"Your father would probably care, for one. He lied to you. I doubt he'd appreciate being confronted not only with his lie but also with the woman herself. Who knows? Since you believed he loved her so much, maybe when he sees her again he can convince her to divorce her current husband and come back to him."

"She's dead!"

"Maybe she could even fly to New York and you could introduce her to all your hotshot friends. Maybe she'd really like to see her granddaughter in Milan. What do you think, Sydney?"

"You're a lying bastard!"

"I wonder how many little stepbrothers and stepsisters you have now? Do you think they're all as smart, beautiful, and charming as you are?"

She struck him hard, with the palm of her hand. His head snapped back. Very calmly Taylor grabbed both her hands in his and held them in front of her.

"I must say I'm delighted you're not my sister-in-law. You probably have some good points, most folk do, maybe even the Son of Sam. However, enough of all this garbage. You won't say a bloody word to Lindsay about her mother. You'll fly home to daddy and tell him that if he opens his mouth, his dead ex-wife will be on his doorstep. If he wants scandal, he'll get it. Do you understand, Sydney?"

"I hope she leaves you."

He laughed. "We're not even on our honeymoon yet. Do you intend to go right out and buy a voodoo doll?"

"She's so screwed up, you'll leave her!"

His laughter died, but his smile didn't. "There is something I'm very grateful to your father for. He never told you about Lindsay. I can just imagine you tormenting both Lindsay and her mother for ten years. Now, go away, Sydney. Go away and keep away."

He released her wrists. She rubbed them. Then, very slowly, she walked away. She never turned back.

Taylor sighed. Jesus, he hoped he'd done the right thing. Actually, it didn't matter what Sydney or her father did. He would tell Lindsay about her mother and real father when the time was right. It seemed to him that taking Royce Foxe out of the father picture should, in the long run, make her feel quite good.

He wondered if Sydney's mother was really still alive.

Thirty minutes later, Lindsay was awake and Barry and Taylor were seated by the bed.

"Okay, Lindsay," Barry said, "we've pretty well knocked any and all of your family out of the running. What Taylor said seems the direction to go."

"And that is?"

"Somebody is after him. They're getting at him through you. Revenge, most likely."

Lindsay felt the dull thudding of her heart, felt the helplessness of ignorance. She looked at Taylor. "Please tell me you have some ideas."

"Yes, several, in fact. Unfortunately . . ." He drew a deep breath, then forced it out. "Oswald is dead. But don't worry, sweetheart, we'll figure this out, and very soon now."

Lindsay wanted to cry. She wanted to howl. It wasn't fair, dammit. She felt so vulnerable her skin crawled. Taylor understood how she felt, the helplessness of it. Very calmly he pulled his .38 from its holster, handed it to her, and said, "Keep it in the bedside drawer. The safety's on, see? If a baddie comes near you, don't hesitate. Flip the safety off, aim, and pull the trigger. Okay?"

Barry wanted to mention that there was a uniformed officer outside her door, but he didn't. The uniformed officer hadn't helped her last time. He patted Lindsay's shoulder and said good night.

Taylor was sleeping here, on his cot. For convenience

and for her protection. He went into the bathroom to brush his teeth and take a shower. He came out in a few minutes wearing a robe she'd never seen before. She raised an eyebrow at him.

"It's new. I didn't want to shock any nurses or doctors. I can't very well wander around nude, the way you like to see me."

"Can't you sleep with me instead?"

Taylor sighed. He wanted to but he was afraid of hurting her.

"Why don't I hold you until you go to sleep? That sleeping pill should be kicking in soon."

He held her loosely, so carefully, and Lindsay sighed and said, "I can't believe Oswald had the nerve to die."

"Me either, the little worm."

"What are you going to do?"

"It's a matter of reviewing all the cases I was in charge of for, say, three years before I quit the force. It'll take me a little time, but I'll figure it out. You're not to worry." The admonition sounded hollow in his ears.

"No, I won't," she said, and nestled closer.

He was amazed that she was here and that she was his wife and that she loved him. He kissed her temple. "You are brave and tough and—"

"The best lay you've ever had?"

"Yeah. There's a story I'd like to tell you, maybe I should have told you sooner, maybe not. It's about this girl—"

"One of your old girlfriends?"

"No. Do you remember me telling you I was in Paris the same time you were in 1983?" She nodded, but he could feel her drawing back, trying to burrow back inside her armor, to hide, to defend herself. He quickened. "Yes, of course you do. I love France; I've told you that. In any case, I was riding my motorcycle in Paris and this damned Peugeot came roaring out of a side street and hit me. I was lucky. I got thrown into some bushes but my arm was broken, that was the main thing. The ambulance took me to St. Catherine's Hospital, to the emergency room. I was waiting for treatment all alone in this curtained-off cubicle when they brought in this young girl who had been raped. She was in the curtained-off room right next to me."

"Taylor, no, damn you, no—"

"Shush. I listened to her screams, her cries, heard what the doctors were saying and how they didn't really give a shit because the girl was a foreigner. I heard how the nurse tried to protect her, but in France, in 1983, the men were doctors and the bosses and they were hassled because there'd been a big auto pileup. And finally I saw her wheeled out. When I was at De Gaulle airport ready to come home, I bought some newspapers and read all about this girl. Practically none of it rang true and I should know because I'd been there, in the emergency room. And I never forgot her name or her. Her name was Lindsay Foxe. I remember thinking that no one should have to bear such humiliation, such lies as the media were telling, and it changed me. I couldn't believe much of what I read because I knew firsthand what had happened."

She was crying silently. He merely held her, his voice pitched low as he continued, saying, "Your rape changed something very fundamental in me, Lindsay. I'd never really been confronted on such a personal level with rape before. Yeah, I'd been called in a couple of times on rape reports, but I hadn't realized the indignity of it, the utter humiliation of it, the hopelessness of it for a woman. In fact, one of the reasons I left the force was a rape, a little girl fourteen years old, raped by her damned uncle.

"You were luckier than she was, Lindsay. She didn't make it. You survived because you're strong and you've got guts. And luckily for me, I found you and it's us now and forever. Okay?"

He felt miraculously purged of something he'd wanted to tell her. "Lindsay? It is over, sweetheart. All over, and very soon we'll get this idiot and then it's Connecticut and a white house and a dog and a half-dozen kids. How does that sound?"

Silence.

Then she said quietly, "There are so many things right here in Manhattan, Taylor. So many new experiences, things I've never done and always wanted to. Can we do them together? I love our apartment. I don't want to leave our apartment."

"I'm easy. You got it."

Taylor and Barry were down at the station, Taylor reviewing old cases. He'd told Lindsay that he'd be back with folders for them to look through together. He'd be back soon now.

Lindsay's arm throbbed and she wanted to rub it, but she'd tried that and it had hurt like hell. Her face throbbed more than her arm, and every once in a while she raised her fingers to the strips of butterfly adhesive that covered the suture lines.

She wanted to get up and pace. Finally, unable to stand it, she threw back the single sheet and thin blanket and swung her legs over the side of the hospital bed.

Even that slight exertion made her dizzy, and she paused, head down, breathing deeply. And that made her ribs hurt. She cursed. She was twenty-six and she felt old and feeble.

It would be over soon now. Very soon. All she had to do was be patient. Lord, she already was a patient. But it was impossible. She lowered her feet to the floor.

She heard the door open quietly and she said as she turned, "Is that you, Taylor? I'm so glad you're back. What did you find?"

A doctor stood in the doorway, wearing his white coat, a stethoscope around his neck. He held a chart in his hand. He was smiling toward her. He simply nodded, then closed the door.

"Who are you?"

"I'm Dr. Grey. Dr. Shantel asked me to see you. He asked me to give you a shot."

"Oh, not another shot! What is it this time?"

"Just an antibiotic." He withdrew a syringe from one of his pockets. He pulled off the safety cap as he walked toward her. "In the arm will be just fine. Could you get back into bed, please?"

She froze. Dr. Shantel wasn't a he. Dr. Shantel was a woman.

The man was advancing on her, a professional smile

firmly in place. She'd never seen him before, never in her life. No, no, she was being stupid. He was a doctor, he was . . . She studied him, but she was certain. She'd never seen him. He shouldn't be here.

He was here to kill her.

There was no place to run. Lindsay did the only thing she could think of. She opened her mouth and screamed as loud as she could. And again and again.

He was on her in an instant, leaping on her and knocking her flat on her back onto the bed, her legs dangling over the side. He was trying to hold her down with his left arm pressed against her chest. In his right hand he was fiddling with the syringe.

Lindsay screamed again.

"Shut up, damn you!" He raised his hand to hit her but she scooted back, bringing her legs up. She was strong in that moment, and when her knees hit him squarely in the back, he yelled and fell sideways.

Lindsay felt raw panic; then she smiled. She smiled as she jerked open the night table beside the bed. She smiled as she picked up the .38 and aimed it at the man. He was shaking his head, and he was pale with rage. He was up in an instant, the syringe high in his hand so she couldn't kick it away from him.

"Now," he said, and then he saw the gun.

"That damned bastard gave you a gun!" And he rushed at her.

Lindsay pulled the trigger. The syringe went flying. He grabbed his right wrist. Blood quickly seeped through between his fingers.

He stared at her. "No, damn you!" he screamed at her. "You damned bitch!" Lindsay fired again. This time nothing happened. "Oh, shit," she said and threw the gun at him. She missed but it didn't matter. She was out of bed and on him in an instant, frenzied, hitting him, a wild keening coming from her throat. He twisted out of her grasp, cursed, tried to hit her, but the pain in his wrist held him up. Lindsay smashed her fist in his throat. He gagged, jerked away, and ran out of the room, holding his wounded wrist. Lindsay stood there panting, staring at the door.

When Taylor and Barry came crashing through the door, it was to see Lindsay standing there, still panting, holding Taylor's gun in her hand. She looked up and said, "Damn, Taylor, you can't trust technology. The thing fired once but didn't do anything the second time." Taylor's heart was careening about in his chest. Dempsey hadn't been at his post and Taylor had been beyond fear. He stared at Lindsay, at the gun that hadn't fired the second time.

"Jesus," he said.

They found Officer Dempsey unconscious in one of the men's-room stalls some five minutes later. Half the staff was in on the search.

They hadn't seen the man who'd tried to kill Lindsay, but it didn't matter. Taylor knew who he was.

Taylor and Barry and two other NYPD cops arrived at the brokerage house of Ashcroft, Hume, Drinkwater, and Henderson on Water Street two and one-half hours later. They'd already converged on the brownstone but found only some bloody towels and an open first-aid box. And an appointment book.

"Bastard," Barry said now as he got out of the car.

"I know where his office is," Taylor said.

"Let's get to it, then."

"My pleasure."

As they rode to the fourteenth floor, Taylor said, "I called to confirm what we read in his appointment book. The executive secretary told me that Brandon Waymer Ashcroft was due in a board meeting in twenty minutes. Just about now, in fact."

"Uncle Bandy," Barry said aloud, shaking his head. "What a nickname."

"You want the truth now or later, Barry?"

"Now, and make it snappy."

Taylor was surprised at how calm he sounded. "Uncle Bandy had been sexually abusing his niece, Ellie, starting when she was about ten years old or so. I came along quite by accident one afternoon to see her mother running out of a very nice brownstone, screaming that her little girl was bleeding to death. She was bleeding. The bastard had just raped her and she was hemorrhaging. I wanted him strung up, and finally I got the mother to testify against him. I got Ellie on tape. Enough to break your heart, Barry. She was such a sweet little kid. So broken . . ."

Barry made a noise in his throat and kept looking straight ahead at the elevator panel.

"Anyway, it turned out Uncle Bandy was rich and powerful and headed up this brokerage house. He was paying the sister's way and evidently that included having her pimp for him, namely, the little girl. You'll recognize this all too well: we arrested him, he was out within an hour, and he got the sister to recant her testimony. He got off scot-free. I played Ellie's tape recording for Judge Riker. I had to do something, but of course it wasn't enough. The judge said chances were good that Uncle Bandy had paid off his sister not to testify against him and that she and Ellie would be long gone. He firmly believed that she would be safe now.

"It didn't work out that way. Two weeks later the girl jumped out of the girls' restroom from the third floor of her private school."

"That's when you quit the force, Taylor?"

"Yeah. But I had to do something to avenge Ellie. I beat the shit out of Uncle Bandy. I got him outside his million-dollar brownstone and I beat him to a pulp. I wanted to kill him, but I didn't. Maybe something you taught me in the academy stopped me, maybe something that was inside me all the time. Who the hell knows? It was later he told me he would get me. I laughed, Barry, I laughed. I didn't look at his eyes. If I had, I would have believed him."

"We're here." The elevator opened onto a huge carpeted entrance area filled with eighteenth-century French antiques, fine prints, and soft recessed lighting.

A woman rose when she saw the two men. She was frowning and Taylor knew well enough that she knew they weren't board members. They didn't look right.

Joanna Bianco, efficient, astute, quickly stepped foward, saying in her smooth calm voice, "Gentlemen, I'm sorry, but Mr. Ashcroft is in a board meeting at present. Perhaps if I could have your names I could—"

Barry flipped out his badge. "Sergeant Kinsley, ma'am. And this is S. C. Taylor. We'll see Mr. Ashcroft right this minute."

"Let me get him, then—"

"Oh, no, Taylor said. "I want him right where he is. At the head of his big mahogany table, feeding a line of B.S. to a whole lot of gentlemen over the age of sixty, right? I want, in short, to humiliate him. He's slime."

Joanna Bianco looked him up and down, her expression unreadable. Then she said, "I gather he's done something rather serious to be slime?"

"Dead serious," Taylor said.

She stepped back and waved toward the doors. "Have at it," she said, and there was a smile on her face.

Barry told the other two officers who had just arrived on another elevator to remain there. "Keep your eyes open, lads. You've seen his photo. If the guy comes bounding out, have a ball, but don't kill him."

Taylor very quietly opened the thick mahogany double doors. They parted soundlessly inward. The room was at least thirty feet long, carpeted in pale cream Berber, wainscoted with dark stained wood. Built-in bookshelves lined the far short wall. The long wall was all windows, covered at the moment with thick pale baize draperies. A long table stood in the center of the room. Silver water carafes sat on silver trays at intervals down the table. A crystal glass stood in front of each person. There was Uncle Bandy, Mr. Brandon Waymer Ashcroft, standing at the head of the table, holding a pointer in one hand, speaking about a chart that was on a stand behind him.

There were ten people seated in the plush chairs that surrounded the table. Only six of them were old men. There were three women, all over fifty, richly dressed, and one older black man. All the men looked affluent, conservative, serious about what they were doing.

Taylor quickly saw that Ashcroft's right hand was at his side. Lindsay had shot him in the right wrist.

"May I?" Taylor asked Barry.

"He's all yours, lad."

Taylor cleared his throat. One by one, all the board members turned to face him. Their faces held only mild interest. Ashcroft, on the other hand, stepped back and turned pale.

"I'm terribly sorry to interrupt your meeting, gentlemen, ladies. This is Sergeant Barry Kinsley. I'm S. C. Taylor. We're here to arrest Mr. Ashcroft for attempted murder."

There were gasps.

". . . what the devil is this?"

"Brandon, what's going on here?"

"Who the hell are these men, Ash?"

Taylor waited for their disbelief to dissipate. Ashcroft remained quiet; he remained pale as death. Taylor said, "I suppose most of you know about the attempted murder of the model Eden in an explosion in Washington Square? Well, Uncle Bandy here—Brandon or Ash—paid a man named Oswald to kill her. When Oswald failed twice, he came to the hospital not three hours ago to do the job himself. Unfortunately his victim is smarter than he is, and braver, and she shot him in his right wrist. Would you like to raise your right arm, Uncle Bandy?"

All the board members were now facing the man at the head of the table, staring at him as if at a stranger, some sort of alien being they'd suddenly realized they didn't understand or even want to.

Brandon Waymer Ashcroft raised his chin. "This is all a ludicrous mistake, gentlemen. As for a wounded hand, that's even more absurd. Now, if you would like to go into my office, I can spare a few minutes to straighten out this ridiculous mistake."

Taylor merely shook his head and addressed the members. "Would you like to know why he was trying to have her killed? Well, let me tell you. A few years ago I was a cop and I came across a fourteen-year-old girl who was bleeding badly after being raped. Her Uncle Bandy had raped her; he'd been sexually abusing her since she was ten. To make it short and sweet, Uncle Bandy here got off, his little niece killed herself, and I beat him up. His only punishment. He promised he'd get even with me. He tried to kill my fiancée, but he's failed. It's all over now and this time justice will come through."

"You're crazy! Get the fuck out of my office!"

"Another thing," Taylor continued easily, "Lindsay Foxe, or Eden, which is her professional name, has a photographic memory for faces. She described you right down to the ear hairs that stick out in a group of three from low in your right ear."

There were more gasps, more astounded speculation, huffs of indignation, murmurs of doubt.

"I suspect, sir," Barry said, stepping foward now, "that we'll find a nice bullet wound in your right wrist. Also, we even have the sketch the police artist drew from Lindsay Foxe's description." Barry pulled a rolled piece of paper from his breast pocket. He unfurled it and handed it to the elderly gentleman who was sitting nearest him.

The old gentleman stared at the drawing. He said nothing. He handed it to the woman next to him.

"It's you, Ash," she said in the most emotionless voice Taylor had ever heard, and passed it on.

Taylor and Barry waited until each person at the table had looked at the sketch.

The black man was the last to look at the sketch. He stared down at it for a long time. He raised his head and said, "He's right about the hairs sticking out of your right ear. I've always thought you should have clipped them."

There was a nervous giggle.

"Now, how about a vote," Taylor said. "All of you who recognized Mr. Ashcroft from the drawing, please raise your hands."

The room was utterly silent. There wasn't a sound. One old gentleman made a disgusted kind of sound and his hand shot up. It was followed by another and then another. All ten board members finally had their arms up.

"Are you ready, Uncle Bandy?" Taylor said.

"This is stupid, crazy. I'm not going anywhere with you fools!"

"Sorry, sir, but you are. Indeed you are." Barry walked around the table toward Brandon Ashcroft. He pulled a pair of handcuffs out of his pocket.

"Do you want to do it the easy way or shall I rough you up just a little bit so you'll know I'm serious?"

"Get away from me, you fucking moron! Damn you! You'll see, Taylor, you'll see! I'll be out of custody in less time than it took me last time! You hear me? And then I'll get that bitch, you'll see!"

"Yes, I hear you," Taylor said. He watched Barry grasp Ashcroft's arms behind him. The man grunted in pain. Barry clapped on the handcuffs, then, smiling gently, leaned close to Ashcroft's ear and whispered, "Now, boyo, you ready to have those nice manicured fingers of yours all blackened with fingerprint ink? Are you ready for a nice big burly guard to strip you down, have you bend over, and make sure you don't have any coke stashed anywhere? I know this one guard who loves his job. Only problem, he's old, not a young girl who's helpless."

Ashcroft broke. He tried to pull lose of Barry. He was frantic, crazy, cursing. "Damn you, Taylor! It's your fault, all your fault! You pig, murderer—you butchered my little Ellie, you made her so unhappy that she couldn't bear things anymore, you made her jump, you're responsible for her death! God, I wanted to get you, and then you beat me up—me! I swore then I'd get you, I'd make you pay by hurting someone you loved, but you were so slow about finding yourself a woman you really cared about. Then you got that bimbo model."

It all came spewing out, filling the heavy silence of the huge boardroom, chilling the air, making the listeners ill and disgusted.

Taylor merely stared at Uncle Bandy, watching as Barry pulled him thrashing and panting through the doors. Ashcroft shouted over his shoulder, "I'll be out soon enough, Taylor! And I'll get you, you damned bastard! Next time I'll get you, and after you're dead, I'll get that damned broad!"

Taylor smiled. "She's not a broad. She's my wife."

# ⤳ EPILOGUE ⤳

"It's all over now, Lindsay. The jury brought in the guilty verdict and Uncle Bandy will be out of the way for so long we'll be able to die and reincarnate at least twice and still be free of him."

"Thank God. It's taken so long, Taylor, so long."

She was right about that. Nearly nine months before he'd gone on trial and two more weeks before the case had gone to the jury. Lindsay had held up well on the witness stand, and he had as well. Taylor scratched his belly and felt relief flood through him. He was naked and still damp from his shower. He felt great. He looked at his wife, at her beautiful face and thick wavy hair. She wasn't quite so thin now, but she was still modeling and it seemed to suit her.

He walked over to the TV and switched it off. He turned, saying even as he climbed into bed, "The media will have a ball for another couple of weeks, sweetheart, and then you and I, Lindsay Taylor, will become nothing more than one of the madding crowd."

She snuggled next to him.

"I was thinking," he said as he stroked his hand down her bare back to cup around her buttocks. "How 'bout you and I flying to Hawaii for a week or two? We can hide out on the beach, let the press forget all about us, and make love until we can't walk."

"That sounds okay." She sighed, moving closer. Her hand was flat on his belly. He wished her fingers would go lower and knew that they would. She always liked to take her time, and it drove him mad and then blissfully happy.

"What do you want if not Maui? It's a long trip, but if you like, we could stop off for a few days in L.A."

She rose on her elbow and looked down at him. "No, it's not that."

"What is it?"

"I want you to show me France."

He stared at her. He couldn't believe it. "France?"

"Yeah, I don't think I gave it a chance to impress me."

"France," he said again. It had been over a year since his last trip there. He felt his blood stir. They'd ride his motorcycle through every inch of the Loire Valley. He'd take her to see the dolmans in Brittany, the Merchants' Table at Locmariaquer, he'd show her the Knights' Hall in the Abbey of Mont St. Michel, ah, so very very much to show her . . .

"How about next Tuesday?"

"France," he said again, then, "Tuesday?"

"Yes, but first things first." Her fingers wrapped around him and he sighed, pleasure flowing through him.

"I don't have much packing to do. We want to travel real light, and—"

She squeezed just a bit, making him groan before he grinned up at her. "You're a hard woman. Let's do it."

Lindsay felt soft and fluid as water. It was Taylor who was hard as a stone. She knew him well now, and if a fire chanced to start in the apartment, they'd both be in dire straits.

She remembered then and said, "Our wedding night has come and gone."

"Sad but true. However, I'm not complaining."

"You shouldn't. Don't you remember, Taylor? You promised you'd tell me what the S.C. meant on our wedding night."

"Your memory is appalling."

"Well? Come on, Taylor, you know all my secrets."

That was certainly true, he thought. He also knew

secrets she might never know, particularly the one about the man who wasn't her father, the man to whom neither of them had spoken since that long-ago time in the hospital. Lindsay had signed over the Foxe mansion not to him, but to Holly. She'd grinned and chortled and rubbed her hands together as she'd done it, and Taylor had been very pleased, not that he thought Holly was such a fine human being, but that Royce Foxe would grind his teeth every time he walked into the mansion that never would belong to him, ever. Also, if he divorced Holly, or if she divorced him, why, then, he'd be out of the mansion on his ear. It was fitting retribution. It had a certain sweet justice to it. Taylor wondered if Royce Foxe still dared to screw around on his wife. Yes, it had a certain pleasant irony to it. The man had never said a word about Lindsay or her mother. Neither had Sydney. Ah, Sydney, she was more famous this year than last. She was seen everywhere with everyone important; she was feted; she was admired; paparazzi followed her. Taylor hoped she was miserable, regardless of all the outward trappings, but in objective moments, he doubted it. As for the prince, he was still in Italy and he was still what he was. Some justice there—he was dependent on his wife for every penny.

Taylor kissed his wife and said, "My real name, huh? All right. A promise is a promise. The S.C. stands for Samuel Clemens. As in Mark Twain."

She didn't say anything for the longest time.

Finally she said, her voice deep and soft, "That's wonderful. Have I married a man whose mother wanted him to be a literary giant? Did you know that Clemens was in San Francisco for a while, way back in the beginning. I thought the S.C. was going to be something ridiculous like Santa Claus."

She giggled against his shoulder. "Did you know his middle name was Langhorne? I learned that in a sophomore lit class."

"So I could have been an S.L.C. Thank God my mom didn't completely lose it."

"What was your mom's name?"

"Her maiden name was Rebecca Thatcher."

"That's grand, Taylor. And what did she name your sister?"

"Ann Marie Taylor."

"After whom?"

"I was the only kid tortured."

"I love you, Taylor."

"I love you too, Lindsay. So you really want to give France a try?"

"Yep. Tuesday. You'll show me everything?"

"Everything," he said, and kissed her.

COU        Coulter, Catherine.

           Beyond Eden.

                    8/5

$20.00